MARGARET MOORE

Tempt Me With Kisses

AVON BOOKS

An Imprint of HarperCollinsPublishers

AVON BOOKS
An Imprint of HarperCollins*Publishers*
10 East 53rd Street
New York, New York 10022-5299

Copyright © 2002 by Margaret Wilkins
ISBN: 0-380-82052-8
www.avonromance.com

First Avon Books paperback printing: April 2002

Avon Trademark Reg. U.S. Pat. Off. and in Other Countries, Marca Registrada, Hecho en U.S.A.
HarperCollins® is a registered trademark of HarperCollins Publishers Inc.

Printed in the U.S.A.

10 9 8 7 6 5 4 3 2 1

Chapter 1

The lord of Llanstephan Fawr looked around the nearly empty hayloft and sighed. There was barely enough hay to last until harvest, and Caradoc had no money to buy more. Worse, he had no money to pay the king's taxes, and hadn't for months.

He glanced out the small window through which the June sunlight shone, over the stone curtain wall of his castle across the valley to the Welsh mountains beyond. Mist covered their crowns and seeped into the valleys, trailing down the slopes like an old woman's unbound hair.

He might end his days living up there a hermit in a cave if things got much worse. That almost seemed a blessed future to be wished for, except that duty and honor tied him to Llanstephan as long as he lived—or until King Richard took it from him.

"Caradoc?"

He turned and saw his friend Dafydd-y-Trwyn peering at him as he climbed up the ladder.

"What is it?" Caradoc asked. "Something wrong with the *ffridd*?"

A damaged sheep pen would be all he needed now.

"No," replied the bailiff of Llanstephan. "I was in the courtyard—"

"Having an ale and bothering the maidservants, I don't doubt," Caradoc growled, although in truth he was relieved that there was not more to trouble him.

Dafydd grinned as he joined Caradoc in the loft. "Aye, I was, I was. And that's when it happened."

Caradoc crossed his arms over his broad chest and leaned his weight on one long, strong leg. "What happened? One of them refuse to be charmed by your honeyed tongue? Had to happen eventually, that did."

Dafydd put his hand over his heart as if mortally wounded. "If you're going to insult me, I'll let you find out for yourself and no warning." He gestured toward the ladder dramatically. "Go you to the yard."

"Just tell me, Dafydd," Caradoc said dryly, quite used to his friend's theatrics.

"It's a woman."

"I should have guessed. Another one after your favors?" Caradoc shook his head. "I don't know how you do it."

And he really didn't, because although they were fast friends and had been since childhood, Dafydd-the-Nose was one of the ugliest men Caradoc had ever seen.

"I'm charming," Dafydd replied cheerfully. "But she's not here for me, odd as that may be, and now that I think of it, insulting, too." He made an exaggerated frown. "I should be offended that she's so persistent about talking to you."

Caradoc uncrossed his arms. "A woman wants to talk to me?"

"Aye, and not taking no, or explaining, either. Just smiles and says she wants to speak to the lord of Llanstephan Fawr." Dafydd ran a measuring gaze over his friend. "There's no accounting for taste, I suppose. If she wants a man who looks like a sheep in serious need of shearing, who am I to judge?"

Caradoc gave him a sour look. "Who is she?"

"Not saying, her, despite my very best efforts."

"She's in the courtyard still, then?"

"Aye." Dafydd pointed at the small window. "See for yourself."

"I will."

Caradoc turned toward the window and, resting his broad hand against the frame, searched the courtyard of his castle, which was a humble one by Norman standards. Beside three large covered wagons, looking about as if surveying the place for taxes, stood a lone woman. Slender and well dressed, she wore a light blue cloak against the morning chill, her face hidden by the hood trimmed with fox fur.

Caradoc had the sudden unsettling sensation that she seemed familiar—from the way she stood so straight and confident, perhaps. Or was it the way she studied the fortress that troubled him? Llanstephan Fawr was no great Norman monstrosity with inner and outer walls and towers to spare.

True, the word *fawr* meant great, but it had been a simple motte and bailey fortress originally, an enclosure of wooden walls surrounding wooden buildings on a hill overlooking a Welsh valley. Caradoc's father had rebuilt the castle with stone and slate, strengthening the walls and adding a second level to the hall for his solar and family quarters, but it was great only compared to the cottages in the village.

Yet it was more than enough for him, and he had sworn to protect it and hold it, and so he would, for as long as he possibly could.

His gaze returned to the unknown woman. If she had been here before, why wouldn't she tell Dafydd who she was? And there was something else. "Where are her drivers, her escort?"

"She paid them and they've already gone."

Brows raised in surprise, Caradoc faced his friend. "She means to stay, obviously. Is she under the impression I enjoy having guests?"

And having to feed and house them as well, when his purse was nearly empty?

"She paid them in *silver*," Dafydd noted significantly.

"So what if she did?" he replied, trying not to be annoyed that a possibly crazed woman had so much money while he, the lord of a Welsh estate, had almost none. "Unless those carts are full of money and jewels and she intends to give it all to me, why should I care?"

"Nobody knows *what* she's got in there."

Caradoc snorted. "Maybe it's nothing at all." He studied her again. "She wants to talk to me, does she?"

Suddenly the woman turned and saw him. She smiled and gave him a merry wave.

Startled, he drew back so fast, a muscle in his back twinged in protest. Ignoring it, he wracked his brain for an explanation, because there was something even more familiar now—something that made him feel . . . happy. He should know that face and her pointed chin and delicate, elfin features. He should recognize the gesture she made, for it seemed to echo another long ago. Deep in his heart, a wee voice told him he should be pleased to see her.

Why should he be pleased to see a woman who arrived uninvited and unannounced, his rational mind argued. "She's a brazen wench," he said aloud.

"That's the general opinion," Dafydd agreed.

"Where is Cordelia?" Caradoc asked. "Maybe this woman is a friend of hers."

"Riding still."

Of course. If it wasn't pouring rain or blowing snow, his sister would be riding, and losing her escort, as often as not. "What does Ganore make of her?"

"Touched in the head, or lost," Dafydd replied. "The woman's got red hair, too."

Caradoc barked a laugh. "I'm surprised she didn't drive her out of the gates." The elderly Ganore hated red-haired women on principle, believing them all witches, or women who would be witches if they only had the nerve.

"Ganore won't go near her. She's watching from the hall, crossing herself every time she takes a breath."

"Lucky for the red-haired woman, I suppose." He glanced out of the window again. The madwoman was still standing in his courtyard, as calm as could be. "Is she Norman?"

"A Scot by the sound of her, which is another reason Ganore won't go near her."

"God help us."

Ganore hated Scots even more than red-haired women.

Caradoc started for the ladder. "Maybe I had best see this woman before Ganore falls into a fit."

Dafydd grinned and nodded and got out of his way. "Aye."

Caradoc checked his step and pivoted toward his friend. "Ask the woman to go to the hall."

Dafydd's merry grin disappeared with his puzzlement. "Why not just meet her in the courtyard?"

Caradoc squared his shoulders and regarded Dafydd with haughty majesty.

"Because I am the lord of Llanstephan Fawr, baron of the march, knight of the realm," he declared in the deep and powerful baritone he could summon when necessary. "I don't introduce myself to unknown women in the courtyard."

Such dignity was completely lost on Dafydd.

"You're going to wash first," he said with sudden understanding, as if this could be the only reason Caradoc wasn't immediately rushing to the courtyard. "And maybe take the shears to that overgrown beard and hair of yours? You know, for a man who's such a dab hand at shearing a sheep, you look—"

"Just go and tell her to wait for me in the hall," Caradoc commanded.

"Right, right, I will, my most sovereign lord, my liege, baron of the march, knight of the realm," Dafydd said, still grinning as he fairly danced to the ladder and descended.

The moment Dafydd was out of sight, Caradoc ran his fingers through the long tangle of his black, waving hair and rubbed his palm over his beard. It had been weeks since he had thought about his appearance, and he wondered if he looked as scruffy as Dafydd implied.

He climbed down the ladder and regarded his reflection in the water trough. Dafydd's comparison to a sheep in need of shearing was not that far off the mark.

Well, he wasn't about to cut his hair and shave or change his clothes for some woman he had never met who rode into his courtyard as if she was the queen and a tax collector combined.

He did splash some water on his face, and wiped it with a handful of hay he grabbed out of the manger, but only because he was sweating—and that had nothing to do with her, either.

Thus prepared, Caradoc went forth from the stable and began to cross his courtyard. As he drew near the wagons, however, he slowed his steps. Tempted by curiosity, he quickly glanced inside, trying to look into them without displaying any overt interest.

He didn't have any luck. He saw barrels in one, but couldn't determine their contents.

Disgruntled, he marched into his hall. Ganore was nowhere to be seen, for once, probably having decamped lest she be tainted by the presence of a redheaded Scot. She would likely have the rushes swept out and replaced and the walls washed before the sun went down.

Otherwise, it seemed every other servant with any possible excuse to be in the hall was there. Meri, Una and Lowri, bolder than all save Ganore, and even shy little Rhonwen stood staring with wonder and anticipation at the woman beside the empty central hearth as if expecting her to burst into flames at any moment. Dafydd was with them, watching, too, and whispering and making them cover their mouths to stifle their giggles.

Envy tweaked Caradoc, for Dafydd had an undeniable way with women, which he most certainly did not.

Apparently not a whit disturbed by being the center of attention, the woman examined everything as if taking stock here, too. She had thrown back her hood, revealing glossy auburn hair, more brown than red, drawn back in two braids gathered at the ends into bronze casings etched in a circular design.

At last the woman realized he was there and turned to face him. Now Caradoc could see the freckles scattered across her nose. Again he felt he should know her, and be happy with the remembrance.

Unfortunately, even this close, he still had no idea who she was.

Her full, beautifully shaped lips turned up into a very friendly, yet speculative, smile. Maybe they hadn't met before. Maybe she simply found him attractive.

Well, what was so surprising about that? Women had wanted to share his bed since he was sixteen.

But only his bed, and only if they had already failed to catch his younger brother's eye, or Dafydd's.

If he lacked Dafydd's way with women or his younger brother's skill at both fighting and seduction, at least he wasn't completely unattractive, or so he told himself.

He approached, bowed politely, and waited for her to speak.

That was not long, for she returned his bow, smiled again, and said, in a very clear and musical voice, "Greetings, my lord. It has been a long time."

Her Welsh was excellent, though she had the accent of a Scot.

"Yes, it has," he agreed, still completely baffled, but demonstrate his ignorance of her identity he would not. "What brings you to Llanstephan Fawr again?"

Her brow furrowed slightly, and he wondered if his puzzlement was obvious, after all. "A proposition."

"Indeed?"

"An important one, so I think we should discuss it in private. May we go to your solar?"

Since Caradoc was in no humor to look ignorant or discuss business in front of his curious friend or the servants, he nodded and proceeded to lead the way to his private chamber at the head of a curving staircase.

Trying to ignore a stab of dismay at the fact that his obvious poverty was about to be revealed, he opened the door to the barren solar. The tapestries that used to grace the walls had been sold long ago, along with the bronze candle stands and silver plate.

As the woman passed by him to enter the chamber, the top of her head came level with his chin. He caught the hint of a delicate scent, like wildflowers. The feminine scent bespoke wealth and leisure and pleasure, too—the sort of pleasure he had denied himself for a very long time.

While that tugged at the edges of his consciousness, he followed her into the room, leaving the door open. He didn't want any hint of impropriety, and nobody could listen at the door if it was open.

"Are you not going to ask me to sit down, my lord?" she asked, a hint of amusement in her dulcet voice.

"Please," he said, gesturing at the chair opposite the scarred and ink-stained trestle table covered with parchment lists and scrolls, a vessel of ink, and the remnants of quills.

The chair was covered in a film of dust, but she sat nonetheless. Her cloak flared open to reveal a beautiful gown clinging to a shapely figure. The garment was made of soft sea green wool and embroidered about the rounded neck and long cuffs with blue and golden threads.

Indeed, she had a very shapely figure. High, rounded breasts just the right size to fit into the palm of his hand. Slim waist. Curving hips.

A jolt of desire hit him right in the gut, and lower, too.

The woman having such a powerful and unexpected effect upon him cocked her head and regarded him with a look of amicable amusement. "You don't know who I am, do you?"

No point lying now, and in truth, it had become rather difficult to think clearly. "No."

"I am Fiona MacDougal. My father was Angus MacDougal, the wool merchant."

Expelling the breath he didn't know he had been holding, Caradoc lowered himself into a nearby chair. Fiona. Of course.

She used to come to Llanstephan with her father. The first time Caradoc had seen her, he had been in this very room, studying with his tutor. He had looked out the narrow window and noticed Fiona Mac-Dougal. She grinned and waved when she saw him.

He had done nothing save swiftly return to his studies, too shy to even wave back. When she came again with her father, he purposefully avoided her rather than be embarrassed and risk being tongue-tied. Yet in time he realized she was sneaking about and following him, the way other girls shadowed his handsome, bold, younger brother, Connor. Flattered, yet still too bashful, Caradoc did not speak to her.

He had never forgotten the girl who seemed to find him interesting. However, she had been forever a girl in his mind, and this was certainly no girl before him now. Fiona MacDougal was a grown woman. He was undeniably pleased to see her again, but she was a bold, brazen and baffling woman, so betray his pleasure like a boy he would not.

"It has indeed been a long time," he said with placid politeness. "How is your father?"

She sobered, and it was like seeing a cloud momentarily blot a sunny sky. "He is dead, two months past."

"I am sorry to hear that." He cursed himself for asking such a question. He should have been more cautious. "My father thought very highly of him."

"I'm sorry about your parents, too," she said softly, genuine sorrow in her green eyes.

It had been a long time since anybody had spoken to him in such a manner. In fact, he could not remember anybody, not even his mother, showing such kind concern. Disconcerted, he fought to keep his expression calm. "Thank you. Now, what is this proposition you spoke of?"

"I have learned that you have fallen on hard times."

He tensed, his pride piqued. But this chamber and the equally barren hall below had already answered for him, so he could not deny it. "Yes."

"I have also heard the taxes on Llanstephan are very high, and you have not been able to pay them."

Was *all* his business common knowledge?

Probably, he grimly acknowledged. People talked, and news of a lordly family's difficulty would be much remarked upon by high and low alike. "Yes, that is so."

"How seriously are you in arrears to the crown?"

Confirming what was already well known was one thing; discussing his debts and obligations were another.

"Why should I tell you?" he demanded, barely restraining his annoyance.

Her bright eyes brightened even more, and a wry little smile played about her lips, as if she was secretly and vastly amused by his troubles, a notion that increased his growing rancor.

"I intend to provide a way for you to pay your debts and to rebuild Llanstephan's prosperity."

His hands gripped the arms of his chair as he examined her face. How could this merchant's daughter, who was little better than a stranger to him, do that?

He steepled his fingers and regarded her as he might a peddler trying to cheat him. "What are you going to do? Give me a good price on this year's fleece, for old time's sake?"

Taking a deep breath, Fiona MacDougal shook her head and looked as if she were preparing to do something astounding. "By offering to marry you."

Speechless, he stared in stunned disbelief. Of all the answers she might have made, he had not expected anything like this.

"You are very poor, my lord," she continued as if the worst were over, or as if she were certain there could be no disagreement. "That is no secret. I am very rich. All I lack is a husband, and what I want is a titled one. If I marry you, your financial problems will be solved, and my desire for a noble husband will be, too."

The reality of what she was proposing crashed into him, propelling him to his feet in outraged majesty. "You want to *buy* me? By the saints, woman, do I look like a *whore* to you?"

She flushed, but rose and faced him squarely, as if speaking man to man, or warrior to warrior. Her green eyes shone with determined spirit, and her breasts rose and fell with each breath.

A vision of her in his bed burst into his head. Her bountiful hair spread upon his pillow, her soft, shapely body beneath him, and her luscious lips parted in anxious cries of desire as he caressed and stroked and loved her . . .

"If I were a titled woman and came to you with the same offer, would you say this?" she inquired, yanking him back to reality. "Or would you be relieved?"

"Unfortunately, you are not a titled woman," he replied, as he tried to focus his mind on the practical reasons for her proposal and why it would never be acceptable despite the furious longing surging through his traitorous body. "You are a wool merchant's daughter, and you are a Scot. Lord Rhys of Wales would not be pleased if I marry a Scot."

She didn't even blink. "He may be the most powerful nobleman in Wales, but you hold your estate by the grace of King Richard, not Lord Rhys. Besides, he rebels against Richard because the king snubbed him after his coronation. If you wish to worry about what such a man will think of your marriage, let me ask you this: What has Lord Rhys ever done for you? Has he offered to help you with your debts? Or does his childish rancor make your life more difficult?"

God save him, for a mere woman she sounded well versed in the politics that interfered with his life.

"And let us not forget King Richard, so busy and indebted with his foreign wars," she continued just as matter-of-factly. "What will he care who you wed, as long as you can pay what you owe, especially when I bring no land or alliances to the marriage? Our union will be for financial reasons, not political, and both Rhys and Richard should appreciate the difference."

She seemed to have anticipated every possible objection.

"My dowry is three thousand marks."

He felt as if she had punched him in the stomach and winded him completely. Such a dowry would tempt the devil himself into matrimony.

"Nobles marry for power and gain all the time," she continued, her gaze even more intense, as if she would stare him into agreeing. "This would be no different, except that I bring no land or titles of my own. Therefore, I am no threat to anyone."

No threat, perhaps, but she was certainly unusual. She made her offer as calmly as if she were trading in a marketplace, not discussing marriage.

What else should he expect from a wealthy merchant's daughter? Awe? Deference?

Surely at least a hint of uncertainty.

"Why am I to be the lucky recipient of your largess, Fiona MacDougal?" he demanded. "There are other noblemen in need of money who could give you a title."

"That's true," she glibly answered. "But you have never been married before, so have no children who could cause conflict between us. Also, my father thought highly of your father."

Nothing of feelings, as he should have anticipated, and he told himself he was glad it was so. This way he could be all business, too. "Perhaps talk of my desperate straits has been greatly exaggerated."

She slowly surveyed the chamber, then him. "Many things have changed since I was last in Llanstephan."

He suddenly saw himself through her eyes: a man no longer in his youth, dressed in an old wool tunic much mended and the color of dung, wearing breeches not much different, with scuffed boots about ten years old and showing every day of their age.

She smiled once more, smugly. "Nor do I see Welsh noblewomen lined up at your castle gate to marry you."

"Which does not mean I have not had other proposals made to me, Fiona MacDougal," he retorted, his pride outraged despite his shabby garments. "I do, after all, have rank, and as you so bluntly point out, a title is a valuable commodity."

"Where is your bride, then, my lord?"

"I have not yet found a woman to suit me," he countered.

She raised a brow in query. "Well, then, my lord, I assume you will be telling me to find another man with whom to share my body and my bounty."

She crossed her arms as she waited for him to answer, just as his father had all those times in this very room.

But he was no longer a little boy anxious for a father's approval, or a youth absurdly flattered by a girl's attention. He was Lord Caradoc of Llanstephan Fawr, and he would remind this bold and brazen woman of that, no matter how much money she had.

"Are you forgetting to whom you speak?" he asked, his voice a rumble as he came around the table and slowly circled her. "I am not some shepherd, Fiona MacDougal, discussing the price of wool. I am Lord Caradoc of Llanstephan, baron of the marches, knight of the realm."

He paused in front of her and leaned forward and

his voice became a low growl as he whispered in her ear. "I do not take very kindly to ultimatums."

She did not avert her steadfast, green-eyed gaze. She did not wrinkle her nose as if he smelled. She did not move at all.

Until she swallowed. Hard.

A brazen, bold woman indeed, but he took a great deal of satisfaction in that swallow. He glanced down at the smooth curve of her jaw where it met her neck and fought a strong, unbidden urge to press his lips there.

Her body and her bounty. A way to pay his taxes and keep his home. Money that would provide a dowry for Cordelia, too, so she could have some choice in a husband. Connor would even be absolved from the need to raise funds, and although he didn't think his younger brother deserved absolution, the notion was tempting nonetheless.

Her body was tempting, too. Lithe and supple, slender and shapely—a man could do much worse.

What would she be like in his bed? Would she be as bold and forthright as she was now, or would she become shy and uncertain?

His blood quickened with these thoughts, until the other part of him—the sensible, rational part—wondered what kind of wife she would make the rest of the time.

Still she regarded him questioningly, waiting for his answer. Then the expression in her eyes suddenly shifted, to one not quite so certain.

She looked vulnerable. Or . . . lonely.

Alone she was, he realized, for alone she had arrived, except for men paid to escort her. He, too, was alone even when surrounded by all the people here. It had always been thus for him.

His gaze drifted lower, past the throbbing pulse in her neck to her breasts, rising and falling with her breathing.

This bold, astonishing woman wanted to be his wife. Would the daughter of a wealthy man, no doubt carefully raised, understand *all* that she was asking for?

He would show her.

He tugged her into his arms and claimed her mouth.

Hot hunger exploded in him. Desire surged and threatened to swamp his senses at the taste and touch of her.

By the saints, he wanted her. Now. Completely. Her legs around him, holding him tight as he thrust inside her. Her anxious moans of yearning sounding in his ears. Her lips crushed beneath his, her breasts against his chest as he took her.

When she wrapped her arms about his neck and pressed her body against his, returning his kiss with equal and insistent passion, he thought he would die if he did not have her.

Was this how it was for Connor and Dafydd when a woman wanted them? If so, he had not envied them nearly enough.

His mouth still locked on hers, he pushed her back until she met the table and could go no farther. He frantically began bunching the soft wool of her gown into his hand, the other splayed against her back, holding her as close as he could. His mouth left hers to slide along her smooth and slender neck. Small sounds of need vibrated in her throat as he kissed lower, and lower still.

She put her hands on his chest and shoved him back.

"We are not married yet," she said, panting, her eyes flashing fires of protest and her lips slightly swollen. "Indeed, my lord—and I do know *exactly* who you are—I do not even know if you are agreeable."

His chest heaving, his whole body ready and anxious to take hers, he stepped forward. She wanted him. He felt her need and desire coursing through her hot and willing body.

She held him back, her lips a firm hard line of decision. "No more until we are married. And you have not yet given me your answer, my lord."

Was this coy refusal after that passionate kiss some kind of game?

If it was a game she wanted, it would be a game she got.

He smiled slowly, as Connor did when he sought to tease a woman into bed. He may not have the experience or the charm of his younger brother, but he had always been a studious boy. Now he would find out how much Connor the fair and winning had unknowingly taught him. "I will have to sleep on it."

Her eyes widened with her surprise, and her full lips parted.

He had taken her aback. Good.

Then her eyes narrowed and that firm resolve returned to her face as she shook her head. "No, my lord. You must decide now. If the answer is no, I will not stay."

So, he had not learned the lessons Connor could teach, not if this bold, insolent creature could so swiftly resume her former manner and ignore what he said about ultimatums to give him another.

No game, this, then, but a haggling in the marketplace. "Three thousand marks, your dowry?" he demanded.

She nodded.

"I want to see it and be sure of its value. I trust it is in the wagons?"

"You will find jewelry, wine from France, fine cloth from Italy, Irish silver and Flemish gold. Also five hundred marks in silver coin."

He tilted his head to study her. "You must be very trusting, Fiona MacDougal, to bring that here and let your escort go."

"If I doubted that you were an honorable and honest man, Lord Caradoc of Llanstephan, I wouldn't have."

Shocked again and undeniably delighted, he nearly grinned like a jester. A compliment was a rare thing in his life. Even his own parents . . . but he would not think of them now. He had to deal with the astonishing Fiona MacDougal, whose naked body he could so easily imagine pressed against his own in the throes of passion. "I would like to see what is in the wagons."

"Certainly, my lord," she said briskly.

She started toward the door, and he followed her just as swiftly. His gaze strayed to the luscious curves of her hips and rounded bottom marching so purposefully before him.

She had offered herself to him. Along with her money. In exchange for his title and the status that went with it.

A trade. A bargain. A sale.

A way out of his troubles.

They passed Dafydd and the servants who were still lingering, as well as elderly pinch-faced Ganore peering out from the kitchen corridor. They continued into the courtyard, which also seemed rather more crowded than it should be.

Big, brawny, black-haired Jon-Bron, his garrison commander, sat outside the barracks apparently polishing his sword. Jon's younger brother, Emlyn-Bron, the sergeant at arms, also big, brawny and dark, likewise supposedly examined a halter. A careful, fastidious man by nature, this might not have been so unusual, except that he wasn't usually quite so slow about it.

Their youngest brother, Bran-Bron, and the only one of the three with light brown hair, was hanging about the kitchen pretending to converse with his troop of bowmen. From the snatches of conversation Caradoc overheard, it was clear none of them were paying any attention whatsoever to what anybody else said. Meanwhile, the scullery maids were busily fetching what looked to be enough water to wash the whole castle top to bottom.

Eifion, the village reeve, must have got wind of the visitor, too, for now he stood near the gate, his long, thin frame in a long gray tunic.

Caradoc subdued a scowl, although at least their curiosity was normal, unlike so much this day.

Glancing at him, Fiona threw back the covering on the first wagon, revealing several barrels with markings on them. "This is the wine. Are you familiar with Bordeaux wine?"

"I prefer ale."

In truth he hadn't been able to afford wine in years, and never anything but English wine, which tended to be bitter and unpleasant.

She let the flap fall, then went on to the next wagon. "In these chests are the fabrics, the silver plate, and the coins are in that smaller box."

"What is in the third wagon?"

"My personal things."

His brow lowered with suspicion. "You have that many clothes?"

She came close to him and smiled a secretive, seductive little smile that made him think she could give lessons to Connor, for he felt the warmth of it along every limb of his body. "There are fine linens and other things to make a bedchamber comfortable and inviting."

His chest constricted, like a landed fish struggling to breathe.

"So, my lord, what is your answer? Will we wed, or not?"

Every person in the courtyard had heard her question. He didn't see Ganore; nevertheless, he was sure she was also watching and listening somewhere, praying to God to strike the Scottish heathen witch dead. He could almost feel her gaze searing his flesh.

Other noblemen would think he had no proper,

lordly pride. His own people would balk at a Scotswoman becoming the chatelaine of his castle.

As for Cordelia, he could imagine how she would react to this proposal. A storm at sea, with waves as high as a mountain, would probably be calmer.

But as he looked at Fiona MacDougal, so bold, so confident, so tempting and so rich, he knew there was really only one answer he could give unless he wanted to lose the castle that was his home and his responsibility. "I will."

A murmur of both surprise and discontent began in the courtyard. If Fiona heard the mutterings, or understood what they meant, she made no sign.

Nor did she smile, or even look relieved. She seemed perfectly, utterly calm. "When?"

Ignoring her lack of reaction, because after all this was but a bargain concluded, he mused a moment. "Tomorrow we have to gather my flocks for the washing before the shearing. We can marry between the washing and shearing—the day after tomorrow."

She nodded, once, then stuck out her hand expectantly. He looked down at it, then back at her.

"We are striking a bargain, my lord, are we not?" she inquired.

"Ah." Indeed they were. He slapped his palm against hers, and thus they were betrothed.

Their gazes met and held for a long moment as he wondered what she was thinking.

And feeling.

He simply could not tell, and once more envy for others' understanding of women nipped at him. If only one of his tutors had been able to instruct him on that subject!

"I will supervise the unloading of the wagons," she said, breaking the silence, "if you will tell me where the goods should be put, and where I may sleep."

"Although I trust everyone in the castle," he answered just as briskly, "the silver and gold should go in my solar, where it can be safely locked away. The cloth will go in the storeroom. As for where you will sleep . . ." He thought of how she looked after they had kissed, and decided to try to gain the upper hand, at least in one way. He dropped his voice to a low, intimate purr. "In my bedchamber."

She flushed, and he felt a surge of triumph. Maybe he didn't need instruction, after all.

Then indignation grew in her green eyes. "My lord, need I remind you—"

"That we are not yet wed?" He raked her with his gaze, only partly to discomfort her. He enjoyed his perusal of her shapely figure too much for it to be just that. "I will sleep in the barracks until we are."

Her blush deepened. "Oh. Very well, then."

Again he felt a rush of restored pride at her discomfort and could not resist pressing his advantage. "I intend to be very well married, indeed."

His gaze locked onto hers, trying to make her silently acknowledge that he was her master.

A movement from the barracks caught his attention, and he half turned. Jon-Bron had dropped the clay vessel of polish.

As he quickly bent to retrieve it, Caradoc scanned the courtyard. Emlyn-Bron still examined the halter as if his eyes were going, while Bran-Bron and his bowmen huddled together in intense discussion. The scullery maids stood by the well, their mouths moving as quickly as baby birds hungry for a worm.

When he turned back, her eyes focused on his with the intensity of a bowman sighting a difficult target.

"I had best tell Father Rhodri about the wedding. The chapel is outside the castle in the village," he said, weary of being a spectacle, and this silent, silly game of staring had gone on quite long enough. Surely he had made his point.

"There is no need to tell anybody else," he concluded as he swiveled on his heel. "They already know."

Chapter 2

$\curvearrowleft \mathbb{O}\mathbb{C} \curvearrowright$

Fiona stood on the threshold of Caradoc's bed-chamber, her hands on her hips and her cloak thrown back over her shoulders. Behind her, grooms and stable boys carried her baggage from the third cart, two large chests and two smaller. The smaller ones were the heaviest, the large ones awkward to hold.

She should not make them wait overlong with their burdens. Nevertheless, she took a moment to survey the small chamber she would soon be sharing with Caradoc of Llanstephan.

And the bed she would be sharing with him, too. Where she would be in his arms, making love.

Fiona put her fingers to her lips and lived again the sensation of his kiss. Never had an embrace aroused such fire and burning need, not even when she had foolishly believed herself in love.

But surely never had a man possessed such a potent combination of attraction and danger as Caradoc of Llanstephan. When he looked at her, heat and dread seemed to blossom in equal measure. From the first moment today, part of her yearned for him to sweep her into his arms and caress her until her cries echoed off the ancient stone walls of this castle. Another part warned that he was not the man she had expected, and he was certainly no longer the boy she had admired from afar.

She had been ten years old the first time she had seen Caradoc. He had been looking out the solar window. She had waved at the solitary youth with black, curling hair, straight nose and prominent cheekbones. He had started and flashed a shy, pleased smile before ducking out of sight.

For the sake of that smile, she had shadowed him afterward, trying to see him smile again. A merchant's daughter, she hadn't dared approach him, but had watched and waited. She had never seen another smile on Caradoc's face, not then or during any of the other visits she made with her father.

More appealing than his handsome looks, though, had been his good temperament. Caradoc the lad had been quiet and reasonable, unlike his brother, who was hot-tempered and spoiled.

Now Caradoc's dark, wavy hair brushed his shoulders and his thick black beard obscured most of his face, making him look more like a wild barbarian than a nobleman. His brilliant, sapphire blue eyes were still a startling and fascinating contrast to his dark complexion, but they burned with a search-

ing intensity that seemed to demand her acknowl-
edgment that he was master here.

Of everything, even a woman who had only just
arrived.

A muffled grunt reminded her that the servants
were holding heavy burdens. Entering the chamber,
she gestured for them to bring the chests inside.

"The largest one should go at the foot of the bed,"
she ordered, "and the other big one against the wall
opposite the window. Set the smaller chests on the
bed, please."

It was large, that bed, with heavy wooden posts
and dingy curtains open to reveal tousled coverings,
as if Caradoc had risen a short time ago. He could
not have, for it was too late in the day, so that suggested the maidservants had not yet been here to
tidy, a notion Fiona found rather shocking. More
surprising, she could see moth holes in the blanket.

Apart from the bed, there was very little furniture. A cheap candle stand, empty of candles, stood
near the bed and there was no sign that any candles
had burned there recently. A chair, very plain and very
small for a man of his size, was by the window. It
was covered in dust, leading her to suspect Caradoc
never actually sat there. The narrow window had no
covering or linen shutter of any kind, and stains on
the wall told her the roof leaked. A battered chest in
one corner completed the simple furnishings.

If she had needed more proof of Caradoc's
poverty, here it was.

Her gaze returned to the messy bed. She doubted
he usually slept there alone. He was too young, too
virile and even with that hair and beard, too hand-

some. Plus, he was half Welsh, and the Welsh were not known for chastity.

She told herself it didn't matter if Caradoc had entertained half the female population of Wales in that bed. She was going to be a lord's wife, and far away from Iain MacLachlann. That was what was important. That was why she had returned, despite the passing years and all that had happened to her.

As for those bed linens, she would replace them at once with sheets she had brought from Dunburn.

After the servants had done as she commanded, they stood looking at her doubtfully, as if they were trying to determine whether she was fish or fowl or something else entirely.

"Thank you. You may go."

The men and boys nodded and filed out, leaving her alone.

She removed her cloak and laid it across the chest at the foot of the bed. She wasn't surprised they didn't know what to make of her. She was a stranger. She was going to marry their overlord, which would give her power over them, and they had never set eyes on her before.

She was also a foreigner. Llanstephan was a small place, with fewer people than her home of Dunburn, so it wasn't hard to guess that the servants and townfolk would be less than delighted by Caradoc's decision.

In spite of her trepidation, her whole body throbbed with the memory of Caradoc standing in his solar. His barbaric hair. His piercing eyes. His powerful body. His lean, strong hands.

His loneliness.

Loneliness—an odd word to intrude on her thoughts as she contemplated the lord of an estate, yet once there, it would not leave.

Was that what she had sensed below the surface of his blue eyes even when he was a boy, the ache of a heart as lonely as hers? Was that why she had been so drawn to him that first day long ago?

She had been lonely all her life. Too well-to-do to fit in with the village girls, not of noble rank to be the acquaintance of the girls of quality, she had inhabited a heaven of material plenty, but a purgatory of solitude. She had desperately yearned for friends and companions, and many a time she had longed to be poor enough to play with the peasant girls.

Since that had not happened, she had found refuge in stories she made up, especially the one about a boy in a tower. He was an enchanted prince and he fell in love with her after she released him from his tower prison. As she had grown up, so had he, becoming a man with dark hair and brilliant blue eyes, broad shoulders and long, strong legs—like Caradoc. She had imagined all this but never the waves of physical longing he inspired.

How could she, when she had never felt anything like that in her life?

Suddenly, an extremely thin, elderly woman marched into the chamber without so much as a knock to warn of her approach. She was clad in a plain brown woolen gown belted about her narrow hips and a white scarf was on her head. The keys tied to her belt jingled as she came to a halt and sneered with impertinent disapproval at Fiona.

Ganore.

Fiona remembered the woman from her visits. Ganore had been younger then, of course, and spent most of her time with Caradoc's mother, or his sister, Cordelia. She had been a harsh, croaking raven of a woman. From her appearance it seemed little had changed, except that now her hair was white and the creases in her cheeks deeper. Unfortunately, the keys she carried indicated that she was of high rank among the servants. A woman like this, of such obvious prejudices and in a position of responsibility, was dangerous. She could make her mistress's life a living hell.

"Hello," Fiona began pleasantly, hoping for the best.

Ganore's suspicious black eyes narrowed. "You're a Scot."

"Yes, I am."

"And you've got red hair."

She spoke as if Fiona had one eye, like a Cyclops.

"It's auburn," she genially corrected, still trying for a truce. "It was much redder when I was younger. I have hopes it will continue to darken. I would love to have black hair before I die."

The woman not only didn't smile, her brow furrowed as if Fiona had personally insulted her. Perhaps it had not been wise to mention death to one of Ganore's years, even in jest. "My name is Fiona, Fiona MacDougal. I used to come here with my father, Angus MacDougal, the wool merchant. He bought Llanstephan fleece."

Ganore sniffed derisively, as if to say, So what of that? "I don't remember you."

She sounded as if she thought Fiona was lying.

Fiona struggled to restrain her temper as she nodded at the keys on Ganore's belt. "I see that you have risen in the world since last I was here, Ganore."

"I am in charge of the household." Ganore's lip curled. "You've got the eyes of your father—sharp and cunning."

There was another implication in this, too: that he was not honest.

Fiona bristled. Her patience, already thinned by her meeting with Caradoc, was rapidly giving way. "It would seem Lord Caradoc's blanket is in need of mending. I am surprised you have been so remiss."

"He never said it needed mending."

"Why should he? Is it not your job to notice?"

Ganore lifted a chin that looked so sharp it could slice bread, and crossed her wiry arms. "He doesn't like anyone coming in here without his permission."

"So you have his permission to be here now?"

The woman's neck reddened, but her blush got no further.

Nevertheless, Fiona was pleased to think she had gotten even that much of a chagrined reaction from Ganore. "I'm sure you've had many responsibilities but now—"

"I was nurse to Caradoc, and his brother and sister, too. I have been in charge of the household since his dear mother, our wonderful *Welsh* lady, passed away."

Once more Fiona reined in her frustration and annoyance, but she was not about to let this woman think she could be bullied by a servant.

"I am your lord's guest," she said evenly, yet with a firmness that would have stood many a nobleman in good stead. "I am sure you have heard that soon I shall be his wife. Do not interrupt me like that again, Ganore."

She watched as her words hit their target, then continued as if nothing of consequence had happened. "As I was saying, I'm sure you've had a position of responsibility for a long time, and that Lord Caradoc is very grateful. However, I am going to be your lord's wife, so I will take over as befits the chatelaine of Llanstephan. After we are wed, you will give me the keys and show me about the castle. Before then, I should be introduced to those servants who have not marched into this chamber as if it were a soldiers' barracks and introduced themselves to me. Do you understand?"

Glare met glare, but Fiona was determined and at last Ganore looked away.

"Yes," she hissed.

"Excellent."

Fiona turned back to the bed and lifted one of the small chests onto the floor. "Now, I need some help to change this linen," she said as she straightened, turned—and found herself alone.

Ganore had quit the field, it seemed. For now, at least, or perhaps merely to regroup before another sortie to try to find her enemy's weak points.

Of which there were many, and one most of all: Fiona MacDougal had been thoroughly, stupidly duped, tricked by a greedy scoundrel and played for a fool.

She didn't want Ganore, or anybody, to discover the other reason she had come back here.

The shame of her folly haunted her still. She had

been tricked by Iain MacLachlann's persuasive manner and words of love, only to discover that he had merely wanted her money in his coffers, a means to raise himself in the court of King William of Scotland.

Humiliated to the core of her soul, she had left Dunburn and gone where he would never find her. She had decided that if she must be seen as only a commodity to be peddled in marriage, she would at least choose where she was traded, and to whom.

Her father had told her of the troubles at Llanstephan before he had died, having heard the stories from other wool merchants with whom he did business. She remembered her old infatuation, and her good opinion of Caradoc, and so she had sold her property and come here to make her offer.

But as Caradoc's shining, intense blue eyes studied her in his solar, she had feared that he could read all of the past six months in hers. It had taken every ounce of courage and determination she had to appear more confident than she was, to seem resolute rather than desperate, as she made her proposition.

It had taken even more effort to meet his steadfast gaze in the courtyard, and to act as if his kiss had not incited hot desire with the force of a smith's hammer striking an anvil.

Then he had agreed to marry her, and it had been another war not to betray her relief.

Or her sudden dread that she had made another mistake coming here, because when all was said and done, he was not the boy she remembered. He was a man, a lord in charge of an estate, mature and tested by troubles. Gruff, grim, stoic, how could she ever understand a man who displayed so little of his thoughts and feelings?

What was there to understand? her mind demanded. She was here, she was safe, she would be titled as she had also envisioned in her childish dreams. Caradoc would take her in his powerful arms, and if that kiss was anything to go by, sweep her into realms of ecstasy that Iain never could. Was that not enough?

It must be. To wish for more was folly, and had she not had enough of that? Had Iain not taught her to beware her fantasies and notions of love? That they were delusions best left to minstrels and silly girls?

Iain had been flesh and blood and flattery. It could be that Caradoc was fantasy and desire made flesh, and to forget that, as grave a mistake as letting Iain into her bed.

She ripped the old, moth-eaten blanket from Caradoc's bed and rolled it, then threw it on the floor. Maybe she should have these coverings burnt.

"What are you doing?" a deep voice asked from the doorway.

She pivoted to see the dark lord of Llanstephan leaning against the frame, his arms crossed, one eyebrow raised in question.

If one of the gods of Olympus had come down to earth in mortal form, he would probably sound like Caradoc, his voice a rich baritone but with a hint of gruffness to give it command. And he would probably look like Caradoc, too—a god trying to appear a mere mortal, and failing utterly.

"I'm stripping the bed."

Oh, good, very good, foolish Fiona! As if he's blind and stupid to boot.

He pushed off from the frame and ambled inside. Toward the bed. Toward her. "So I see. Why?"

"I have other linen in that chest," she said as she pointed to the one at the foot of the bed. "Fresh linen. *New* linen."

He came to a halt about three feet from her and his gaze shifted to the bed and the tick, which had several holes with straw poking through. "There are servants for such tasks."

Her pulse began to race, just as it had in the solar when he had whispered in her ear. "I would have asked for Ganore's assistance with the linens, but she left."

He strolled around the bed. "I don't think she approves my choice of bride."

Fiona thought that was putting it mildly, but said nothing. She wasn't going to begin by informing on the servants, no matter how they irritated her. She wanted their respect, not their hatred.

"I came for my clothes, to take them to the barracks. Or would you mind if I changed here?"

She fought to keep her reactions to herself, her voice serene and steady, as her mind's eye conjured invisible hands stripping him as she had ripped the linens from his bed. "I would mind."

"Pity," he murmured, the low purr of his voice making her feel hot to the soles of her feet. "I think you will need some help to put this room to rights with all your personal goods."

"Yes," she answered. Again she managed to

sound calm and businesslike despite his disconcerting presence.

"I'll send Ganore back."

Anybody but her! "I would prefer another maidservant, if you please."

For a moment, she feared he was going to insist, but instead, he conceded with a nod. "I'll have Rhonwen come help."

"Thank you, my lord."

He sauntered over to the battered chest in the corner—mercifully away from the bed—and lifted the lid. "Ganore will get used to it."

"It?"

"You."

Hardly flattering to be an "it," but again, what else could she expect?

Given that kiss, something more, her heart argued.

She silenced that hopeful little voice. This marriage was a bargain, and if he craved her body, that was no more than to be expected.

He pulled out a pile of clothes, then shoved the lid closed with his elbow so that it fell with a thunk. "Ganore doesn't approve of red-haired women, or Scots, either."

"She made that very plain."

"Redheaded women are the devil's chosen, to hear her tell it. And a Scot cheated her once out of half a mark when she was young. She's borne a grudge against your entire country ever since. Unfortunately, her notions seem to get more set and settled with age."

Fiona sat on the bed. "So I should not take her rudeness as a personal insult, then?"

"Well, how you take it is your business," he said, coming closer. "But with that red hair of yours she would feel the same way if you were the queen of Wales. In that case, she'd probably tell everybody you had bewitched your way to the throne."

Was that a jest? She couldn't tell.

She also thought it had been a mistake to sit on the bed as he loomed over her. He cocked his head and studied her until she felt like reminding him it was rude to stare. "I am the lord here, Fiona, not Ganore. I decide what I do, and whether or not anybody else approves is not important."

She suspected that he was setting limits and boundaries with her and making his leadership plain, just as she had with Ganore. "I understand, my lord."

A look passed across his face, as if *he* didn't understand, but it was just as quickly gone. "Since we are to be wed, call me by my name."

"Yes, Caradoc."

Again that look crossed his face, and then he frowned. "I am not a harsh overlord, Fiona, and I do not expect to be harsh with my wife, either."

For the first time since he had accepted her offer, she felt that she could breathe, and for the first time since she had seen him today, she saw something of the quiet youth who had captured her attention. "I remember you as a boy, Caradoc, and if I had not believed that to be so, I would never have come here."

Something flickered in the blue depths of his eyes. Pride and pleasure, she thought, and inwardly she exalted that perhaps he was not so unreadable as she had feared. She rose so that she faced him, and as she did, she wondered what else she could say that would make the quiet boy appear again, if only in his eyes.

He went to the door. "I shall see you below in the hall for the evening meal."

He paused on the threshold and looked back at her. "I should warn you, Father Rhodri's grace is probably not going to be a pleasant one. He does not approve of my betrothal, either."

If so many objected, and despite his vow that he alone decided what he did, he might yet change his mind and call off the marriage. But as if he could read her thoughts he said, "He does not rule Llanstephan either, Fiona."

Trying to let his words lift the burden of dread that had settled upon her, she nodded and walked toward the window.

Then she waited, her whole body tense, to see if he would offer words of solace or encouragement, or perhaps take her in his strong arms again and press his warm, surprisingly soft lips to hers, to have his wonderful mouth tease hers into opening like a bud coming into flower so that his tongue could slip inside—

The heavy door closed with a thud.

She glanced over her shoulder. She was, indeed, alone.

She should be glad he had gone and that he had not tempted her with more amazing kisses. She should be more wary of him. It had been years, after all. He had changed, and so had she. He was no longer a boy, and she no longer a maid.

Therefore, it was better he had gone without a kiss or caress, so that she did not have to struggle against the astonishing desire he aroused and act the affronted maid. For her past to remain in the past, she must convince Caradoc she was a virgin still. Then he would not be curious about the man who had taken her maidenhead, and as good as sent her here.

Ask of me no questions, and I shall answer with no lies.

At the clatter of hoof beats on the cobblestones, she again looked into the courtyard. A dark-haired woman in a blood red cloak rode hell-bent through the gate, her head bare, her black hair loose and tousled, her red cloak streaming behind her like a pennant in the breeze. She yanked the white beast to a halt, and despite its prancing, jumped nimbly down. She tossed the reins to one of the stable boys who came in answer to her call, and then hurried into the hall.

Cordelia, Caradoc's sister.

Fiona recognized her by her manner as much as her looks and the raven hair. As a girl, Cordelia could barely sit still. She never walked, always ran, and teased her brothers unmercifully.

Connor had teased back. Caradoc had looked pained, as if she gave him a stomachache, and he never said a word.

She had assumed Cordelia would be married and gone from Llanstephan by now. Dismay filled her as she realized she was not, for she could well imagine that Cordelia's reaction to news of her brother's betrothal and impending marriage would not be cries of gladness.

Another battle was probably going to be waged there, too.

Sighing, she turned and leaned back against the sill.

The marriage had not happened yet. She could always leave.

And go to some strange place to be preyed upon by other men seeking only a rich wife?

She pushed off the sill and marched toward her chest. She threw open the lid and yanked out a linen sheet.

For good or ill, the bargain had been made and sealed. It would take more than a sister's disapproval and a servant's animosity to make her break her word and flee.

A chill fog shrouded the stone buildings of Dunburn. The bell in the village church tolled a death knell, and a small group of the bereaved huddled in the churchyard. Otherwise, few souls ventured outside.

However, neither the weather nor the solemn clang of the bell dampened the spirits of the boisterous band of young men whose sudden appearance on the main street shattered the hushed calm. Oblivious to the sullen mourners, they pulled their equally high-spirited horses to a halt outside a tavern near the wharf and wooden piers. Light oozed out of the small windows and beneath the rough door of the stone building and, like the laughter from within, was almost immediately smothered in the mist. They dismounted, their cloaks and *feileadh mor* swinging about their legs clad in buckskin *cuarans*.

"Wait for me here. I willna be long," declared one

of them, his voice loud in the street. He was a comely fellow, with red-gold hair that waved about his face, and brown eyes that could be pleasant if he was happy, or cruel if he was not.

"You'd better not be," his stocky friend warned as he took hold of the reins of his friend's horse to lead it through the wide arch to the stable in back. "King William expects us back 'ere the week is out."

Iain MacLachlann laughed, and it was boastful and vain, like the man himself. "Since he knows I'm bringing him a thousand marks from my bride's dowry to buy back more land from that Norman bastard Richard, he won't begrudge me the delay."

His companion made a low, appreciative whistle. "I ne'er knew Fiona MacDougal was worth as much as that," Fergus muttered, "or I might have courted her myself."

"Aye, but you didn't, and I did, so she's going to marry me. I've made certain of it, too, so don't go sniffing round her skirts." Iain's hand moved beneath his black cloak, toward the hilt of his sword.

"No fear of that," Fergus quickly replied. "No need for temper, either."

Iain smiled, but there was no mirth or joy in it. It was a threat, that smile, as much as if he held a knife to Fergus's throat.

"I willna be long," Iain repeated before turning away. "I haven't been here for over a month, and my bride-to-be will surely be missing me," he finished with a hint of a smirk lifting the corner of his sensual mouth, which was almost feminine in its fullness. "Later, for King William's sake, I'll tear myself away."

Careful not to slip on the slick cobblestones, Iain started down the street. He wrapped his cloak tighter about himself and silently cursed the mist that dampened his hair and wet his face. Much better it would have been to rejoin King William's court without stopping in Dunburn, but he needed to see if his future bride had sold all the fleece her father had left in store. The major portion of her dowry must be in coin, easily transported. The property here in Dunburn he would rent out, to provide a steady source of income after they were married.

Mercifully it was but a short way from the tavern to the large walled enclosure that housed both Mac-Dougal's warehouse and the living quarters, which the old man had shared with his daughter before he conveniently died.

A man who craved power had to be willing to make sacrifices to get it, and if that meant marrying a merchant's daughter for the dowry she would give him, so be it. A wise man who wanted the merchant's daughter would also do what he must to ensure that she was his, even going as far as seducing her.

Fiona MacDougal had taken some persuading, but at last she had succumbed.

Thus it was with a feeling of immense confidence and satisfaction that Iain MacLachlann pounded his fist on the MacDougal gate and waited for a servant to let him in.

His foot tapping impatiently, he waited some more, then pounded again.

Strange.

Fiona's servants were better trained than this.

The fog became a steady drizzle, further souring

his mood. He would have cursed and returned to the tavern save that soon he would have Fiona on her back beneath him.

Iain smiled to himself as he thought of the night they had finally shared in her bed. A surprising woman, Fiona. He had never guessed she could love so well.

But then, he knew what he was doing when it came to bedding a woman.

At last, as even the taking of Fiona began to lose its appeal, he heard the shuffle of footsteps crossing the puddled cobblestone yard. The grill in the smaller door in the gate creaked open. An unfamiliar man's head appeared in the aperture. The fellow's face was wrinkled and weather-beaten, and a thick thatch of matted gray-blond hair stuck out from beneath a sodden hood.

"Who are you and what do you want, banging fit to wake the dead?" the big oaf demanded, his slightly German accent marking him as a loathsome Saxon.

What in the name of Scotland was Fiona doing hiring a Saxon? He would have the impertinent lout dismissed.

"I am here to see Fiona MacDougal," he announced. "Let me in."

Beneath his grizzled brows the man's watery blue eyes narrowed with suspicion. "Don't know nobody by that name."

Although all Saxons were stupid, this dolt must be simple in the head, too. "Fiona MacDougal, fool! The woman who hired you."

"I've been Heribert of Hartley's man for neigh on ten years."

His soaking cloak now weighing on his shoulders, Iain didn't trouble himself to hide his impatience. "Who, in God's name, is Heribert of Hartley?"

"Who wants t'know?"

"A kinsman of King William of Scotland," Iain haughtily retorted. A distant kinsman he was, but a kinsman nonetheless.

"Heribert of Hartley be a wool merchant," the Saxon grudgingly explained. "He bought this place to ship his wool south a month ago."

Iain couldn't believe his ears. "Then where is Fiona MacDougal—the woman who owned this property?"

"Oh, her. She left Dunburn a fortnight back."

Once over the initial shock, Iain's mind worked swiftly. As Fiona was her father's legal heir, she had the right to sell the property. But the wench had done so against his very specific wishes. "When did you say this was?"

"The sale was a month past and she left a fortnight ago," the man repeated as he started to close the grill.

Iain swiftly shoved his gloved hand in the opening. "Not so fast, my friend."

Marshaling his talents other than martial, Iain made his expression sorrowful.

"Have a little mercy," he pleaded as if his heart was broken, "and forgive my manner. Fiona is my betrothed. We quarreled the last time I was here. I had to leave on business for the crown before I could make up with her, and I've only just got the chance to come back. Now I find she's gone and left."

"Women," the Saxon muttered, shaking his head as if he would never understand the creatures.

Although pleased with his clever deception, Iain was careful not to display his satisfaction. "You have no idea where she went?"

"No."

"I tell you what, my friend," Iain suggested with his most persuasive manner, "if you let me rest a bit and try to get the wind back in my lungs, I'll stand you an ale for my thanks."

The man's eyes gleamed at the thought of a free ale, and after he fumbled about with the keys, the gate swung open.

His shoulders slumped as if overwrought, Iain followed the man into the small gatehouse. A tiny hearth glowed with burning peat, and nearby stood a table and chair. Iain took the chair and the man waited by the hearth. Steam and the stink of wet wool and sweat arose from the Saxon.

"Nobody knows where she went?" Iain asked again, hating the fellow for his Saxon stench, and the devious Fiona even more.

"Lot o' talk in the taverns about how she cleared out so quick and mysterious," the Saxon replied. "Hired a guard as far as York, they say, and then after that . . . ?"

He shrugged his brawny shoulders.

York. She could set sail from there to . . . anywhere. That homely bitch.

He had promised a thousand marks to King

William, and he was going to bloody well provide it. Fiona MacDougal was not going to ruin his plans. No woman was going to make a fool out of him.

By God, he would find her, and he would get his money, one way or the other.

Trying to keep his boiling wrath under control, Iain got to his feet. "I'm ready for that ale now."

The Saxon turned to open the door, and as he did, Iain slid his hand around the man's head to cover his mouth. Then he plunged his dagger between the Saxon's shoulders. He smiled with grim delight as the fellow uselessly struggled and the life left his stinking carcass.

One less insolent Saxon in Scotland.

Chapter 3

Instead of going directly on to the barracks after leaving Fiona in his bedchamber, Caradoc ducked into his solar. He did not want to see anyone until he was once more in complete control of his wayward emotions.

As he tossed his clothes onto the messy table, he battled to subdue the surges of impassioned desire coursing through him.

Long ago, in a vain attempt to stop Connor and Cordelia from teasing him, he had learned how to hide his outward reactions. If they couldn't goad him, he had reasoned, they would tire and stop.

That had not worked, but by the time he had decided it was ineffective, he had come to appreciate the privacy and protection his stoic mask created. People did not know what he was thinking or feeling, and that gave him an advantage. It also made him feel strong and in control of one aspect of his life, at least.

Then, as the years had passed, he had learned how to control more than just the mask. He could control his emotions as well as their display.

At least so he had believed, until today.

What was wrong with him now that he could not subvert the desire coursing through him? Why could he not remove the image of Fiona and her bright eyes and soft lips from his mind, or stop envisioning her remaking his bed with clean, fresh sheets, and silken pillows that a man could sink into? Why could he not prevent the picture of her beneath him, naked and anxious, making small sighs of love and arousal as he slowly pushed inside her, from forming in his head?

He strode to the window where he drew in great breaths of air.

It had to be because she had surprised him with her offer, he told himself. She had disrupted the pattern of his days.

As having her beside him in his bed would disrupt the pattern of his nights.

He must control such thoughts and the feelings that went with them. He must be strong, not weak. He must rule, not be ruled.

He was the lord here. It was the role he had been born and bred for. It had been his destiny from the time of conception. It was what he had worked for.

He did not realize that his hands had balled into fists so tight, his knuckles whitened.

Looking out the window, he surveyed his castle

and forced himself to consider the dowry and all
that it could do.

He could see at once to the repairs of the roofs and
walls. He could purchase new shears for his shepherds and new weapons for his garrison. New
horses, too, and cows from the south.

He began to make a mental list of all that he
would do with his newfound wealth, and his desire
slipped away. Once more, he was Caradoc, the lord
of Llanstephan, and master of himself.

Then Cordelia rode into the courtyard. As always,
she was alone, and must have escaped her escort.
The two men detailed to ride with her would un-
doubtedly return some time later and complain of
having to chase her all over the hills.

She would smile and shrug, vastly amused and
proud of her prowess as a rider and the speed of her
fiery mount, Icarus.

She stared at the wagons, then jumped from her
horse and hurried into the hall.

He could imagine how she would react to the
news surely flying around Llanstephan. A few moments later, he had his confirmation. Her booted
steps sounded on the stairs, for she was taking them
two at a time.

He sat behind his table and prepared for war.

The door to his solar crashed open and Cordelia
burst into the chamber like an irate whirlwind.

"Have you gone *mad*?" she demanded. "Utterly,
totally mad?"

Her gray eyes snapping, she faced him with feet
planted and arms akimbo, her cloak flaring. "What's
this I hear about you getting *married*? To a *Scot*. A

redheaded creature who just appeared out of nowhere with three carts like some kind of brownie. And the day after tomorrow! I told Jon-Bron he must be making it up, and a very poor jest it was."

In her anger, she was the female image of Connor in one of his rages, and Caradoc's ire burned the hotter for it. Always Connor had gotten his way because he could make life a misery when he was thus enraged.

Caradoc forced away the past and faced the angry present. "Then you owe Jon-Bron an apology, for it's true. I am getting married the day after tomorrow to a Scot who appeared as if by magic in the courtyard, with three carts and three thousand marks for her dowry."

Cordelia's jaw dropped. Then it just as quickly snapped shut before she spoke. "So that's it? Three thousand marks and the lord of Llanstephan is sold?"

"Watch your tongue, little sister," he growled as he rose. "I don't recall asking your opinion, and I don't have to ask your permission to marry—but you will have to ask mine."

"Why should I?" she demanded, crossing her arms, like Connor in that, too. "Surely I will choose better than some Scot who arrives unannounced and unlooked for and convinces my brother to sell himself!"

Her angry denunciation cut Caradoc like a dagger's thrust. He had worked and worried for her sake, yet she would stand there and hurl such words at him.

He strode toward her until he was nearly nose to

nose with her, for she was tall for seventeen. "I am the lord of Llanstephan and *no one* tells me what to do, or how, or when. I have made my decision, and you will simply have to abide by it."

She didn't back away. Cordelia never backed away.

"Oh, yes, Caradoc, the mighty lord of Llanstephan Fawr, who sells his title for some Scots coin," she retorted, her fists on her hips. "How could you do something so shameful? Have you no pride? No honor? Do you forget you are Welsh?"

Glaring at her, he crossed his arms over his broad chest and fought to keep from shouting. "Listen to me, little sister, and listen to me well. I have sense, and pride, and honor, and we are but half Welsh. You would do well to remember that before you use that sharp tongue of yours to upbraid me again. What I do, I do for the good of Llanstephan, and you, and everyone who depends upon me for their safety and their livelihood. Have you forgotten that we are not rich, thanks to Connor? That we have little power, thanks to Connor? Or would you rather I found some rich and ancient Welsh knight who craves a young and beautiful bride? You are so lovely, Cordelia, I could have offered a pittance for your dowry, I'm sure, and then used your *amobr* to pay our debts."

She reared back as if he had struck her. Instantly, his heart wished he could take back those final words. Yet his mind rebelled against regret, for what he had said was a truth, albeit an ugly one. She was beautiful enough that he would have a fine profit between a small dowry and the *amobr*, the Welsh bride price.

Cordelia's nostrils flared as she sniffed with disgust, although not with the same vim. "How foolish of me not to be grateful that you did not sell me off to the first knight who came calling."

"You should be. And I think you are angry because you will no longer be the chatelaine here once I wed."

He immediately realized this was a mistake. The expression on her face declared that she had not thought of what this marriage would mean to her beyond the shame of being the sister of a man who would sell himself for money.

She marched over to the window and looked out a moment, thinking—something she had not done prior to marching in here like an enraged shrew, he was sure—before she whirled around to face him again. "What of Lord Rhys? Do you think he will stand idly by afterwards? He will say you are betraying the Welsh, as many others will."

"What has Lord Rhys ever done for me? Or these other Welsh you speak of?" he countered as he leaned his hip against the table, Fiona's argument coming easily to his lips. "They will not pay the taxes for us, will they? As for Rhys, he's too busy weaving his own plans and nursing his grudge against Richard. Nor should King Richard care who I marry, as long as he gets his money. You see, little sister, I did not make this bargain without thought."

He waited for Cordelia to try to disagree with him.

Her frown deepened and suddenly, he saw a hint of pity in her eyes.

"Do you hear yourself?" she asked. "A bargain, you call it. A trade. You might as well be speaking of horses at the fair."

His anger spiked again. He didn't need anyone's pity. There had been a time he ached for a kind word, or praise for a lesson well done, but it had not come, and he had learned to live without it. "So what if it is? All marriages are business agreements."

"That's a lie and you know it. Our parents' marriage was not a bargain."

Lingering grief cooled his hot anger to practicality.

"Our parents are dead and we are in danger of losing our home," he said with more restraint. "Marrying Fiona will prevent that, and that's what I intend to do, whether you approve or not."

Storm clouds gathered again on her brow and in her smoke gray eyes. "I know our parents are dead, and so you are the overlord here. I know full well that we are not rich anymore, and if you want to do this thing, I cannot stop you. So do what you will. Just don't expect me to like it, or that brazen Scot."

"Fiona. Her name is Fiona."

Cordelia's lip curled, barely perceptibly, but he saw it nonetheless. "If you say so."

She marched to the door, then looked back at him. "If you *had* to sell yourself, it's too bad you couldn't at least have been purchased by a *pretty* woman."

With that she went out and slammed the door behind her, the sound echoing through the solar.

Caradoc ground his fist in his palm as he stared at the back of the door. What else had he expected? That she would welcome this news and gladly give up her position as chatelaine of Llanstephan to a stranger, and a Scottish one at that? That she would understand the problems he faced? That she would have a moment's compassion for him?

God save him, every time he tried to reason with his sister, he only made things worse. When he tried to talk to her, it was disastrous. He should join a holy order of monks under a vow of silence.

But then he would have to give up Fiona, too.

He ran his hand through his hair and threw himself in his chair, slinging one leg over the arm as he leaned his head back.

Could Cordelia not see that he agreed to this marriage out of duty? That most of what he did had little to do with his own desires or needs or wishes?

This was not the life he had dreamed of during all those long hours here with Brother Adolphus droning on in Greek and Latin, staring at figures on the parchment, tallying profits and gain and taxes until the numbers swam before his eyes.

Then he had longed to leave Llanstephan, to travel the world and see the things he'd read about—elephants, the great pyramids of Egypt, the Roman Coliseum. Paris. Florence.

Instead, he had done his duty as the eldest son while Connor got to go, sent off on Crusade with great fanfare and at such great cost, only to have it end in disaster. Connor had quarreled with King Richard and been sent from the royal retinue in disgrace. Then the taxes on Llanstephan had been tripled, so that now they had scarcely a coin to their name.

To be sure, it could be much worse. Connor could have been killed.

And he could have been born a poor peasant . . . a poor peasant who had only himself to think of, not a sister who argued, and a castle and village full of people who looked to him for safety and security.

Sometimes he thought of leaving Llanstephan, going out into the dark of the night, away from responsibility and duty. He'd go to some place where he could think and plan and dream for himself alone.

Alone, but no more lonely than he was here.

Then he thought of Fiona standing here in this chamber making her incredible proposition. The physical desire she stirred within him. The fierce, passionate kiss they had shared.

No matter what he said to Cordelia, in his heart he knew he had not agreed to this marriage solely because of money. Nay, nor lust, either, as he remembered Fiona's frank, bold manner. She addressed him as an equal, not a lord to be feared or an annoying sibling. A small part of him hoped he could find some measure of happiness with such a woman as his wife.

Perhaps he was wrong to entertain even a tiny sliver of hope. He had been disappointed often enough in the past.

And yet, as he remembered Fiona's kiss and her passion, the hope that had taken root dared to grow a little more.

Dafydd surveyed the group of men sitting in the barracks of Llanstephan Fawr.

At this time of day, when the sun was nearly set, the chamber was dim and would have been empty except for the rows of cots, the long table at one end holding basins and ewers of cold water for washing, and the pegs near the door where cloaks and various bits and pieces of armor hung. Each man had a wooden chest beside his bed for his personal belongings. In the evening, light was provided by torches in sconces on the walls, as well as by a fire lit in the small open hearth in the center of the room.

The loopholes, windows only wide enough for an archer to take aim, provided little ventilation, so the scent of smoke, pitch, horse, and sweaty soldiers lingered.

Jon-Bron and his two brothers sat glumly on one of the cots, looking like three statues of mournfully martyred saints. Eifion, called the Eel for his tall, slender build, leaned against the wall, thoughtfully picking at a small hole in the nearest stone with his long, narrow fingers. Dafydd paced down the room and back again.

"There's nothing we can do, then?" Jon-Bron repeated for what must have been the twentieth time since they had gathered there.

"No, nothing. He's decided and there's an end to it," Dafydd replied as he halted. "He went to the priest like his britches were on fire. We should be glad he didn't marry her then and there, I suppose. Maybe the gathering and washing will give him time to cool his ardor and reconsider."

Bran-Bron thoughtfully rubbed his chin. "How long has it been since he's had a woman? He should have called for Bronwyn."

The brothers exchanged sage looks. It was well

known that their sister Bronwyn was very talented in some regards, and they were justly proud.

"You know why not. He won't go with a girl from here," Dafydd said. "It would only cause trouble, he says. Jealousy and accusations of playing favorites. Who knows? Maybe he's right."

"Then you should have told him to go to Shrewsbury," Eifion declared as a small avalanche of dust fell from the hole he had picked in the stone. "It's too hasty, this marriage." He lowered his voice to a suitably somber tone. "I foresee trouble."

Dafydd gave him a look of disgruntled disgust. "Quit picking at that wall as if you're trying to break from prison. And considering the usual way of your predictions, I feel a lot better. You said there was going to be a great snowstorm last winter and we had the most mild weather in years. You said we'd only have two hundred lambs and we had nearly three times that. You said two years ago your mother-in-law was going to be in her grave in a week and here she is still hale and hearty at eighty, although nobody blames you for being hopeful. You said Richard was going to take Jerusalem and our Connor come home covered in glory and . . . well, he didn't. You should give over making predictions, Eifion, before you're the laughingstock of Llanstephan."

"I've got a bad feeling about this," the reeve stubbornly insisted.

"You don't need to be a seer to have that about this," Jon-Bron noted, shaking his head. "A Scot. A merchant's daughter. God save me, I never thought

Caradoc would stoop so low. It's a disgrace, that's what, and we've got to stop him."

"He's been that worried, I was afraid he would do something drastic, but never anything so terrible as this," Dafydd admitted as the others nodded in agreement. "We've got to save him. The question is, how?"

"Kidnap Father Rhodri?" Emlyn-Bron suggested.

Dafydd frowned. "You know he doesn't *need* a priest. He could just announce it and there you are."

"We could kidnap *her*."

Dafydd grinned at Emlyn-Bron. "Now there's a thought. Get her out of the tower somehow and onto a horse and take her to somebody's farm until Caradoc has had time—"

"To do what?" their lord asked as he strode into the barracks.

The men jumped as if he had thrown a bucket of freezing water at them, and Caradoc could tell from their guilty faces that whatever they had been discussing, they didn't think he would be pleased.

His impending marriage, no doubt.

There was an empty cot near the door, the last ever taken because it was colder there from the draft and farthest from the hearth. He put his clothes on it and sat, facing them with his hand clasped and his elbows on his knees.

"Look you," he said, ready to explain because these men were his friends, and they led his people, too, "she's brought a dowry of three thousand marks."

He thought Dafydd was going to faint as he wobbled to the nearest chest and sat down. The three men already seated stared at him with their mouths open, looking like fish in a stall at a market. Eifion leaned back against the wall as if he was holding it up, not the other way around.

"Th-three thousand marks you said?" Dafydd finally managed to stammer. "Three *thousand*?"

"Aye, three thousand in wine and cloth and gold and silver and jewels. That's what the men unloaded from those wagons."

Jon-Bron slowly came back to life and cleared his throat. "That's, um, that's quite a sum, Caradoc."

"Isn't it?" he genially agreed. "So how could I say no? None of the Welsh nobility have gone out of their way to help us, or make a marriage offer I could accept, so it's marry Fiona or give up Llanstephan to the crown." He spread his hands. "It's as simple as that."

Dafydd studied the toe of Caradoc's left boot. "Well, understanding I am about the money, Caradoc." He raised his eyes to his friend's face. "But what about *her*? She's a Scot."

"I know."

"Not Welsh."

"Yes, I understand that."

Jon-Bron looked at him with eyes full of sympathy. "Money or not, it's a terrible sacrifice you're making, Caradoc. Are you that sure it's necessary?"

"Yes, I am."

"A *merchant's* daughter," Eifion mumbled.

"Since she isn't noble, neither Rhys nor Richard will be able to say I'm making potentially dangerous political alliances, will they?"

"Aye, there is that," Bran-Bron noted in a more hopeful tone.

Dafydd delicately cleared his throat. "Well, Caradoc, even if she's got money and no political entanglements, it's not as if you're going to be bedding a pile of coins, is it? I mean, she's not very . . . You could do better, that's all."

Like Cordelia, they didn't think Fiona was pretty. Maybe she wasn't in the way they meant, yet he found her attractive. Her bold spirit, her shining eyes, her kiss, her way of making him feel that he was the most desirable man in the world—these were things not to be taken lightly.

Yet he wasn't about to reveal his innermost feelings to anybody, not even Dafydd. "I like her well enough."

"And Cordelia? What about her? How did she take the news?" Jon-Bron asked.

Caradoc's good humor diminished. "Ah, yes, Cordelia. She doesn't approve, but that doesn't matter. I must marry or risk losing Llanstephan, so marriage it will be."

"What does Father Rhodri say?" Dafydd asked.

Caradoc fidgeted. He really didn't want to talk about his discussion with Father Rhodri, either. The priest had immediately denounced the marriage as hasty and wrongheaded, a bad decision Caradoc would come to regret. Caradoc had stooped to reminding the priest that while Father Rhodri served God, *he* served the king and his people as well as God, and to do that, he needed a castle. To keep his castle he needed Fiona.

Unfortunately, Father Rhodri had stood stubbornly firm and refused to sanctify the marriage on the holy ground of his chapel. Only reluctantly had he agreed to bless the joining of hands in the hall.

The men exchanged knowing looks.

"What?" Caradoc demanded.

"He tried to talk you out of it, didn't he?" Dafydd said.

"He thought I should pray on it and ask for God's guidance."

"Wise man, Father Rhodri," Eifion remarked to no one in particular.

Caradoc fixed his steely gaze on the reeve. "I told him Fiona must have been sent by God in answer to my prayers to keep me from losing Llanstephan."

Which he had. The rest had come after, when Father Rhodri had looked at him as if Caradoc had declared his intention to turn heathen. "Now, if you don't mind, I would like to wash and change for the evening meal."

There was no need for them to stare at him as if he had never washed before and wasn't expected to. "Nothing wrong with wanting to be clean, is there?"

"No, no," Jon-Bron and his brothers muttered as they got to their feet. "We'll be seeing you in the hall, then, Caradoc."

"Aye."

The men filed out, all but Dafydd, who toyed with a thread from the blanket covering the cot beside him.

"You're going to make a hole," Caradoc remarked as the brothers exited and closed the door.

Dafydd stopped fiddling and clasped his hands.

Caradoc decided to ignore him. Nothing Dafydd could say was going to make him change his mind.

After removing his old tunic, he went to one of the jugs beside the basins and poured out some water. He rinsed his face in the frigid water, then threw back his head and ran his fingers through his hair. Maybe one of the men had a comb he could use. And a dagger to scrape the whiskers from his face. He wouldn't put himself at risk of Dafydd's teasing by cutting his hair, but he would shave off his beard and try to look more like a lord and less like an unshorn sheep.

"Caradoc?"

He tensed at the serious tone of Dafydd's voice. "Yes?"

"How can you marry her? You just met her today."

"I knew her years ago, and so did you. Her father was Angus MacDougal, the wool merchant."

"I don't remember him, or her, either."

"I do."

"You could have had your pick of half the unmarried noblewomen in Wales, and they've got dowries big enough to pay off the worst of the debt."

Caradoc faced his friend. "Half the unmarried noblewomen in Wales have hardly been beating a path to my door, have they? Besides, even if they did, I'd have to pay their families the *amobr*. Fiona doesn't know about that, or I think she would have mentioned it. Even if she did, she has no family to pay. So I get all her considerable dowry, and have nothing to pay myself.

"As for her being pretty or not, she's pretty enough for me." He slid his friend a glance and decided he could say a little more about her. "And she's, um, not shy."

Dafydd's eyes widened and he let out a low whistle. "Aye, I should have guessed that from her arrival. Brazen in many things, is she?"

Caradoc saw no need to confirm Dafydd's opinion with examples as he went to the nearest chest and lifted the lid. There was a comb made from bone right on the top. If he were like Eifion, he would take this as a sign, and a good one. "Whose is this? Do you know?"

"No. Jon-Bron will. Are you going to try to comb that tangled mess on your head?"

"Is there something wrong with that?"

"Not at all, provided you don't break the comb. Will you have me fetch the shears?" he finished with mock gravity.

Caradoc was glad to hear his friend's jesting query. It made his marriage seem a much less serious undertaking. "No, I don't want the shears. Nobody would recognize me if I cut my hair. It'll be enough if I comb it and get rid of my beard."

"You're cutting off your beard?" Dafydd cried, genuinely shocked.

Caradoc frowned. "And you it was telling me I looked like a sheep in serious need of shearing."

"Well, yes, I did."

Caradoc raised his brows questioningly.

"All right, all right, off it goes. And here's just the thing to do it with." He pulled his dagger from his belt and held it out. "Sharp as can be, that is. Be careful."

With a scowl that wasn't completely bogus, Caradoc accepted it. "I am not so clumsy as I was."

"I know that." Dafydd went back to toying with the thread and slid Caradoc a look out of the corner of his eye. "So, tell me. How did you discover she wasn't *shy*?"

"That's for me to know, and you to puzzle over."

"You're not going to tell me, your best and oldest friend? The one who taught you how to shear? The fellow who took you to the Bull and Crown in Shrewsbury and introduced you to that fine girl who giggled all the time, even when you were—"

"I'm *not* going to tell you," Caradoc sternly interrupted before Dafydd went any further with his reminiscences.

Despite the merriment in his eyes, Dafydd managed to look mightily affronted. "Varlet."

"Cur."

"Blackguard."

"Nit."

Dafydd got up and came closer to examine Caradoc's progress. "Watch what you're doing there, Caradoc, or you're going to slit your own throat."

"Then be quiet and let me get on with it," the lord of Llanstephan growled as he continued to scrape the heavy black whiskers from his face.

Chapter 4

Later that night, Fiona followed Rhonwen down the steps to the great hall. The petite young woman had been quiet and efficient, and was so delicate in her movements that, coupled with her light brown hair and brown gown, she reminded Fiona of a sparrow or wren, a tiny creature that flitted about its business unnoticed and unremarked.

In that, Rhonwen was blessedly different from Ganore. She wondered if Caradoc had chosen this girl to help her for precisely that reason, or if he had thought about it at all. Perhaps Rhonwen was used to waiting on ladies. Or perhaps she was simply the first maidservant whose name had come to his lips.

Either way, the bed was now remade with clean, fine linens and covered in a scarlet coverlet of silk. Matching scarlet velvet curtains had replaced the old. A dressing table now stood across from the bed, covered with Fiona's combs, a few small glass bottles holding perfumes and unguents, and the sandalwood box in which she kept her ribbons and the bronze casings for her hair. A cushioned stool was underneath it. Tapestries depicting a hunt and a couple in a garden graced the walls, hiding the water stains. Two large candle stands holding expensive beeswax candles would provide ample light, and a bronze brazier stood in the corner, ready to be filled with glowing coals to heat the room against the evening's chill. There were even carpets on the floor—a luxury the returning Crusaders had introduced, and her father had enthusiastically adopted.

Their work completed, Fiona had washed and dabbed on a bit of the expensive perfume her father had given her as a gift. Then, with Rhonwen's help, she had donned one of her finer gowns, a delightful garment of rich creamy velvet embroidered about the neck and cuffs with delicate greens, golds, and reds, which she thought brought out the green of her eyes. Wearing this gown, she felt equal to any noblewoman, even if she was no beauty and had no title. Or rather, no title *yet*.

They entered the hall. Tables and benches were set up for the meal, and the high table on the dais was covered with a white linen cloth.

As Rhonwen slipped into the crowd of people waiting there, Fiona paused a moment to survey them. Ganore stood at the head of a phalanx of maidservants like a general on the battlefield. Her expression was just as fierce as Fiona imagined a general's would be if he were facing a detested enemy.

There were soldiers milling about, too, and what

appeared to be three brothers were obviously leaders among them. Cordelia stood on the dais beside her brother and a priest. If Ganore looked angry, it was nothing compared to the animosity fairly shooting from Cordelia's gray eyes.

The priest, a middle-aged man in the black robe of a Dominican, seemed tense and extremely unhappy.

She saved Caradoc for last.

Wearing a simple black tunic that reached to his knees, black woolen breeches, boots and a wide leather sword belt, he stood with his feet apart, his hands clasped behind his back, commanding as befitted the lord of a castle. He needed no fine clothes to show that he ruled here; the mantle of leadership hung about him like a cloak.

But that was as she might expect. It was his face, clean-shaven and more handsome than she had ever imagined—and she had imagined him very handsome, indeed—that took her breath away.

Over the years the soft planes of his cheeks and the line of his boyish jaw had developed into an angular, altogether masculine, incredibly attractive face. His lips had felt wonderful upon hers, and seeing them without the hindrance of his beard, she knew why. They were full, sensual, yet as undeniably masculine as the rest of him.

If she had known just how good-looking Lord Caradoc of Llanstephan had become, she would never have dreamed of coming here to offer herself to him, for she would have been quite certain he would laugh in her face. Skin-and-Bones Fiona, Freckled Fiona whom the other children laughed at, would never have presumed to think so handsome a man would marry her even if she came to him with ten times three thousand marks. Nor would he have to. Women of rank would be lined up a hundred deep outside the castle gates for the opportunity of finding favor with the dark lord of Llanstephan.

She nearly turned tail and ran. But what fate awaited if she did that? Besides, she had given her word. Her father had shown every day by word and deed that honor did not rest solely with the nobility. Indeed, a merchant needed to be more honest and trustworthy than they if he was to have the respect of the world.

A title would give her a certain amount of respect. Some of her other attributes might win her more from these people. But more importantly, she needed to prove her worthiness by earning their respect, and that she was determined to do.

Yet still she hesitated, the taunting laughter of her childhood ringing in her ears. And then she found her strength where she so often had in those days. She told herself to forget the dowry that made their marriage possible and the shame that had sent her here. She imagined instead that Caradoc had chosen her from a horde of beauties for her looks, her wit, and her wisdom. She was Fiona the Fair, and he was the Dark Prince she had saved from the Lonely Tower.

Her shoulders straightened, her chin lifted, and she began to cross the hall. She ignored the stares, the questioning looks, the whispered comments. She was Fiona the Fair, sure of her value, confident of her worth, and such things could not touch her.

Not even the lack of expression on the face of the man she was to marry could upset her.

She reached the dais and bowed. "My lord."

He came forward and took her hand to lead her toward the priest and Cordelia. Despite her resolve to be as calm and serene as a statue of the Holy Mother, the first touch of his flesh against hers made her instantly aware that she was very mortal indeed, and as full of original sin as Eve. Caradoc's grasp released a coil of heat and fervent desire within her that destroyed the inner calm she had managed to achieve and sent it spiraling away into the ether.

"This is Father Rhodri. Father, this is Fiona," Caradoc said in his deep, rich voice as he introduced her to the priest.

While she was struggling against lust, he spoke as if he felt nothing at all.

"Father Rhodri," she replied, still struggling.

The priest rudely stared at her.

When Caradoc ignored the priest's obvious insolence, the excitement in her shifted to the beginnings of anger. Did he not notice the man's rudeness? Did he not see the lack of respect? Did he not care?

"Cordelia, this is Fiona," Caradoc continued. "Fiona, my sister."

"I know who she is," Cordelia snapped as she ran a scornful gaze over Fiona and her fine gown.

Fiona felt a hot blush spreading on her face. There was nothing she could do about that. Nor had she expected to be welcomed with open arms by Caradoc's sister, especially under these circumstances. Nevertheless, she would not accept being treated as if she were some kind of outlaw or thief, unworthy of courtesy. Nor would she wait for

Caradoc to intervene. As with Ganore, this would have to be a battle between *them*.

"I know who you are, too, sister-in-law-to-be," she said with a serenity distinctly at odds with the anger burning in her breast. "Your rudeness tells me that you are in need of an older sister's guidance. I shall do my best, although it is a sad day when the daughter of a Scottish merchant must teach the daughter of a Welsh princess how a lady should behave."

Ignoring the shocked gasp from those nearby, and the growing outrage on Cordelia's face, she continued to regard the young woman steadily.

"Are you going to let her talk to me like that?" Cordelia demanded of Caradoc after the initial moment of surprise had passed.

"Since she is right, yes. Your greeting was not polite, Cordelia."

Cordelia's eyes blazed and her hands balled into outraged fists. "If you don't mind, I'll go sit with Dafydd and Fifion," she declared.

"I don't mind at all," he replied with placid calm.

A moment's pleased relief passed through Fiona as Cordelia marched past her and took a place at another table. Caradoc had not taken Cordelia's side against her.

Then, disaster.

Caradoc turned to face everyone in the hall and raised his voice so that it rang out like the bell of a cathedral calling sinners to prayer. "This woman is to be my wife. You will *all* respect her and treat her accordingly, because she is my wife."

Fiona wanted to howl with frustration. While a

look or a brief word to the priest would have been welcome, she did not want this imperious command to the entire household. Fitting in here and earning their respect was going to be difficult enough, but it was for her to do. By doing this, he had only increased their wariness of her.

But what could she say to him? The deed could not be undone.

She might not be in a position to chastise her husband-to-be, she decided, but she must try to find a way to repair the damage he had unwittingly inflicted.

"Now, Fiona, I will introduce you to the others here."

Fiona the Fair steeled herself and went forth into the lion's den of Llanstephan.

As Caradoc led his bride toward the people waiting at the tables, he surreptitiously studied her. She was stoically staring straight ahead as if she were made of marble.

It wasn't hard for him to guess why.

God save him, he hated his sister sometimes. She had no thought beyond what she considered right and proper and befitting a Welsh nobleman. She had no concern for finances or necessities. She had been too coddled and spoiled for too long, doted on because of her beauty and spirit.

Fiona had spirit of a different sort, for there was humor and generosity in it, too. Cordelia would not have found his lack of recognition amusing; she would have found it offensive in the extreme. While Cordelia could probably face any man in defiance, he doubted she could plead her case so fluently and so well as Fiona had, putting her request in reasonable terms that were difficult to disagree with. She never remained calm in the face of another's anger, but lashed out.

He had had little joy in his life these past few years in no small part because Cordelia couldn't accept that he stood in the place of their father. It was his right and his duty to command everyone here, including her. Worse, she would always compare him to Connor of the merry smile and winning charm, a contest he was always bound to lose.

Putting his sister's displeasure from his mind as best he could, he again glanced at his future wife. She carried herself with the pride and dignity befitting a noblewoman, and better than some he had seen. If he had had any fears about how she would act in noble company, they were dispelled. Yet while he appreciated this dignified lady, he preferred the confident, spirited woman of the solar and bedchamber.

His bedchamber, where soon they would join as man and wife. Again his burning desire rose up and threatened his self-control. He could barely prevent himself from tugging her into his arms and kissing her right then, regardless of where they were or who would see. More, he wanted to sweep her into his arms, dash up the steps to his chamber, kick open the door, lay her on his bed and—

Keeping any hint of the visions playing about his mind from his face and his voice, he introduced Fiona to Eifion, who tonight looked like a man who had lost his last hope. Fortunately, Fiona seemed to find nothing wrong with his demeanor as she nodded regally and gave him a small smile.

As Caradoc escorted her toward Jon-Bron, Emlyn-Bron, Bran-Bron and the other soldiers, a silent recitation of his oath of fealty further subdued his vivid imaginings.

He needed no such thing to keep his mind focused when he introduced Fiona to the servants, for they were barely civil.

He hadn't expected a warm welcome, but he saw Ganore's hand in this, and anger filled him, replacing everything else.

But he didn't show that, either. Instead, he silently reassured himself that Ganore must come to accept Fiona one day and treat her as his wife deserved.

Or, considering how she usually treated him, better.

After that, they went toward Dafydd. He had left his friend for last, fearing that Dafydd might say something undignified or tell some outrageous tale from his childhood, like the time he had gotten his head stuck in a bucket. Now, he thought they could all use a little touch of levity, and it might help lessen his smoldering ire. "Fiona, this is Dafydd. He is my bailiff, and my friend."

Dafydd grinned and bowed low. "A pleasure it is to meet you, Fiona MacDougal," he said, sincerity in every word.

Fiona must have heard that, too, for her haughty grandeur fled, and with it, the last of Caradoc's anger. Now she was again the woman in his solar. The woman he had kissed.

The woman who had so eagerly kissed him back.

"I am pleased to meet you, too, Dafydd," she said.

"If you're going to live here married to this shaggy fellow, you had best know my full name. Dafydd-y-Trwyn." He tapped his nose and his brown eyes shone with mirth. "Dafydd the Nose, that is, because God saw fit to give me enough for two."

Fiona clearly didn't know what to make of that.

"Of course, the women know that it means I have enough for two of something else," he said with a sly wink.

As Fiona colored, Caradoc wished the stones beneath his feet would heave, splinter, open up and swallow him—aye, and Dafydd, too.

"Dafydd," he growled, his tone warning that his friend had gone too far. Relief from anger and tension was one thing; such rude implications were something else again.

"I thought it was a man's ears that indicated that," Fiona remarked, apparently gravely serious. "Yours seem quite small, although very attractive."

Then she turned and tucked Caradoc's hair behind his right ear, her touch so much like a caress, his whole body warmed with it. Her lovely lips turned up into a devilish smile that made his heartbeat skip. "Whereas my lord's seem . . . quite substantial."

Caradoc didn't know what he felt more: shock, distress, pride, or glee to see the look of stunned surprise on Dafydd's face.

Countless times he had yearned to pay Dafydd back for all his teasing, and here she was doing it for him.

He could not let her have all the fun.

"You've hurt his feelings, Fiona," he noted, apparently equally serious. "Proud of his prowess with women is our Dafydd."

"I can see why women would like him," she said as if Dafydd wasn't there. "He is a very charming fellow. Impertinent, of course, but one cannot take offense at what so merry a man says, even if it is most improper."

Caradoc wanted to laugh out loud. He wanted to grab her and kiss her. Passionately.

"God save me, boy, she is a wonder," Dafydd muttered, his face so red, Caradoc almost pitied him. He might have, had Dafydd not embarrassed him a hundred times or more.

And Dafydd's heartfelt words were a great compliment, whether Fiona knew it or not.

"We had best return to the high table. Father Rhodri is starting to fidget," he said, moving before he started grinning like a drunkard getting free ale.

But by the saints, he hadn't felt this lighthearted in months.

Fiona was indeed a wonder. He could hardly wait to be alone with her again. To stifle his building laughter by kissing her. To tuck her marvelous thick hair behind her shapely ears with a similar caress, and to let that caress linger and slip lower . . .

When they had reached their places, Father Rhodri stepped forward to say the grace. As everyone bowed their heads expectantly, Caradoc saw the look on the priest's face and all propensity to laughter fled. Dreading what was to come, he readied himself as a warrior before battle, for he was sure it would be a challenge to keep his emotions under control as Father Rhodri spoke.

"Oh, God and St. David, patron saint of this blessed land of Wales," the priest began in a mournful voice more suited to a funeral oration. "Look down with mercy on all here as we prepare to partake of Your blessed bounty. Forgive decisions made in haste, based on earthly need. Pardon the worship of mammon, oh God, and the lusts of the flesh. Show all those tempted into sin the error of their ways and lead them onto the path of redemption and reconsideration. Have mercy upon the impetuous, oh God, and teach them the wisdom of patience. Blessed heavenly Father, take pity on the weak and give them strength.

"Grant us these things, we pray, in the name of Your beloved Son who first made known His divine nature at the wedding feast at Cana where He was a guest, a ceremony not agreed upon in haste and leading to disaster. Amen."

Caradoc shifted and mentally rolled his eyes, frustrated nearly to speaking. He had guessed the man's grace was going to be bad, but this was beyond anything he had anticipated.

Yet he would not reveal his anger. Father Rhodri had been here too long and was too beloved by the people for him to chastise. Besides, Father Rhodri would take his complaint all the way to the pope if Caradoc even tried.

"Thank you, Father," Caradoc said, managing to keep his voice level with great effort.

"You're welcome, my son," Father Rhodri replied, sounding very well pleased with himself.

It was tempting to send the man on a long pil-grimage, preferably somewhere that would take years to reach.

"This food smells wonderful. I didn't realize how hungry I am," Fiona remarked as the aromas of fresh bread and roasted mutton filled the hall. She was ap-parently no more disturbed by Father Rhodri's im-pertinence than she was by Dafydd's comments.

A wonder indeed, thank God. He had known from the moment he had agreed to marry her that it was not going to be easy for her to be accepted. For-tunately, it seemed she wasn't going to let that trou-ble her. It appeared he need not fear complaints and grumbling or hot-tempered demands from his wife.

That would be pleasant.

Of course, a far more pleasant change to his cir-cumstances awaited him at night. Thinking of that and emboldened by her comments to Dafydd, he didn't resist the impulse to put his hand on her thigh.

Her muscle tightened and he imagined her legs gripping him, holding him to her as he loved her.

"My lord," she said as she lifted his hand away, her voice low so that only he could hear, "perhaps my response to your friend, made in the same jesting spirit as his remark to me, has caused you to think I am somewhat wanton. I am not."

Despite her chiding remark, he was not willing to return to polite distance yet. "If I think you are somewhat wanton, it is because of the kiss we have already shared."

"Be that as it may, I must remind you that we are not yet married," she retorted, sounding surprisingly prim considering what she had said to Dafydd and in view of that breathtaking kiss. "Although I have given my word and mean to keep it, I will not be treated like a piece of merchandise to be pawed over."

He had heard that critical tone too often from others and he hated it.

Nor did he deserve such severe censure for a relatively harmless gesture. "We have made a bargain, Fiona," he likewise reminded her, his voice as stern as when he passed judgment in his courtyard.

She did not seem overly impressed. "I know that as well as you, but you do not own me yet, so please do not treat me as if you do."

"As you wish," he replied. "Besides, my people already think you very brazen, and perhaps it would be best not to confirm their impression. And what would Father Rhodri say? His next grace would surely condemn you as a Jezebel."

"*I* am brazen?" she countered, her eyes fairly blazing with indignation. "I am not the one putting hands on thighs."

He leaned slightly forward, his gaze dropping to her luscious lips. "You are the one who proposed to me, Fiona, not the other way 'round," he whispered, his voice deep and low and intimate.

"But you are the one who needs my money."

It was as if she had slapped his face, or risen to berate him in his hall.

Feeling that same horrible sense of deficiency as when he had failed to please his father or his tutors, he scowled and took a gulp of her fine French wine.

* * *

Would that he had scowled thus at the priest after that insolent, outrageous blessing! Fiona thought as she watched the goblet meet Caradoc's shapely lips. If Father Rhodri had raised his hand and struck her, she couldn't have felt more humiliated and embarrassed. If that was his idea of a blessing, she didn't want to imagine his curse. What would he say at the marriage? That they deserved excommunication and eternal damnation? Or would he refuse to bless it at all?

Why had Caradoc accepted the insolence without a look or word of criticism? After all, the priest didn't seem to be limiting his disgust to her, but obviously sought to criticize Caradoc, too.

On the other hand, she reminded herself, she had not admired Connor of the fiery temper, so how could she condemn Caradoc for being more moderate?

Caradoc took another huge gulp of the wine. "God's wounds, that's good."

She sipped hers and realized it was the Bordeaux. "You have already opened the French wine?"

"Why not?"

Why not indeed?

In an attempt to have some sort of normal conversation—for surely then she would *feel* normal—she nodded toward the three dark-haired men sitting together at a table full of raucous soldiers. "Those three brothers have unusual names. Is Bron a family name?"

Caradoc wiped his lips after another gulp of wine. When he spoke, his accent was broader and

he seemed far more relaxed than he had been before. "In a way. It's from their older sister, Bronwyn. Famous is our Bronwyn, you see, for her
talents."

Since she was in Wales, Fiona made a guess. "She
is a fine singer?"

She had the sudden sensation he was doing his
best not to burst out laughing, which was almost as
disconcerting as if he had.

He leaned close again, bringing his broad shoulders nearly to hers, and whispered as if revealing state
secrets. "She makes a kind of music. An earthy lass is
our Bronwyn, and liking men, especially young ones
ready for their first time. In other places they say such
lads are sowing their oats. Here we say the lad's gone
to Bronwyn, because most times, he has."

This was not what she had expected to hear. At all.

"She was the most popular tavern wench between Cardiff and Shrewsbury," he continued, as if
he were proud of Bronwyn, too. "She made enough
that now she owns the tavern in the village."

"Then she was a—?"

"Whore, aye. A good one."

He sounded so proud and happy for the woman,
he must have been a frequent customer.

Then the corners of his mouth slowly curved up
in a secretive smile that seemed to say he had read
her thoughts. "No, not me. I went farther afield."

She stared down at the table, blushing like a green
girl who didn't know men had needs, especially virile men like Caradoc. And after all, he would not be
her first, either.

But he would be far and away the best.

She silenced that knowing little voice, so confident and keen.

"She doesn't mind the reputation, and neither do
they."

"Then the stories are true about the wild Welsh in
their mountains," she replied, fighting to sound
matter-of-fact. "I had believed them exaggerations,
but obviously they are not if those men take part of
her name as their own."

"That isn't the way it works. Others give you the
name."

She fingered the base of her goblet. "And they still
don't mind?"

"No. Not so delicate, the Welsh," he replied, by
his tone condemning not the Welsh but everyone
else. "It's part of living, isn't it? Nothing to bring
shame."

Unless you were too easily won over by empty
flattery and even emptier promises. That would
bring shame, far more than the act itself, although in
the eyes of the church, the act alone was a serious
sin. "Father Rhodri surely doesn't think so."

"Father Rhodri understands there is a time to condemn and a time to forgive."

No wonder he had not chastised the priest—he
thought the man's disapproval only temporary. She
hoped he was right.

And then a new fear slipped into her consciousness. "Do they nickname everybody?"

"Mostly, yes," he replied, ripping apart a loaf of
brown bread with his lean fingers. "Sometimes it's
from a feature, like Dafydd, or something to do with

the family like Jon and his brothers, or a quality, like piety."

Holy Mother, what would they call *her*?

Not Fiona the Fair, that was certain. "Does the lord of Llanstephan have a nickname?" she asked.

"Aye. Connor and Cordelia gave me a name. Would you like to hear it?"

His low, proud growl of a voice seemed to challenge her to ask. Yet in his eyes, she saw something that made her hesitate: a pain as old as the first cruel taunt of childhood.

"They called me the troll. I stayed so long in the solar at my studies, I was like a troll in my cave or under a bridge somewhere, they said."

Appalled, she exclaimed, "You are far too handsome to be likened to a troll!"

A spark kindled in the blue depths of his eyes and he once again put his strong, broad hand on her thigh. "Calm yourself, my champion. They have not called me that in a long time."

Once more she felt that leaping excitement. When he had put his hand on her knee the first time, she had nearly jumped out of her skin, and not just because she was surprised. His simple action engendered a shockingly powerful excitement.

As for the way his kiss made her feel . . .

Despite her own volatile reactions, however, she had to act as if mightily offended when he touched her in that intimate manner. She must pretend to be the virgin bride unless she wanted him to ask a lot of questions.

So she had, even when his incredible deep, luxuriant voice seemed more thrillingly intimate than his caress. He could seduce her with his voice alone.

No, he didn't even have to speak. He didn't have to do anything at all except look at her, and she was like chaff in a strong breeze, helpless to resist the winds of desire sweeping through her.

He took his hand away before she had to tell him to. "Did you ever have a nickname, Fiona?"

The churning excitement died with his question. She had no desire to humiliate herself by confessing that she had. Nevertheless, his questioning gaze compelled her to answer.

"Skin-and-Bones," she admitted quietly, so that only he would hear. "Freckled Fiona. Cows-eyes. They would moo when I walked past, or cluck like chickens."

His expression softened. "It must have been difficult."

Nothing had prepared her for that different look in his blue eyes. She had not anticipated his sympathy or his understanding. Suddenly she saw again the Caradoc of his youth, when he had been shy and unassuming.

"If your own brother and sister called you a name like that, no wonder you stayed so long in the solar," she said, grateful for that glimpse, and hoping young Caradoc would not retreat behind the cool facade of Caradoc the man for a while yet.

"I did not stay there to avoid them. I had my lessons to learn and work to do. Did you hide at home, Fiona, or did you ignore the taunters?"

Caught in the warm swell of his unexpected sympathy, she was proud to answer, "I ignored them."

"I knew it."

His lips curved up a little into a smile that told her he understood the courage she had been forced to muster to face her tormentors daily. More, he admired it. She heard that in his voice and saw it in his brilliant blue eyes.

Iain would never have understood. For him, courage was something that only a man could feel, and only then in a battle.

"What of Rhonwen? What is her nickname?" she asked, trying to clear her mind of Iain, hating the intrusion of her folly into this moment.

He regarded Fiona steadily, and to her sorrow, the shutters closed once more. "She is only and always Rhonwen."

This lack of a nickname was obviously not something good, yet she saw no reason that Rhonwen should be so excluded. "She is Welsh, too, isn't she?"

Caradoc took another sip of wine before answering. "Nobody knows. She was abandoned here by her father, a tinker, whose woman died in childbirth. The woman was not cold in the bed before he was gone. We never even knew her mother's name, and her father never came back."

"That was not the babe's fault," Fiona said, upset to think that the shy, quiet young woman was faulted for the circumstances of her birth.

"So my mother thought. She paid a farmer's wife to nurse and raise her, and believed Rhonwen well taken care of. It was only years later that we found out otherwise. She was treated little better than a slave by that woman and her husband. That is why she is here now."

Yet not accepted, either, although Rhonwen had been born there.

Dismay settled upon Fiona, like a blanket dank and damp, overwhelming the other emotions Caradoc had stirred into life.

For if Rhonwen was not accepted, what chance had she?

Chapter 5

⌒~oᐤo~⌒

The next morning Fiona awoke with a start to find Rhonwen standing silently at the foot of the bed, her expression as unreadable as her lord's and a tray covered with a linen cloth in her hands.

Yawning, Fiona rubbed her eyes and sat up. Tired from her journey, her thoughts and emotions a jumble, alternately excited by the memory of Caradoc's kiss and touch, troubled by anger and shame at the past, wary of what the future held, her mind had been active far too long after she had retired.

Even when she finally fell asleep, her dreams had carried on the conflict. Caradoc, Iain, Cordelia, Dafydd, Ganore, Rhonwen . . . all had paraded through her slumbers like a troop of angels and demons bent on waging war for her heart and happiness.

She glanced at the window and realized the sun

was beaming in. It was a fine day, and already further along in the morning than she was used to rising. "What hour is it? How long have you been
waiting for me to wake?"

"It's nearly midmorning, my lady," Rhonwen answered as she balanced the tray against her stomach
and lifted the cloth to reveal sliced bread and cheese
and a mug of what smelled like cider.

"So late?" Fiona asked, appalled that she had
slept so long, and yet distracted by the food. Her
stomach growled loudly, and she smiled sheepishly.
"It is much later than I usually wake. And I am not a
lady, Rhonwen. At least, not yet."

The young woman's brow furrowed in confusion.
"Lord Caradoc says I am to be your maid. What am I
to call you?"

"Fiona, I suppose."

"Th-that doesn't seem right," Rhonwen stammered, and Fiona felt sorry for making an issue of
how she was addressed.

However, if her name sounded lacking in deference, "my lady" was certainly presumptuous, and if
she thought that, she could easily imagine what
Ganore and the rest of the household would make
of it.

"For now I think you should call me 'mistress,' "
she replied, using the term the servants at home had
called her after her mother had died and she had
taken charge of the household for her father.

She thought of something else and her smile died.
"What of mass? Have I slept through that?"

Rhonwen nodded again.

The people of Llanstephan would surely think

she was lazy and irreligious, too. In his next grace Father Rhodri would probably condemn her for a pagan and suggest she be purified by being burned at the stake. "In the future, wake me at dawn with the rest of the household."

Rhonwen blushed and stared at the floor, and immediately Fiona regretted her sternly commanding tone. That might be appropriate for Ganore, but not for this quiet, obedient young woman.

"Forgive me, Rhonwen," she said, hugging her knees. "I am a stranger in a strange place where the people do not know me. Apparently many have already taken a dislike to me. I don't want to do anything to make that dislike grow."

She laid her chin on her knees and eyed the girl with sympathy. "I think you, of all in Llanstephan, know what I mean and how I feel."

Rhonwen raised her head and regarded Fiona steadily with her big brown doe eyes. "They do not hurt me here."

Despite her brave words, Fiona saw the loneliness lurking within the girl and sat up straighter. "But they are not kind to you here, either."

The loneliness flickered and died out, replaced by an expression of stoic acceptance as Rhonwen set the tray on the table beside the bed, then plumped up Fiona's pillows. "Those who raised me hurt and starved me, so it is enough."

Fiona shifted backward until she was sitting against the headboard. Rhonwen could say it was enough; she might even believe it, but Fiona did not. Nevertheless, she wouldn't press the girl anymore, lest she embarrass her.

Rhonwen set the tray on Fiona's lap. As she began to eat, Rhonwen tidied the room.

This morning, it was easier to think of the good things, such as her jest with Dafydd, Caradoc's sympathetic understanding of her childhood troubles, and Rhonwen's friendliness. Indeed, if there was anyone here she could be close to besides her husband, she suspected it would be the quiet maid.

Yes, there were reasons to be pleased today. Caradoc was not what she had expected, but there were signs that he was still the same in some ways, and her marriage might be pleasant.

Maybe even *very* pleasant, at least when they were alone.

Blushing, she sipped her cider and glanced at Rhonwen, glad to see that the girl was too occupied with her tasks to notice or wonder what had brought that blush to her mistress's face.

There was another good thing. Dafydd and Rhonwen seemed willing to accept her. She hoped it was a beginning.

But maybe Dafydd only acted as if he did because Caradoc was his friend. Perhaps Rhonwen was simply better at hiding her animosity than the other servants.

Fiona dearly believed she was wrong as she surreptitiously studied the young woman's face, trying to gauge Rhonwen's true opinion of her new mistress. Unfortunately, the girl's long brown hair curtained her face as effectively as a veil.

"Last night Lord Caradoc spoke of gathering the sheep," she noted as she nibbled on the excellent cheese and attempted to engage Rhonwen in conversation.

"Aye, they do that today and maybe start the washing if the weather stays fine," Rhonwen replied as she put the bronze braid casings back in their box.

"We are surrounded by hills and mountains. I assume gathering all the sheep that pasture on the estate isn't easy."

"No, it's not," Rhonwen agreed as she gathered up Fiona's comb and mirror and put them in a small wooden chest on the table. "It takes most of the morning and all the men and dogs that can be spared. Lord Caradoc takes the high point most times."

She paused in her tidying when she saw Fiona's bafflement. "They make a line, you see, the men and the dogs, stretching up and across the mountain. Then they move toward the pens, sweeping the sheep before them like they are a giant scythe."

Fiona had assumed noblemen simply sat in their halls and waited to be told what was being done on their estate. She had also assumed Caradoc's humble clothing was the result of his poverty. Now, she realized they could be the garments of a man who worked as hard as any laborer on his land.

"You could wait at the pens to see them bring the sheep down," Rhonwen said, her expression shy but eager, too.

"I would like that," Fiona replied, pleased by Rhonwen's burst of confident eloquence and delighted by her suggestion. She also welcomed the chance to get out of the castle, which felt very much like enemy territory. "Will you wait with me?"

"If you like, mistress."

"Excellent." Fiona set aside the tray, rose and went to the window. Although the sun was shining brightly, mist still crowned the highest reaches of the mountains in the distance.

Rhonwen joined her. "Hard to tell, you see, if the mist will stay mist, or disappear, or turn into rain clouds. Difficult it is to gather the sheep in a fog, as I'm sure you can imagine."

"Difficult, and dangerous, too," Fiona surmised, for the Welsh hills could be little more than broken rock and bracken, both equally slippery in the wet.

"Aye. Dafydd broke his leg two years ago at the gathering for the lambing."

Rhonwen's expression revealed nothing, but Fiona had harbored a secret yearning for years, and thought she detected something similar in the young woman's tone.

"It mended well," Fiona remarked, for the man had had no limp that she could detect.

"Yes."

"He seems an amusing fellow, and well liked," Fiona noted, doing a little impromptu investigation.

"Everybody likes him," Rhonwen murmured as she went to make the bed.

Meaning there was a lot of competition for his attention, and a quiet girl like Rhonwen probably stood little chance of being noticed.

She knew exactly how that felt.

She also suspected that if Rhonwen thought she was too nosy, she would reveal nothing more. Her sympathetic curiosity, however, made her unwilling to abandon the subject of Dafydd entirely.

"He is not married, is he?" she asked as she went to the large chest near the window and opened it. She wondered what she should wear that would be suitable for walking in the hills, yet fine enough to remind the servants that she was no pauper come begging for a husband like scraps at the gate.

Rhonwen raised the silken covering and let it fall, unwrinkled, back into place on the bed. "No."

The blue wool was too plain. "I suppose his looks make him less than popular with the young women."

"He has never lacked for female company, my lady."

Fiona glanced up from her contemplation of the light brown gown with the green ivy embroidered along the square neckline. "Really?"

Rhonwen colored as she tucked the coverlet under the tick. "He's said to be very . . very . . ."

Fiona laughed as she drew out her light green gown. It laced at the sides, and was wider in the skirt than most, so she could take long strides in it. "So he told me himself last night, but I thought that merely meant he has a high opinion of himself."

Rhonwen came to help her lift the gown over her head. "He does, but for more than that," she said. "He knows more about sheep and their illnesses and injuries than most shepherds twice his age, and there's nothing he won't do when it comes to work. Him it was taught Lord Caradoc to shear as well as any man—"

"Caradoc can shear a sheep?" Fiona interrupted, pausing in her adjustment of the gown over her shift.

"Aye, mistress, and he's quick as Dafydd, and rarely nicks."

Here was more of the unexpected—a lord who could shear sheep.

"Dafydd must be a fine man if he is as good a friend to Lord Caradoc as he seems."

"Oh, he is!"

Rhonwen smiled, and Fiona realized how pretty the girl really was, with big, soft brown eyes, long lashes and pink cheeks.

She wondered if Dafydd had ever noticed her loveliness, or if he had ever seen her smile. She could believe that Rhonwen was always too shy to do so in his high-spirited presence. Maybe she followed Dafydd around whenever she could, hiding in the shadows and ducking behind corners, as a certain other girl had done years ago following the object of her secret desire, never realizing just how attractive and desirable he was going to become in his maturity.

With that thought warming her, she tied the lacing at the sides of the gown. "What do you think, Rhonwen?" she asked when she was finished. "Is this a good choice for tramping in the hills?"

"The pens are near the river for the washing, so we do not have to go far up."

"Oh, good," Fiona said with a relieved sigh as she sat on her stool before her dressing table and began to comb her hair. "I would hate to trip or fall in front of everybody. Then they would surely say I was clumsy as well as homely."

"You aren't homely, mistress," Rhonwen protested.

"Well, I am no great beauty, either."

Rhonwen did not disagree, but Fiona wasn't offended by the girl's silence. She had accepted the truth about her appearance long ago. Only once had she forgotten it, when Iain had lied and told her she was beautiful.

"I think simple braids today, and fastened with those two green ribbons," she said, gesturing at the finery in an open box on the table.

"Yes, mistress," Rhonwen said, picking out the green ribbons as Fiona did the first braid.

Fiona tilted her head and looked up at Rhonwen as she held out her hand for one of the ribbons. "I have often been lonely, Rhonwen, as I think you have been," she said as she tied the ribbon around the end of her braid. "We have something in common there, and since I was not born a lady, I am hoping that we can be friends."

Rhonwen nodded, then another shy smile stole onto her face. "I would like that very much."

As the daughter of a wool merchant, Fiona was familiar with fleece and sheep in pens. Rarely had she witnessed a shearing, though, or the washing that went before it to remove the grease and dirt from the fleece.

Now she waited with Rhonwen on the stone wall of a huge pen close to the river. They had trudged up the hill to this place, and although the distance wasn't far, the angle of the slope had tired her quickly. Rhonwen, however, looked as if she had somehow flown there. She was not winded in the least, and as they walked, she had told Fiona many things about the raising of sheep on Llanstephan.

There was no sign of men or dogs or sheep, but Rhonwen had told her it would be a little while yet before they appeared.

"When they come, the sheep all go to the big *ffridd* here and then they're sent down that way to the river, one by one," she said, pointing to a large gate at one end of the stonewalled pen and then to another smaller gate on the opposite side. The small gate opened onto a narrow enclosed path leading to a pier in the slow moving river, which had been dammed to form a deep pool.

"A man stands on the pier, picks them up and throws them into the water," she continued.

"He picks them and throws them in?" Fiona repeated incredulously, for sheep were not light.

"Otherwise they don't get their backs under the water." Rhonwen gave her a little smile, and her eyes sparkled. "Your husband-to-be generally starts, and when he is tired, Dafydd takes over, and after him another shepherd, and so on."

Fiona stared at Rhonwen with blatant surprise, then recalled Caradoc's strong arms. That walk up the side of the hill told her why his legs were so muscular, too.

"He likes to do such work," Rhonwen explained. "I heard him say once to Dafydd that it gives him something to do instead of thinking about his troubles."

It was folly perhaps to ask questions of a servant, even Rhonwen, yet Fiona couldn't resist the opportunity. "Has he many other troubles besides his debts?"

Rhonwen looked as if she regretted saying what she had, so Fiona did not wait for her answer. "I remember that he did not get along well with his brother, or his sister, either."

Rhonwen pulled out a bit of grass growing from the wall as she shook her head. "No, they used to argue all the time, worst of all when Sir Connor came back from the East after the king raised the taxes."

She shivered, as if a chill breeze had just blown by. "That was a terrible time. He has not heard from his brother since Sir Connor left, and Lady Cordelia still says he all but banished him from Llanstephan."

"Did he? Or did Sir Connor leave in a huff? I saw him march from the hall once when the stew was not to his liking."

Rhonwen threw away the bit of grass. "More like that, I think."

Fiona could easily imagine how difficult it was for Caradoc if Cordelia blamed him for the breech between the brothers.

And then she had arrived, and made things worse.

She had not seen Cordelia today. Likely the gathering of sheep was nothing new to her, so she had taken herself elsewhere, perhaps purposefully avoiding her future sister-in-law.

Ganore was certainly giving Fiona a wide berth. As soon as she had set foot in the hall this morning, Ganore had marched out the door leading to the kitchen.

Well, she was happier out of their hostile presence, too.

"Mistress?"

Fiona came out of her reverie and realized Rhonwen was looking very serious and very worried. "What is it?"

"Ganore loves Cordelia like a daughter and believes everything she does is perfection. Ganore leads the other servants by the nose, and I fear she has taken a dislike to you."

Fiona smiled to put the girl at ease. "I know, and I will deal with Ganore."

Somehow.

"She would have taken a dislike to any woman not Welsh born and bred," Rhonwen continued. "A few Norman lords brought their daughters here, and that was a disaster. The Welsh ones she would fawn and fuss over. Lord Caradoc mostly ignored them all until their fathers took them away."

She had thought Caradoc's claim that there had been others seeking his hand in marriage an exaggeration to assuage his pride, but apparently it was not.

Yet why, if this were so, would Caradoc want *her*?

Because as time passed he must have gotten more desperate and more in need of money to pay his debts.

As this thought rankled in her bosom, Rhonwen suddenly straightened and looked up the hill. "They're coming."

Fiona followed her gaze, and in the distance saw what had to be a flock of sheep and lambs and rams rushing down the slope like a wide, white waterfall. Behind and to the east was a line of men, and between them and the sheep rushed the dogs. She scanned the men for a familiar face and dark wild hair, and finally spotted Caradoc in the middle of the top line, with Dafydd beside him.

The thunder of her excited heartbeat was nearly drowned by the thunder of the approaching flock, but not quite.

Even dressed in the same simple tunic and breeches as the others, Caradoc was clearly a lord among them. Everything about him proclaimed it: his bearing, his commanding mien, the way everybody's gaze would drift toward him.

To think that tomorrow, she was going to be this man's bride. After their wedding night, she would be his legal wife, and no man could come between them.

Yet it was not the legality of it or the pride of being a lord's wife that thrilled her as he came closer. It was the inward image she had of being in his powerful arms, making love.

Surely then the memory of Iain's lustful embrace would be forever purged, and her shame likewise.

She watched with silent fascination as the flock came closer. The dogs barked and yipped and raced about chasing any sheep who looked to break back through the line. The bleating of the sheep mingled with the dogs and the calls of the men, for sometimes, a sheep did manage to break free. Then, with a bark that sounded like a canine curse, one of the dogs rushed after it and herded it back.

Caradoc was so deep in discussion with Dafydd, he did not notice her. Of course, he did not know she was going to be there, so there was no need for her to feel disappointed.

A few of the men spotted her, and the word went up the line. Caradoc looked in her direction, but he didn't indicate in any way that he saw her.

Well, what had she expected? That he would cheerfully wave and call out her name?

As for the other men, whenever they looked her way, they seemed perplexed, clearly wondering what she was doing there.

Fiona and Rhonwen jumped down from the wall as the sheep were herded into the pen. The animals milled about, annoyed at being compelled to leave their pasture, and sounding like querulous old women disturbed after a nap. Behind the gate, the dogs sat with their masters, barely still, their haunches quivering. Other men leaned on the wall, looking at the flock with great satisfaction—when they were not glancing at their lord, and her.

Still Caradoc did not acknowledge her presence. He continued to speak to Dafydd, his expression grave. Perhaps there was a problem with the sheep.

She almost hoped that was so. Otherwise, she would have to admit that he was purposefully ignoring her.

"If you will excuse me, mistress," Rhonwen said, bashfully backing away toward the castle. "You don't need me, so I'll go back and see to the . . . to the . . . laundry."

Before Fiona could stop her, she hurried away.

Puzzled, she looked at Caradoc and Dafydd still deep in discussion. Maybe Rhonwen was upset that Dafydd hadn't noticed her, either, but that didn't seem likely.

Then another possible reason for Rhonwen's bashful flight appeared.

A group of servants, led by Lowri, a middle-aged,

stout serving woman with a face that looked as if she brooked no nonsense, came trudging up the hill. The grooms who had helped Fiona unload her wagons bore trestle tables to be assembled, and more women carried baskets and small casks of ale. Una, not as old or as stout as Lowri, but round-faced and dark-haired, carried a basket full of mugs. Mercifully, there was no sign of Ganore or Cordelia among them, but when she saw the expressions on the serving women's faces as they realized she was there, she sympathized with her maid's desire to flee.

Fiona straightened her shoulders. She didn't belong there, and Caradoc acted as if she didn't exist, yet she wasn't about to run away. And maybe helping the women would be a start to earning their respect. She certainly wasn't afraid of a little hard work. She had helped around the household whenever she could.

Her decision made, she went toward the tables and approached Lowri. "I will pour the ale," she offered.

Lowri's eyes narrowed. "We don't need *your* help."

The back of Fiona's neck prickled, as if a thunderstorm or other natural phenomena loomed close behind her.

"You don't have to do that," Caradoc said, and she turned to find him so close to her elbow, she might have hit him with hers if she had turned too quickly.

She blushed, and knew she was, and wished she wasn't. She probably looked silly petitioning a servant for the right to pour ale. "I want to help, as you do."

"If you like."

His mellifluous voice and sapphire eyes should be condemned by the church for temptations to sin, or declared illegal by the crown for leading women to indulge in wanton behavior. He didn't have to smile before waves of hot desire swept over her. The promise of a passion such as she had never imagined seemed to emanate from him, drawing her close.

Maybe she shouldn't linger here. Maybe she should hide herself away lest she betray her far-from-innocent hunger and give him cause to wonder.

Caradoc looked at Lowri, not condemning or chastising, but calm and purposeful in a way that would not allow protest. "Lowri, you set out the mugs and my bride-to-be will pour."

Then he turned and walked away.

Chapter 6

❦❦

"Showing off, are you?" Dafydd demanded later. There was a grin on his face but gravity in his eyes as he pushed his way through the sheep crowding the narrow enclosure leading to the river.

Caradoc paused in the act of pitching a sheep into the deep water. Sweat poured off his forehead, naked chest and back, and it dampened the waist of his breeches. His arms and legs and shoulders ached from the lifting, and his throat was as parched as if he hadn't had a drink in days. He hadn't felt this physically exhausted in years.

That was not so surprising, considering he had been tired when he had started out that morning. It had taken him even longer than usual to fall asleep last night. Normally, it was worrying about how he was going to pay his taxes and feed his household that kept him staring at the ceiling well after everyone else slumbered.

Trying to fall asleep in the barracks with all the noise the men made would have been difficult enough at the best of times. With all that had happened that day rushing through his mind creating eddies of desire and whirlpools of dread, fervently anticipating his wedding night while fearing he would rue accepting Fiona's offer, sleep had eluded him.

Finally, toward the dawn, he had dropped off into an uneasy rest, to dream of Fiona naked in his arms while around his bed, Father Rhodri and everybody else in Llanstephan chastised him for a stupid, silly little boy whose father would be justly ashamed of him.

Despite that nightmarish aspect of his dream, when he had awakened, he had been astonishingly aroused and it was the memory of Fiona in his arms that lingered longest.

He heaved the bleating, struggling sheep into the river, then turned to Dafydd, who nodded toward the tables set near the big *ffridd* where Fiona and the maidservants were clearing away the food and drink. "For her, is it?"

"She's still there?" he asked, his voice a rough croak as he tried to sound unconcerned, although he knew full well she was.

He had not expected her to be at the river, but when he had seen her, he had been undeniably pleased. Too many highborn women cared only about the finished wool and the income it provided, not the way it was obtained, or the work that went into caring for the animals that produced it.

He had almost waved and called out to her, until it had occurred to him that she might be appalled a lord would do such labor. What if she thought helping his shepherds beneath him?

If that proved to be, he had decided, he wouldn't trouble himself to explain that he enjoyed being out in the mountains with men who were his friends as well as his tenants. Here he felt free and happy, unencumbered by his cares and worries and duty.

When she stayed, he began to think she must not disapprove. He had even begun to hope that she was impressed.

Not wanting to be teased by Dafydd or any of the others, though, or seem as if he was becoming too enamored of a woman he had only just met, he had ignored her for as long as he could.

When he couldn't do that anymore, he walked over to the tables where she was speaking to Lowri, allowing himself the simple pleasure of watching her as he did. Her auburn hair glowed in the sunlight, and her supple body had a grace such as he had never seen before, as if she were dancing even when she stood still.

He had overheard Lowri's insolent response and braced himself for Fiona's answering burst of temper.

None came. Instead, she replied calmly, yet with a hint of iron in her voice that was most impressive.

Obviously Fiona MacDougal was not a woman to be trifled with, yet she was willing to help with a menial task when she could have stayed in the castle doing whatever it was well-bred women did.

He hoped that would go some way toward showing his household that he had not made a disastrous choice of bride.

"Of course she is still here," Dafydd said, "and she keeps looking at your manly form, as I'm sure you know. That is why you're going to do this until you drop, aren't you, fool that you are?"

Caradoc wasn't about to admit that there was some basis for Dafydd's observation. "Since you've finally stopped talking with the women and come, now I'll go."

"Oh, my fault, is it?" Dafydd asked sarcastically as he stripped off his tunic, revealing a body as lean and hard as Caradoc's. "That's right. Blame me—but go and talk to her before her eyes fall out of her head."

Caradoc gave him a critical look that didn't fool his friend for a minute, as Dafydd's good-natured laughter showed. "But wash yourself first, Caradoc. You stink worse than these sheep."

God's wounds, he did. "Varlet," he muttered as he pulled off his boots.

"Bastard."

He shoved his boots into Dafydd's hands. "Blackguard."

"Nit."

With a farewell scowl at his friend, he jumped off the pier into the river. The water was freezing, and he had a moment's pity for the sheep, but they had their wool to warm them. He swam for as long as he could stand it, then climbed out onto the shingle of the bank.

He shook his head like a dog and sluiced off as much of the water from his chest as he could with his hands before Dafydd tossed him his boots. He nearly didn't catch them because his hands were numb from the cold.

He glanced at the western sky. The sun was more than three quarters through its downward course. Still, they should be able to finish the washing today.

Resisting the urge to look and see if Fiona was watching, he headed for the wall of the enclosure and his dry tunic, all the while trying to look as calm as if he worked himself like this every day.

When he was dressed, he sauntered over to her, still affecting a far more casual air than he felt.

God save him, he was like a green lad feeling the first pangs of love-sickness.

No green lad was he, but he had never been as attracted to a woman before. Connor and Dafydd had fallen in and out of love with surprising frequency, at least in their youth. He had always observed their dramatic trials of the heart with disapproving skepticism. He had believed love must be a shallow pond the way they dipped into it.

Now, though, as he wandered toward the woman who was to be his wife, he began to think that maybe he had been very seriously mistaken. He was starting to understand how a feeling, a yearning, a desire that built into an intense need, could lead a man to do unusual things.

He came to a halt behind her, and once more the subtle aroma of her perfume stirred his senses.

"Will you be going back now?" he asked her as she finished packing away some of the leftover bread.

She started and looked back at him, obviously surprised.

He would not be disappointed by the possibility that she had not been watching him as often as he thought.

She faced him, a calmly quizzical expression on her face. "Will *you* be returning?"

She didn't respond with bashful maidenly modesty like most of the girls who swarmed around Connor and Dafydd.

But then, he hadn't liked those girls much, and not just because they ignored him. They were silly, flighty, vain creatures whose affections seemed even shallower than Connor's and Dafydd's. "Not yet. I'll stay until the last sheep is done."

He fought the urge to clear his throat or brush his toe across the grass like a bashful boy. "You are welcome to wait with me."

He looked past her to the mountains, where the mist still lingered. Fortunately, it had not thickened into clouds. "The weather looks to hold."

She smiled, and he thought he had never seen a prettier one. "Then I will stay. There is nothing for me to do at the castle anyway. Besides, I find this all very interesting, especially the dogs."

What had he expected? That she was going to tell him that she had been admiring him?

He became aware that it had grown quiet, save for the constant noise of the sheep bleating and moving about the enclosure. A quick glance sent the women and men who had been watching and listening back to their business.

Suddenly he wanted to be somewhere private. Very private.

Well, not too private, or that would set the tongues

to wagging. Once they were married, though, he would get Fiona alone as often as he could.

He put that incredibly arousing thought from his mind. There was a little rise a short distance away, still within full view of the *ffridd*—a perfect place to talk quietly and not be heard, yet still be within sight of the rest of the people.

He held out his hand to her. "Come."

As she put her hand in Caradoc's and again experienced that surprisingly intense reaction his touch inspired, Fiona wasn't quite sure where he wanted to lead her, or for what purpose.

But the words to ask would not be spoken. She was too aware of the powerful, commanding masculinity of the man leading her away from the others. The memory of his naked back and rippling muscles, the ease with which he picked up and tossed the sheep into the river, made it even easier to imagine being in those arms, her body against his, naked and intimate.

Indeed, she had been so fascinated and intrigued and excited watching him, she had not minded that few save Dafydd had spoken to her. Let them leave her alone. She would far rather indulge in passionate fantasies about the man she was going to marry.

Although it would have been most improper for Caradoc to take her out of sight of the others, considering they were not yet wed, she couldn't help being sorry when he didn't. Instead, he led her a short distance away to a small rise that overlooked the large pen.

He gestured for her to sit. When she had, he sat beside her, over a foot away.

She waited for him to speak. When he didn't, she decided to say something—anything, rather than sit here as if she were too timid to talk to him.

"I noticed that you don't have a dog. I mean, a sheep dog," she amended, not referring to the hounds in the hall.

She had paid little heed to the hounds because they were always in any nobleman's hall, kept for hunting and to eat the scraps of food that fell into the rushes.

Caradoc shook his head, and it made his damp hair curl even more. "No. A courtyard is not big enough for their need to run and herd, and there are no sheep there. I did try once, but the poor beast kept trying to herd the chickens."

She wished she could tell if he was serious or not. What he said sounded amusing, but he did not smile. "Dafydd's dog is very good, is it not?"

"Aye, as well he should be. There's not much Dafydd doesn't know about dogs or sheep." Caradoc pointed down the hill to three men who were involved in a heated discussion near the sheep pen. "See them arguing there?"

"Yes."

"The tall one is Merlyn-of-Gwendwr, the short one is Cadwallader-from-over-the-rise and the other's Peulan-who-limps. They quarrel like that every gathering. We always find some sheep with earmarks that don't belong to Llanstephan when we gather. You know what an earmark is?"

"Rhonwen told me about the cuts and nicks you make in the animal's ear to show who owns it."

Caradoc nodded. "A few sheep range far and sometimes we find them, so the earmark is not familiar. Cadwallader, Merlyn and Peulan consider themselves experts, you see, so they will argue about where it belongs until dark, if we let them. Watch you now, for here comes Dafydd to set them straight."

The bailiff walked up to the men, pointed at the sheep, said one word, gave them a smug, insolent grin, and sauntered off again.

"He's just told them who owns it, and he is never wrong," Caradoc explained.

By the time Dafydd returned to where Lowri and the other women were preparing to leave, the three men were arguing again, about another sheep.

"So do you shear the ones who don't belong to Llanstephan or let them go?" Fiona asked.

Caradoc lay flat on his back, his head pillowed in his hands as he looked up at the sky. She was secretly pleased because this way, she could study him all she wanted without encountering his intense and inscrutable blue eyes.

"Got enough of our own to do," he replied. "We'll pen them with the lambs and let them go when we're done."

She raised her knees and wrapped her arms around them. "You don't shear the lambs, then?"

"Some do, because the wool can get caught on branches or in the rocks, but I prefer ours to have it for the winter. Besides, they can kick like the devil and they wiggle so much, they're harder to get a hold on."

"Rhonwen told me that you shear. I was surprised that you would do something like that, but Rhonwen says—"

He sat up and regarded her suspiciously. "What did Rhonwen say about me?"

What if her impetuous remark meant trouble for Rhonwen? She should have kept quiet. "Only that you like to work. Nothing more you should be angry about," she assured him. "She said it keeps you from thinking about your troubles."

"Aye, it does."

Inwardly pleased that he felt comfortable enough to reveal this, his answer raised another question far less pleasant. "Do you have troubles other than those I have already heard about?"

He shook his head. "No more than we discussed yesterday. You are very well informed."

She was happy to hear that.

He pulled up a bit of bracken and twisted it around his long, slender, strong fingers. "You are not ignorant of politics, Fiona," he said, not looking at her. "What do you think of our sovereign, King Richard?"

Fiona wasn't sure what to say. Like many people, she had no great love for Richard, who was bankrupting his kingdom with his foreign wars. But she was not yet Caradoc's wife and until that came to pass, she might do well to keep most of her opinions to herself. "I try to think of him as little as possible, my lord."

Caradoc lifted the corner of his well-cut mouth in a sardonic grimace. "A fine answer. You would probably do well at court. Like Connor, before he lost his temper and criticized the king to his face."

It was obvious he disapproved of his brother's action and, given the results, she certainly didn't blame him. "I remember your brother's temper."

"Do you, now? Still, a fine lad, our Connor, for all that."

She plucked up a bit of bracken herself and pulled it apart.

"What, surely you must agree?" he asked, fixing his intense gaze upon her. "All the girls liked him."

She didn't answer. Even if he and his brother hadn't gotten along as children and had parted on bad terms, a man as proud as Caradoc probably wouldn't welcome any condemnation of a family member.

He put his hand on her arm, so that she had to look at him. "Does this silence imply you did not?"

"I found him too lively for my taste," she prevaricated as he moved his hand away.

Caradoc's brows lowered, as if he wasn't pleased with her response.

Fortunately, his displeasure, if that's what it was, did not last. "It has been a long time since you last came here with your father," he observed, and she was relieved he had changed the subject of their conversation to one less fraught with potential trouble. "You were a little girl then."

"The last time I was here, I was ten years old and you were fourteen."

And tall even then, and dark and mysterious.

"So, twelve years ago." He studied her. "And in all those years, no man has wanted to marry you?"

Less fraught? Merciful Mary, she was in a bog. One false step, and she would sink in quicksand. "That is hardly a polite question to ask a woman."

Was he blushing as he bent down to brush some mud from his boot?

Emboldened by that sudden hint of remorse for his question, she continued, using his own words. "Perhaps I never found one to suit."

He glanced at her sharply. Embarrassed? Not likely.

She flushed under his scrutiny and turned the talk away from her past. "Is Cordelia betrothed?"

"Not yet."

That was unfortunate. Cordelia would leave Llanstephan when she married, and take her animosity with her.

"She hasn't found anyone to suit."

With a look that seemed suspiciously like smug satisfaction, he lay back down again. "I confess I have my doubts she will ever be wed if she keeps on the way she's going, ignoring my orders and riding about the countryside like some sort of bandit. I always send two soldiers to accompany her, but she usually loses them. It's a game with her."

"But that's dangerous!"

She didn't particularly like Cordelia, given her reception, yet she hated to think of any woman in the hands of outlaws.

"My lands are safe enough, and I pity the man

who tries to catch her. Icarus is the fastest horse in Wales, and she's an excellent rider."

"An arrow can go faster than a horse."

He frowned and didn't answer.

She had said too much too soon about his sister and her behavior. She must remember that, for the time being at least, she was in no position to offer her opinion, especially if it was critical.

Worse, he had seemed disposed to talk, and she had inadvertently silenced him.

Upset with herself, she surveyed the area below. The sheep pen looked nearly empty. "I think they are getting near the finish," she observed, breaking the heavy silence.

Caradoc sat up and followed her gaze. "It takes longer than it looks toward the end. The sheep have more room to run in the pen and avoid the gate."

She was relieved that he didn't sound angry. "Why don't they send in the dogs?"

"Too small for that. Look, they'll send in Dafydd now."

Dafydd clearly would have made a fine jester. He scampered to and fro like a madman, bowing majestically when he got a sheep through the gate. He threw himself headlong after some, and picked up lambs and handed them out of the pen with a flourish, as if they were gifts he was bestowing.

Watching his antics, her tension lessened. "He's very funny."

"Oh, a thousand laughs Dafydd gives us," her future husband replied dryly. "As long as he's not making sport of *you*."

Another thing for her to fear?

"He won't," Caradoc said.

"I beg your pardon?"

He inched closer and reached out to toy with the end of the lacing at the side of her gown.

"He won't make fun of you," he replied, his voice placid despite what he was doing. "My good friend is Dafydd, and he might tease me nearly to madness, but he'll leave you alone."

"I do have a sense of humor, Caradoc. I can laugh at myself as well as the next person," she said, not nearly as affronted as she was aroused by the realization that if he untied that knot, the lace would loosen and he could slip his hand inside her gown.

"That may be so," he answered, still fiddling with the lace, "but you proved your mettle the first time you met him. He won't be quick to tease you again."

"Maybe he *should* tease me," she said, wondering how long Caradoc was going to keep toying with her lace and if she should order him to stop. "I don't want people to think I'm going to be angry or cry or be upset if he does. I assure you, I have a sense of humor and I have been teased plenty of times in my life."

Caradoc stopped playing with her lace and looked up at her in a way that made her heart spin. "I remember what you told me, so it shall be as you desire. If he starts to tease you, I shall not try to stop him."

"Good," she said, telling herself it was also good that Caradoc had stopped fiddling with the lace without having to be asked, and the desire he meant was not the kind coursing through her now.

He tilted his head to regard her solemnly. "He is

not the one who will give you trouble. That will be Ganore."

His words doused her mood as effectively as a leap into the river.

"Patience it will take, and time, but I think she'll come 'round eventually."

Fiona wasn't so sure, but she didn't want to contradict him.

He got to his feet and held out his hand to help her stand. "Come now, the washing is nearly finished and it's getting to be dusk. Dafydd and I always toss the last sheep together."

She took hold of Caradoc's hand and let him pull her up. Very strong he was, his grip like iron, and yet not so strong he hurt. As always, his touch thrilled her, even more when he did not immediately release her.

Wondrously, he grinned like a boy sharing a secret, almost marvelously mischievous.

Almost, because he was very much a mature man.

"And then I'm going to shove him in."

Delighted and tickled by this unseen side of him, and having seen the altercation with the boots, she smiled. "Or perhaps he will push you in."

Caradoc's infectious grin grew and his eyes sparkled with determination as well as high spirits. "He can try."

She was suddenly very sure Dafydd was in for a swim.

That night, as the mist came up from the river and down from the hills, Caradoc strode toward Dafydd's stone cottage.

He rapped sharply on the rough wooden door and went inside when bidden, relieved Dafydd had not yet retired for the night. His friend sat beside the small glowing hearth, a mug of ale cradled in his hands. His face glowed bronze in the dim light, and the rest of his body seemed a part of the shadows.

"Ah, the mighty lord of the Llanstephan Fawr!" Dafydd declared, raising his mug in salute and half rising before Caradoc gestured for him to sit back down. "What the devil are you doing here this time of night? Not a problem with the sheep, is it?"

"No, it's not a problem with any of the sheep," Caradoc replied.

"If you've come to see if I've dried off yet, you're a little late."

"No, it's not that," he answered as he accepted the mug of ale Dafydd poured for him.

A look of comprehension dawned on Dafydd's face, and he grinned so broadly, he looked like a gargoyle. "Questions for the wedding night, is it? Come to the right man you have, then, indeed."

Although this was exactly the reason he had come, Caradoc scowled. Maybe he should leave . . . but as chagrined as he was, he wanted Dafydd's advice too much to go.

Dafydd's grin disappeared as quickly as it had come and his eyes widened in genuine surprise. "Is that really why you've come, Caradoc?"

He might as well admit it. "As a matter of fact, yes."

Dafydd let out a low whistle and devilish delight shone in his dark eyes. "Well, well, well, an honor this is, and no mistake. Caradoc come to ask my advice about a woman. I never thought I would see the day the mighty lord of Llanstephan Fawr would humble himself to ask me, a simple bailiff with the biggest nose in Wales, for advice. Why, a man could swoon with the shock—"

Caradoc started to stand up. There was a limit to his patience and his tolerance at being the butt of Dafydd's humor. "If you're going to waste my time prattling—"

"No, no, I won't, I won't!" Dafydd cried, tugging on Caradoc's tunic to pull him back. "Still, you must admit, Caradoc, the day you ask advice about anything from anybody is a rare one."

"I've never been married before," Caradoc dryly noted. "So this *is* a very rare occasion."

"Aye, just so." Dafydd set down his ale and assumed a very studious demeanor. "Now, to business. What do you want to know?"

Caradoc reconsidered and once again started to stand.

Once again Dafydd pulled him back. "Caradoc, I am here and you have a question, so you might as well speak. I promise you I will not tell anybody."

"You said that about the time I got my head stuck in the bucket."

"Different that was, Caradoc. I had to say what had happened to your hair. Otherwise, your father might have thought I took the shears to it for no reason at all."

"It would have been better if you had told me that there had been honey in the bucket and you hadn't cleaned it before you put it on my head."

"I forgot."

Caradoc gave him a disgruntled look. He had always believed, and believed it still, that Dafydd had let him put that honey-coated bucket on his head for a joke. *Let's play knights. Here's your helmet.* He should have been more suspicious.

"Look you, Caradoc, are we going to talk about that, or your wedding night?"

Caradoc took a swig of ale, set down the mug and rubbed his hand over his stubbled chin before answering. He thought himself prepared to be matter-of-fact, but when he opened his mouth, the words stumbled out. "Since Fiona is a virgin—"

"She told you that?" Dafydd interrupted, shocked.

He shook his head. "No. I just assumed. The Scots hold their honor dear, and like the Normans they are in this."

"Aye, I've heard that, too."

"So assuming that she is," Caradoc continued, "I don't want to . . . you know . . . be too quick."

Dafydd's brow furrowed studiously as he silently regarded his friend.

"I don't want to hurt her," Caradoc elaborated. "I want it to be good for her."

Especially after their conversation by the *ffridd*. Despite his stupid awkwardness and his lack of facility with words, he had never enjoyed such a talk with a woman. It gave him hope that his decision to marry her was one of the better ones of his life.

Still Dafydd looked at him as if Caradoc were speaking a foreign language.

"God's wounds, Dafydd," he growled, "don't play the fool with me. You understand what I'm talking about well enough."

His friend grinned mischievously. "Aye, I do. Just wanted to know why you wanted to take your time. That's important."

"It is?"

"Aye. Virgin or not, a good lover thinks of the woman as much as himself, if not more. Glad I am that you have figured that out for yourself."

Caradoc felt a flush of pride at his words. Nevertheless, he was also glad it was dark so that Dafydd wouldn't see it. "So, what should I do?"

Dafydd made a great show of stroking his chin and appearing to be musing deeply. "Well, my friend, as you have realized, it is best to concentrate on *her* pleasure, not your own. You must make sure she is very ready for you, if you follow me, so that the pain is not too bad. And lots of tender love talk I would be saying."

The first suggestion was fine. And the second. But the third? "What do you mean, tender love talk? I am not Connor, you know."

Dafydd gave him a wry look. "Aye, I know. He was forever trying to tell *me* how to handle women, the arrogant pup."

"So let's forget any notion of tender love talk."

"You don't have to be a bard, Caradoc. Just tell her she's the most beautiful woman in the world, that sort of thing."

"Everyone keeps telling me she's not pretty, and Fiona herself is no fool, so I don't think she'll believe that."

Dafydd stroked his chin some more. "Tell her she's very exciting, then."

"That's true," Caradoc reflected.

Dafydd's mischievous grin returned twofold. "Really?"

Caradoc wished he had kept his mouth shut about that. "Anything else?"

"Listen, and listen well. Let her guide you."

"If she's a virgin, she won't know what to tell me to do."

"Are you a dolt, Caradoc, or what?" Dafydd demanded, exasperated. "You would think you had never been with a woman before, and since I was losing my virginity at the same time you were thanks to those two sisters at the Bull and Crown, I know you have. Women make *noises*, boy."

"I knew that." He just hadn't noticed for a long time. For the past few years, his couplings had been swift releases and nothing more.

"Listen to them. That way you'll know what's working."

Dafydd rose and began pacing just as Father Adolphus had when he was trying to drum a Latin verb into Caradoc's head. "Listen and she'll teach you what excites her most. Every woman is different, my friend."

Unlike Father Adolphus, who always clasped his hands behind his back when he paced, Dafydd gestured expansively. "Some like one thing, some another. Some scream, some make only the smallest of whimpers. It is your task to discover what will—"

"I understand, Dafydd," Caradoc interrupted, having heard what he needed. "I don't need a lecture. I've already endured enough of those, thank you."

Because Dafydd had known Caradoc all his life and seen the way things had been at Llanstephan when they were both lads, he nodded and answered without rancor. "Aye, I suppose you have at that."

Chapter 7

ᕲᕲ

Fiona watched the activity in the courtyard below as she waited for Rhonwen to return with
fresh, hot water. She had put on her finest shift of
thin white silk, and her wedding gown of deep, rich
burgundy velvet. Gold and silver flowers had been
embroidered around the curving neck and along the
hem of the long flowing sleeves lined with cloth of
gold. Her girdle, made of gilded leather, lay ready
on the bed, to be put on after Rhonwen returned and
tied the laces at the back of her gown.

Only a short time remained until the wedding,
and from her vantage point, Fiona could watch the
servants coming and going as they completed the final preparations for the wedding feast to come.

Last night as she had supped in the hall beside
Caradoc, he had warned her that the feasting and
drinking and singing was likely to last a long time

today. She had wondered if he was telling her that as a warning not to expect him to come too soon to the bridal chamber.

She hadn't asked. Indeed, she hadn't said much of anything. Her emotions had been in a tumult and seemed to be getting more tumultuous every moment she was with Caradoc.

It wasn't only that he stirred her passions when they were together. Caradoc's effect upon her was something more than the mere excited desire she had felt for Iain. It was deeper, stirring the depths of her heart rather than simply skimming the surface the way a stone could be made to skip across water.

Surely, because of that, she was not wrong to hope that this marriage could be more than a mere bargain.

Ganore bustled out of the kitchen and across to the storeroom where the ale was kept. Fiona didn't have to see the woman's face to know that she was nearly apoplectic with annoyance. When she had seen Cordelia earlier in the day, the girl hadn't looked any happier, either.

Except for Rhonwen, it was the women of this household who gave her the most trepidation about her chosen course of action. They might never accept her, and she would be as isolated as she had been in Dunburn.

It would help if Father Rhodri would quit condemning her and her marriage during grace. Last night he had referred to the plagues of Egypt as if she were one of them. And again, Caradoc had been stonily silent. Maybe he thought the man would cease his thinly veiled denunciations after the ceremony.

Maybe Caradoc was right, but in view of the level of Father Rhodri's hostility, she doubted it.

The chamber door creaked open. Holding her untied bodice to her chest, she turned, expecting to see Rhonwen with the water.

Caradoc stood on the threshold, his face full of wonder as he surveyed the refurbished chamber.

Despite his openmouthed surprise and his plain clothing, he looked marvelous. His simple black wool tunic fit as if it had grown on him. His breeches hugged his muscular thighs, and his boot were polished so well, they shone. He had shaved again, and his dark, curling hair had been combed into smooth waves.

Her rational mind told her it was improper to be alone with him since they were not yet wed, yet she couldn't find the words to tell him to leave.

Tonight, this incredibly handsome, virile man would return with her to this chamber, and he would remove those clothes. He would take her in his arms and his lips would touch hers . . .

He stopped surveying the room and his blue-eyed gaze came to rest upon her as the door swung shut behind him. Her vision of being in his passionate embrace was still strong upon her, and she suddenly feared he knew exactly what she had been imagining.

And that it pleased him.

She would have backed up if she had had anywhere to go other than out the window.

"My imaginings fell short," he said as he came farther into the room.

I don't think mine will.

His utterly masculine presence made her very

aware that her bodice was untied. One gentle tug, and it would fall, exposing her body clad only in her very thin silken shift.

She struggled to be calm, or at least look it. "What are you doing here, my lord?"

Passionate heat seemed to shoot out of his sapphire blue eyes, catching her directly. "I came to fetch my bride."

Her mouth dried. It wasn't fair that one simple statement and a pair of blue eyes could have such an effect on her, and her whole body. It was as if every muscle clenched, including those in her toes.

She must be serene. *Act* serene. "I am not quite prepared."

"No?" he asked, his eyes seeming to shine even more. "May I help?"

Only if you want to see me swoon.

Despite her efforts to be calm, a hot blush crept up her face. "My bodice needs to be tied."

"Turn around."

Swooning was a definite possibility.

Telling herself not to be so silly, or inflamed, Fiona slowly turned so that her back was to Caradoc, her future husband, who was going to marry her this day, and that night make love to her in the bed she could see out of the corner of her eye.

Not now. Of course not now.

Still trying to be calm, she swallowed hard when his hands pulled the lacing tighter at the back of her gown. His breath warmed the bare nape of her neck and his knuckles brushed her flesh.

Deciding to take a chance on a forgotten dream seemed like a simple thing compared to having to act as if his presence and touch did not affect her as it did.

But only until tonight. After the marriage was consummated, she wouldn't have to act the ignorant virgin bride. Then he would not wonder why she was not, or demand to know about her past.

When he was finished, he did not step away. For what seemed an eternity, as her breathing became erratic and her whole body tensed with anticipation as if she were being pulled from above and below, he simply stood behind her.

Then his strong hands took hold of her upper arms and his lips brushed across the back of her neck.

Oh, sweet merciful Mary!

If that could make her feel this way, what thrilling wonder would the wedding night hold?

His mouth slid lower, to the edge of her gown. Delightful waves of pleasure washed along her spine, all the way to the soles of her feet.

Ignoring her blossoming need became a Herculean task when his lips found the slope of her neck where it joined her shoulder. With exquisite, torturous leisure he feathered the tiniest of kisses there as with equal slowness he drew her back so that her body was flush against his.

He was as aroused as she.

She stepped forward, out of his grasp, away from his lips and his kiss, and the sensation of his mouth on her warm and willing flesh.

She forced herself to speak. "You are too forward, my lord. I am not yet your wife."

She turned to face him and saw the blatant desire still lingering in his face.

She wished she could tell him how he thrilled and aroused her. She wished she could confess all that she had done so that there was no secret between them forcing her to act contrary to the heated longings of her heart and her body.

Yet caution held her tongue. When they were safely wed, then she would gladly give in to the passion he aroused, and she would rouse an even greater passion within him. She must, certainly for the first night. She had to distract him so that some things would pass unnoticed.

"Forgive me," he murmured.

She hated this ruse she was perpetuating. She hated Iain for making it necessary.

She hated herself for having been so gullible.

Wherever the blame lay for this deception, it did not lie with Caradoc.

"You were too forward," she admitted with a small, shy smile, "but I liked it. I fear you could seduce me here and now with very little effort."

That was as true a thing as she had ever said, even if her choice of words belied the overwhelming hunger and desire he inspired within her.

"That is an effort I am willing to make," he said, his voice low and husky.

He didn't have to make an effort. He was seducing her right now, just standing there and looking at her. Iain had cajoled and pleaded and begged at the last, until she had finally given in. Caradoc needed to do none of that.

Feet came pounding up the stairs and in the next moment, male voices muttered in loud whispers outside the door.

"What is it?" Fiona asked nervously, moving back to the window's edge.

Caradoc ran his hand through his hair, mussing the smooth waves. "My friends have already been into the ale. Maybe the *braggot*, too."

Fiona had heard of *braggot*, a potent Welsh blend of mead and ale. The voices did sound rather the worse for drink, and the men obviously believed they were whispering. If so, it was a whisper that could be heard across the courtyard.

"If they've been drinking *braggot*, they'll pay for it tomorrow," Caradoc noted without so much as a hint of sympathy.

She had heard that, too—that the resulting sickness from drinking too much of that brew was misery itself because it was so sweet. "Why are they here?"

"It's the bidding. They've come to escort us to the wedding."

Fiona wasn't delighted by the prospect of an escort of drunken men, but these were Caradoc's friends and countrymen, so she held her tongue about that. "Are you not going to open the door?"

"Not yet."

She gave him a puzzled look.

"They are supposed to sing a verse of a song that they've made up," he explained, "about us or our wedding or some such thing. Then I am supposed to sing back. Then they will answer with another verse, and so on."

"For how long?"

"Until they've run out of verses."

"How many are there?"

"It depends how many they've made up." He shrugged. "It's a custom."

If it was a custom, she didn't dare to question it.

He swore softly. "I hate singing."

Shocked, she stared at him. "But you're Welsh."

"Not every Welshman can sing."

"You have a lovely speaking voice." *That alone could seduce a woman.*

He did not appear to appreciate the compliment. "I am . . ." He gestured at his ear, seemingly searching for an explanation. "If it's just a chant you want, I can do that, but anything more, I can't get the proper pitch."

She could imagine how humiliating that must be in a country whose people prided themselves on their musical ability. She had heard that Lord Rhys was so proud of Welsh accomplishments in music and poetry, he had started a competition called an *Eisteddfod*, awarding honors and prizes for music and poetry, too.

"Oh, hail the bride and groom within," Dafydd suddenly sang in a very pleasant, mellow tenor, slightly muffled by the door. "We come to give you joy, and you must answer— *What?*" he demanded peevishly, interrupting himself. "That's what we said. Bran-Bron came up with that line, and me the next."

An unintelligible mumble followed.

"Don't tell me what I said. I know full well it was

about him . . ." Dafydd's voice became incoherent, and it was clear from the harsh whispers that they were arguing.

Caradoc put his arm around her shoulders in a companionable gesture that delighted her. "Thank God, they're so drunk, they'll never remember the verses, and I won't have to sing. Now I'll send them on their way, or we'll be here all day." He raised his voice. "Since you louts have no song or subtlety, leave it and wait for us in the hall."

"Caradoc!" Jon-Bron called.

"What?" he bellowed back.

"Not fair, that," Jon-Bron loudly slurred. "We've got some fine verses all ready here. Took us all night. Give us a little time, will you? If Dafydd would quit being so stubborn about it—"

"I'm not stubborn. I'm right, that's all."

Caradoc gave Fiona a wry, long-suffering look that brought a sympathetic smile to her face. "Who is guarding my castle, Jon-Bron?"

"Oh, you know. Some of the lads."

"Leave me alone, you men. I am busy with my bride and we don't wish to be disturbed for a little while yet." He bussed Fiona's cheek with a hearty smack. "I hope they heard that. Then maybe they'll leave us in peace."

"Do you really want them to go?"

"Don't you?"

If he didn't want such an escort, that was all she needed to hear. A plan presented itself, and she acted upon it at once.

"It sounds as if they are right up against the

door," she whispered, taking his hand and pulling him until they stood close to the door, yet far enough away that it wouldn't hit them when it opened.

Turning him to face her, she reached out with one hand and pushed down on the latch. The next moment, without one word of warning, she threw her arms around Caradoc, pressed her body against his and kissed him passionately.

The door swung open and the men all gasped as one.

She scarcely heard them as Caradoc's mouth moved with incredible, wonderful leisure over hers. His lips seemed to tease and cajole, promise and deliver at the same time. Her whole body softened, limp with desire, in a way that was certainly not planned or feigned.

Caradoc broke their kiss and if he hadn't been holding her in his powerful arms, she would have wobbled.

Still holding her, he looked at his friends, who were staring wide-eyed and openmouthed. He raised one brow. "*Now* will you leave?"

"Sorry, Caradoc, sorry!" Dafydd muttered, stumbling back and nearly knocking Bran-Bron over.

Caradoc caressed her back, the sensation of his broad hands on her body promising even more than his lips.

"I will see you below," he said to his friends. "Is Father Rhodri here yet?"

"Aye, aye, he is."

"Good. Good-bye."

Caradoc put his hand on the door and gave a

slight shove. It swung slowly back, but didn't latch, so they could clearly hear the noise of several pairs of feet stumbling drunkenly down the stairs.

Caradoc pulled her close again and looked down into her upturned face. "Interesting plan."

She wanted to kiss him, but she restrained herself. She dare not be any bolder until after the wedding night, she told herself.

Then, as she continued to look at his shapely lips, she decided she could tease and cajole a *little*. "I thought so."

"They're probably telling everybody about our amazing passion," he said, his deep voice low and amused.

Unfortunately, his comment did not amuse her, for suddenly her clever plan didn't seem so very clever. She could easily imagine what condemning things Ganore and Cordelia would say, and passion or anything other than base lust would not enter into it.

He inched closer so that she could feel his hips and thighs against her. "No need to look so worried. I will take the blame, if blame there be. And now those men will all think twice about why I am marrying you."

She felt a little better, and then her dread was forgotten as he bent his head to kiss her again.

Just as his lips met hers, the door swung open. Rhonwen stood there, a bucket of water in her hands.

"Oh!" she squeaked, and the bucket fell to the floor, spilling its contents across the threshold.

"I'm so sorry!" the little maid cried, her face bright red. "I'll . . . I'll get a cloth to wipe it up," she spluttered before she turned and ran away.

"Stranded by a flood," Caradoc remarked with astonishing aplomb, while she felt as if the very floor beneath her was starting to give way.

His lips slowly, seductively, curved up into a smile. "What shall we do until we are rescued?"

At least a dozen ideas burst into her brain, each one more exciting than the last.

But practicality—or at least the reminder that some people would dearly love to find fault with her—forced her to lock those ideas away. For the time being.

"I think if we stay up here alone any longer, my reputation will be in complete tatters," she observed, successfully sounding much cooler than she felt.

"Aye, that could well be," he agreed. "Then I suppose we should go and get married."

The next thing Fiona knew, he had put one arm around her shoulder, another under her knees, and picked her up.

She threw her arms around his neck and held on for dear life. "What are you doing?"

"Carrying you over the threshold. Backwards, I know, but you don't want to get your gown wet, do you?"

Since she didn't, she let him carry her through the puddle and out the door, but once they were past that obstacle, she tried to wiggle out of his arms. "I would prefer to walk."

He only held her tighter. "I won't drop you."

"It's not that. This isn't very dignified, and Ganore will probably start a rumor that I am too feeble to walk."

"Ah, you may be right. Later on, I may not be so dignified, but for now, I will."

He set her down, letting her slip along his body in a way that sent new waves of desire unfurling through her.

With great effort, she managed not to kiss him.

He held out his arm to escort her. "And I wouldn't want anybody to think there's anything wrong with your legs."

Nervously twisting the silken coverlet in her fingers, Fiona glanced again at the single candle burning in the stand. She had blown out the others just before she had gotten into bed. How long ago that had been she could measure by the difference between them, and the candle still flickering.

Caradoc had said he didn't intend to linger after the wedding feast, but that had been before the dowry wine had been served. From below, she could hear the sounds of men's voices raised in song, and she had to admit he was right about his singing. His voice was the tuneless drone.

At least they were married—or at least partly. They wouldn't be considered irrevocably wed until the marriage was consummated.

Tonight. In this very bed . . .

She nervously rearranged the ties at the bodice of her shift. She studied the effect, then loosened them a little and pulled her bodice down a bit more, until her cleavage was visible. She was no beauty, but her body wasn't without merit.

Maybe she should be naked. That would probably surprise and distract him.

Once more she cursed the day she had met Iain MacLachlann and wished she really was coming to Caradoc with no past follies to darken her desire, free and unencumbered, a virgin to the nuptial bed.

For a moment, dismay and shame clouded her thoughts and feelings. She could imagine Iain standing before her, mocking her for a fool if she thought she could forget him and trick Caradoc into believing she was a virgin.

At that vision, energy and determination shot through her. She could forget Iain and what he had done, how he had made her feel used and stupid.

He had been so triumphant the morning after he seduced her—so proud of himself, so sure of his worth, so confident he had completely conquered her and that her money would soon be his. He had spoken of what he intended to do with her dowry as bluntly as if she were his steward keeping track of his coin. She had known then, fully and completely, that he had never wanted her for herself alone. He had wanted her money, and by seducing her, he was sure he had it.

She had not let him defeat her. She had left him and found another, more worthy man to marry, and she would do everything in her power to make certain Caradoc of Llanstephan never knew of her past, or regretted marrying her, despite his people's objections.

Father Rhodri had both looked and sounded as if

he were condemning them to eternal damnation when he blessed both their union and the simple gold band she now sported on her left hand. Cordelia had fidgeted as if standing on hellish coals, and she wouldn't have been surprised if Ganore had shouted denunciations all the way through.

Mercifully—or perhaps in view of Caradoc's fiercely determined expression—nobody had said a thing. Not before, not during, not after. Indeed, it had been one of the grimmer marriage ceremonies Fiona had ever experienced, until her Bordeaux wine began to flow. Then had come the laughter and the merriment and the singing, from everybody except Cordelia and Ganore, and Father Rhodri, who had not even stayed to eat.

Footsteps. Coming toward this chamber.

Caradoc!

Her heart started to pound and her hands felt clammy. She chewed her lip and slid lower beneath the coverings.

The door to the chamber opened. The lover of her girlish dreams stood there, illuminated by the spluttering rushlight in his hand, while the sound of men singing came louder through the open door.

The dull light flickered on Caradoc's face, across the planes and angles, reminding her once more—as if she needed it—that the boy was a boy no longer, but a man in his prime.

So different from Iain, in so many ways. So wonderfully, excitingly different.

She would make Caradoc glad she had come. She would make him happy that she had offered him her body as well as her bounty, and in doing so, she would cleanse even the intimate memories of Iain from her mind, as they had been banished from her heart the moment he raised his head and smiled his smug, satisfied smile that had nothing of love in it at all.

Caradoc did not enter. As her heartbeat quickened and abated, then quickened again, he simply waited there, until she began to wonder if he was drunk or expecting her to say something.

Finally, before she could guess what might be the appropriate thing to say, he came into the room and closed the door. His steps were firm and steady, so she knew he was not drunk. Indeed, she realized he was as sober as she, and that was *very* sober.

He crossed the room and set the light on the windowsill.

He hesitated again, looking out the window, but she didn't get the impression he was looking at or for anything specific.

Why, he seemed . . . shy!

By the saints, after his previous behavior, shy would have been the last word she would have used to describe Caradoc of Llanstephan.

The worst of her anxiety dissipated like smoke in the open air. "I feared you were going to stay below and sing all night."

"No."

He seemed so like a lad both dreading and hoping for a girl's first kiss, she took pity on him and threw back the coverlet. She rose and went to him, wrapping her arms about his waist and laying her head against his broad, muscular back, the wool warm against her cheek. "I'm glad you're here. I missed you."

He was so tense! It was tempting to tell him to relax, that she was not a timid girl who did not know full well what was about to happen.

She dare not, but she could tell him something of her feelings. "I didn't come here just because you were the only poor nobleman in Britain, Caradoc. I had very pleasant memories of you."

She crept around him, her arms still holding him, until she was between him and the window. She tilted her head and smiled. "Don't you want to kiss your bride?"

He didn't answer with words. He gathered her into his powerful arms and kissed her. Gently. Tenderly. Wonderfully, his mouth sliding over hers, teasing her senses, arousing her passion. Desire, pent-up and eager, pushed against the edges of her control, urging her to lose herself in his arms.

Not yet, for her mind persisted in comparing him to her first lover, who was the loser in that contest.

Until Caradoc shifted, holding her tighter, his mouth claiming hers with sure purpose and blatant desire, and at last the memory of Iain's kisses and his touch upon her skin sank and departed, drowned and destroyed by Caradoc's lips and hands and passionate attention.

Delicious trills of sensation skittered about her body, settling at last where a new throbbing began. This felt so good, so right, she shivered with the delight of it and leaned into him, relaxing into his embrace, giving herself to him, and all but begging him to take her then and there.

"You are cold." He let go and she almost whimpered with frustration. "Get into bed."

That was not why she shivered, and she wanted nothing more than to caress his strong arms and warrior's body, to tell him how he aroused her. But she was an actor tonight, and so must act as if this was all new and unexpected, which was not going to be nearly as difficult as she had feared. With him, it was as if she had only sipped before, but now was going to drink deep.

She watched him disrobe. Surely a bride watching the groom was not strange. Besides, he was so attractive, she could not bring herself to look away as his body was revealed in the light of the candle and rush.

He was simply magnificent. His shoulders were broad, his chest and back muscled, his waist lean. He bore no scars of battle or injuries. His long hair brushed his naked shoulders as he ran his hand through it in a gesture that seemed at once self-conscious and natural before he bent down to tug off his boots.

"Why is your hair so long?" she asked, unable to contain her curiosity.

"I like it that way," he answered, his voice muffled as his second boot fell upon the floor.

He turned away to remove his breeches, again giving her the impression he was shy, and suddenly she wanted to giggle with delight.

That urge passed when he faced the bed. Shy? She

had thought him shy? If he had been, that had certainly fled.

This time, *she* looked away, abashed by the glory of his naked body.

He went to blow out the rushlight and the candle, enveloping them in a welcome, intimate darkness.

She shifted when he lifted the covers, letting in a brief blast of cool air as he slid beneath them. He did not immediately embrace her. "In truth, I seldom think about my hair and nobody except Dafydd dares to tell the lord of Llanstephan that he is as shaggy as a sheep before shearing. I will have it trimmed tomorrow."

His voice came from the darkness as if he were a spirit. She vaguely remembered a legend about Cupid, the god of love, who had come to his wife invisible. It was not difficult to imagine Caradoc as the god of love. For years he had been the god of her daydreams.

"No, not if you do that for my sake," she answered. "I like it."

It made him different from Iain in one more way, and she would have all the reminders she could of the disparity between them.

"Do you?"

"Yes." It was more a sigh than a word.

"Come to your husband, Fiona," he whispered as he ran his fingertips down her bare arm.

Her whole body started to quiver like a drawn bowstring as she turned toward him.

"I promise I will be as gentle as I can," he murmured as he put his arm around her.

He was mistaken about that, too, for she trembled

not with fear, but with anticipation, excited even beyond the expectations that had burst into life the moment she saw him approaching her in the hall the day she had arrived.

His warm breath stirred her hair brushing her cheek just before his mouth took hers as if asking for permission, not demanding his rights or in fierce and boastful conquest. She gladly gave him that permission, returning his kiss with the passion he called forth from deep within her.

She tried not to be too eager at first, but she could not hold back. She leaned against him, feeling the length of his body against hers, the only barrier the thin silk of her shift, and gave herself up to his soul-stirring and amazing kisses.

With a low moan of pleasure, she let him part her lips with his tongue, masterful and yet still gentle. His tongue slid inside her mouth, making their kiss yet more intimate.

She ran her fingers through his thick dark hair and pulled him even closer, as if she would consume him with her yearning. Still kissing, he laid her on her back and began to loosen the tie of her shift.

Thinking of his pleasure, she slowly lowered her hands, letting them drift and brush and caress his chest, her fingertips grazing the hairs, then discovering his nipples.

He stilled.

"Should I not touch you there?"

"I like it," he murmured as the tie came undone and he nuzzled her garment lower with his chin. "Very much."

Gripping his arms, she raised herself and flicked

her tongue where her fingers had been at play. He threw back his head, and groan rumbled from his throat.

"You like that, too?" she whispered.

"Aye. So will you."

He pushed her back and swiftly bent to kiss the valley between her breasts. As he leaned his weight on one arm, he pleasured one breast with his gentle touch while he licked and kissed the other, sending torrents of excitement through her along taut lines of wondrous tension.

His hand left her breast and traveled lower, then lower still.

He must be more excited than I. With that thought on the fringe of her consciousness, she reached for him. She, too, let her hand move lower, then lower still.

By the saints! She snatched her hand away. He was . . . not like Iain, and for the first time since she had seen the heartless triumph in Iain's eyes, she was glad she was not a virgin; otherwise, she probably would have been terrified to think of what Caradoc was going to do with his magnificent body.

"It will not hurt much if you let me prepare you," he said, his voice low and tender as he raised his head and looked at her, his hand still making its leisurely progress over her body. "I will not force you until you are ready."

Again, he misunderstood, but once more, she was not about to tell him that, or why. "What of you? Do you not need to be prepared?"

"I am already prepared. *Very* prepared."

His hand slipped beneath the hem of her shift and began to slowly push it upward, baring her to his fingers. "You have lovely legs, Fiona."

She let herself enjoy the exquisite sensations that built and built the higher his hand went. "How do you know?"

His hand returned to her ankle. "By this," he said, circling her ankle with his fingers. "Slender and supple." His hand slid along the curve of her calf "And this." Past her knee. "Not too bony." To her thigh. "Wonderful," he breathed.

She could not prevent a wiggle as his fingertips moved between her thighs. Prepared? She was more than prepared.

But it was too soon yet. He was still thinking too much of her. "What of you, my lord? Have you not fine legs, too?"

She had to sit up a bit to reach his ankle. "Firm and strong." She trailed her hand up his calf. "Excellent muscle." Past his knee. "Not bony, either." To his thigh. "More excellent muscle." He sighed as she moved her hand again to encircle him.

Pleased, she stroked him, then used her tongue to pleasure his nipples, tentatively at first, so that he did not suspect she had some experience in these matters.

After what seemed a very brief time, he pulled her to him, then rolled so that she was beneath him, her shift bunched about her waist.

"I thought your kisses were marvels," he muttered as he settled himself between her legs.

His mouth swooped down upon hers, hot and

passionate. She tried to think, to maintain some level of awareness that would enable her to control this, but it was impossible. In an instant, she was lost on an ocean of sensation, guided only by his lips and his touch as he kissed and caressed and stroked.

Making her ready. Aye, and more. Desperate. Demanding. Anxious. Needy. She moaned and sighed and whimpered as he stoked the fires of her passion, until she was ready to beg him to take her and end the exquisite torture.

She didn't have to ask, for he sensed it.

She felt him prepare to enter her and from the desire-drenched core of her mind came a warning that this was the moment when she must take the most care.

A moment that should have been wonderful, spoiled by that thought, and her own foolishness.

He hesitated again, as if trying to read her thoughts, her feelings.

Should she make the first move now, or leave that to him?

Him. He must be the experienced one here.

She ran her hands over his chest, touching, teasing, inflaming him more, wanting him to be so immersed in arousal he paid only slight heed to her as she waited, waited, waited for his thrust. His face twisted with the hunger, and at last he entered her.

She moved suddenly, bucking to disguise the missing resistance. That was not hard to do, for the sensation of his body filling her was as wonderful as she had expected.

She remembered to cry out as if in pain.

He did not pause as if suspicions were aroused

with the rest of him. He continued to move, slowly, gently, obviously afraid of hurting her.

There was no fear of that and she would not have the rest of this night tainted by deception. She reached up and brought his lips to hers in a burning, fervent kiss, claiming him as he was claiming her.

He started to move faster and as her hands slid down his cheeks and neck to his broad shoulders, she felt the corded muscles, tight with desire.

She began to move her hips, matching the driving rhythm of his strokes, and not only to reassure him that she felt far more pleasure than pain. She could not have stayed still if her whole fortune depended upon it. His body was too potent, too incredible. Tension, wondrous, unfamiliar tension, blossomed and stretched along her body.

His movements grew faster, sweeping her away on waves of passion. He became all in all, the lover of her dreams and fancies. Perfect. Wonderful.

Her whole body sang. Her heart soared. She had no thoughts beyond the pleasure. And still the tension grew, spreading, seeking. Stronger. Tighter.

Until it snapped and shattered. She cried out, but the marvelous sensations did not diminish. Caradoc thrust harder, deeper, and it was as if although the wave had broken upon the shore, she was yet carried along by it.

Then Caradoc growled, a low, deep sound primitive and powerful, masculine and virile, pure male in all its glory.

Panting, he stilled, and his anxious gaze searched her face a moment before he withdrew and rolled to lay beside her.

She lay motionless as her own hoarse breathing returned to normal. Virgin or not, it was done. They were wed, and the union consummated. She was Caradoc's wife, and no man could come between them.

His deep, gentle voice seemed to come from the darkness and warmth surrounding her, as if she had just experienced a fabulous dream and lingered in that dreamlike state yet. "I hope I did not hurt you much. I tried not to."

"No, you did not hurt me too much," she said.

"Glad I am to hear it."

She lay still, wondering if he was going to kiss her or hold her, or do anything more. She held her breath as his fingers once more caressed her arm. Then he turned, and in a little while, she heard the slow, even sounds of a man asleep.

She could not yet rest. First, she must feel for the hidden needle and prick her finger and put the blood where a virgin's blood should be.

Caradoc might not look for it come the morning, but she was sure Ganore would.

Chapter 8

‿‿‿∞‿‿‿

Caradoc awoke to find Fiona's arm draped over his naked waist. The neck of her silken shift, a wonderful creation that slid and slithered over her shapely body like a second skin, was still untied and her bare shoulder glowed in the dawn's light.

Young she looked, and soft and lovely in her sleep, her mouth forming what could almost be a pout, kissable and irresistible. To think that only days ago he faced ruin and despair, utter failure and loneliness. God must have heard his fervent prayers, as he had told Father Rhodri, and sent him salvation from far more than poverty and disgrace.

Fiona stirred, sighed, and snuggled against him, making him feel strong and protective, blissfully contented as he had never been before. He wanted to laugh with the joy of it. Only the fear of waking her and breaking this spell stopped him, for he would have this bliss last as long as possible.

A lock of her hair brushed her cheek, and he caressed it away so that he could see her face. Pretty? No, she wasn't pretty. She was lovely—lovable. Soft and welcoming, almost a wanton in her desire, arousing him as no woman ever had.

Perhaps they could make love again this morning—except that Dafydd and the others would be waiting for him.

Surely the men could gather the flock again without him, and start the shearing, too, even if more than a few would be the worse for *braggot*. Walking would do them good, and he could join them later, for the shearing would take all day.

Fiona shifted and more of her body pressed against him.

Of course the men would understand why a bridegroom might not be anxious to rush from his bedchamber in the chill early morning mist.

He gently slid his mouth over hers, back and forth until his whole body tingled with the delight of it. The texture of her soft lips teased his senses, reminding him of all the tender places of her body. He left her mouth and tasted the soft skin of her cheeks and chin, then lower to feel the warm pulse of her neck against his lips.

Lowering himself more, he brushed his palm across her breast.

Then she moved, stretching as languorously as a cat in the summer sun. Her eyes fluttered open, and they seemed to sparkle when she looked at him. "Caradoc?"

He raised himself on his elbow to look at her.

"Were you expecting to find somebody else in your bridal bed, Fiona?" he teased.

Her lips turned down and a little wrinkle appearing between her shapely brows. "Of course not."

"I meant no offense," he said, the warm mood momentarily sullied by his vain attempt at teasing.

Leave the wordplay, boy, he told himself, *for you are not like Connor and Dafydd*.

She sighed and ran her fingertip around his ear in a way that seemed to set his whole body alight with desire.

"I know very well who made love with me last night," she whispered, her voice low and sultry and incredibly seductive. "A very handsome fellow he was, with dark, wild hair like a Norseman. He claims to be the lord of an estate, but I think not, for it is clear by the sunlight that it is past dawn, yet he still lingers in bed like a lascivious rogue, even though I heard his men saying at the feast last night that there was much to be done today. They expected this lord to be there."

He moved back until he was sitting up, his back against the headboard, the sensual spell surrounding them broken for him by her implication. "I know my responsibilities, Fiona. I do not need reminding."

Shifting upward, she stroked his chest lightly with her fingertips. "I meant no offense either, my lord."

He sighed and closed his eyes, and wondered why he had been so annoyed a moment ago.

"It's just that if you stay too long in the bridal chamber to the neglect of your duties," she explained, "I doubt anybody will blame you. They will blame me. Indeed, can you not hear Father Rhodri denouncing me for a sinful Eve leading you into the pit of irresponsible decadence, and Ganore saying I must have slipped something into your wine?"

His happiness restored, his desire building, he gazed into her brilliant green eyes as he ran his hand over the curve of her shoulder toward her breasts. "As a matter of fact, I can. And you are right. But surely we can linger for a few moments before I am damned into the eternal flames of hell."

She sighed and closed her eyes, the lashes fanning upon her soft, flushed cheeks. He could gaze at her and caress her all day.

"If it will make you feel better," he murmured as she began to explore his body with her supple hands, "I shall announce in the hall that I stayed in our bedchamber because I enjoy being alone with you so much."

"Ganore will say I've bewitched you," she whispered as she pressed gentle kisses where her hands had been.

He groaned softly. "I think she might be right," he growled, his jaw tense with the pleasure she invoked. "You have bewitched me."

"Not the way she means."

"No, in a better way."

He maneuvered her onto her back.

"What are you doing, my lord?" she asked, her voice both amused and excited, and her eyes bright with anticipation, which enflamed his desire even more.

"I am going to make love with my bride again," he said in a low husky whisper.

"So soon?"

He hesitated a moment, unsure and uncertain, willing to wait if she deemed it necessary, or even preferable. "Are you too sore? Would you rather not?"

"Since you are where you are," she said softly, toying with the hairs circling his nipple as a smile lit her face and welcome blossomed in her eyes, "it seems a shame to stop you."

He laughed, a low rumble of pleasure. "I think you want me as much as I want you, Fiona MacDougal." His hand cupped her breast and her nipple pebbled beneath his palm. "I can feel that here." He moved his hand between her legs. "And here, too."

He looked back at her face. Her eyes were closed, and her delectable mouth was slightly open, her breathing fast. "And you are breathing as if you had run here all the way from Scotland."

"I might have, had I known what awaited."

His hand stilled a moment as he let himself simply enjoy the sensation of her palms gliding over him, imitating his motions and demonstrating how effective they could be.

She opened her eyes and regarded him with mocking accusation. "Is this some form of torture you have devised, Caradoc, to get me so stirred, and then stop?"

"Not at all," he replied as he lowered his head and teased her breasts with his lips and tongue.

"Yes, it is," she gasped, squirming beneath him. She put her hands on his shoulders and pushed, surprising him. She continued to push. "Roll over."

Despite the tone of her voice and the circumstances, he did not immediately do as she ordered. He did not take kindly to being told to do anything by anyone now that he was overlord.

"Please."

Not an order, then, but a request—and that was a very different thing. "Far be it from me to refuse a lady," he said as he complied, his excitement beginning to build again.

"I am a lady now, aren't I? Funny, I don't feel like one at the moment. I feel like quite the wanton wench."

He held his breath to see what she would do next.

She straddled his hips, her eyes agleam with triumph while his whole body reacted to the sensation of her above, and vulnerable. Without fighting it, he ceded control to her as easily as snow drifted down when there was no wind.

"I am going to give you a taste of your torture," she crooned before she leaned forward and pressed the softest of kisses upon his chest, so light as to be like the brush of a moth's wing. And so arousing, he thought the growing tension would make him snap like a dry twig if it didn't end soon.

Her hair stroked him like her fingers and when she continued to move her mouth still lower, he had to press his lips together to keep from groaning so loud, they would hear him in the hall below.

"Oh, sweet heaven, Fiona," he growled as the desire swept over, through and around him. "I yield. You win. Don't stop."

But she did.

He opened his eyes, to see both sure purpose and ardent need on her face. With a smile of blatant exultation, she moved forward and raised herself. Then she guided him to her and with deliberate leisure lowered herself until he was sheathed by her, joined in a union of flesh and desire.

Better was yet to be. She placed her hands beside his head and began to rock.

It was exquisite agony. Wondrous torment. Her tongue swirled around the peaks of his nipples, and soon he had no thoughts beyond Fiona and the sensations she aroused, and no need but that of completion.

In what seemed a scant few moments, the tension snapped and broke.

As the waves of release subsided, he drew her down and kissed her deeply. Somehow, by some miracle, an amazing woman had come to Llanstephan and married him. If he had not stayed here, despite the yearnings of his heart, he would not be holding Fiona in his arms. Never again would he doubt that duty would be rewarded, and God indeed knew best.

She sighed and sat up, then slowly moved away from him.

"Where are you going?" he asked as she threw back the bedcovers and got out of bed.

"To get dressed, of course. It's nearly time for mass, I'm sure."

"It cannot be. It is just past the dawn."

Getting purchase with his heels, he pushed himself back until he was once more against the head of the bed, his head pillowed in his hands. He watched as Fiona walked toward the chest where she kept her gowns. She moved so gracefully, her body straight and yet supple as a willow. She was supple in other marvelous ways, too.

"I assure you it is," she said. "Look out the window."

He did as she suggested, and what he saw ruined his lazy, pleasant mood. With a curse, he climbed out of bed and, naked, strode to the window.

"What is it?" she asked as she took a rust-colored gown out of the chest.

"Rain. Not yet, but probably soon." His gaze scanned the sky. "If it rains, we can't shear. The shears get caught in the wet fleece."

After quickly pulling on the gown, she joined him. The sky was dull, dark gray, like heavy smoke. "Maybe it will hold off until you're done."

"It might," he agreed grimly, "but I doubt it. The clouds are too low and dark. We have about ten days or then we'll have to wash again, and I assure you, my shoulders will not appreciate having to do it a second time."

He turned away and went to dress in what looked to be very old clothes from the very bottom of his battered chest: worn woolen breeches, a much-mended brown tunic and heavy boots. "We will have to start at once."

She began to swiftly braid her hair. "After mass?"

He nodded. "We'll take our bread and cheese and eat on the way to the gathering." He ran his gaze over her, and her untied gown. "Since I told Rhonwen not to disturb us this morning, I will be your lady's maid. Let me help you with that gown."

He came up behind her. His hand glided into the

opening at the back of her gown, his palm warm against her skin. Sighing, she leaned back, momentarily caught up in the sensation of skin upon skin. Then he circled her with his arms, pulled her back against him and nuzzled her neck.

"I thought you were going to help me, my lord," she murmured as his hands glided along her breasts to her waist and then her hips. "I don't call that helping."

"I'm smoothing it down."

"Whatever you wish to call it, please stop and tie the lacing."

"With great pleasure, my lady."

It was the first time anybody had called her by the title, and she was delighted. It was the reason she had given for this marriage, of course, so it should have pleased her. Yet in her heart she knew it was the title spoken in Caradoc's deep, velvety voice that made it so wonderfully thrilling.

He made everything so wonderfully thrilling.

How much she wanted to spend the whole of the morning here with him—no, the whole day. Unfortunately, unless she wanted gossip and rumor to take her to task, she dare not.

She stepped away from her handsome husband's roving hands and thought to keep the talk to something . . . not intimate. "Why didn't you just keep the sheep in the pens after you wash them?"

"We would have to feed them if we did," he said as he sat on the bed and pulled on his boots. "But they wouldn't eat what we give them. Too rich it is for them, when they are used to foraging on the mountain. Like drinking that fine French wine when you aren't used it. Two goblets and I knew I should avoid it on my wedding night."

He raised his eyes to look at her, then frowned. "What's wrong?"

She continued to braid her thick hair and wished she had been more guarded. "Nothing."

"Something is. The wine was excellent—"

"No, it isn't that," she confessed, interrupting him. "It's just that when you are out with the men, I'll be here alone."

"There is a household of servants for you to get to know," he reminded her.

The household was the problem, but she didn't want to start their marriage off with whining.

He came to her and pulled her into his arms, a most comfortable and comforting place to be. "It may take some time, Fiona, but I'm sure you'll win them over."

"I'll do my best."

"I ask no more." He bussed her lightly on the forehead. "Now we had best get below, before Ganore comes pounding on the door and demands to know if we're sick with the plague."

"At least she would knock for you," Fiona replied, pulling away. "If it was just me, she would probably walk in without a single rap on the door."

Then, before they moved another inch or said another word, the heavens opened the way a dam burst its banks and rain poured down so hard and so fast, by the time they turned to look outside, water was already dripping from the leaking roof and running down the wall.

Caradoc swore, while Fiona hurried to take down

the tapestries before they got wet. After helping her, he sighed and raked his tousled hair. "No shearing today."

So he would not have to leave her. She tried to look sorry.

And obviously failed, as his frown changed to a sly smile.

"A pity, that," he said. "I'll have to find something to do to pass the time. Any suggestions, wife?"

"First, we must go to mass. Then break the fast. Then, I must begin my life as chatelaine of your household. When I have seen to my household duties for today, then, my lord," she said, a seductive smile blooming, "I may have a spare moment or two for you."

His breathing labored, his muscles taut with exertion, his body sweat-slicked, Caradoc continued to circle Jon-Bron in the empty stall. Both men held broadswords in their two hands, and each crouched and waited for the other to strike a blow. Like Caradoc, Jon-Bron was half naked; unlike Caradoc, his chest and back was scarred with ancient wounds, both large and small, and some from when he had tumbled from a tree and landed on a holly bush that had torn right through his clothes when he was a boy.

"Hold it up higher, Caradoc, to protect your chest and face. That's right," Jon-Bron coached.

One of the horses whinnied with what sounded like curiosity to know why two men, friends for years, were fighting each other in the stable.

"Don't be distracted, Caradoc," Jon-Bron warned

after he glanced toward the other stall. "That will give your opponent an opening. Watch and wait. Be ready for any chance, and let nothing interfere—"

Suddenly the stable door creaked open, letting in the wind and rain with a whoosh. Immediately ignoring Jon-Bron's caution, both men straightened and looked expectantly at the entrance.

They lowered their swords as Dafydd stumbled over the threshold and stared with unmasked surprise at the sight that met his eyes, as if he had never seen Caradoc half-naked and sweating with a broadsword in his hand and Jon-Bron teaching a man how to fight. "Caradoc, what the devil are you doing?"

Jon-Bron tossed down his sword and leaned over, resting his hands on his knees as he caught his breath, while Caradoc slumped against the empty stable wall. "We're practicing."

"What for? Are you expecting an attack?" Dafydd demanded. He ran his gaze over the pale garrison commander, whose eyes were so bloodshot, they looked like glowing coals. "Or is this a punishment for Jon-Bron's drunkenness last night?"

"I told you, we're practicing."

Dafydd's own bloodshot eyes narrowed with sudden suspicion. "Ah, more showing off, is it? I must say, Caradoc, if that is what you were after, the hall would be a better place."

Showing off had been the farthest thing from Caradoc's mind when he had asked Jon-Bron for a practice while Fiona bustled about the castle. He didn't want Fiona to realize how incompetent a warrior her noble husband was. While he was one of the fastest, most efficient shearers of sheep—and justly proud of that skill—that was hardly something a nobleman could brag about.

"It's raining, so we can't shear, so I thought I'd practice with a sword," he said. "Nothing wrong with that, is there?"

"I didn't say it was wrong," Dafydd said. "Just strange."

"He's better than he used to be," Jon-Bron noted as he picked up his sword. "Why, I remember the days when he could barely lift—"

"Years ago, that was," Caradoc interrupted, his pride piqued. "I was younger then."

"Aye, and scrawny as a bird with the ribs poking out of you. Remember, Dafydd?" Jon-Bron replied nostalgically. "What was it Connor called you sometimes? The starving vulture?"

Caradoc didn't deign to respond as he lifted a bucket of water and took a gulp.

Dafydd cocked his head as he studied Jon-Bron. "You look terrible."

"No more than you," Jon-Bron shot back. "You had as much *braggot* as I did—or probably more, since I fell asleep before you did."

"Passed out, you mean," Caradoc said, glancing at both of them as he put the bucket back down. "I've never seen either one of you sleeping with your head on the table and a mug clenched in your fist before. And I would not be too quick to tell Jon-Bron he looks the worse for it, Dafydd, because you don't look any better."

"Then you should be showing Jon-Bron here some mercy, for we were celebrating your wedding, after all," Dafydd replied as he plopped himself down in the straw.

"Well, so you were," Caradoc admitted more genially. "Jon-Bron, I think we're finished for the day."

He sheathed his sword, which had not been out of its scabbard in so long, it had taken three tries for him to pull it free. "If it's still raining tomorrow, we'll meet again after the noon and practice some more." He put a condemning expression on his face. "And stay away from the *braggot*."

"You don't have to tell me twice," Jon-Bron said as he, too, sheathed his broadsword. His tunic, like Caradoc's, had been tossed over the wall of the stall, and he took it down to put on. "Well, maybe you do. If only I could remember the afterward when it's put before me, but it tastes so good."

"And costs so much," Caradoc added as he slung his sword belt over the stable post and reached for his tunic.

"But money no trouble now, my friend," Dafydd jovially observed. "You've seen to that."

"Aye, but it's money I don't want spent on *braggot* or wine. Debts I have that must be paid, and more taxes to come," he said as he sat heavily beside Dafydd.

His action sent motes of dust and bits of straw into the air, tickling his nostrils and reminding him to send Rhonwen into the village when the rain let up a bit, to buy a featherbed.

He could so easily imagine sinking into a featherbed with Fiona's soft, welcoming body beneath him . . .

"Have no fear," Jon-Bron said, bringing him back

to the here and now, away from the contemplation of lovemaking. "Ale will suit me and my men fine."

He left the stall and went to the stable door. Opening it, he threw his arm over his head to shield it from the rain and dashed out into the courtyard.

"Eifion said last night he was sure the rain was going to let up by tonight," Dafydd remarked.

Caradoc sighed as he bunched up his tunic, then put it behind him to cushion his back as he leaned against the stable wall. "Then it's rain for days. At least it will keep Cordelia home."

Dafydd nodded, then his gaze went to Caradoc's broadsword. "What's this really about, Caradoc? Since when do you decide to pick up a sword? Always better with a quill, you were."

"I just thought that I should practice. Now that my finances are not such a worry, I have more time for such things."

"Then it's nothing to do with your wife at all?"

"Of course not."

Dafydd shook his head. "Liar."

"Blackguard."

"Varlet."

"Nit."

"At least when I'm after impressing a woman," Dafydd noted as he began to plait some straw, "I don't come up with some pathetic excuse about plenty of time on my hands."

"Your wits are still addled by that *braggot*. How is this to impress Fiona? First of all, she cannot see me," Caradoc said as he closed his eyes. Maybe he had worked a bit *too* hard.

"That's true—for now. Maybe you're planning

on revealing your warrior glory later, after more practice."

Caradoc slid Dafydd a critical glance under his half-open lids. "I don't have to reveal my warrior glory to her. She's my wife, isn't she? Why would I have to trouble myself to impress her?"

"Because she's your bride, man." Dafydd's expression altered, to one of understanding. "Because Connor was always better at this than you, and it galls you still. Now you have saved Llanstephan from the tax collectors, so you think you will succeed in this, too, at least in your wife's green eyes."

Caradoc frowned. "Now you sound like Eifion. Your predictions are no more accurate, either. I decide to practice with a sword on a rainy day, and suddenly there are all sorts of deep, dark reasons thrown at me."

Which may be true, but that was not for even Dafydd to know.

Dafydd didn't answer directly as he looked at the straw in his hands. "I wonder where Connor is right now."

"I don't know and I don't care," Caradoc declared, telling himself that was true.

They said nothing for a while, each in their own thoughts. Then Dafydd grinned, and Caradoc knew peace was restored between them.

"I know where your wife is," he announced.

"In the hall. Where else?"

Dafydd tossed aside the straw he had been playing with and once again his expression grew serious. "She's in the kitchen, laying down the law to Gwillym about the meals, with Ganore looking daggers at her. I stopped in there looking for you."

Ganore's fierce countenance was not unexpected, and he doubted there was little he could do about it anyway. "And the others? How are they treating Fiona?"

Dafydd shrugged. "About how you'd expect. Silent as stones, the lot of them, while she talks on, pleasant as can be. Myself, I don't know how she's managing it. I would have given up long ago, for I gather this has been going on since you broke the fast this morning."

His expression just as grim, Caradoc nodded. Where Ganore led, the other servants would follow— at least until Fiona somehow proved herself.

It wasn't going to be easy winning over Cordelia or Ganore, but if anybody could overcome Cordelia's fierce Welsh pride and Ganore's prejudices, he believed it would be the amazing, astounding, delightful Fiona. Fiona the Fair, come to rescue him from the dungeon of his despair.

"She started off asking for the keys from Ganore," he explained to his friend, "which of course she had every right to do. She asked nicely enough, but you would have thought Ganore had been ordered to give up her hand with them." He shook his head. "Maybe I should have stayed. But the household is for Fiona to manage now, and I thought I'd done enough."

"Oh, I think you did plenty that first day, all right," Dafydd agreed, so seriously that Caradoc could hardly believe it was Dafydd speaking.

"Made her a threat to them, you did, with your harshness and order to respect her. That did not smooth her way. It would have been better to say nothing. She felt that, too. I saw it in her face."

"I didn't," he replied defensively. "I had to say something, didn't I? I only came to her defense."

As he thought back, though, he recalled that she had not looked as pleased as he had expected.

But Dafydd couldn't have more of an understanding of Fiona than he did, not after last night. "She didn't say anything to me about it."

"What did you expect her to do, criticize you in front of everybody? She's not like Cordelia, you know."

"Thank the Lord for that."

"I don't think she's like any woman we've met," Dafydd gravely warned. "Take care, Caradoc."

"Now you make her sound like an assassin."

"A man can be wounded without a drop of blood being shed."

"You think she will hurt me?" he demanded.

"I think she could, and you've only just been married. A warning is all, before you are blinded by love."

"Love?" Caradoc scoffed as he got stiffly to his feet, and despite the hope that had taken root in his heart. "Have I said I *love* her?"

"No," Dafydd conceded as he, too, rose. "But you scarcely know her, when all is said and done."

"And you are the expert, of course," Caradoc mocked as his hope seemed to feel the blight of frost.

"Enough that you sought my advice before,"

Dafydd reminded him as they faced each other. "I don't mean to pry or ruin your happiness. I just want you to be careful."

"Aren't I always?" Caradoc snapped as he grabbed his sword belt. It caught on the post.

"Well, once I would have said yes without hesitation. Now I'm not so sure. I have made plenty of mistakes when it comes to women, Caradoc, and I don't want you to make any with your wife."

Caradoc glanced at Dafydd over his shoulder as he tried to get his sword belt off the post. "This is certainly an unfamiliar modesty."

"It's the truth, and I wouldn't be saying it to anybody but you, and if I didn't think it was important. So you will take care, my friend?"

As his sword belt finally came free, Caradoc realized that it had taken something for Dafydd to admit his failings. His annoyance fled, replaced by gratitude that Dafydd was worried about his happiness. "Aye, I'll take care."

Dafydd smiled, and the familiar merriment came back to his dancing eyes. "So, was my advice a help last night?"

Caradoc didn't answer with words. Instead, and to show that all was well between them, he did something he hadn't done in years.

He winked.

Chapter 9

I ain MacLachlann thrust hard into the harlot, driving himself further and further in his pleasure. She moaned and whimpered and perhaps called his name, but he wasn't listening. He was enjoying her willing flesh; beyond sating his lust, nothing else intruded into his consciousness until, with what sounded like a snarl, he climaxed.

Sweat-slicked and panting, he collapsed against her, then rolled off. He slowly grew aware of the trollop's ale-soaked breath and the lice in her tangled, filthy hair. She stank, too, as much as the fusty linens in this rundown tavern. Water from the leaking, bug-infested thatch stained the wattle-and-daub walls, bringing with it the smell of mold, decay, and the aged dung used to make the daub. It had fallen away in places, exposing the woven twigs of the wattle.

Fiona had smelled of flowers, and her thick auburn hair had been like silk in his fingers.

That whore—and he wasn't thinking of the woman lying beside him now.

The harlot inched closer, all too horribly visible in the moonlight coming in through the open shutter on the small window. She laid her hand on his chest. "I heard you Scots were fearsome lovers, but I wasn't expectin' ya to be as fast as that! Will we wait a bit, then go again?"

With a scowl, he threw her off. "Leave me. My friend waiting on the stairs will pay you."

"I'm in no hurry," she purred, nipping at his chest with her blackened teeth. "Not at all. Ain't you going to stay and let me enjoy meself, too?"

As if he cared about a whore's pleasure! He shoved her so hard, she tumbled from the bed and hit the wall of the small room. "I'm finished wi' you Get out."

The woman adjusted her filthy shift and gathered up her equally filthy and ragged gown stained with ale and gravy. "Fine way to be, I must say. Just wantin' a bit more fun, is all. No need to be so rude."

Iain laughed, enjoying her anger as much as he had her body. "Go away, that's a good girl. Do as I say, and maybe I'll come back."

"Don't bother. You ain't so much anyway."

He was out of the bed in an instant, fierce rage twisting his face that could be so attractive when he smiled. He grabbed her and threw her hard against the wall.

Terrified, she stared at him helplessly as he

grabbed his dagger from the pile of clothes on the rough wooden floor. Hugging her tattered garments to her chest, she inched toward the door, but he caught her, pinning her beside it, the tip of his knife at her throat.

"What did you say?" he demanded.

"Nothing, sir, nothing," she mumbled as tears oozed out of her red-rimmed eyes.

His features contorted with wrath so that he didn't even look human anymore. "I'm the best you've had, aren't I?"

"Aye, sir, aye. The v-very best," she stammered.

"You would do me for nothing, wouldn't you?"

"O' course I would."

"Right. Now get out." Regardless of his nakedness, he lunged for the door and threw it open, then pushed her through. He slammed the door behind her and strode to the pile of his clothing. He just as swiftly and angrily dressed himself. What did that harlot know, anyway? Women begged for his embrace.

A soft rap at the door interrupted his disgruntled ruminations and he turned toward it, a smug smile on his face.

She had come back to apologize. Of course she had, and he would dearly enjoy making her beg for forgiveness. "Enter."

Fergus warily stuck his head inside the door.

"That whore didna dare ask you for more money, did she?"

"No. Douglas is back. With news of Fiona."

"About bloody time," Iain growled, angry and yet pleased, too. His men had ranged all over the south of Scotland and north of England trying to find out where his money had gone. Fiona had led them all a merry chase, hiring new men every twenty miles, doubling back, staying a day or two in some places, and apparently sleeping by the side of the road others.

He put his hands on his hips and glared at Fergus. "Well?"

"She may have gone to Wales."

"Wales?" he demanded incredulously.

Then he remembered she spoke Welsh, as well as French and even some of the gibberish of the Norsemen. "What the devil would she be doing there?"

Trepidation in his eyes, Fergus shrugged.

The answer came to him. Getting as far away from him as possible. *That bitch.* "What part o' Wales?"

"The march."

"Well, that makes it easy," Iain muttered sarcastically. He fastened his cold glare onto Fergus. "What part o' the borderlands?"

"Probably the north."

"Then that's where we're going."

Fergus shifted uneasily. "But King William—"

"Can damn well wait! I'm no' going back until I've got my money!"

"Oh, God, Father in Heaven, we give thanks to you for stopping the rain at last," Father Rhodri intoned as he said the grace. "We pray that all those who should have, have recalled the great flood, when You washed away the sin of the world. We pray they pay heed to this warning and sin no more or act with impulsive haste. Help us to remember the light of Your countenance and benevolent mercy in the sun shining upon the hills, oh God, a reminder that mistakes can be remedied."

Alone at the high table, Fiona shifted her weight from one leg to the other. Since their marriage Caradoc had stood beside her for every grace, sometimes even surreptitiously rolling his eyes as Father Rhodri reminded them yet again that he didn't approve of their marriage. He was obviously still quite convinced God didn't, either.

Today, however, Caradoc and most of the men had gone to shear, for the rain had finally abated, at least for the time being, and thankfully before they had to wash the sheep again.

Father Rhodri's lips narrowed even more as he continued. "Be kind to your servants, oh Blessed Savior, who seek to do Your will and walk in Your ways, with fortitude, humility and chastity."

At first, Caradoc had taken the continuing rainfall with good grace. So had she, for it meant he was always close by, even though he spent a great deal of time with the soldiers of his garrison, or with Dafydd, discussing the shearing to come and the possible amount of fleece they would get.

Yet as the rain had gone on, even Caradoc began to get tense. Finally, last evening, it had stopped. Caradoc had sent out word for the men to be prepared to gather and shear beginning at dawn the next day. He had been too restless to sleep, even after making love, and had gotten up several times to make certain the rain wasn't starting again. It had not, so immediately after mass, he and the other men had grabbed bread and cheese and left for the hills to gather, hoping that the rain would hold off long enough to get the shearing finished.

Fiona hoped so, too, for her husband's sake, although the sky was still dark with heavy clouds of moisture.

"And finally, oh God . . ."

She nearly groaned with relief.

"We also humbly ask that You bless this food, and all who eat it, that they may know when they are sated so they do not fall prey to gluttony or greed, of any kind. We ask this in the name of Your Son, Jesus Christ the Righteous, who fasted forty days and nights resisting the devil's own tempting. Amen."

Fiona muttered an amen and sat down. Eight days, and Father Rhodri still managed to make every blessing and grace a curse upon her head.

Eight days, and the servants still regarded her as if she were the serpent come to ruin Paradise, watching her with barely disguised scorn and obeying her orders as if it would simply be too much bother to protest, or they certainly would. She had been polite, she had been friendly, but nothing seemed to thaw the frigid, rigid Welsh.

Ganore, of course, was the worst, and the others followed her lead. Unfortunately, short of dying her hair black and announcing she was a changeling really born in Wales, there didn't seem to be much she could do to change the woman's feelings about her. There was one other arrow in her quiver, but she did not want to use it yet. She wanted the servants to see that she was worthy of respect because she knew how to manage a household, even one of this size.

It wasn't only the servants and Father Rhodri who made her days a trial. Cordelia barely spoke to her and refused to sit at the high table. She spent most of her time riding about the hills like some sort of merry vagabond.

Fiona almost envied her that freedom. She would have, if she didn't truly believe this behavior was a dangerous thing for a woman.

Fiona could console herself that there had been no outright mutiny so far, but that was small comfort as the days went on.

Indeed, if it wasn't for the nights she shared with Caradoc, her new life would have been misery itself. Outside of their bedchamber, Caradoc was brusque and gruff, the commanding lord of an estate. Alone with her, however, it was like their first night and early morning. He seemed years younger then, and free of the burden of his responsibilities, while she escaped the animosity surrounding her everywhere else in Llanstephan.

After the meal concluded and the servants dispersed, she detained Rhonwen a moment.

"I was thinking that perhaps we could go see the shearing today," she said. "I've never actually witnessed such a thing, and I would be glad of your company."

She knew, but did not say, that Dafydd would be there as well as Caradoc.

Rhonwen bit her lip nervously, and looked around as if she feared they were being spied upon. "I have much to do, my lady."

"Tidying our bedchamber won't take long."

"There's your shifts to be washed, and . . . and other things."

It was clear the girl didn't want to go. "Very well. I'll go by myself."

Fiona watched her quiet little maidservant hurry away, her head bowed. Then she sighed. So far, she hadn't made much progress figuring out what she should do about Rhonwen and her attraction to the friendly bailiff, if anything. He seemed a nice enough fellow and not simply interested in making a number of conquests like some sort of merchant tallying his coins. No men of that ilk remained friends with their lovers once the relationship was over, but from the things Rhonwen had said, and her own observations, it seemed Dafydd did.

Dafydd also took his duties seriously. The times she had seen him in discussion with Caradoc about the sheep, such as when a fox had killed several of the lambs and Dafydd had organized a hunt despite the rain, she had been very impressed by his serious attitude.

She could understand why he, seemingly so merry, and Caradoc, seemingly so grim, could be friends.

But would Dafydd and could Dafydd make Rhonwen happy, or would she be better off waiting for another man who offered marriage? She could ask Caradoc what he thought, but that would reveal Rhonwen's secret. Rhonwen herself had never said anything about her feelings, so perhaps it would be best to keep quiet.

She headed for the kitchen to speak to Gwillym

about fish for that evening's meal. Gwillym was under the impression that only on Fridays should they have fish. She, however, liked a nice fresh fish at other times, and planned to ask him to prepare one for the evening's repast. Unfortunately, she could already imagine the look on his broad face. Friendliness seemed to be ineffective, so she would order him if necessary, although she hoped it didn't come to—

"I tell you, it's unnatural," Ganore declared, her harsh, firm voice audible through the slightly open kitchen door. "She's put some kind of spell on him, that's what, to make him marry her."

Fiona hesitated, taking a deep breath as she prepared to enter.

"Besotted, that's what he is—like he's drunk or insensible," Cordelia said, just as firmly and just as loudly.

Delightful. She should go inside and break up the "condemn Fiona" conversation they were having. She really should.

"Aye, or too long without a woman in that big bed of his. I told him time and again he should find a wife, a good Welsh lady like his sainted mother, but did he listen? No! Just growled like a bear and paid me no mind!"

So, Caradoc had not married when or who Ganore told him to. Obviously the woman took this as a personal affront—but really! Why should Caradoc listen to her?

"And look where it's got him," Ganore continued. "He's being led around by the nose by that redheaded Scot. Mark my words, if she's not bewitched him, he'll wake up soon enough when he's had his fill of loving her and realizes what he's done. I wouldn't be in her shoes then, I can tell you!"

"There are ways to have a marriage ended," Cordelia noted with grim satisfaction.

"Aye, it's easy enough," Ganore agreed. "*And . . .*"

Fiona held her breath.

"We should all pray hard she doesn't get with child. Not that I think she will. Barren she is, and I can tell. Her hips are too thin and she's too pale by far under those spots on her face. That's another reason Caradoc should get rid of her."

She had not gotten with child by Iain, thank God, but she would love to bear Caradoc's offspring. And it was far, far too early yet to be speculating about being barren. Why, they had not yet been wed a month.

"Otherwise, he'll feel duty-bound to keep her," Cordelia added, "and there won't be a word anyone can say to make him change his mind."

"I'd even wager she knows she's barren and that's why she came here bragging of her money, shoving it under Caradoc's nose. Sly and deceitful, that's what she is."

She *had* been deceitful, not telling Caradoc about Iain. But that relationship was in the past, forever in the past. She had been so careful coming here, surely Iain would never find her, and the past could stay buried.

"He'll turn her out if she is," Ganore said. "He needs an heir."

"I think that, of all things, he would make her go if she were barren," Cordelia confirmed.

She suddenly felt sick. What if that were so? What if Caradoc sent her away?

She had left Dunburn by her own choice, but to be sent off. . . .

Her pride rebelled against that distressing thought.

And what was she doing anyway, listening at the door like a silly girl? She need pay no heed to whatever those two spiteful women said. She should be ashamed of herself, and if what she heard distressed her, that was a fitting punishment.

She pushed open the door and marched into the kitchen, ignoring everyone save Gwillym.

"We shall have fish tonight," she said in her most commanding manner, one that would brook no protest. "Whatever is freshest."

"Doesn't know what day it is," Ganore muttered behind her, followed by a stifled chorus of snickers.

Fiona fixed her steely gaze on Ganore. She had tried to be understanding and patient, and all she got was disrespect and scorn. "I rule this household the way Caradoc rules the estate, so we will eat what I decide. Do you understand me, or must I make it simpler for you?"

The woman shrugged, her expression still impertinent.

It was past time that Ganore learned once and for all that things had changed, at least as long as Fiona was at Llanstephan.

"Do you forget how to address your lord's wife?" she demanded, her voice as firm and sure as if she were commanding an army in battle. "And how dare you sit while your lord's wife speaks to you?"

Their gazes met and held, old, shrewd brown eyes against snapping, younger green ones that would not yield. Finally, Ganore got to her feet. "I understand, my lady."

"Good," Fiona snapped as she marched out of the kitchen into the courtyard.

The wind whipped her gown around her legs as she strode toward the gate and struggled to regain control of her seething emotions. Above, heavy gray clouds scudded across the sky, a fitting heaven for her dark mood.

Why couldn't these people accept their marriage, or her? What had she done that was so very bad? She could not help where she was born, or the color of her hair. She had married their lord and allowed him to keep the estate. Were they really so ignorant of what would have happened if Caradoc had lost it? Did they think some other Welsh lord would get it? Richard would turn it over to a Norman nobleman who would surely have little sympathy and even less mercy for his Welsh tenants.

Nevertheless, a horrible sense of defeat tugged at her. She would probably never win over the servants or Cordelia or Father Rhodri. They would always be cold and distant and critical, and she would be virtually alone again.

At least she had Rhonwen to talk to, and her time with Caradoc to look forward to.

By the time she reached the *ffridd* near the river and realized where she was, her pace had slowed from its furious march.

She looked about as she surveyed the hectic activity before her, not sure what to do. It was like a crowded market on fair day. Men ran about with struggling sheep in their arms, while others cut off the fleece. Boys tore up and down the line of benches where the shearers sat, handing out leather strips or collecting them. Others picked up the shorn fleeces and took them quickly to women folding and rolling them at wide trestle tables. The noise was incredible, from the sheep bleating in the pens, to the men and boys shouting unintelligible commands or answers, to the women chatting at the tables.

She looked for Caradoc, an anchor in this storm of motion.

The men shearing either sat on benches or stood, bending over the sheep in such a way that Fiona's back ached just to look at them.

At last she spotted her husband straddling a bench near the big enclosure and shearing a sheep. Dafydd was next to him, also shearing.

Like the others, Caradoc was too intent on his task to do much save cut. He might never notice her here. She took a few steps forward, then hesitated. He might not want to be interrupted at his work. And what was she going to interrupt him with? Complaints.

He didn't need to hear them when he was so busy, if ever. She didn't want to sound like a weak, helpless woman who couldn't manage her household, or who whined that people didn't like her. After all, servants weren't necessarily supposed to like their mistress; she just wished they would.

She wrapped her arms around herself and contemplated going back. But returning to the castle meant returning to a tense and uncomfortable household, and she didn't want to do that. She had told Rhonwen she wanted to watch, so watch she would.

Unnoticed by anyone, she sat on the little rise of the hill where she had been with Caradoc on the day of the gathering and observed the frantic activity below.

Some men had the unenviable task of carrying a sheep from the pen to the shearers. Back and forth they fairly ran with their burdens, one arm around the neck of the sheep, the other holding the wool of the side.

The actual shearing itself seemed to go incredibly fast. She kept her eyes on Caradoc after one of the carriers brought him a sheep. First he trimmed the fleece on the animal's belly. Then, when he was nearly done and without looking up, he called out a single word and one of the running boys handed him a thin leather strip with which he swiftly bound the animal's legs. Then he laid the sheep on its side on the bench, its head between his muscular thighs. Arching over it, he started to cut the wool from the neck to the rump, moving back and forth between belly and back with amazing speed, the cut fleece folded over the side like a piece of cloth.

Next, as easily as if the sheep weighed little more than its fleece, Caradoc flipped it over onto its other side and started to clip until the whole fleece was kept on by a few strands that Caradoc quickly snipped, freeing the fleece to fall to the ground. He untied the animal's feet and, now shorn, it scampered off back up the hill.

By the time a young man collected the fleece, another man was already depositing another sheep on Caradoc's bench.

What had seemed chaos was actually a well-regulated procedure. At one point, Caradoc looked up and she waved, but he didn't see her. He was checking the cloudy sky, and as he did so, there was an ominous roll of thunder.

More rain would be disaster for the shearers, she knew, so she tried not to pray or even hope for it, although more rain would mean Caradoc would have to leave what he was doing, and come back to the castle with her.

Then she heard another unexpected sound: running footsteps and Rhonwen calling her. "My lady!"

Fiona scrambled to her feet and hurried to meet her. Maybe Ganore had taken sick, she thought hopefully, then condemned herself for that selfish wish.

Her face red, her forehead beaded with perspiration, Rhonwen came to a halt. "A visitor has come, my lady," she said, panting.

Merciful Savior!

Her whole body tensed, as if someone had shot an arrow through her, and her stomach lurched with dread.

"A Norman, Sir Ralph de Valmonte."

Not Iain, thank God. A Norman. Not Iain. "Did he say why he has come? It is about the taxes?"

"I don't know, my lady. He doesn't speak Welsh, and I don't understand the Normans."

Thunder rolled again, close this time. In its wake,

there was a moment's silence until the voices began again, sounding even more urgent. She looked at Caradoc, whose hands were moving faster. Still nobody had seen her on the rise, or Rhonwen, either. If they had, they obviously thought it of no great significance.

"I shall go back and greet him. You wait here, and when the men stop work, tell Caradoc about Sir Ralph—not before. They should keep shearing for as long as they can."

One look at the man waiting in the hall was enough to tell Fiona that Sir Ralph de Valmonte was a typically well fed, pompous Norman nobleman, certain of his worth and place in the world. She had seen his sort many times in the cities where her father went to trade. Now as then, she wanted to wipe that satisfied smirk from his face.

Unfortunately, given his rank, she had to be polite.

As she approached him, he ran an impertinent gaze over her, measuring her beauty and her worth, and probably finding her lacking in both. Well, this would not be the first time she had fallen short in a man's estimation.

She, in turn, scrutinized him. His thinning, mouse-colored hair cut around his face in the Norman fashion only made his plump face look rounder. He was finely dressed in a long indigo tunic of velvet, belted with a wide leather strip embossed with silver studs and clasped with a huge silver buckle. She suspected the belt was intended to make him look slimmer or rope in his girth, but instead he looked like a barrel with a band around it. The shirt beneath his tunic was pristinely white, and his black leather boots shone from polishing.

There was a loud crash of thunder, and a heavy rain began to fall. The men would have to stop shearing, so Caradoc would be here soon.

She stifled a sigh of relief. She was too new to her status as a lord's lady to be as confident in this situation as she wished to be.

However, until Caradoc arrived, she would do the honors as befitted her station as best she could, and hopefully in such a way that neither this Norman, or the servants peeking out of the kitchen corridor, would find fault with her.

"Greetings, Sir Ralph," she said in Norman French as she reached the dais and bowed. "I bid you welcome to Llanstephan Fawr."

The Norman gave her an insolent little smile to go along with his equally insolent scrutiny. "And who might you be, sweeting?"

"I am the wife of Lord Caradoc, Lady Fiona."

The man's eyes widened and his smile disappeared. "Sir Connor said nothing about his brother being recently wed."

"I do not think Sir Connor yet knows of his brother's marriage."

The Norman's brow rose in more surprise.

"We have not been married long," she said by way of explanation.

She spotted Una peering out of the door to the kitchen corridor and signaled her to come closer. "Would you care for some wine?" she asked as the woman reluctantly obeyed.

He looked doubtful.

"It's from France," she assured him.

"If it is from France, I will."

Fiona wasn't about to bellow the request across the hall, so she waited until Una drew near. "Please bring wine for our guest."

Una looked as if she would rather eat a sword.

Sir Ralph leered at the maidservant. "What's *your* name, sweet?"

Una was far from the first blush of youth, and while she had a pleasant enough face—when she wasn't sneering—she was not particularly attractive. Sir Ralph had to be one of those men who flirted with maidservants as a matter of course, treating them as objects for his amusement or perhaps practice.

He could use all the practice he could get.

When Una didn't answer at once, Sir Ralph frowned and turned to Fiona. "Hasn't she been taught to reply to her betters?"

"She's Welsh, Sir Ralph," Fiona calmly answered. "She cannot understand you."

But she understood the tone well enough, Fiona was sure. Any woman would—and be just as disgusted as Una looked to be.

"Please fetch some wine, Una, for this fat fellow," she said in Welsh, smiling a false smile all the while.

Una was clearly taken aback by Fiona's epithet. "Aye, my lady," she mumbled as she bowed. "At once."

Bang!

The door to the hall burst open and an obviously disgruntled Caradoc came striding in, dripping wet. Behind him came an equally sodden Rhonwen.

Caradoc came to an abrupt halt when he saw their guest, then marched forward. Between his plain clothes and soaking state, he looked more like an irate shepherd than the overlord, and it was quite clear from Sir Ralph's sneer that he assumed that was indeed the case. "What does this fellow want?" he demanded, as if Caradoc stank.

In truth, her husband did smell rather strongly of wet sheep.

"Sir Ralph, allow me to present—"

"I am Lord Caradoc of Llanstephan Fawr. Who the devil are you?" her husband growled, crossing his arms and glaring.

Sir Ralph looked as if he'd soiled himself.

She pitied the hapless Norman more than she would have thought possible only moments ago. He could not be faulted for assuming a man dressed that way, soaked to the skin and with hair like a Norseman, was nobody he need regard. Besides, no matter how upset Caradoc was because the rain interrupted the shearing, this was no way for a lord to behave to a guest.

She smiled, trying to lessen the tension. "My lord, this is Sir Ralph de Valmonte."

Caradoc's eyes flicked to her, then back to their guest. "And what, pray tell, does Sir Ralph de Valmonte want?"

The man went as pale as his white shirt.

"If it is about the taxes," Caradoc growled, "you may tell Richard they will be paid the next time the king sends his tax collectors, and the full amount owing, as well."

Unless Caradoc knew for certain that this man

was a minor noble with no particular ties to the king, it surely was not wise to address him this way. "My lord, perhaps you should get into dry clothing—"

Caradoc's look silenced her.

"I-I'm sure King Richard will be glad to hear that . . . that your financial difficulties have been alleviated," Sir Ralph stammered. "But th-that's not why I've come."

Sir Ralph seemed to recover when he remembered why he was there. "I was traveling to my estate north of here, and Richard commanded me to bring you this, on your brother's behalf."

A direct request from the king? Merciful Mary, this was not good. Caradoc must be more polite.

Unfortunately, one glance at Caradoc's face told her that if anything, he was even more annoyed.

His hands trembling slightly, Sir Ralph reached into the pouch tied at his waist and pulled out a scroll. "Normally, of course, I do not do this sort of thing, for I am no messenger. But as the king commands, I obey."

The king would not *command* a friend. Then she recalled what she had heard of Richard and his imperious manner. Maybe he would. Either way, upsetting this man was probably a grave mistake.

"Thank you," Caradoc replied with the barest hint of sarcasm as he snatched the parchment from Sir Ralph's hands.

"Won't you sit down, Sir Ralph?" she asked, gesturing to the chairs nearby and wondering what else she could do to repair the damage. Maybe invite him to stay a few days . . . no, considering this household, that was probably not a good idea.

A gift, perhaps? Yes, she could give him some of the fine Italian cloth. It would not be a bribe, exactly—

"*I don't believe it!*" Caradoc bellowed.

Fiona started as if he'd grabbed her and Sir Ralph sat heavily, practically collapsing into the chair.

The very embodiment of outraged majesty, Caradoc crumpled the scroll and waved it at the Norman. "What took you so bloody long to get here? Connor wrote this weeks ago and only now do I receive it?"

"M-my lord, I didn't think there was any need to rush," Sir Ralph stammered, pale to the lips, practically cowering in the chair.

Fiona stared, aghast. Whatever this message was, Sir Ralph came from the king. Besides, he was their guest.

She opened her mouth to urge peace, but Sir Ralph spoke first. "I understood your brother merely wished to inform you of his marriage," he all but whimpered. "I didn't think the message was anything urgent."

Fiona went to stand in front of Sir Ralph, determined to end this confrontation now, before Caradoc did something rash, like strike the man.

"My lord, whatever news you have had, it should be discussed in more privacy." Ignoring his scowl, she addressed their visitor. "Please, have some wine, Sir Ralph, and if you will excuse us, I must speak to my husband about his display of temper."

With that, she took Caradoc's arm in a firm grasp and sailed toward the steps to the solar, towing him like a barge.

"Let go of me, Fiona," he muttered under his breath.

She gripped his arm tighter. "No. Act like a child, and like a child I shall treat you."

"I said, let go of me!" he repeated, pulling his arm.

She wound her fingers into his sleeve. "No."

"Why must I be surrounded by stubborn women?" he charged as they started up the stairs.

"Perhaps it is the air of Wales, for the men are just as stubborn," she retorted.

Once in the solar, she yanked her hand free, shoved the door closed and faced him. "I don't know what exactly was in that message—"

Glaring at her, Caradoc shook the document as if he would squeeze the very ink from the parchment. "My damned brother has married a Norman heiress. He's rich, he's got an estate. He's paid Llanstephan's debts and managed to convince the king to lower the taxes."

Now his anger really made no sense. "Isn't that good—?"

"He's been married for *six weeks!* Six bloody weeks, while I was thinking every day I was going to lose Llanstephan and getting more desperate every day! Six bloody weeks while this fool wandered around the country probably sleeping with every tavern wench between here and Westminster, and me here suffering! Six weeks when I could barely sleep for worry, until I finally sold myself like a whore!"

When she gasped, he fell silent and stared at her as if he had never seen her before. Maybe he never really had. Perhaps all he had seen when he looked at her was a pile of money, and a body in his bed.

But that was the bargain you made, her mind charged as humiliation swept through her. *You knew that when you came here and made your proposal.*

At first, her heart retorted, *at first it was a bargain. But afterward, when he loved you—*

What? Did you think he was falling in love with you? Maybe she hadn't really seen him either, but only what she wanted to see, her dream lover made flesh, and loving her.

Foolish, foolish Fiona! You should know that men make love without giving their heart. Did Iain not teach you that?

Then her pride arose, burning as hot—hotter—than her humiliation.

Mustering her dignity, she drew herself up. She would not let him see her shame or hurt. "I insist that you apologize to that Norman before he makes trouble for Llanstephan."

Her husband planted his feet and crossed his arms. "I will not apologize to that fat dolt."

All her emotions boiled over and she returned his angry glower with equal animosity. "*You* are the dolt if you don't! Think, Caradoc. Why did the king send such a man on such an errand? Sir Ralph himself said the king asked it of him. Why would Richard do that?"

Caradoc leaned his weight on one leg, as if her questions were wasting his time. "Because Sir Ralph was coming this way."

"You are smarter than that, surely," she countered. "Richard probably sent that man because he wants to know how things are here, and how loyal you are to the crown. He wants to hear it from a man he has some kind of faith in, whose loyalty he does not doubt, or he would simply have sent a messenger. If Sir Ralph goes away offended, what do you think he will say? He will claim that whatever your brother may be, you are a barbarian who insulted the king's representative. Have you forgotten that Richard can raise the taxes again as easily as he lowered them?"

"Since you seem so well versed in politics, why don't you apologize for me?" Caradoc demanded.

"I am not the lord of Llanstephan Fawr who commands this fortress. I am not the one who acted like a child. You made the mistake. You fix it."

Glare met glare, pride against pride, until finally Caradoc went to the door. He yanked it open, making her jump out of the way.

"By God, woman," he snarled as he looked back at her, "what have I ever done *but* consider the good of Llanstephan? As you should well remember, that is why I married *you*."

With that he went out, slamming the door so hard, the furniture rattled.

Fiona pressed her hands against her eyes, willing herself not to cry despite how upset she was. Tears were a weakness, and she would not have red-rimmed eyes and tear-stained cheeks for Ganore and Cordelia to gloat over.

They would have enough to gossip and snicker about already.

Chapter 10

s Caradoc marched down the stairs, hot anger flared and burned with the heat of a smith's forge. Wife or no wife, Fiona had no business telling him what to do.

Apologize to that fat fool? He would sooner lick the man's boots.

He was Caradoc of Llanstephan Fawr, baron of the march, knight of the realm. He was a lord, a powerful man, not a boy whose brother, though younger, seemed to be everything he was not—bold, glorious, the pride of his family.

He was not Connor the tempestuous, the handsome and the demanding. He was Caradoc the patient, the wise—Caradoc the fool, who had just reacted with as much irrational anger as Connor ever had.

He halted and leaned against the cool stone wall.

Yes, he was frustrated by the rain that forced them to stop shearing before they were finished. Yes, he saw Sir Ralph as a representative of the greedy king he hated.

Yet to quarrel with Fiona as he had . . . to have his control shatter and disappear, his raw emotions on display . . . Not since he was a child had he lost his temper.

In a way, it was her fault. She had aroused his emotions, and not just his desire, since she had arrived.

But that was no excuse.

Then to tell her that she made him feel like a whore . . .

Fiona had looked as if he had thrust a dagger through her heart when he said that.

New and deeper shame overwhelmed him. What he had said to her was worse than reacting as arrogant, spoiled Connor always had.

Because he had lied.

He had not sold himself to her. He had gladly given.

Yes, he needed the money she had brought for her dowry, but more than that—far more—he had wanted her as he had wanted no other woman in all his life. From the moment he had seen her in his courtyard, even that very first time when he was but a youth, Fiona had opened his heart and claimed a place there.

Perhaps that was why no other woman had ever really captivated him. Maybe that was why he could not understand Connor and Dafydd's fickle ways. He had belonged to Fiona MacDougal from the first time she had smiled at him and made that cheery, friendly wave.

The money was but the excuse he needed to justify his decision to everybody else.

That was the real, secret truth. He wanted her, and yet he had not been able to admit the weakness of his need. He could not confess to anyone, not even himself, that he was lonely and afraid, and she offered the end of both.

What was he going to do now?

He turned and looked up the steps, back to his solar where Fiona still remained. He should return and apologize. He should say . . . what? How could he begin? What could he say to make her understand?

Words were his enemies, more so than Richard or Rhys or anyone. Words betrayed and hurt him far more than helped, and he could not trust them.

What if he only made things worse?

It would be easier to apologize to Sir Ralph first, he decided. After all, he didn't really care if Sir Ralph forgave him or not, just so long as he smoothed things over enough that the Norman would not send a scathing report of the lord of Llanstephan to the king.

He trotted down the steps and strode into the hall—to discover that Sir Ralph wasn't there.

"Where is the Norman?" he demanded of Ganore, who appeared at the entrance to the kitchen with a bucket of water and a rag in her hand.

"Gone, and good riddance," she snapped as she marched to the dais.

Gone? In this rain? He felt like a slowly closing

bellows, all the air pushed out along with his rage. Rain was nothing to a Welshman, but it would be different for a pampered nobleman of the sort Sir Ralph looked to be.

"Damn the man," he muttered while Ganore plunged the rag into the bucket and began to vigorously scrub the chair in which Sir Ralph had been sitting.

He went to the door and surveyed the courtyard through the torrential downpour.

Sir Ralph wasn't there, either. He and his guard were already out of the gate.

Ah, well. He would go to Fiona and say . . . what?

As he contemplated the words he would use to apologize, he turned back into the hall. Fiona came gliding toward the hearth as serene as an angel, her sewing box in her hands. She sat near the fire and ignored both Ganore still scrubbing and him as she began to embroider a band that would eventually be used to trim a gown, he supposed.

He wasn't about to apologize with Ganore close by, or in such a public place.

Maybe Sir Ralph had taken refuge at the village inn. If that were so, he could still apologize.

With a sigh, he plunged into the rain and headed toward the stable.

"I don't care if you're the king of France and Italy besides," Bronwyn declared in very passable Norman French, having learned it from several young men who passed through Llanstephan.

The black-haired and voluptuous beauty, who

was past her prime but still could make men's heads turn, lifted Sir Ralph's hand from her buttocks. "I said no."

Sir Ralph closed his gaping mouth, obviously taken aback by so much irate, full-lipped, full-breasted pulchritude glaring down at him.

"If you can't keep your hands to yourself, Sir Rodent or whatever it is you call yourself, you'll have to go."

"A man gets lonely traveling," he pleaded.

"I've heard it all before, so save yourself the trouble," she snapped, her hands splayed on her hips.

Sir Ralph seemed to recall where he was, and who he was. "I am a Norman knight, my girl, and after the reception I received from your overlord—"

"Which was very rude," Caradoc's deep voice rumbled from the doorway.

Sir Ralph turned to see the man's body almost filling the doorway and he began to tremble. "My lord, I—"

"I ask your forgiveness," Caradoc said as he came inside, closing the door behind him. "I was upset about the rain, and then my brother's message, and I took out my ire on you. For that, I beg your pardon."

Caradoc tried not to notice the stunned and slightly disgusted look on Bronwyn's face, and the blatant shock on those of the laborers and shepherds gathered there as he sat on the bench beside Sir Ralph. "Will you allow me to pay for your refreshment here, and then return to my castle with me?"

Sir Ralph shook his head. "No, no, my lord. That's

not necessary. I really must be on my way to my own holding. As you so justly point out, I have been taking rather too much time."

Caradoc swore silently. He would try once more nonetheless. "It may rain for some days. Hardly suitable weather for travel."

"I have not far to go. Only another hundred miles or so."

Not far? For a man who liked his comforts as much as Sir Ralph probably did, that was surely an epic journey.

But if the man really didn't wish to linger, there was nothing he could do. He certainly wasn't going to beg.

"As you wish," he said, rising.

Perhaps there was one thing he could do to try to make amends. "Bronwyn, I shall pay for Sir Ralph's stay here."

She nodded, and never had he seen less respect in her eyes as she looked at him.

Maybe he shouldn't have come after the Norman; maybe he should have let the man go, and damn the consequences. At least then he wouldn't be standing in Bronwyn's tavern humbling himself like a beggar at the gates.

"Godspeed, Sir Ralph," he said as he turned on his heel.

"Farewell, my lord," Sir Ralph said as he watched the savage Welshman leave.

That night, as she lay in bed tense and expectant, Fiona wondered if she should even try to sleep, or simply accept that she was too anxious. Ever since her confrontation with Caradoc over his treatment of Sir Ralph, her whole body had seemed poised on a sword's edge with her pride on one side, and hurt and humiliation on the other.

She still felt as wounded and raw, her hopes as dashed and destroyed, as when he announced that she had made him feel like a whore. What man of his pride, his stature, could truly care for a woman who made him feel thus?

She should have subdued her temper, just as she had told him to conquer his. Although she was still sure she was right—it was a mistake to offend Sir Ralph or any man who came from the king—she should have found a more diplomatic way to upbraid him. She should have stayed with Sir Ralph and done all she could to persuade him that not everyone in Llanstephan was an enraged, wildhaired Welshman. Instead, she had acted no better than Caradoc.

Afterward, she had wanted to tell him that she was sorry for her outburst, but she never got the chance. He had charged out of the hall into the rain like an enraged bull, and when he had returned, soaked through once more, the servants had been preparing the hall for the evening meal. By the time he had changed, it was time to eat.

Father Rhodri had given another one of his "blessings," this time denouncing the moneylenders at the temple, a thinly disguised jibe at both the Normans and anybody who traded for a living, like her father. This was his most upsetting grace yet, for she had loved her father dear, and to hear him equated with greedy, blasphemous men enraged her. Nevertheless, she had stayed silent, but only with much effort and because she had already quarreled with her husband once that day.

During the grim and silent meal, Cordelia kept shooting them both scornful looks, her lip practically curling all the way to her nostril. There was no denying that their quarrel had not been dignified; perhaps she should consider this a part of her punishment.

Caradoc, of course, seemed to take it all in stride, as he did any of his sister's reactions, and if he was still upset by their argument, he made no sign. He made no sign if he was sorry, either.

Indeed, he betrayed no feelings at all, and he sat far enough away that he couldn't even touch her by accident.

At last the bedchamber door opened. She instinctively clutched the bedclothes to her chest as Caradoc strode into the room, the rushlight in his hand illuminating his fierce face from below, making him look like the very embodiment of a savage warrior race.

Her heart quailed in view of his expression, and she waited with dread for him to speak.

He didn't say anything. He set the rushlight on the table near the door very slowly and very carefully, as if he was afraid he might accidentally set something on fire; then, without so much as a glance in her direction, he began to disrobe.

Perhaps he was no longer angry.

That was a hopeful thought.

Of course, the cooling of his rage didn't diminish the fact that his display of temper might have put everybody under his rule in jeopardy.

Caradoc took off his tunic. He threw it over the chest, then his shirt followed.

She tried to banish any critical thoughts. She was his wife, he was her husband and lord over her as well as the estate.

That didn't make him wise, though.

Still, for the sake of what they had already shared, perhaps silence and apparent wifely docility was the best path to take.

Even if the notion was far from pleasing.

She had to move out of the way quickly as he sat on the bed to remove his boots.

Was he planning to ignore her all night? What would she do if he did?

As she held her breath, he lifted the bedcovers and joined her. He lay still, not moving.

A horrible, terrible thought stole into her mind. What if Ganore was right and his ardor was beginning to cool—and his apparent affection for her with it?

Foolish again, she may have been. And desperate to come here, still dreaming of the dark prince in the tower, and believing that once wed, she would be happy ever after.

If Caradoc wanted this marriage annulled, he could find a way, especially now that he had her dowry to pay an unscrupulous clergyman to find an obscure blood tie that would make their union illegal in the sight of God and the eyes of the law.

If he annulled their marriage, she would be left

penniless. She had not signed any agreement before the marriage guaranteeing her any rights to even a portion of the money.

She would be all alone in the world, and penniless. Cast out and abandoned. Not loved as she had hoped, but rejected. She would not be the one leaving of her own choice and volition; she would be banished like a criminal.

She could not let that happen.

Nor could she believe that all she had shared with Caradoc was merely lust. That he had her bounty and her body, and gave nothing in return.

He cared for her. She saw it in his eyes, heard it in his voice, when they were alone. He was not like Iain, whose words meant nothing. Caradoc spoke volumes, but not only with his voice.

So would she. She would show him that she was sorry she had lost her temper. She would tell him, without words, that she cherished him and rejoiced that they married. Most of all, she would convince him that she belonged here, in his household and in his arms.

She slid close beside him and laid her hand on his muscular chest. He turned his head and looked at her, his expression unreadable in the darkness.

Watching him, trying to gauge his reaction, she began to caress his chest, brushing her open palm lightly over his nipples. His lips parted as his breathing quickened, and then he closed his eyes as she continued her gentle assault.

She laid her leg over his hips and inched closer, pressing her warm, willing body against him. She leaned over him and teased his mouth with hers.

No, she would not give up, any more than she had accepted that what Iain offered was the best she could ever expect from a man. She needed Caradoc, and the way he made her feel cherished and necessary in a way Iain never had.

She deepened her kiss, slipping her tongue between Caradoc's firm, soft lips to plunder his mouth. With wanton abandon she stroked and caressed his body, arousing him as if her life, her hopes, her future depended upon what she did now.

With a loan moan, Caradoc shifted so that she was beneath him. He cupped her face in his strong, broad hands.

Incredibly soft hands, especially for a man, she thought vaguely as his mouth crushed hers in a passionate, heated kiss. She had heard that the lanolin in sheep's fleece, used as a base for so many salves and ointments, made the flesh of a shearer's hands as soft as a baby's, and now she knew that was true.

His hand combed through her hair, spreading it around her. His fingers skimmed over her heated flesh with the lightest touch, as if she were too delicate for more. His hips, the fulcrum of his strong body, pressed against her, the sensation intense, and welcome.

Yes, oh, yes, her mind and her heart cried, a chorus of bliss and relief and pleasure, as her passionate need increased.

He wanted her, at least like this.

At least for now.

She would not think like that. She would believe their marriage would last forever. She *must* believe it.

As his firm, soft hands meandered over her flesh

like a trickle of water seeking a downward course, she surrendered to the excitement he created. She sighed as he broke the kiss to slide his lips along the side of her neck, then below to pleasure her breasts.

Feverish, anxious need exploded within her. It was as if all the emotions of that day had been bottled up and changed in the heat of an alchemist's fire into sharp craving. She shoved away the remorse of mistakes or words said in that different heat. This was her lawful husband, and she would gladly do her duty as his wife. If there was one thing she did not regret, it was having the right to be in this bed with this man.

She could not get close enough to him, could not feel enough of his naked, straining body.

She must be naked, too.

With blatantly hungry eyes he watched her as she sat up and yanked up her shift, the sensation of the silk as she removed it adding to her ardor.

She fell back and pulled him to her, seizing his mouth and thrusting her tongue between his virile lips, ignoring the rasp of the stubble around his mouth. She kissed and stroked and caressed and touched as if they had only moments to love and she must make the most of it.

She touched his shaft, hard and anxious, and swiftly positioned herself. He pushed inside her and she met him thrust for thrust, her hips instinctively bucking. With furious, wild passion, she loved him as if they were doomed never to be together again. He, too, caught the fever of her passion, and responded in kind, with primitive, glorious abandon.

It seemed to last forever, this powerful, surging

union, with her poised on the precipice of release. Like a long, keening wail, her body stretched, so anxious with hungry need every muscle was tight with it.

At last, with a strangled cry and throat-deep growl, release broke like waves tearing down a wall.

In the next moment, Caradoc groaned, his whole body tense, before he collapsed against her, sweat-slicked and panting.

She lay still, her own breathing rushed and shallow as the tension ebbed away.

This sating of mutual need and desire would not be the sum total of all that was between them. It was but the beginning, she assured herself as she put her arms around him and held him to her.

Please, God, do not let it be all that is between us . . .

"Married?" Iain demanded as he stared at the wool merchant he had befriended in the tavern near Shrewsbury. It took every bit of self-control he had not to shout the word. "She's married? To a nobleman, you say?"

Having encountered Heribert of Hartley in a wayside inn, and graciously subdued the urge to run the man through for purchasing the property that should have been his, Iain had steered the conversation all the way from the weather to the state of the roads to the price of wool and finally to any news of a fellow wool merchant's daughter. He had been delighted that the man had news of Fiona MacDougal—until he learned what it was.

"I agree it's astonishing," Heribert said, shaking his head as he lifted the mug of ale, oblivious to how close to death he had been. "I didn't believe it myself the first time I heard it."

"A nobleman marrying a merchant's daughter seems like a fable," Iain replied with a false smile. He managed to sound merely interested in a bit of choice gossip, instead of seething with anger and frustration.

"I've heard it from more than one now. She arrived at his estate practically on her own, and two days later, they were wed."

"She must be a beauty, for that to happen so fast."

More than a little drunk, the merchant leaned forward and spoke in what was supposed to be a conspiratorial whisper. "Oddly enough, she's not. Why, she's nothing much at all. Looks too much like old Angus MacDougal for my taste, and then there's her red hair." He made a face to show what he thought of red hair, then gestured at Iain with the mug he held. The ale slopped unnoticed over his hand. "I thought you said you're from Dunburn, too. *You* must have seen her."

"I didn't have anything to do with the Mac-Dougals. I am a poor soldier, you see, and MacDougal was well to do."

"I'll say he was—and that's how she got her husband. I heard she came with twenty carts full to the brim with gold and silver. If I had known the old buzzard had left her so well off, I wouldn't have paid so much for their warehouse, and I would have asked for her hand myself, red-haired or not." He chortled and winked.

Iain knew full well that Fiona wasn't rich enough to fill twenty carts with gold and silver. He began to wonder if this tale was really true. He would have to endure this fool's company a little longer to be sure.

"Twenty carts? It was a mercy then that she wasna set upon by thieves."

"Well, perhaps it was not twenty—but the dowry was three thousand marks."

Iain's jaw clenched at the mention of the familiar sum. "No wonder the Welshman jumped at the chance to marry her. What was his name again?"

"Lord Caradoc of Llanstephan, and he needed the money bad." Leaning on his elbow, Heribert held up his hand, his thumb and forefinger an inch apart. "He was this close to losing his home because he couldn't pay his taxes. Lucky for him she came along."

"I dinna think it was luck," Iain said with a genial smile.

Had Heribert been sober, he might have noticed that the look in Iain's eyes was anything but friendly. "Her father used to buy a lot of wool from the Welsh, and she used to travel with him," Iain said. "Maybe she met this Caradoc before."

"Indeed?" Heribert muttered as he looked at the bottom of his mug, clearly more concerned with the fact that it was empty than Fiona's past.

"This Llanstephan, is it near here?"

"Oh, about fifty miles over the hills. The roads are muddy—Wales, you know—but not too bad this time of year." Heribert's bleary eyes narrowed with suspicion. "Who did you say you were again?"

"Oh, just a soldier heading north for home," Iain replied amicably. "I'll certainly have a tale to tell when I get there."

"That you will," Heribert agreed. "Well, good luck

to her, I say, even with that much money. Takes more than money to make a marriage and with him for a husband . . ." He let his words trail off suggestively.

Iain's ears pricked up. "What's that?"

"Weeelll, he's not a, um, civilized man at all. Not like yourself," the merchant added, glancing down at his empty mug again.

"More ale here for me and my friend!" Iain called to the serving wench, a plump little dumpling of a woman he wouldn't mind bedding. It would be worth another ale to hear about the man who had robbed him of more than some property.

"Ah, that's kind of you, sir, very kind. He would never do anything like that, even if he had the money. He's close with his coins, that one. Always has been," Heribert said, shaking his head.

Probably drove a hard bargain, Iain thought with disgust for all merchants and other money-grubbers. Still, it was pleasant to think of Fiona married to a miser. "Is he a handsome fellow?"

"Oh, not nearly so good-looking as yourself, sir," Heribert replied at once, grinning drunkenly. "Big, hairy brute, he is. Hair past his shoulders, black beard—he looks more like a bear than a man. And gruff! Sounds like a bear, too. She must have been desperate for a husband."

Iain leaned closer, and asked the question that had been skulking in his mind for days now. "Maybe she needed a father for her child?"

"Oh, I doubt that. He never would have wed her then, by God. He may look like a bear, but he's a proud man if ever there was one. The whole family is as proud as if they were kings. His brother got into trouble with Richard for arguing with him. I mean, that tells you something right there! Imagine the gall to upbraid the king to his face! And he's the *younger* brother," Heribert finished, obviously considering pride and arrogance to increase with rank in the family, as it generally did among nobles.

The serving wench arrived with more ale.

"Ah, Bessie my beauty," Heribert cried as he eagerly reached for the ale before the plump young woman had a chance to hand it to him.

"Thirsty work, all this chat," he said by way of explanation when he caught the look of contempt on Iain's face.

"Of course it is, and I've certainly pestered you with questions," Iain replied, once again settling his features into a genial mask.

He looked across the room, where Fergus and the others were sitting in a morose little group. His men had not been pleased coming here, and even his promise to share some of his recovered wealth was beginning to lose its luster.

But they were his kinsmen, and he had his wounded pride that must be assuaged, one way or another. Besides, they were cowards, the lot of them, so they would never dare rebel against a man like him.

He looked back at Bessie and gave her his very best smile. Now that he knew exactly where Fiona was, he could take a little time for his own amusement— until he could really amuse himself by introducing himself to Fiona's proud and noble husband. Surely this Caradoc or whatever his name was would like

to meet the man who had taken his wife's maidenhead.

Or maybe he would give Fiona the chance to keep
her little secret.

For a price.

Chapter 11

A fortnight later, Caradoc sat in the solar and studied the scroll in front of him listing the names of all the tenants and the tithes they owed him. He had always been as lenient as he could be with those who had trouble paying through no fault of their own, and in view of his recent prosperity, he was considering ways to lessen their obligations even further.

Despite his belief in this necessary mercy, every time he tried to concentrate on the task, his thoughts returned to his wife and the horrendous chasm that had opened between them.

Although they still loved passionately and often, something had been lost after their argument. He had assumed, after the way she welcomed him into their bed that night, that she had forgiven and forgotten. As the days passed, she said no more cross or angry words and gave him no scornful looks. All was as it had been before.

Or so he had tried to convince himself. Now, he could not find comfort in that pleasant delusion. Things were very different. They had lost that wonderful intimacy that went beyond the physical, and with every day that passed, the barrier between them seemed to grow.

Time and again, he opened his mouth to speak of their quarrel and apologize for losing his temper. But always his fear that he would say the wrong thing rose up to silence him. He told himself that she would understand without him having to speak; that he could show her, as he held her in his arms, that he was sorry.

Unfortunately, he could not even tell if she noticed anything amiss. Maybe she didn't speak because she thought there was nothing to discuss, and the sense of loss was only on his part. Perhaps their mutual desire was enough for her, and she neither felt nor suffered the absence of anything more.

He did. A hope for a life beloved and cherished, accepted and at peace, had taken hold of his heart the very day she arrived and flourished at the beginning of their marriage. Now that hope could not simply be plucked out of his heart to wither and die. It had grown too powerful, and more to be sought than the mere sating of his lust.

Sighing again, he stared at the parchment and raked his hand through his hair. What he would not give to have Connor's smooth fluency or Dafydd's merry charm for just half a day! Then he would confront Fiona and speak.

"Caradoc, there's trouble."

He glanced at Dafydd waiting on the threshold, then once more returned to his scroll as if what was written there was completely absorbing and vitally important.

"What kind of trouble?" he muttered as if he begrudged rather than welcomed the interruption. "A lover's spat? A leaking bucket in the kitchens? I haven't heard a call to arms, so I don't think we're under attack from marauding Norsemen."

Dafydd came inside. "I'm serious, Caradoc. We're missing sheep. I make it half a dozen from the lower slopes at least, and probably more."

Shocked and regretting his selfish attempt at levity, Caradoc growled a curse. Although there was no way to keep an accurate count of the sheep that ranged in the hills, he knew better than to ask if Dafydd was sure about the number. "Another fox?"

"No," Dafydd replied, shaking his head as he drew closer. "No bodies where they graze. Just trampled grass and bracken. No blood, so it wasn't animals or arrows or throats slit."

Caradoc's frown deepened. "What, like they've just vanished?"

Dafydd grinned at that. "Now you sound like you've been listening to Ganore too much." He sobered as quickly as he had smiled. "If they've been slaughtered, they've been taken to be killed elsewhere, probably where there's plenty of water to wash away the blood, like on a riverbank. Clever it is, but I've seen it before."

"A band of outlaws?"

"Could be."

"Normans run wild?"

That suggestion made Dafydd grin again. "Normans don't run wild. They get drunk. Besides, most of them wouldn't know how to get hold of a sheep if they tried, I'm sure."

Caradoc hated to ask it, but the question hung in the air regardless. "Welshmen, then?"

Dafydd shrugged, but Caradoc saw the dismay lurking in his friend's brown eyes. "Could be, although ashamed I am to say it. Whoever it is, they're quick and they're good. Nobody's seen anything or anybody suspicious, and I've asked."

Caradoc rose. "I'll order more patrols, starting today. I'll lead one out right now."

"What about what you were doing?"

Gesturing for Dafydd to follow, Caradoc marched to the door. "That can wait. For too long I've had to stay at my scrolls like a clerk. Thank God those days are done," he said, meaning it.

It was important that he lead by more than hunching over his lists and calculations, but when he had to account for every ha'penny, he had had little choice about it. Now he had the freedom to ride with his men and see for himself what was happening on his estate.

It didn't take them long to mount a patrol, for Dafydd had already mentioned his suspicions to Jon-Bron before going to the solar. The garrison commander had a troop of ten mounted and was waiting for orders by the time Caradoc and Dafydd entered the courtyard.

"I'll lead us out," Caradoc announced. He ignored the flare of surprise on Jon-Bron's face as he strode past him to the stable and ordered a horse saddled. The groom leapt to obey.

His horse was ready by the time Dafydd had retrieved his. Mounting, Caradoc briefly wondered where Fiona was and what she was doing, then berated himself for letting his mind wander at such a time. Right now, the most important thing was finding whoever was stealing his sheep.

He raised his hand and signaled the men to follow him out of the gate. They made a silent and grim group as they followed, for every soldier appreciated the seriousness of the crime Dafydd had discovered.

"Show me where you first realized the sheep were gone," he said to his friend as they rode through the village.

Dafydd nodded and led the way, coming to a halt near a large boulder on the low slope. "Remember that big white ewe with the one blind eye? That was her place."

Caradoc nodded. He did remember that ewe, for a more nasty tempered beast he had rarely encountered. Like the other sheep on his land, she grazed where her mother had, as her mother had before her, each sheep seeming to inherit their grazing ground the way Caradoc had inherited Llanstephan, which was why they did not need fences in the mountains.

"When I saw she wasn't there, I started to search. I couldn't find her, or her body, or her lamb. No sign of them at all, and then I realized more sheep were missing."

"All from the lower slopes?"

"Aye," Dafydd confirmed. "Easier to catch the sheep there, without climbing or having to bring them down."

Caradoc stood in his stirrups and surveyed the slope that was covered in bracken, then the wood near the river a short distance away. "If they killed them, they probably took them through the wood to the river there."

"Aye."

Jon-Bron likewise nodded his agreement.

Caradoc turned his horse and headed for the river, where they all dismounted and searched.

They found nothing. No churned up mud, no fleece clinging to branches, no blood, no footprints or hoof prints.

Holding his reins in his hand, Caradoc stopped studying the ground to look at his friend. "Maybe they're planning to sell them far away from here."

"Aye, or they've eaten them."

Caradoc straightened. "Let's hope the patrols find something."

"If it's outlaws, they may already have moved on," Dafydd proposed hopefully.

That was true, and while Caradoc hated to think of outlaws getting away with theft, he would be happy to learn they were off his land. Warning messages to the other estates nearby would alert them to the brigands, and if they were still in the area, soon they would be caught.

Then they would be hung, for stealing sheep was a crime punishable by death.

"Let's ride up to that ridge there," Caradoc ordered, pointing. "Maybe we'll see something. Smoke, or other sign of men where men ought not to be."

Once at the top of the hill, Caradoc raised his hand to halt them. Again he stood in his stirrups and surveyed the area.

No smoke. No encampment.

But a rider on the road below heading for Llanstephan, on a white horse galloping as fast as the winter wind howling down from Snowdon.

Cordelia on Icarus, with her hair streaming out behind her, and her ruby red cloak likewise.

As always, she was alone. He could not see her guards anywhere.

A shaft of chilling fear stabbed him. Very vulnerable she looked, despite her speed. Cordelia's sex alone put her at risk of attack, and her fine clothes and beauty added to her value, whether for outlaws or men who would sell her to Norse slave traders, or rebels who might decide to hold a Welsh-Norman lord's sister for ransom. Fiona had been right to warn him that it was dangerous for Cordelia to be alone and unprotected when she rode, even on their estate.

He might not be able to find a way to mend his marriage, but he could do something about this. At once.

A short time later, Caradoc turned away from the solar window as Cordelia marched into the chamber without so much as a tap on the door.

"Ganore said you wanted to speak to me," she declared.

"I do. Sit down."

She threw herself in a chair like a squire and not a young lady of rank. Her long hair had come partly out of her braids, and she had not troubled herself to tidy it upon her return. Her saffron yellow woolen gown smelled of her horse, and her boots were caked with mud and manure. She must have come directly from the stable, and he supposed he should take some comfort in Ganore's swift summons and his sister's equally swift obedience.

She was not going to be pleased with what he had decided, so there would be another skirmish, one of a multitude. This one, however, he was absolutely determined to win. He had been blind not to see the jeopardy she put herself in with her headstrong ways.

Yet because what he had to say was so important and because he was partly to blame for the state of things, he must try to be patient. After all, he should have reined her in long ago.

"So speak," she ordered dismissively, as if he was her lackey.

At her tone, the frustration that was simmering beneath his surface arose and he fought to control it. "Since you insist upon endangering yourself by losing your escort, I have decided you must not leave this castle without telling me, and when you go out you must have a guard of ten men."

She sat up straight and stared at him with disdainful disbelief. "What sort of jest is this?"

"It is no jest. It is too dangerous for you to be riding alone, Cordelia. You are a woman, and of high rank. You have fine clothes and a fine horse, all of which make you a tempting target for brigands, and somebody is stealing our sheep. I will not let you risk being robbed, or worse."

"Who would dare to steal sheep from Llanstephan?"

"If I knew that, I would have them in my dungeon already. Yet Dafydd is quite sure somebody is."

"No sheep thief would dare to touch the lord's sister."

"As they have not dared to steal our sheep?" he countered.

"I am perfectly safe on our lands!"

He crossed his arms over his chest, as if that could keep his temper in check. "No, I do not think you are."

She glared at him, her gray eyes smoldering. "Our parents were admired and respected. No brigands would dare attack their daughter."

"Perhaps once that was so, but our parents have been dead for some time now, and things are different. You cannot be certain of your safety, and neither can I."

"So I must beg to ride out?" she cried, her face reddening as she jumped to her feet. "And with ten men who surely have better things to do than play nursemaid to me? Why not just throw me in the dungeon and be done with it?"

"I gave you more freedom than most ladies of rank ever enjoy, and you have put yourself at risk," he said, sitting behind the table and attempting to be as cool and composed as their father had always been when chastising his son.

He ignored the fact that his youthful dismay had been all the worse for his father's frigid calm.

"And do not think to sneak away," he continued. "Every sentry, every soldier, every person here will know of my command, and that I will not look kindly on anyone who does not report it if you try to ride out without my leave. I have been too lenient, and the time for lenience is past."

"Your wife has told you to do this," Cordelia accused, jabbing her forefinger at him, "to punish me because I did not welcome her with open arms."

He wondered if Fiona had warned Cordelia, too. But Fiona would surely have mentioned it to him if she had.

When? When did they ever *talk* as husband and wife?

Besides, Cordelia would have complained of it if she had.

"No, she has not," he said. "I rule here, Cordelia. This is my decision and mine alone, and the men stealing sheep on our land make it vital that you obey me."

"If there is an danger here, it's not because of what *I* do," she declared, still defiant, "but what *you* have done with your foreign marriage."

"The *foreigner* I married made it possible for us to keep our Welsh home, a fact you seem determined to forget. Now you will stay in the castle or the village. It simply isn't safe for you to ride about the countryside like some kind of merry Gypsy. Besides, you are not a child anymore. It's time you began to act like the lady you are."

"I do, *brother*," she retorted, indignant and insolent, her tone the same as when she had called him a troll.

Staring at her with righteous, ancient indignation, he put his hands on the table and slowly rose. "When you speak to me, remember you address the lord of Llanstephan Fawr, *sister*."

Cordelia tossed her head and frowned, feet planted and arms akimbo. "Why don't you just marry me off and be rid of me?" she charged, her voice rising almost to a shout.

Her accusation, as well as her tone, cut him to the quick.

"Because I have been forced to do too many things in my life, things I did not want to do, but was told I must," he said, still trying to restrain his anger and his hurt. "I will not have that fate thrust upon you, as you should have guessed, or you would have been married by now."

Her steadfast gaze faltered for the briefest of moments before her more familiar contempt returned. "Perhaps you will not—but I'll wager *she* would. I would wager that wife of yours was already planning how to get rid of me before she had your ring on her finger."

Now she would accuse Fiona of scheming selfishness, too?

He strode toward her and stopped inches from Cordelia's recalcitrant face, glaring into her gray eyes. When he spoke, his voice was hard and stern. "Fiona has not put these things into my head, but if she did, I wouldn't blame her. This is the *troll* you're talking to, Cordelia. You and Connor made my life miserable, and now you are doing the same to her."

"Because I do not trust her, and neither should you!"

His anger boiled up and he ground his fist into his palm as if to shove it down physically. "I would trust Fiona with my life."

"Why not? She already rules you. She has changed you, Caradoc. You suddenly speak to me of acting like a lady. What else am I to think but that you are planning to marry me off to further her ambitions. Or yours."

"Ambitions?" he repeated, dumbfounded. "When have I had the leisure to have ambitions? All my time has been spent trying not to lose Llanstephan."

"And doing whatever it takes, no matter how shameful," she countered, her whole body quaking with ire. "But I forget—you nobly sacrifice yourself for my welfare. How dutiful, how good, how wonderful." She made a mocking little bow. "I am forever in your debt. And the fact that you have comforts you couldn't afford only a little while ago, and a warm body in your bed at night, that is nothing, of course. You do it all for me."

"Fiona is more than a warm body in my bed, and so help me, Cordelia," he said, his jaw clenched even tighter than his fist, "if you don't start acting like a lady and treating her better, I'll send you to a convent myself!"

"Why don't you?" she cried, tears starting in her eyes. "I am just a millstone around your neck, another mouth to feed. She is everything, and I am *nothing*. I have never been anything to you. You never paid the slightest bit of attention to me until now, and only then because I upset your wife."

God save him! Was that why she was so cruel to Fiona? To get his attention?

As he stared at Cordelia, he suddenly saw not the outraged young woman, but the little girl after their parents' deaths. For days afterward, he had stayed in the solar, afraid that someone would see him cry. He knew Ganore would look after her, and he did not think he could offer her better comfort. After he had learned to hide his grief, he had yearned to go his sister and try to offer her a brother's solace, but she always asked for Connor, who was not there, and Ganore who was. She had never, ever asked for him.

That was not all her fault. He had locked himself away, and not only in his solar. He had locked away his feelings, too, until Fiona had arrived and set them free. All of them.

Regret, remorse, dismay and lingering despair overwhelmed his anger. She was his little sister still, and he loved her dearly. Surely there must be some way to make a truce with her, if not outright peace.

He held out his hands in a placating gesture. "Fiona is my wife, and you are my sister. I would have you both live here in harmony. There doesn't need to be a war between you, or between us."

She marched to the door, then whirled back to glare at him again. "Oh yes, there does. Her wiles do not blind *me*. I do not trust her, and neither does anybody else except my besotted brother. So as long as either that Scot is here, or I am, there can be no peace."

She went out, slamming the oak door with all her might.

Caradoc sat in his solar alone for a long time after that, considering all that was and might have been.

As Dafydd entered the dim confines of the village tavern several days later, he spotted the huddle of men waiting for him—the brothers of beautiful Bronwyn, who was carrying cool ale and steaming meat pies to them, as well as Eifion looking as miserable as it was possible for Eifion to look, which was like he had worse troubles than Job.

The air was scented with ale and roast mutton, and the small windows didn't do much to dispel the perpetual gloom.

"Thank you, my beauty," Dafydd said as he attempted to grab one of the mugs from Bronwyn's tray.

She swerved and ducked out of his reach. "Spill it, and you've still got to pay, my buck. Wait till it's on the table, will you?"

Dafydd sighed and followed her to the corner table

"No work to do today, is it, the lot of you?" she charged as she set the tray down in front of Jon-Bron and waited for him to pay. Brothers or not, she gave out no free food and drink. There was only one thing Bronwyn ever gave freely, and then only if she decided to. "The sun shines, yet you would sit here in the dark in the middle of the day."

"Having to eat and drink, aren't we?" Jon-Bron said defensively. "I've got ten patrols out there in the hills. They don't need me watching over them like the angel Gabriel. Go about your work, woman, and leave us to have our meal in private."

She gave him the sort of disdainfully dismissive look only a sister can give. "Very well, then. Clear the table when you're done, and give a shout if any more customers come in. I'll be out back sitting in the sun like I have no work to do—the Queen of Sheba, me—or like you."

With that, Bronwyn sauntered from the room laughing, her womanly hips swaying.

Dafydd sighed again as he sat on a bench at the scarred oak table, while her brothers and Eifion each took an ale and a pie. "I'm glad I had no sisters. Torments they are, the lot of them."

Bran-Bron shrugged as he shoved his doe-colored brown hair out of his eyes and reached for a pie. He held it up, examining it as if he were a goldsmith pricing a necklace. "You will be thinking different when you bite into one of these. A great cook, our Bronwyn. Worth a little teasing for the food."

"As your belly attests," Dafydd agreed, glancing down at Bran-Bron's rotund torso. "And she's a beauty, too, and talented as few are. But I am thinking of Cordelia. You've heard what's happened now, of course."

Their mouths full of pie or ale, the men nodded, their expressions grave.

Jon-Bron wiped dripping gravy from his chin and set his half-eaten pie on the table. "Not to go without permission, and with ten of my men if she has it. Hell to pay when he told her, I heard—shouting and doors banging and the sulks, as always. There's still a hell of a lot of trouble over it. Cold as the top of Snowdon in winter, that hall is these days, despite the warmer weather."

"Aye," Dafydd agreed with another long-suffering sigh. "It's like the trouble between them has burned so bright, only cold ashes are left. And then there's his trouble with Fiona."

"Has he talked to you about it yet?" Jon-Bron asked.

Dafydd shook his head. "No, and not likely to now, it's been so long." He regarded his ale thoughtfully, like a seer seeking visions. "I never thought I'd see the day Caradoc would quarrel with his wife or lose his temper like that. They could hear him shouting in the hall, Una said. They have not made it up yet, either. A wall there is between them that I confess it pains me to see."

"A wall there may be in the day, but at night they breech it," Emlyn-Bron calmly observed, delicately picking up a piece of crust and putting it in his mouth.

"How do you know that?" Dafydd demanded.

"Rhonwen. Takes the linen off the bed, doesn't she?"

Dafydd looked skeptical. "She told you this?"

"I asked."

Dafydd's brown eyes lit up. "Well, that's a hopeful sign, at least." He hesitated a moment, then asked, "What else does Rhonwen say?"

"Lady Fiona's not with child."

The men exchanged wary looks.

"Early days yet, isn't it?" Eifion offered. "At least he's trying. That's what I call a sacrifice."

Dafydd frowned. "Look you, I am no beauty, either, but I don't think any woman's ever had cause to complain about what we do when we're alone."

"Well, aye, of course," Eifion quickly agreed. "But you're . . . well, you're *you*."

"Oh, that's helpful," Dafydd retorted.

"We're not here to talk about you and your conquests, Dafydd," Jon-Bron pointed out, peeved. "Something has to be done about what's going on. Caradoc's too distracted by all this turmoil, and it's got to stop. He's got enough to worry about with the theft of his sheep. He doesn't need his hall to be a misery to him, too."

"Any more gone missing?" Bran-Bron asked the bailiff.

"No, thank God and all his saints. Or," he amended, "none that we know of. We've had so many patrols out, I think we would know. Hoping they've moved on, I am. The bastards," he finished in a rancorous mumble.

Eifion hunched over and looked around nervously. "You don't think it was . . . it was brownies, then?"

Dafydd gave him a sour look. "Since when have brownies taken to sheep stealing?" He waggled an accusing finger at him. "You've been listening to Ganore. I'm surprised she's not accusing Lady Fiona of stealing them and hiding them in their bedchamber or doing sacrifices by the light of the full moon."

He realized the three brothers were exchanging nervous glances. "Don't tell me she's saying something like that?"

"She would if Lady Fiona ever went out of the

castle alone," Jon-Bron replied. "But I've been hearing Ganore mutter about witchcraft and red hair."

"If Caradoc ever gets a whiff of that, there will be hell to pay," Dafydd said firmly, "and I think even Ganore realizes that it wouldn't be wise to cross him about his wife."

"That's why she's only muttering."

"There's no doubt in my mind that it was the work of men, and I've said so all along," Dafydd declared. "Clever ones, maybe, but if they're still nearby, we'll catch them now that Caradoc's sending out more patrols."

"And taken to riding out with us, too," Bran-Bron noted, shaking his light brown hair out of his eyes, "so he's that worried."

"Or trying to get some peace and quiet. I've never seen him look so weary," Dafydd said. He looked pointedly at Emlyn-Bron. "And that has nothing to do with what goes on in the bedchamber. We never saw him look more rested than he was the first days after the marriage, did we? I had real hopes then, I can tell you, despite Cordelia and Ganore. Foolish, I guess. Nor can we blame Fiona. She's been more patient than most."

The men all nodded.

"I tell you, he was silence itself when we were practicing yesterday, like when Connor was about," Jon-Bron said after he swallowed the last of his meat pie. "A nod, a shake of the head, a grunt."

Eifion paused as he lifted his mug. "Maybe it's time Cordelia was married, or sent off to a convent."

"He won't make her marry, and there's no man asking for her," Dafydd replied after he wiped his mouth on his woolen sleeve. "And he would die before he sent her away from home. You know that as well as I."

"Spoiled she is," Bran-Bron muttered, his leather jerkin creaking as he rubbed the crumbs from his hands. "Always was, always will be."

Dafydd nodded and wrapped his hands around his mug. "That may be, but that's the way it is, and he knows it better than we do. What else can we say to him?"

"*We?*" Eifion squeaked. "I'm not going to try to tell Caradoc what to do when he's like this. Value my head, I do."

"He's got a point, you know, Dafydd," Jon-Bron said, toying thoughtfully with his mug. He glanced at the bailiff. "He won't like having anybody telling him he should be doing something. Stubborn like that, isn't he? We were, um, discussing this before you got here, and we think it would be best if *you* talked to him. Man to man, you know. Maybe you can suggest something to help. You're his best friend, after all, and an expert with the women."

Dafydd frowned. "I thought this was to be a united effort, not just me alone to beard the lion in his den."

"But you would be *best*," Jon-Bron insisted. "You have to see that."

Dafydd sighed and downed the last of his ale before he replied. "Aye, I suppose I do," he conceded. "Very well, I will speak to him. But what am I going to suggest he do? He won't send Cordelia away, and I have to tell you, lads, quarrel or not, I don't think he wants to send his wife away."

"There's those sheets," Eifion reminded them sagely.

Dafydd grinned for the first time since he had arrived. "Aye, the sheets. Whatever bump they've hit in the road, I believe he likes her more than we know, and probably more than she does, either." He sobered. "But they'll never be able to make it up the way things are now, not with all the conflict in the hall. Peace has to be restored, so I think Ganore ought to go."

Emlyn-Bron whistled. "By the saints, Dafydd, that's almost like asking him to send away Cordelia."

"Almost," Dafydd replied, "but not the same. Ganore's been a thorn in his side and a cross to bear all his life. She's getting worse, too, in her old age, and she's encouraging disrespect. The time has come for her to leave Llanstephan."

"You think Caradoc will agree?" Bran-Bron asked warily, clearly believing he would not.

"I think he already understands that, but doesn't want to upset Cordelia any more after their last quarrel," Dafydd replied. "He loves his sister dear when all is said and done, maybe too dear. He's given her her own way too many times."

Eifion ran his long finger around the neck of his tunic, as if it had suddenly grown too tight. "You'll tell him that?"

"I don't have to. But knowing a thing and doing something about it can be two different notions," Dafydd pointed out as he folded his arms on the table and leaned forward.

"She'll have another fine fit if he tells Ganore to go," Emlyn-Bron noted with a sigh.

"Aye, and that's the problem. If it was just his misery, he would never do it. But it's a choice he'll have to make—try to make Cordelia content, or his wife."

The others exchanged glances, as if they weren't sure this was a good enough reason.

"As you say, I am his best friend," Dafydd said as he straightened, determination in his brown eyes, "so trust me in this. He cares for Fiona, and if he won't send Ganore away for his sake, he may do it for hers. I think that's the only way to have a hope of peace in the castle."

The men gravely nodded their assent.

"So we'll leave it to your tender care, Dafydd, eh?" Eifion asked, obviously glad he wasn't the one who was going to talk to Caradoc.

"Aye."

"He should be in a good humor after we have a practice, or as good as he gets these days," Jon-Bron noted as he got to his feet. "Very well he's doing with his sword. He used to be so clumsy, I can't think what happened."

"Age, maybe," Dafydd said as he, too, stood. "Or maybe it's not having the glorious Connor about to be compared to."

"Aye, could be," Bran-Bron agreed, glancing at his brothers. "Not easy to be compared."

Jon-Bron began to gather up the mugs. "Help me clear or Bronwyn will have our heads. Caradoc's not the only one with a sister with a temper."

* * *

Caradoc surveyed the large sacks of wool in the storeroom with some satisfaction. The stacked sacks reached all the way to the top of the stone walls, piled one on the other in rows.

Whatever else was amiss in his life—and there was much—between Fiona's dowry and this year's fleece, his financial troubles were definitely over.

"Are you trying to hide from me or what these days, Caradoc?" Dafydd demanded from the door.

Caradoc turned. "What is it? More sheep missing?"

"No, thank God," Dafydd said, giving him a grin. "I think the thieves must have seen the error of their ways and repented. Either that, or the sight of the fearsome lord of Llanstephan riding about his estate has sent them scurrying away."

"As long as they're gone," Caradoc replied, overlooking Dafydd's jibe in his relief.

If the sheep thieves had taken themselves elsewhere, that would be one less worry to darken his days.

"Impressive," Dafydd noted, nodding at the wool sacks as he sauntered inside—and it was, considering each sack held over two hundred pounds of fleece. "Remember the time you hid in here and fell asleep, and when you woke up in the dark, you thought you were surrounded by ghosts and screamed fit to make the walls fall down?"

Caradoc did remember. He had been terrified, for he had forgotten that freshly shorn wool was warm, so in the cooler night air, a mist would rise off it. Not only that, the fleeces stirred, making noises like soft whispers. He had been certain that a legion of evil spirits had surrounded him, ready to carry him off to hell.

He had been ten at the time, and Connor eight, and Connor wasted no time in telling the tale to anyone who wanted to listen. Caradoc wouldn't be surprised to find out that Connor had regaled King Richard with the story on the road to the Holy Land.

His relatively good humor slightly spoiled by the recollection, Caradoc leaned back against the wool sacks and crossed his arms and ankles. "I don't think you've come to reminisce."

Dafydd likewise reclined against the stuffed sacks. "Why not?"

"Because it's a fine sunny day and the village women are doing their washing at the river. Surely one or two of them should be claiming your attention, not me."

"Maybe I've sworn off women," Dafydd replied with an airy wave of his hand.

Caradoc raised a skeptical brow. "Oh, and the sun will not rise tomorrow?"

"Cur."

"Varlet."

"Blackguard."

"Nit."

Caradoc realized Dafydd must have something on his mind, or he wouldn't be in the storeroom in the middle of the day. "Then I'll wager you've come about Cordelia and our quarrel about her riding alone."

Dafydd nodded. "Aye, that's part."

"I've made my decision about that, and thus it will be—and about time, too," he finished firmly.

"Not criticizing you there, Caradoc."

He didn't show his relief that Dafydd agreed, although he was glad to think Dafydd didn't consider him overly cruel for the restrictions he had finally placed on his sister's freedom.

"I've come to talk to you friend to friend, Caradoc."

Dafydd looked so serious, a sliver of dread scurried down his spine. He didn't want to have a serious talk with Dafydd, especially when he feared he knew where this conversation would lead.

His relationship with his wife was his business, and nobody else's, not even his best and oldest friend's.

"We're all worried about you, Bronwyn's brothers and Eifion and me," Dafydd explained. "You're exhausted and your patience is as thin as an apple peel these days. That's not surprising, though, considering somebody's been after the sheep and your household is like a battleground. But the loss of some sheep, even to thieves, shouldn't have you looking worse than when you had no money for your taxes. We lose more than a few over the winter. So, it's the battleground, isn't it?"

He spoke of the household, not his wife. Caradoc's pride still urged him to deny that there was anything wrong, but he had suffered in silence for days.

"God save me, Dafydd," he said with a sigh as he slid downward to sit on the floor, "I think my household has more conflict than the East."

"Aye, I know," Dafydd said sympathetically, sitting cross-legged beside him.

"Ganore's the worst, of course," Caradoc admitted. He rubbed his jaw, then shrugged his shoulders. "She simply won't give Fiona a chance."

Dafydd cleared his throat delicately. "Then don't you think it's time she left? It's true Cordelia and some of the others would fault you for it, but surely you can see that your wife doesn't stand a hope of being accepted here until Ganore is gone."

He slipped into an uncannily accurate impersonation of the elderly woman. " 'Silken coverlet, pillows, carpets on the floor. Sinful luxury, that's what it is, the brazen hussy! Incense it will be next, and all manner of decadence! I never thought I would see a Scot so free with money. Why didn't she just throw it at Caradoc and then go away!' "

His imitation might have been funny, if it didn't ring so true. "She said that?"

"Near enough. And she's whispering about witchcraft, too. Nobody's paid much heed to her—yet—because everybody knows she would claim Mary Magdalen was a witch if she knew Mary Magdelen had had red hair. But in time, Caradoc, especially if more sheep go missing and we don't find the thieves . . ."

He didn't have to finish.

Caradoc sighed and raked his hand through his thick hair.

"I can't send her away, for Cordelia's sake," he said, voicing the justification he had given himself since Fiona had come. He also continued to hope that Fiona would be able to tame the surly Ganore. "She misses Connor, and our parents. I won't force her to lose Ganore, too."

Now Dafydd didn't look nearly so sympathetic. "You may have to choose between making your wife happy, or your sister, Caradoc."

An ultimatum. Friend or no friend, he hated ultimatums. Copy that scroll or go without food. Memorize every Latin irregular verb and repeat them without error or miss the Christmas feast. "I have already made Cordelia feel like a prisoner in her own home. It would be too much to send Ganore away, too."

Dafydd laced his fingers, clasped his hands and regarded Caradoc with a serious intensity that was rare indeed. "Look you, Caradoc, I know you love your sister dear, but what about your wife? If you will not think of your own peace and happiness, what about hers? She's suffering, Caradoc, a great deal. Can't you see that? How long must it go on? Until she leaves you?"

Caradoc got to his feet, too agitated to sit. He knew Fiona was having a difficult time, but he had hoped—continued to hope—that she could overcome the animosity. That the time she spent alone with him would be enough to counter the struggle of the days. That she would know, somehow, how much he cared for her. Aye, and how much he needed her, too.

"It will come to that eventually," Dafydd persisted as he, too, rose and watched Caradoc pace restlessly, like a caged bear. "There will come a point when whatever pleasure Fiona finds in your arms won't be enough to overcome the torment of her days. If you wait too long, it may be too late and she will leave you. You do care about that, don't you, Caradoc?"

Caradoc halted and rubbed his chin. What if Dafydd was right, and he ran out of time before he could regain what he had lost with Fiona? "I know she's not had an easy time of it," he admitted, "but I thought I could make up for it when we're alone. That's what I've been trying to do, anyway."

"Is it working?"

That was the question, wasn't it? "I think so. I hope so."

Dafydd sighed with undisguised exasperation. "But you don't *know* and I daresay you haven't asked."

Caradoc looked at his worn boots and shook his head like a chastised boy.

"Why the devil not?"

Caradoc shrugged.

"Afraid to talk to her, are you? Afraid to let her know how you feel, is that it? Thinking that makes you look like a besotted boy and not a man? Pricks your pride, maybe?"

"I never said that."

"You don't have to. I've known you since birth, and it wouldn't surprise me to learn you would rather be tortured than tell a woman how you feel, even if she's your wife."

He didn't need Dafydd to point out his failings when it came to women, especially talking to one. He knew them well enough already.

"Look you, Caradoc," Dafydd said, ignoring Caradoc's annoyed expression, "you must choose between your sister's happiness, or your wife's. And one day, Cordelia may marry and leave here. If she has forced Fiona out, what will be left for you? Come, man, think of that. You have a chance for real happiness with your wife, Caradoc. I saw it in the first days of your marriage. If you think that there'll come another chance like this, think again, or look at me. You don't want to wind up as I am, my friend— loved by many, but beloved by none."

Caradoc saw the pain in Dafydd's usually merry eyes, and heard the ring of sincerity in every word he said. To think he had known Dafydd all his life and never suspected he felt like this.

His annoyance fell away like the mist from the fleece. "You're right. I've got to choose."

And then and there, he did.

Ganore was going to have to leave. Dafydd's heartfelt words seemed almost like the permission he had been seeking and removed the impediment of his doubts.

It was as if the weight of Llanstephan's walls had been lifted from him, and he clapped a hand on Dafydd's shoulder. "Since you are so keen to speak of matters of the heart, my friend, I overheard Rhonwen talking to Fiona about you the other day. While I myself don't understand it, since she seems an intelligent young woman, I think Rhonwen likes you."

Dafydd gave him a genuinely startled—and shyly pleased—look such as Caradoc had never seen on his face before, and for once, Dafydd didn't declare a woman's attraction inevitable. "Really?"

His delighted expression altered to a wary one. "You're not teasing me?"

"If I were, it would be a just return for all the times *you've* teased *me*. But no, she really does," Caradoc said as he started toward the hall.

Dafydd hurried after him. "Wait for me, you varlet. What exactly did she say?"

"I can't remember *exactly*, but I think she called you a cur."

"Blackguard!"

"Or maybe it was nit."

Chapter 12

⎯⎯⎯ ❦ ⎯⎯⎯

Caradoc awaited Ganore in his solar. He had sent Lowri to fetch her and knew Ganore was taking her time. The woman had no notion she was really only making him more sure of his purpose.

He also contemplated Father Rhodri, who was still demonstrating a distinct lack of Christian charity where Fiona was concerned. He had let that go on too long, too, hoping it would resolve itself, having faith in Fiona's ability to overcome the poor opinion of others—or, as he now realized, using that excuse to avoid another conflict in his household. Well, he would not put that burden on Fiona any longer, either.

At last there came a single sharp rap at the door and Ganore marched into the solar before he answered. She came to a halt and looked at him expectantly, and with all the respect she would accord a six-year-old boy.

Another mistake, Ganore.

He lifted up the purse of silver coins he had taken from Fiona's dowry and set it on the table with a dull clink. "Ganore, because you have served this household well, this is yours."

Her eyes narrowed and her lips thinned, as they had done for years every time she was about to criticize him.

"This is your reward for your service here," he said, "which is now at an end."

Her mouth opened and she paled, but only for an instant before her eyes got the fierce look he knew so well.

"It's her, isn't it?" she charged. "Casting me out of my home like I was a leper when she's the one who ought to be going! Look you, Caradoc, she's a no-good, lying, cheating Scot. She bought her way into this household and into your bed. She's cheated you there, too, if you think she was a virgin. That old whore's trick of blood on the sheets wouldn't fool anybody with half a bit of sense and—"

Caradoc's anger rose, bringing with it the bitter taste of bile. Ganore had not been there on his wedding night. She knew *nothing* about Fiona, and her speculations were all based on ancient prejudices and superstitions.

He was around the table in an instant to confront her. "Anybody with half a bit of sense would not spread false rumors of witchcraft just because a woman has red hair. Anybody with half a bit of sense would see Fiona for the woman she is, and not the creature you make her out to be. Look *you*, Ganore, she is my wife, and anybody with half a bit of sense would beware what they say to a man about his wife, especially when the man is a lord."

"But you cannot understand, can you?" he demanded, his rage finally breaking free of the restraints he had placed upon it for years upon years. "I am the lord of Llanstephan Fawr, not the child you terrorized while exalting my brother and sister before me."

A plea rose unbidden from the depths of his heart. "Why was that, Ganore? Why have you always hated me?"

Ganore's whole body trembled with emotion, and her eyes were wild with fury. "Me? It wasn't only me. Did you never wonder why your father was so hard on you, and your mother did not come to the aid of her firstborn?"

"My mother didn't know there was anything to save me from," he retorted, his hands curving into fists of tension.

"Of course she did! My lady knew everything that went on here."

"She didn't. She couldn't have." *Or she would have told you to be kinder to me. She would have stopped Connor and Cordelia from teasing me. She would have got me out of the solar, and told my father to praise me.*

Ganore went behind the chair, her skeletal fingers, knuckles white, gripping the back of it as if she would break it if she could. "Where do those blue eyes of yours come from, eh? Connor's are brown like his father's. Cordelia's are gray, like your mother. No one in your family has ever had blue eyes."

A sudden terrible fear grabbed Caradoc's heart, as strong as her grip upon the chair. "What does that matter?"

"A Norman *raped* my sweet lady," she cried, bending forward, the spittle flying from her thin lips, "and you are *that* man's son."

Everything except shock drained from him as he stared at her.

Then pride and denial, tough and strong as the mountains beyond the walls of his castle, formed a bandage over the gaping wound she made.

He would not believe this tale he had never heard before. She must be lying, trying to hurt him one last time before she went away.

"There was a feast at her uncle's manor. A Norman squire named DeFrouchette caught her in the garden, alone and unprotected," Ganore continued, a mad gleam of triumph in her dark and beady eyes. "He took his pleasure of her and left her insensible. By the time she was found, he had fled to France."

Holding the arms of his chair, Caradoc lowered himself to sit. "If that is true, why have I never heard it?" he asked, his voice cold as ice, hard as iron.

"Because her parents had great plans for her, an important match with a Norman lord, and the Normans are particular about virgin brides. She had put them off for as long as she could, wanting a Welshman for her husband, but when she realized she was with child, she finally gave in. She said she might as well make her parents happy, if not herself. Because of you, she was forced to marry your Norman father, who had been after her for months to no avail, until she was attacked."

Ganore raised a bony finger and pointed at him as if she was the judgment of God. "You're a Norman's bastard, Caradoc, and if it weren't for you, my sweet lady would have married a proper Welshman!"

"Still your lying tongue, old woman!" he cried, and with some triumph himself, for he had found the flaw in her story, the element that gave him hope that this was just a lie. "If it was a Welshman she wanted, he wouldn't care if she was a virgin."

Her black eyes gleamed with twisted pleasure. "No Welshman with any pride would want her once she bore a Norman's brat."

Sweet heaven. That had the ring of truth.

"Believe it or not as you will, it is what happened. I was her most trusted maidservant. She had no secrets from me."

Yes, Ganore had been his mother's nurse, and that was why he thought his mother kept her close, despite the woman's harsh, judgmental nature.

If Ganore knew her secret, perhaps his mother did not dare to tell her to go lest she speak of it. Perhaps that was why she would not cross Ganore, or come to the aid of her son.

But to think that was to admit that Ganore was telling him the truth, and that he would not accept. He couldn't.

As his mind desperately grappled with what she said, he found another flaw in her story.

He steepled his fingers and regarded her steadily, his lip sneering. "If I am a bastard, how am I the heir of Llanstephan? Or will you tell me my father never knew?"

"Of course he knew," she replied, and her triumph and pleasure did not lessen. "But what Norman would admit he was so besotted over a woman he would marry one bearing another man's brat?"

She came around the chair, moving toward the table like a snake slithering through the grass in the meadow. "They learned to care for one another, but not you. How could they? You were the reminder of another man who had taken her first. You were the proof that they had not come together in love. Most of all, you have Rennick DeFrouchette's eyes."

Smiling cruelly, she splayed her hands on the table and leaned closer, her dragon's breath full of bile. "In your heart, you know I speak the truth, Caradoc. Why else were you never your father's pride?"

Repulsed by her, full of hatred and anguish, he stood up so swiftly, his chair toppled over backward.

"Even if this lie has one grain of truth in it, is not Connor a Norman's son?" he cried, despair creeping into his voice and wrapping itself around his heart. "Is not Cordelia a Norman's daughter?"

Ganore rocked back, still smiling her thin, cruel smile. "But they are like my lady, merry and charming, with the voices of angels when they sing. You are a Norman through and through—proud, arrogant, no voice to sing, no words for poetry! You are half Welsh by blood, but you are pure Norman in your soul."

She stabbed her skinny finger at him. "You know it. You feel it. That is why you don't belong here any more than your wife. That is why you ached to leave Wales, to get back among your own kind where you *do* belong!"

He stumbled back as if she had struck him, for how often in his heart had he felt alone and outside, as if he did not belong there? Yet his aloofness was no secret, and this woman had lived here all her life to see it. Indeed, she had often been the cause of his keeping apart from others. This lie absolved her of any blame for that.

Strengthened by that thought, he straightened. "Who else has heard this little tale? Have you told Cordelia why her mother married a Norman? She is so adamantly Welsh, I am sure she would like to know it was done out of necessity rather than love, as she believes."

The woman blanched, and with horrified, remorseful eyes she stared at him for one long moment before she threw herself on her knees and, humbled and pleading, grabbed his hand. "No, she doesn't know and you must never tell her. I swore to my lady that I would take the secret to my grave, because she wanted it to be so. She was too proud to have her children know that she had been forced into marriage. Oh, why did you make me so angry I spoke of it?"

His world had blown apart and he was hollow inside. Nothing Ganore had said convinced him that she spoke the truth more than this.

No wonder he could never please the man he thought was his father. No wonder his mother never came to his aid, or championed him.

He shook Ganore off and pushed the bag of coins at her. "Get out, Ganore. Take this and get out of Llanstephan. Out of my castle. Out of my village."

As she sobbed and protested, he felt not a jot of pity

for her. He felt nothing at all except a great vast emptiness, as if he were all alone in the middle of a desert.

No, not alone. Fiona was apart and different, too. Fiona was not accepted, not wanted here. He had her to cling to, to love.

And there were others.

Rhonwen. She, too, had been held apart by Ganore and the others. He had Dafydd, his friend. And Bronwyn's brothers. Even Eifion.

He drew himself up, the lord of Llanstephan Fawr once more, and not a lonely, isolated child. "Make your farewells to Cordelia, pack your bags and be gone. I never want to see your face again."

Ganore clutched the money to her skinny breast. "Give me your word you won't tell Cordelia about your sainted mother."

"The word of a Norman's bastard is good enough for you?" he asked, his voice soft and low, and the more frightening for that. "Have no fear, Ganore. I am not like you, happy to hurt. I will not tell her, for there is no need for her to know."

He would not have Cordelia's world shattered, too.

Fiona helped Rhonwen adjust the silken coverlet over her bed. She enjoyed sharing such quiet, simple tasks with her maidservant. During that time they would sometimes talk about Dafydd. It was, she suspected, one of the few indulgences Rhonwen allowed herself, although Fiona feared it was the closest Rhonwen ever got to voicing her attraction to the man. She was fairly certain Rhonwen was far too bashful to say anything to Dafydd himself.

Nor did Fiona consider lingering in the bedchamber hiding, exactly. It was just that she saw no reason to go quickly back to the hall, where Ganore still ruled by subterfuge and disrespect despite her continuing efforts, and Cordelia still sneered at her as if she were a Scottish harlot.

It was getting more difficult to get through the day without losing her patience, and it wasn't only the situation with Ganore and Cordelia and the ever-condemning Father Rhodri that made her tense and edgy.

It was her marriage.

Her relationship with Caradoc seemed fine on the surface. He was polite, so was she; they made love often, and with passion and desire.

But beneath that placid surface was a sense that they had lost the lovely intimacy they had shared after their wedding. As the days passed, she began to wonder if they could ever restore the growing affection their quarrel had seemingly blighted.

Caradoc never spoke of the argument, though, and she was loathe to mention it first, afraid she might make things worse.

Indeed, he never spoke to her save for inconsequential things. She learned of the missing sheep from Rhonwen, as well as the growing belief that the sheep thieves had fled Llanstephan.

Perhaps if she could bear Caradoc a child, their delightful and affectionate intimacy would be restored and he would begin to confide in her. Unfortunately, she had already had one menses since she had arrived, and while Caradoc had not acted as if he was troubled by that, she could not forget what

Ganore had said—that if she didn't bear him a son, Caradoc would make her go.

She realized Rhonwen seemed distracted this morning, too. She wasn't going about her tasks as efficiently as usual, and she looked anxious.

She suspected the girl's agitation had something to do with Dafydd, but she wasn't sure what she should ask, or if she should interfere at all. Rhonwen might consider questioning an unwelcome intrusion. Fiona did not want to risk the one female friendship she had.

Suddenly a great commotion erupted in the courtyard. Fiona recognized Ganore's harsh, condemning voice. She was so loud, it sounded as if she was berating every single inhabitant of the castle.

Wondering what this boded—and sure it was nothing good—Fiona hurried to the window and looked out. Ganore stood near the stables, where one of the grooms was trying to hitch a donkey to a cart. She gestured wildly, nearly striking him. Her face was fierce and every word seemed a denunciation. A little crowd of maidservants had gathered around her, and a few of the soldiers. Cordelia was there, and although she didn't speak, she seemed to be just as frantically upset.

Absolutely baffled, Fiona turned to look at Rhonwen, and found the girl wringing her hands with dismay.

"What is it?" she demanded, upset by this mystery. "What is going on?"

"Ganore is leaving Llanstephan today," Rhonwen replied, her voice little more than a whisper.

Fiona stared at her. Her prayers had been answered! Then she glanced again at the commotion, and thought perhaps her joy was premature.

It was.

"Lord Caradoc has sent her away," Rhonwen clarified, to Fiona's dismay.

That must have been why he did not break the fast with her. She had assumed it was estate business that had sent him to his solar so quickly, and in so businesslike a fashion.

Instead it was a disaster, at least for her. Cordelia and the others would blame her and resent her even more. "Where is my husband?"

"Still in the solar, I think."

Fiona did not wait to hear more, but left the chamber at once.

She found Caradoc sitting in the solar with his parchment scrolls and records before him as if nothing was wrong.

"It is a mistake to send Ganore away," she began without preamble, too concerned for what this boded to be cautious and polite.

The look in his eyes! Fiona had never seen his expression so bleak, never imagined that it could be. Immediately any concern for what Ganore's banishment would mean for her fled like dust before the wind.

Yet why had he done it, if it was going to hurt him like this?

He rose and went to stare out the window. His shoulders slumped as if he bore the weight of the world upon them— or terrible guilt. "The woman gave me no choice. There could be no peace in my household until she was gone."

She should have found a way to get along with Ganore! For his sake, she should have done anything it took to endure the woman's animosity.

"I regret that I couldn't overcome her prejudice against me," she said, meaning it more than she would ever have thought possible.

He turned back, his brow wrinkled quizzically. "You have done nothing wrong and you must not blame yourself in any way. It was not only you she did not like, you know. I kept her here for Cordelia's sake, and by God, I am sorry I did.

"Indeed, Fiona . . ." His voice broke and he turned away as if ashamed of the depth of his feelings. "I am more sorry than I can say."

She stared at his broad back, dismayed and anxious. But why was he so stricken? Ganore had not treated him with the respect befitting his station, either, and—

And she had probably said terrible things to Caradoc because he was making her leave. Horrible, hurtful things, based on long years of knowledge. Every foible, every mistake—she would know them all, and Fiona did not doubt for a moment that Ganore would use each one as a weapon against him.

Her heart full of sympathy, she took a step toward him, determined to offer him all the comfort she could, as best she could.

Cordelia burst into the room.

"How could you?" she cried, glaring at Caradoc and ignoring Fiona. "How could you order Ganore to go?"

Anger and frustration surged within Fiona when she saw Caradoc flinch. She opened her mouth, ready to chastise her, when Caradoc pivoted on his heel and looked at his sister. The expression on his face was no longer hurt, no longer vulnerable, but stern and forbidding, and that look made Fiona hold her tongue.

"I have ordered her to go, and go she will," he said, firm conviction in every word. His sister might try to argue, but he was not going to yield.

Cordelia must have seen that, too, for she said no more to him. Instead, she turned on Fiona.

"It's your fault!" she declared, shaking her fist at her. "You made him do this! Don't think I don't know!"

"I did not ask him to do it, but I cannot be sorry that Ganore is leaving," Fiona replied, righteously indignant for Caradoc's sake. "I think he should have done it long before I came."

"Why should *she* be banished? You came here like some sort of Lady Bountiful with your money and your jewels, to marry my brother like he's a stallion you want for stud. If anyone should go, it should be *you*."

Fiona glared at the furious young woman, equally enraged as her patience shattered. "What of the way that woman treated your brother all these years? Good God, I have never met a girl so willfully blind, so incredibly selfish! He put up with Ganore for your sake, and yours alone, and what thanks does he get? Nothing but conflict because of the wife he has married—again, for your sake.

"If you had an ounce of wisdom, you would realize all that he has done for you. You would see him for the kindhearted brother he is, one who spoiled you and gave you your own way too often and for too long, even though you treated him worse than he ever deserved. How could you call him troll? How could you tease him all those years and not see the hurt you caused?"

Cordelia stared at her, incredulous, her face reddening. "How dare you!" she cried. "How dare you upbraid me! I am not your servant and you are not—"

"I will tell you what I am," Fiona said, very slowly and very deliberate as she interrupted. "I am your good brother's wife. Whatever else I am, this is what should be first and foremost. For his sake, you should not be rude. I do not expect you to be my dearest friend. I do not ask for that. I ask you to be friendly, as a noble lady should be to anyone in her hall."

"I will not be criticized in this manner! I am not a child!" Cordelia retorted, stamping her foot.

Fiona looked down at Cordelia's foot, then back at her face. "No?"

"Enough!" Caradoc thundered, and both women stared at him, shocked by the force and commanding power of his voice. "I have decided the woman must go. There will be no discussion, no argument. If she is upset, she need look no further than her own sharp and bitter tongue for the reason why, and she should be grateful I allowed her to stay as long as I did. Do you understand, Cordelia?"

When Cordelia didn't answer, he bellowed, *"Do you understand me?"*

Her eyes puddled with tears as she silently nodded.

"And this woman is my wife," he declared.

He strode forward and put his arm around Fiona, drawing her close. But his grip was gentle for all that, and more wonderful and welcome than she could say. "You will respect her, you will obey her. Like her or not as you will, you are to treat her as is her due."

He let go of Fiona and pointed at the door, his hand steady, his gaze resolute. "Or you, too, can leave with Ganore."

With a cry of anguish, Cordelia ran from the room.

As Fiona stood dumbfounded, Caradoc returned to the window, gulping great breaths of air as if he found it hard to breathe.

She didn't know what to say. Everything that had come before this day, the quarrel and the distance between them, suddenly melted away. She cared for this man, and ached to see him in such pain.

She had always cared for him, from that first day when he had seemed so lonely and apart.

Now she must hold him. Embrace him. Comfort him. Show him that she sympathized with his pain and wanted to do what she could to make it dwindle.

She went to him and slid her arms about his waist, and laid her head upon his heaving chest.

He sighed raggedly as he encircled her with his arms and held close. "Fiona, I'm sorry for what I said the day Sir Ralph came." He spoke haltingly, as if unsure of how his words would affect her, and yet they gave her only joy, a joy more boundless and delighting than she had ever felt in all her life. "I did not marry you just for your money. No one has ever made me as happy as you do. If I had said no, I would have blighted my life."

Thrilled to be in his arms and feeling as close to him as she had in those first days of her marriage, her embrace tightened.

"I think I have loved you since that first day I saw you in the courtyard when you waved at me," he murmured.

She eyed him warily even as her heartbeat tripped like a dancer on midsummer's eve. "But you did not remember me."

"I remembered the girl. I did not recognize the bold and beautiful woman, at least not with my mind. My heart knew you the moment you waved again, and it told me I should be glad. I am glad you came back, Fiona, and very much more than glad that we are wed. Can you forgive me for what I said, and how I lost my temper?"

She sighed, leaning against him, cherishing him more than she had ever even imagined. "Of course."

He drew in another great, quavering breath.

"What is it?"

"Cordelia," he said wearily. "I did my best with her, but I've failed. She hates me now, when all I was trying to do—"

His breath caught in a way that made Fiona's heart ache even more for him.

"All I was trying to do was get her to like me as much as Connor."

"*I* like you, Caradoc. More than like," she offered, looking up at him and willingly revealing the depths of her affection. Letting herself be vulnerable, because she could do nothing less. "I love you. I have loved you from the first time I saw you."

His eyes widened, and then, in the shifting, brilliant depths of his eyes she saw what she had longed to see—the depths stirred by love, and love for her.

"You love me?" he asked, as if afraid to believe it.

"So much, I cannot bear the thought of ever living without you." She took his face gently between her hands and sealed her vow with a soft, slow kiss.

"I could not bear living without you, either," he whispered.

She had no words to say how she felt at that moment, yet it was there in the language of her kisses and her caresses. She was tender as she had never been before, yet passionate, too. She leaned against him, relaxed and bending like a willow in the wind.

For a time they kissed and did no more, wordlessly comforting each other with the tender touch of their lips. Then, after a time, their kisses deepened. Their feelings called for more than kissing, and their hands began to rove and explore.

His caresses grew more heated, and so did hers, until she tore at his clothes, greedy for the more intimate touch of flesh upon flesh, while her legs weakened with the strength of her yearning.

She was his, in love as well as law, and she would prove it.

With hungry eyes she led him to the nearest chair and pushed him down to sit. His tunic was already untied and exposed much of his chest, and his breeches were half undone. Her bodice gaped, her breasts available to his eager eyes and hands.

In the next moment, she was straddling him, guiding him inside where she was wet and waiting.

His breathing hoarse, his mouth pleasured her

breasts as she rose and fell, while anxious murmurs slipped from her throat.

She kissed him again and again, paying no heed to the rough stubble of his beard. She wanted him, she needed him, and she would show him. Throwing back her head, wanton in her desire, she gripped his shoulders as she rocked against him.

Suddenly, he tensed, his arms tightening about her, the sinews of his neck taut as he gasped, and climaxed.

Pleased, she stilled, resting her forehead against his shoulder.

"Fiona," he murmured as his breathing returned to normal.

She raised her head and he brushed her braid back over her shoulder. She shifted, feeling him still inside her, and closed her eyes a moment to enjoy it.

"Fiona, you did not cry out."

She opened her eyes, to find his steadfast gaze upon her, his eyes still dark with desire.

"You did not cry out," he repeated, his eyes locked onto hers as he took her hips in his hands and gentle pulled her forward, then released her.

The sensation made her gasp.

Still watching her intently, he did it again. She could hardly breathe with the excitement of it. Again, he did it while he kissed her throat, then let his lips trail down her neck to her breasts. Still moving her, his tongue swirled around the hardened tip of her breast and he sucked her nipple into his mouth.

As he moved her and pleasured her breasts, she

lost track of everything except the incredible sensations rippling through her. It was as if he knew every single thing that could and would excite her. Hot, anxious passion seared and burned and built, until her body tensed like a drawn bowstring.

Then the arrow was loosed.

Wave after wave of pleasure took her as she cried out, her back arching and her toes curling as the climax seized her.

When the throbbing gentled, she fell against him.

An intimate silence, warm and comfortable, surrounded them, and she floated there, blissfully happy.

Caradoc sighed raggedly, and whispered as he laid his head against her shoulder. "I have never had anyone champion me before, Fiona. Thank you."

"I said no more than the truth, and no more than you deserve." She, too, sighed as she looked at his beloved face. "I cannot understand the people here, Caradoc. Can they not see all that you do and how you worry? Why has no one ever chastised your sister or Ganore before? Granted the servants could not, but how could your parents—?"

"Ganore told me this morning that the man all the world believes was my father may not have been."

She stared at him, shocked and incredulous.

But he believed it. She saw that in the tormented depths of his eyes.

"She said my mother was raped by a Norman before she married my father, and I am that man's son."

He was in such pain, such anguish! Anger at

Ganore and her spiteful spirit reared up within Fiona, as hot and powerful as her passion had been moments before.

"Ganore was a hateful old woman full of malice. She just told you that to hurt you." Her gaze searched his face. "And she did, didn't she?"

"I don't want to believe her." With another deep sigh, he pulled Fiona close and buried his face against the curtain of her hair, as if he could not bear to look at her. "But I do. I even think a part of me hopes it was so. That would explain why I was never good enough for my father, and why my mother let Ganore treat me as she did. It would mean the fault or lack was not solely mine, as I have always thought."

She took his face gently between her hands to ensure that he saw her face as she answered, firmly and without reservation. "Whoever your father was, you are Caradoc, lord of Llanstephan Fawr. Everything you have done, everything you do, everything about you, proclaims that.

"Even more important to me," she said, her voice dropping to a tender whisper, "you are Caradoc, my beloved husband. *Nothing* can change that."

The torment left his eyes, replaced with joy, and all the affection she had ever hoped to see in the eyes of the Dark Prince of the Lonely Tower. "And you are my beloved wife, Fiona, who came to me in my hour of need, and stayed to give me far more than relief from my worries. You have made me happier than I have been in my life." He kissed her with the same wonderful joy and affection. "I am glad I shared this with you, Fiona. I would have no secrets between us."

She embraced him tightly, closing her eyes as if to close out her shame.

Now is the time, her heart commanded. *Tell him. Tell him about Iain. Have no secrets from this man who cherishes you as you have always dreamed.*

Yet the same strong pride that had refused to accept Iain after she learned his true nature, the same fierce self-respect that had led her to leave her home and seek a better happiness elsewhere, held her tongue. She could not confess to that stupidity and vanity, not when they were so close to what they had shared before, and more. She would not risk losing that because of what was in the past, and over with forever.

The sudden cry of the sentry at the gate made her start, as if her very thoughts had conjured a Scots man at the gates.

"What is it?" she asked as she got shakily to her feet, all her hopes and desires suddenly as tenuous as the first thin tendril of a new plant.

"I don't know." With a scowl of displeasure, Caradoc quickly tied his breeches and went to look out the window.

"Not what," he muttered as she waited, too full of dread to breathe. "Who."

Not Iain. Please, God, not Iain!

Then she realized he looked more disgruntled than confused or angry or suspicious.

Despite that hopeful observation, she trembled as she went to join him. Looking out the window, she saw a troop of mounted men in the courtyard. One of them held a standard, and upon it a red and green banner fluttered in the breeze.

Not Iain. Oh, praise God, not Iain. Weak with relief, she leaned against the sill and wondered how many more days, weeks or years must pass before that dread finally left her.

"Who is it?" she asked as her heartbeat returned to normal.

Caradoc turned to her with a grim frown. "Lord Rhys of Wales himself, in all his glory, and I do not think he comes to wish me joy upon my marriage."

Chapter 13

Wishing Lord Rhys far away—preferably on the other side of Wales—Caradoc sighed as he watched the arrogant and fiercely Welsh nobleman dismount.

Why did he have to come today, of all days? His household in upheaval, Ganore surely cursing him to the heavens with every step she took as she left, Cordelia upset . . . and his amazing, loving wife here beside him, having made the worst of this day disappear with her heartfelt words and the bliss of making love with her. He wanted nothing more than to sweep her into his arms and take her to their bedchamber to love her again.

Unfortunately, Lord Rhys's arrival rendered that impossible.

"I think I should go and fix my hair," Fiona murmured, turning toward the door. "As a married woman, I should cover it."

"You look lovely," he said as he held her back and tucked a stray wisp of her marvelous hair behind her ear. "I would have you by my side to greet our important guest."

Smiling wryly, he half-jokingly continued, "Besides, I may need you to remind me to keep my temper. I was annoyed when the rain interrupted the shearing. I am far more frustrated by Lord Rhys's arrival."

Although he saw trepidation in her brilliant eyes, she gave him an answering smile. "Very well."

He held out his arm to escort her. "I don't think Lord Rhys shares Ganore's prejudice against redhaired women," he said by way of encouragement, "and I suppose his arrival will give Cordelia something else to think about, at any rate."

Fiona said no more as they left the solar and went down the steps toward the hall. No doubt her thoughts and emotions were as jumbled as his after all that had happened this day.

They entered the hall just as the tall, imposing Lord Rhys entered. Curious servants appeared at the entrance to the kitchen and unfamiliar soldiers followed the man inside.

It had been some years since Caradoc had been in Lord Rhys's presence, but the man was little changed save that his hair was now iron gray. He still had the broad shoulders and narrow waist of a fit man used to riding and fighting, and from the shrewd intelligence of his face, only a fool would think age had dulled his wits.

"My Lord Rhys," Caradoc called out as they approached him, "welcome again to Llanstephan Fawr."

Beaming, Lord Rhys shrugged off his cloak. One of the soldiers behind caught it neatly before it fell onto the floor. "Caradoc!" he cried happily, striding toward them.

They clasped forearms, and Lord Rhys's powerful grip also assured Caradoc that the older man was as healthy and vital as he had ever been. Then Lord Rhys took him by the shoulders and smiled.

At least, his lips smiled. His shrewd gaze looked far more searching than pleased. "It has been a long time, Caradoc of Llanstephan Fawr. I thought perhaps to see you at my *Eisteddfod* last summer."

"I have not had the leisure to travel, my lord," Caradoc replied evenly as he stepped back, trying not to show how much he resented the Welsh lord's scrutiny, or his slightly condemning tone.

"And now you are wed, or so I have been told."

"Yes, my lord, I am." Caradoc proudly presented Fiona. "This is Fiona. My wife."

Lord Rhys barely glanced at her. "I suppose you did not have the leisure to inform me of such important news, either," he said, his tone suddenly cold.

Irritation, already simmering within him, began to boil again. However, the memory of Fiona's words when they had quarreled over Sir Ralph held his tongue. She had been right to point out the larger implications of his actions then, and she would be right to do so now if he forgot.

And in his heart, the doubt that he did not have the right to rule here caged his temper.

"I bid you welcome to my home. Surely you can forgive him his lapse and understand that a bridegroom might take rather too much leisure," Fiona spoke brightly, apparently not a whit disturbed by Lord Rhys's rudeness, but Caradoc knew her better, and he could see the subtle signs of anger at the corners of her lips and lurking in the sparkle of her eyes.

Lord Rhys ran a measuring gaze over her, then addressed Caradoc, as if Fiona were one of the hounds in the hall and not a person capable of understanding him. "So, this is the Scot. I did not know she could speak Welsh. Had you thought to inform me of this marriage yourself, I might have."

Caradoc's hands balled into fists. He dearly wanted to strike the man for his rude insolence, until Fiona put her hand gently on his arm. She didn't look at him, though. She kept her gaze on Lord Rhys and smiled still.

"I daresay there are many things about me you do not know, Lord Rhys," she said with just the slightest hint of condemnation beneath the calm politeness. "Now that you are here, you can get to know me, and I shall get to know you, too. However, if you will excuse me, I must have refreshments prepared for you, and a chamber for your use, so I shall have to leave you. Is there anything you especially prefer for the evening meal, Lord Rhys? Fish, perhaps?"

"That would suit me well, my lady."

"Excellent! I shall inform our cook at once."

Still smiling, with her back straight and her head held high, she did not wait for Lord Rhys's leave to go.

The Welsh nobleman looked rather stunned as he

watched her head for the kitchen corridor, probably because few men and fewer women would ever dare address him in such a manner. Although she had said nothing rude or intemperate, she had made her displeasure obvious.

It was all Caradoc could do to keep from chuckling with proud satisfaction as he calmly gestured toward the chairs on the dais. "Will you sit, my lord?"

His noble guest regally inclined his head, then led the way as arrogantly as if this were his own home.

As he followed, it occurred to Caradoc that Ganore must already be gone, or she would be here. She thought Lord Rhys walked on water.

He also pondered Cordelia's absence. Either she was sulking, in which case she might not come down until the evening meal, or she did not yet know Lord Rhys was come.

Once seated, Lord Rhys wasted no time with genial preamble. He fixed his eyes on Caradoc and said, "You should have consulted with me before you wed."

Caradoc did not appreciate being treated without deference any more than Fiona did, especially in his own castle. Whatever the exact circumstances of his birth, he was no peasant or serf. Besides, as Fiona had so aptly pointed out, Lord Rhys had never come to his rescue, in any way. "What you mean is, you would rather I had sought your approval."

Rhys did not look pleased that Caradoc had answered in such blunt terms. His eyes flashed with ire, and his lips thinned. "If that is the way you wish to put it, yes."

"Who would you have had me wed?"

Rhys folded his arms across his chest. "There are Welsh heiresses."

"Aye, my lord, and I have met a few. Of course, I might have paid off the worst of my debts had I wed one of them, but I might also have made an alliance that neither you, nor Richard, would look on with favor. Instead I have married a merchant's daughter who came to me with moveable goods, not land or political allegiances or secret ambitions. Since our marriage has no political repercussions, I saw no need to ask you for your permission, or Richard, either."

The nobleman's eyes flared with sudden pleased satisfaction.

So that was it—he had wondered if Caradoc had sought Richard's approval, and not his.

"What is important to consider is that if I had refused this marriage," Caradoc said, "and the dowry that went with it, I would have lost my home eventually—and you know as well as I that Richard would have put his own man in my place."

"Perhaps the choice of bride was wiser than I thought," Lord Rhys conceded.

For the sake of Fiona's pride, Caradoc gave the man a secretive smile. "I had other reasons for my haste. She has many excellent qualities not immediately obvious, my lord, and I found I did not want to wait."

"Well, every man to his own taste, of course."

He really should leave the levity to Dafydd.

Rhys sat back and studied him a moment. "I heard your wife sought *you* out."

The man's tone implied that this utterly baffled

him and Caradoc struggled not to reveal how offended he was. "I may not sing like Connor, but apparently I have other qualities not readily apparent, either."

Rhys's brow quirked upward. "I wonder if your brother will offer a similar explanation for his marriage to a Norman."

So, it wasn't only *his* marriage that had brought Lord Rhys to Llanstephan.

"I know little about it," Caradoc honestly replied, "save that the heiress was a reward for saving Richard's life. Since Connor is a knight of the realm, that is what he had sworn to do, just as I have."

"I have no criticism of Connor's action with regard to Richard. Assassins are dishonorable rogues who deserve death. It is his marriage that concerns me."

"I do not recall that Connor ever swore an oath of loyalty to you. Neither have I."

Lord Rhys's eyes narrowed and he looked far from pleased by this reminder. Before he could speak, however, Cordelia appeared. She had put on her finest garment of rich, scarlet velvet, and dressed her flowing hair with scarlet ribbons.

Caradoc studied her face, looking for remnants of her tears, and saw it in the puffy skin about her eyes. But she was too lovely to be much marred by that, and that was not what affected him as she glided toward them, her bearing as regal as Fiona's. Indeed, she seemed to be imitating his wife's natural grace and proudly poised head.

He had told her to act like a woman and by the saints, she was. Suddenly, he saw and truly understood that Cordelia was no longer the little hoyden who used to tease him and call him troll, but a beautiful woman men would desire. Aye, and fight over, too.

That realization hit him like a punch in the gut. It hit him even harder as his gaze swept over the men in the hall, who were all looking at his sister with blatant admiration.

Especially Lord Rhys.

The man had been fast falling in Caradoc's estimation since his arrival and rude reception of Fiona; his repute slipped yet more the closer Cordelia came, and his expression grew more lascivious.

God save him, if Rhys didn't start behaving better, powerful nobleman or not, and whether it was wise or not, he would order him to leave.

Rhys rose and bowed to Cordelia as if she were the queen, far more deferential than he had been to Fiona.

"My lord, my sister, Cordelia," Caradoc said, fighting to keep his growing wrath in check.

"My lady Cordelia," Rhys said, giving her a warm smile. "It has been many years since last we met, and seeing you now reminds me of my age, for you were but a child then and you have grown into a beauty."

Cordelia flushed, all trace of her bold manner subverted. "Thank you, my lord."

He had never seen Cordelia act the coy maiden before.

He didn't like it. He preferred the spirited woman, even if she aggravated him, to this pale imitation of Cordelia before him now. It was like having a ghost there, and not a person of flesh and blood.

Then Cordelia glanced at him, and for once, he was relieved to see the flash of ire in her eyes. She was still fiercely angry with him for sending Ganore away. She would probably be fiercely angry about that for the rest of her life. While that troubled him, it wasn't as disturbing as seeing her act little more than a pretty doll.

"I would like nothing better than to visit with you, my lady," Rhys continued. "Unfortunately, I fear your brother and I have other business to discuss. Perhaps you will wait here while we go to his solar?"

Cordelia's eyes showed her displeasure, but she did not protest. "As you wish, my lord."

Since he had been given no real choice, Caradoc led the Welsh nobleman to the solar. He glanced at the chair in which he had been with Fiona a short time ago while Lord Rhys sat behind the table, again as if he ruled here.

Reminding himself that he must control his temper, Caradoc clenched his jaw as he sat opposite him.

"I did not want to speak of this in front of your sister," Rhys began, "although it is part of what we were discussing before, that is the subject of marriage. Your sister should be betrothed soon."

He gave Caradoc a pointed look. "To a Welshman, eh, Caradoc? Your brother has a Norman wife, and you a Scot. Surely you can spare your sister for a fellow countryman."

"I would be hard pressed to spare my sister at all, my lord."

Rhys steepled his fingers and laid them against his lips. "I do not want to hear of the lovely Cordelia wed to some Norseman or other foreigner at a later date."

"She will marry whoever she chooses, my lord," Caradoc answered, struggling to remain calm. "I have always intended that it be so."

His guest lowered his hands and regarded Caradoc as if he wasn't sure if he had heard aright. "I can understand if you will let her have her opinion, but surely the choice must be yours."

"The permission will be mine to grant, but she will have her choice, and I will not withhold it without serious cause."

Rhys stared at Caradoc as if he had suddenly declared that the earth was round. "Why, just think, Caradoc, if we let women marry whoever they wanted, what chaos it would be! My sister—who is a fool if ever there was one—would have run off with a shepherd had my father not had the presumptuous lout killed."

Caradoc tried not to show how this comment repulsed him, but he couldn't. He had held himself in check too long as it was. "No man deserves to die for falling in love, and no woman, either."

Rhys reclined in his chair. Despite his relaxed attitude, his gaze was still intense, a reminder to Caradoc that the man before him wielded considerable power of his own and might not hesitate to use it. "You may be no singer, Caradoc, but perhaps you have the makings of a poet, eh?"

Ganore had not thought so. To her, he was a Norman to the core. "I doubt it very much, my lord."

"A pity, that."

"Perhaps you can think of someone appropriate for my sister, my lord," he suggested, not at all serious, "and send him to visit us."

"Why, that's a fine idea, Caradoc, a fine idea."

In truth, it was a stupid, useless idea. Cordelia would not welcome a parade of suitors. Indeed, he could almost hear the jibes she would hurl at them. "Of course, it may be that it will take a wild Norseman to tame her."

"Whoever it is and however he is found, when she is betrothed, I expect to be informed."

"I will inform you, my lord, as you ask, but it will be for me to grant permission or not, as I see fit."

Rhys straightened, his intense gaze suddenly hostile. "Are you saying you will pay no heed to the duty you owe your countrymen?"

He had endured enough, been patient long enough, and put up with more than he should have to. He rose and regarded the nobleman coldly. Sternly. As the lord he was. "Are you challenging my right as her elder brother and the lord of Llanstephan Fawr to make decisions as I see fit?"

Rhys's gaze faltered. "Of course not. Please, sit down, Caradoc."

The man obviously realized he had gone too far, so Caradoc did as he asked.

"Of course it is for you to choose, or give permission, or whatever aspect of agreement you prefer when it comes to your sister's marriage. However, the marriage of a noblewoman is an important thing and must not be undertaken lightly, or in haste."

Rhys sounded just like Father Rhodri.

"My marriage may have been made in haste," Caradoc retorted, his temper flaring once again, "but I assure you, I did not undertake it lightly, whatever you or anyone else may think."

"Good," Rhys said. He leaned forward and fixed his fierce gaze on Caradoc. "Since you have brought up the question of loyalty and allegiances, let me ask you this: if it came down to a choice between Richard or me, who would you choose to follow?"

"Are you asking me to make that choice here and now, my lord?"

"Do you have to think about it?"

"Do you have to ask? My father was a Norman, and I am a Norman knight, a baron of the kingdom. My first duty must be to Richard. My second will be to you, since my mother was a princess of Wales. But know you this, my lord, no matter what oaths I have sworn, my first and foremost loyalty is to God, then my family and Llanstephan."

Whether his answer pleased Rhys or not, it was the truth, and nothing that should have taken Rhys by surprise.

"Yet what of this Scot you have married?" Rhys demanded. "She ties you to that land, and their king."

"I married Fiona, not Scotland, and she is here, not there."

"A good answer." Rhys studied Caradoc. "So, it shall be England first, then Wales, then Scotland with you?"

"As I said, my lord, it shall be God and then my family and my land. Those I will protect, from anyone who tries to attack them or take them from me, whether they are Norman, Welsh, Scot or something else entirely."

"You tread on dangerous ground, Caradoc."

"I have done so for many years, my lord, and I do not seek any man's enmity. I want only to be left to live in peace."

"So do we all, but these are troubled times."

Caradoc did nothing, said nothing, as Rhys continued to regard him steadily for a long moment. He had been honest and truthful, and now it was for the man before him to make of that what he would.

Rhys smiled, a genuine smile that was guarded, but with honest acceptance in it, too. "Very well, Caradoc. I seek no enmity with you. All I ask is that you do not fight against your fellow Welshmen."

"I have no intention of doing so," he answered honestly, "unless they fight against me. Or steal my sheep."

"Ah, yes, I have heard that some have gone missing from your hills and others nearby. It's probably Norsemen or the Normans, their cousins, when all is said and done. They are all pirates at heart."

"If it is Welshmen and I catch them, I will punish them as the king's law allows, my lord."

"Of course. I would do the same. I merely ask that you do not start feuds with your countrymen "

"As I said, my lord, I seek to live in peace."

Rhys nodded, then got to his feet. "Now, let us go below. We have left your charming sister alone long enough."

The lord of Llanstephan Fawr saw little of his wife for the rest of the day. She flitted about, with Rhonwen trailing her like a faithful puppy, as she oversaw the preparations for a sumptuous evening meal and accommodations for their guests.

Caradoc kept watch out of the corner of his eye as Rhonwen trotted through the hall going from the stairway leading to his bedchamber to a section of the hall behind a painted screen that Fiona had designated as Lord Rhys's while he stayed. Rhys's men would bed down in the open portion of the hall.

First the young woman went by carrying a brazier, then a candlestand, then linens and what looked like a bronze ewer and basin. In fact she made so many trips that he wouldn't be surprised to find their bedchamber stripped when he retired that night.

Barren bedchamber or not, he would be with his wonderful Fiona. As long as they had something to lie on . . . sit on . . . even lean on.

He let his mind drift to such thoughts while Rhys unfavorably dissected the king of England and his military campaigns. Cordelia sat with them, also listening, apparently raptly, as the man went on and on.

How he wished Ganore had been as silent that morning! Whether what she said were horrible lies, or the truth, he wished she had simply taken the money and gone.

Lies, or the truth. He had no way of knowing. His parents were dead, and he had never heard of this De-Frouchette. The man could be dead, for all he knew.

Besides, what good would it do for the truth to be revealed now? He had been named heir by his father and nobody disputed it. Connor had his own estate; he did not need this one, as well. Caradoc decided he would let the past stay buried, as his mother had wanted, and he would bury the emotions Ganore's story aroused beneath the happiness he found with Fiona.

Finally the servants began setting up the tables for the evening meal. Several other guests arrived, including Dafydd, who needed no special invitation. The brothers of Bronwyn entered with their men, and after acknowledging Lord Rhys, went to their customary places.

Eifion and his family appeared. Eifion's wife was as stout as he was thin, and pleasant and well liked by all. Usually she preferred to eat in her own home, but clearly the lure of a famous man like Lord Rhys was too great. She came clutching her husband's arm, more than a little flustered.

Only when the hall was prepared and most of the people in their places did Fiona appear. She wore the lovely dress of ivory velvet that he liked so much, although he had never told her. In what might be considered a breach of etiquette, she wore no scarf or wimple. Instead, her flowing, waving auburn hair hung loose about her shoulders like a living cloak. It shimmered and gleamed in the light of the torches now lighting the hall, and memories of it spread upon their pillows teased him. Her eyes were so bright and glowing, it was as if she were lit from within.

He couldn't take his eyes off her as she politely greeted Lord Rhys, then directed him to sit at the center of the high table, the place of highest honor as befitted his rank.

He was to sit at Lord Rhys's left, she gravely informed him. She came to stand beside him, while Cordelia went to Lord Rhys's right. Father Rhodri would sit beside her.

As Caradoc waited for the priest to arrive and say the blessing, it was all he could do not to touch his lovely, exciting wife. Indeed, he lost the battle when she looked at him, her slightly curious expression seeming to ask if he remembered that morning, when they had been alone in the solar.

Aye, he did. The memories had tempted and tormented him while he listened to Rhys and even when he pondered all that Ganore had said.

He took her hand in his and squeezed lightly.

Father Rhodri came bustling into the hall, at once deferential because of their mighty guest, and yet pompous as always because he represented God. He smiled at Lord Rhys as if that alone conferred a blessing while Caradoc introduced him to the Welsh nobleman.

Then, after slowly raising his hands and pressing them together, he began to pray in his most sonorous tones, obviously with an eye to impressing Lord Rhys. "Oh God, His Son, and blessed St. David, look down on us mortals as we prepare to partake of Your generous bounty. We give You thanks for the fine leadership of this great nation of ours. Grant all here, both high and low, native and foreign, wisdom, mercy and *chastity.* Remind them that we are put on this earth to overcome our mortal coil, and the sins of the flesh—"

Caradoc cleared his throat. Loudly.

Father Rhodri's eyes flew open. He glanced at

Caradoc, who raised his brows and gave him a glare, silently ordering the man to cease such "graces" unless he wanted to follow Ganore out the gate.

The priest swallowed hard and resumed. "The sins of the flesh . . ."

Caradoc kept glaring, and Father Rhodri's eyes cracked open a bit, to encounter his hostile gaze.

"Bl-bless our friends, oh God and smite—"

Caradoc coughed as if he had a rock in his throat.

Lord Rhys opened his eyes and looked around curiously, obviously wondering what was going on.

"I beg your pardon. I fear I am catching a cold," Caradoc whispered by way of explanation.

Then he went back to glaring at Father Rhodri.

"Bless all here and the food before us. Amen," the priest finished swiftly, his face red and his bearing much more honestly humble.

Satisfied, Caradoc slid a glance at Fiona as they sat. She looked as calm as she had that afternoon when Lord Rhys had arrived, and she did not meet her husband's gaze.

Maybe she was thinking he had been rude again and acted improperly. Well, he did not regret anything except making her endure Father Rhodri's rudeness for as long as she had.

Then, as the maidservants began to serve the meal under the watchful eye of Lowri—when she wasn't staring at Rhys, for Ganore was not the only Welshwoman who thought the majestic older man a marvel—he suddenly felt his wife's hand upon his thigh. *High* on his thigh.

He couldn't have felt more shocked if she had suddenly stripped naked.

"Thank you," she whispered.

"I should have caught a cold sooner," he quietly replied, covering her hand with his.

"It's too bad you're sick. Of course, I shall have to nurse you back to health," she finished in a low, sultry tone that made him wish the meal was over.

When she moved her hand away, he brushed his fingers lightly over her thigh, keeping his face perfectly placid, as hers had been.

She stiffened, then relaxed. "My lord," she murmured while apparently fascinated by the top of Jon-Bron's head, "you had best move your hand. You will need it to eat."

Unfortunately, she had a point. He could probably manage with one hand, but it would soon become obvious to anybody who cared to look that he was caressing his wife's leg.

Reluctantly, he stopped, consoling himself with the thought that eventually, they would be alone.

Unfortunately, not only did the meal promise to take forever, Fiona clearly having exhorted Gwillym to extraordinary culinary exertion, but he knew Rhys would not retire without some kind of entertainment first.

"A pity it is your brother is not here," Lord Rhys said to Caradoc when the meal was finally at an end. "I would like to hear him sing again. A very fine voice he has, I recall."

Unlike me, Caradoc thought grimly as he washed his hands in the basin Lowri set before him.

"Cordelia sings well, my lord," he noted, putting aside his humiliation over this lack.

"Ah!" the man cried, turning eagerly to Cordelia. "Will you grace us with a song, my dear?"

"I would be happy to," she said, flushing with pleasure.

Yet still she did not look at her brother.

"I have a musician who always travels with me. Cynvelin is a most excellent harpist," Rhys declared. "He has won the *Eisteddfod* two years running now. I'm sure he will be delighted to accompany you. There must be a song you both know."

Cordelia smiled, and Rhys signaled a man to come forward. A slender youth came forward carrying a fine-looking harp, obviously well cared for. He was tall and long-fingered, with an otherworldly look about his eyes that made Caradoc think of stories of men who were given magic musical gifts.

Cynvelin sat on the edge of the dais, then turned his gentle and intelligent brown eyes toward Cordelia.

She named a well known ballad about Tristan and Isolde. Cynvelin nodded, then put his hands on the strings as if they were the most delicate things in all creation.

While his sister sang, Caradoc simply let himself enjoy it. As the music filled the hall, it was as if all the troubles between them disappeared, rendered unimportant by the beauty of her voice and the music. She wasn't his sister calling him names, or disobeying him, or treating him with disrespectful insolence. She was the voice and the song, blending together in wondrous union.

The last notes died away, and brought him back to the hall. Like everyone else, he stamped his feet and clapped his hands with approval while, flushed with pleasure, Cordelia returned to her seat.

"Marvelous," Rhys declared. "There is nothing to equal a proud Welsh voice raised in song."

Fiona rose abruptly.

Caradoc stared at her. Her eyes flashed with fiery determination and her back was straight with pride as she waited for everyone in the hall to fall silent and realize she was on her feet and waiting.

For what? She had put up with much, and more since Rhys had come. What the devil was she going to do, denounce them all?

Fearing disaster, he put his hands on the arms of his chair, prepared to rise and stop her.

Then she closed her eyes and began to sing.

He sat back with wonder as her smooth, honey-sweet voice filled the hall. Finer than Cordelia. Better than Connor. Rich and warm, full and perfect, the notes soared and dipped, powerful and then soft as a mother's whisper to her baby, in a language he didn't understand. She sang with no accompaniment, Cynvelin as stunned as them all, at the virtuosity of Fiona's voice.

If his sister's had been the union of voice and ballad, Fiona's was the union of voice and song and feeling, for she imbued the words with such emotion, they seemed to explain his own. Although he did not understand the words, he knew it was a song of longing and desire, of hope and need—all the feelings that he had tried to conquer, only to know now, as he listened, that they were powerful and strong beyond conquest.

Then the longing ended, for it had been satisfied. He heard that in the joy and rapture in her voice, the trill of happiness, the pure bliss of pleasure.

Suddenly he felt as he had on their wedding night, and the morning after until, with a final, triumphant note, her song ended.

There was a moment of stupefied silence. Everyone in the hall must feel as he did, sharing her feelings, caught in the same web of sorrow and triumph.

To think he had no idea—none at all—that she could sing, let alone like that. That might have mollified even Ganore.

Lord Rhys began to clap. Around them, the hall burst into applause and shouts and stamps, from all except Cordelia. Her face burned red, and her hands didn't move in her lap.

Unfair, Cordelia. Petty and unjust.

"Wonderful, my lady," Rhys said. "That was Gaelic, was it not?"

"Yes, my lord," she replied as she faced him. "It is a song about Scotland, for I am as proud of my country as you are of yours."

"You must come to my *Eisteddfod*."

She gave him a haughty little smile and lifted her chin a bit. "But I am not Welsh, my lord. I am a Scot."

"Married to a Welshman."

"So while I am not good enough to be treated with courtesy for those things alone," she said, her voice strong and proud and firm as the mountains, "once I prove that a fine voice for singing is not unique to the Welsh, apparently I am worthy of your regard. I should have been worthy of your respect simply because I was Caradoc's wife, if for no personal reason, just as he is worthy of your respect because he is a noble lord. Indeed, he is worthy of respect for more than that—by virtue of his concern for his people that led him to marry for their sake rather than his own, and a hundred other things he does for them alone. There is not a more just, conscientious overlord in the land, and the people here should thank God for him every day and not take him for granted."

She shot Cordelia a stern look. "*No one* should take him for granted. Now if you will excuse me, my lord, I believe I shall retire. All this *Welshness* is overwhelming for a poor little Scot like me."

With that, she did not wait for a response but marched from the hall, leaving another stunned silence in her wake.

Caradoc wasn't angry as he watched her go. He was delighted and prouder than he had ever been in his life, even the day he was knighted.

He turned to Rhys and made no effort to mask his proud pleasure. "As I told you, my lord, she has many qualities. Now if you will excuse me, I believe I shall retire, too."

Chapter 14

Caradoc had no idea what to expect when he opened the door to their bedchamber. Fiona standing there like an irate goddess? Fiona acting as if nothing was the matter? Fiona naked in bed, waiting for him?

A quick glance revealed that whatever Rhonwen had taken from the room, the bed had been untouched. The room was dimmer than usual, for the candlestand was gone, but he could see Fiona plainly enough.

She sat at her dressing table clad in her silken shift and combing her long auburn hair. The candle on the table cast a pool of golden light upon her face, and with her unbound hair and simple white shift, she looked like an angel.

By the saints, she was lovely, and as today had

proven, an even more wonderful bride than he had assumed on that first day.

He wanted so much to kiss her and touch her, but first he *must* speak of what had happened tonight. "Why did you not tell me that you could sing?"

Although she kept combing, her shoulders tensed. "You never asked."

He had not meant to sound critical, but he must have. Damn his stupid tongue and awkward manner.

Yet he would try again. "You might have told me anyway." He tried to make a joke. "I could have died of shock."

"You didn't."

She still sounded angry, but perhaps not quite so much. "Fiona, I was proud of you today."

"Because I can sing."

"Not just for that," he protested as he took the comb and set it down. Gently taking her hands in his, he pulled her to her feet to look into her face. "Before that. Because you stood your ground like a warrior and did not let Rhys snub you. Because you will not be intimidated by him, or Cordelia, or anyone, including me. Because you showed Lord Rhys better than I ever could with a thousand words why I am not, and should not, be ashamed of my foreign wife."

"Because I can sing," she repeated, and he heard the distress beneath her words. "I am not pleased to think that if the people here now agree with your choice of bride, it is only because of that. That is not how I wish to earn their good regard. I wanted to show them that I could be a lady by my acts, if not by birth."

"If they do not yet, as I do, at least your voice is a beginning," he said softly. "But your music is not why you made me glad that I had married you. I was glad the day you came, and more the night we wed. I have been glad ever since, in many ways. But I am not good with words, Fiona, and didn't know how to tell you."

"Now you have," she whispered, smiling with such warmth and happiness, the world seemed newly made and fresh, with all the past pain and insecurity taken away.

She leaned against him, and never had he felt so wanted, not even when she had made love to him. "Caradoc, I do not need flowery speeches or poetic explanations. You have made me happier than I had ever hoped. You even made me feel beautiful."

"You *are* beautiful, Fiona, in a hundred ways the poets never sing of. They would put a woman on a pedestal, to admire from afar. I would admire you here, in my arms. Or as I watch you go about your day. I see your grace in the way you open that chest at the foot of our bed. I see the beauty of your pride in the carriage of your head. I see loveliness in the fierce sparkle of your eyes, brighter by far than the jewels another wears around her neck. I heard the beauty of your soul tonight when you sang. I am a lucky man, Fiona, because you choose to marry me. You blessed me beyond hope, when I thought I had none."

She did not speak. She could not. What words could *she* find to describe how he made her feel? There were none.

"Fiona, are you . . . are you crying?"

She nodded her head, her throat tight with emotion as a tear rolled down her cheek. She had come to Llanstephan angry and desperate, determined to repair a shameful error as best she could, yet now she could believe it was divine providence that had brought her here, because God knew that they needed each other.

He brushed the tear away with the tip of his finger. "I did not mean to make you cry."

"It is a happy tear, Caradoc," she whispered. "Like you, I find it hard to speak of what I feel most deeply. The words will not come, or if they do, they are not the right ones. So let us have no more words tonight, my husband." She smiled tremulously. "We have managed all right without them when we are alone."

He laughed softly, a low, deep sound of joy that echoed within her heart. His hand brushed her shoulder and swept down her arm, sending thrills of pleasure through her body.

She sighed as his hand skimmed her breast, moving toward the lacing of her shift. Her breathing quickened with anticipation when he untied the knot and pushed her garment from her shoulders. His lips glided over her skin as she clutched him, ready to surrender to the wonder of his mouth and body, liberated at last from the past and all the insecurity that went with it.

This night, they loved gently, as if marveling at their blessed fortune. They loved long, taking time to explore their bodies and their reactions to lips and caress. They loved playfully, free as they had never been with each other before.

This was a new beginning, and the past was unimportant.

It was indeed like the start of a new season, Fiona thought as she rode contentedly behind Caradoc the next morning. As if to also herald her happiness, the sun had risen in a cloudless sky, blue and free of so much as a hint of rain.

Even more wonderfully, for the first time mass did not seem a personal assault. Apparently Father Rhodri had indeed seen the error of his ways. Afterward, Lord Rhys had greeted her with all the deference she could ever want when she joined him to break the fast.

Cordelia had not been any more welcoming, but she had not expected that, and was simply grateful that the young woman had chosen to ignore her. Indeed, she believed Cordelia would never accept her, although the young woman was finally learning how it felt to be second-best. Considering how Cordelia had treated Caradoc, this was a lesson long overdue.

She herself would learn to live with her sister-in-law's hostility. After all, she had Caradoc's love, and that was far more important.

As recalcitrant Cordelia might prove, the servants now looked at her with guarded respect. Perhaps she should have performed for them sooner, but she had truly hoped she could win them over without having to entertain them first. She might never have sung at all, except that Cordelia looked so smug and Caradoc so ashamed that he could not.

After mass, Lord Rhys suggested a hunt. Caradoc readily agreed, inviting her to accompany them, and she gladly assented. She was no horsewoman, but it was a beautiful sunny day, and she did not want to stay inside.

Cordelia fairly leapt at the chance to ride out. Caradoc gave her a warning look, then announced that Jon-Bron and some of his soldiers would come, too. He said nothing about the thieves that might be stealing sheep, no doubt to keep an eye on his sister. Surely Cordelia would not dare to try to flee when surrounded by Jon-Bron, his men and such of Lord Rhys's retinue as cared to accompany them.

Now, she rode beside Fiona, the fiery Icarus fairly chaffing at the bit, the impatient look in his eye not very different from that of his mistress.

Regardless of Cordelia's perpetual, petulant frown, Fiona vowed to enjoy the day. Iain was locked in the past, where he belonged, Ganore was gone, Father Rhodri subdued, and the people respectful at last.

Best of all, though, was the new depth of understanding and emotion she shared with Caradoc. As she watched her handsome husband, she marveled to think that all she had ever hoped had transpired.

Well, except for one. Children.

But there was no reason to fear that could not also come true. Indeed, on this beautiful, glorious morning, she could easily envision herself with several of their children gathered about her, some with dark hair, some with auburn, some with blue eyes, some with green.

She sighed with happiness. It had been a long time—or so it seemed—since she had ridden along this road headed toward Llanstephan, trepidation and fear dogging her with every lurch of the cart. She had been afraid Iain was hiding behind each bush or tree, waiting to leap out and demand that she marry him.

Her gaze returned to Caradoc, so tall and fine, his hips moving forward and back with the motion of his horse, reminding her of other times his hips moved like that. She smiled to herself, knowing that the heat coursing through her body was not solely from the sun.

A pebble struck her horse's rump, hard enough to draw blood.

The normally placid mare whinnied with pain and reared. Panic seized Fiona as it galloped off the road at a breakneck pace.

The horse tore across a bracken-covered hillside. Panting, winded from the jostling that threatened to send her toppling to the ground, Fiona could scarcely see where they were going, or find her breath to scream.

Every impulse, every thought congealed into just one thing: hold on, with a grip tight as a death throe.

She heard other hoof beats, not just the mare's.

Praise God! Caradoc had come.

The horseman came beside her and reached for her reins.

Like some vision from a nightmare, Iain MacLachlann tried to grab hold of her reins.

New determination burst through her panic, and she tugged on the reins not to pull the horse to a stop, but to turn away from Iain.

Iain snarled a curse.

She dug her heels into the mare's side, paying little heed to where they went. Over another hill, through a meadow, toward a wood. The beast was winded, but she didn't care. She kicked again and again, trying to get away.

But the mare was no fiery stallion like Icarus; Caradoc had told her this horse was a gentle beast, perfect for someone who was not used to riding. Perfect for a slow ride on a fine day. Terrible for getting away from Iain.

He caught hold of the reins and steered them toward the wood. She raised her hand and tried to hit Iain's arm. She missed.

He laughed in that mocking way he had. Laughed at her futile efforts. Laughed like the demon he was come to destroy her happiness.

Where was Caradoc? Would he come to her aid? What if Iain killed her?

They reached the wood and plunged into the sudden dimness. Dappled sunlight lit the ground, and she realized they were on a path.

Did Iain lead her into this wood on purpose? For what reason? To kill her for leaving him, out of sight of prying eyes?

Oh, God, she prayed as they finally slowed, *protect me. Send Caradoc, even if he sees Iain. Even if I must tell him everything.*

At last Iain brought the mare to a halt in a clearing. Where it was in relation to Llanstephan or how far they had come, she had no idea.

All she knew was that she had to get away from Iain. Again.

Anger nipped at her fear, and fought to overcome it. She was married. She was the wife of the lord of Llanstephan Fawr, and there was nothing Iain could do about that. She must make him see that he would gain nothing by hurting her. The vain, arrogant bully should let her go.

"What do you want, Iain?" she demanded, breathing hard as she glared into his detestable face.

"I wanted to speak with my betrothed alone. I thought you were never going to leave the castle, but my patience has finally been rewarded. Fergus has a fine aim with a stone, does he no'?" Iain said with a loathsome smile as his stallion snorted and refooted.

"You are not my betrothed," she declared, all the while trying to decide what to do. Get down and run? He would give chase, and he would be faster than she could be, for she was weighted down with skirt.

Try to ride away? Her horse was exhausted nearly to collapse, sweat streaked and breathing as hard as she.

She must buy some time. Surely Caradoc would come after her, with Jon-Bron and his soldiers. "Iain, this is madness. What little there was between us is finished. If you are wise, you will let me go."

His expression altered, to one of unmasked fury and scorn. "Finished? I am not finished with you, my love."

"I am not your love, and never were. All you loved was my dowry, and it belongs to another now."

Iain swung down from his horse and approached the mare, grabbing its bridle and glaring up at her. "So I have heard. You have taken from me what was mine and given it to a Welshman. What am I to think about that, eh?"

From her saddle, she looked down on him as if he were made of dung—as he had made her feel. "You should think that you erred when you made it so clear that you wanted my money far more than me."

"How can you say that when we shared your bed?"

"To my eternal shame! You seduced me with the sure and certain belief that once you had done so, my money was as good as yours. You made that very clear afterward, bragging how your money would be welcomed by William, and wondering aloud what titles he would reward you with once you had bought them. Did you think I was too stupid not to understand what that really meant? Did you believe I was too infatuated to care? If I was a fool—and by God, I was!—you were a greater one, and by following me here, you prove you are a greater one still. You will get nothing more from me, ever. I have wed another, and that is the end of it."

"No, it is not," Iain snarled as he grabbed her arm and hauled her, struggling, from the mare.

He shoved her up against the horse's quivering, sweaty, blood-streaked flank, blocking her escape with his body. "What, no kiss? And once you could not get enough of them."

Triumph gleamed in his eyes as a cruel smile

curved his lips. "I want what you owe me, Fiona. I have already taken a small payment in some sheep, but that is not nearly enough."

She would not look away. She faced him squarely, hatred and pride strengthening her. "I owe you *nothing* and the penalty for stealing sheep is death."

"Will your husband agree, do you think?" Iain asked with a vestige of his sly, seductive charm. "Or do you think he will agree with me that a broken betrothal is worth some kind of compensation, especially when he learns how close we were? And I must say, Fiona, I thought you would at least wed a clever man. Neither he nor his men have come close to finding us or the sheep we've slaughtered."

She should have told Caradoc about Iain the day she arrived. She should have been honest from the start. With her secrecy, she had given Iain the power to make this threat.

Iain's eyes gleamed with cruel jubilation. "Ah, he does not know about me and all that we have shared, does he? I heard he was a proud man. Welsh or not, a proud man might not want a bride who was not a virgin. You must have tricked him into believing you came a maiden to his bed." His eyes hardened. "You condemn me for deception, but what else would you call what you have done?"

God help her, he was right.

And his presence here and now must be the punishment sent down from heaven.

"Tell me, Fiona," he asked with smooth mockery, "has he heard of me at all?"

She did not answer. She was trapped, trapped by

her own unwillingness to tell Caradoc the whole truth about why she had come to Llanstephan.

"Better and better," Iain murmured, his voice dripping with vile delight. "Well, then, my dearest, darling Fiona, unless you want him to, you should make it worth my while to quietly creep back to Scotland."

Her head snapped up. "Like the snake you are!"

Her insult meant nothing to him. "If you do not want your husband to know *all* about us, you will bring me a thousand marks. I know you've got that much in coin and jewels alone. You showed me, remember? There is a village a few miles from here, Pontyfrydd. Go to the tavern there in two days with the money and wait for me."

He believed he had won. That by following her and threatening her, he was triumphant. That she would pay for his silence rather than risk her husband's wrath.

He knew nothing of love. He would never comprehend that feeling and the strength it could imbue.

And the trust. As Caradoc loved her, he would understand.

She had made a mistake not telling him of her past, but she would confess all, and gladly, for she had faith in his love.

"You haven't grown any more intelligent since I left you, I see," she replied, scorn in every syllable. "Even if I wanted to pay for your silence, the lady of Llanstephan can hardly ride to a tavern and sit waiting."

"I think the lady of Llanstephan is clever enough

to come up with an explanation." Iain grabbed her upper arms and held her so tight, she had to bite her lip to keep from crying out. "I mean it, Fiona. I'm not leaving until you pay me."

He moved suffocatingly closer and ran his hand over her breast, a gross parody of Caradoc's gentle caresses. "Otherwise, my dearest darling, I might just as well kill you as I have your husband's sheep and that one over there."

He smiled another terrible smile as he nodded to something to his right. She followed his gaze, to see Ganore's limp body hanging from the limb of a chestnut tree.

Her knees buckled and bile rose in her throat. That was why he had led her here—to show her this. To prove how vicious he could be, as if she needed it.

She closed her eyes and struggled not to faint.

"I met her yesterday at an inn near here," he said as calmly as if he were discussing an old friend. "Very irate she was, and most uncomplimentary toward you. You must have had a hard time with that one in the household. So I thought to give you a wedding gift, my love, by silencing her hateful tongue.

"It was a mistake to leave me, Fiona," he continued, pressing his body up against her, his voice hoarse with lust, as if her distress inflamed him. "You must have realized that on your wedding night. After me, your husband was surely a disappointment."

Her eyes blazed open, and fierce vitality returned to her limbs.

"What I realized that night, Iain," she said with

cold and determined disdain, "was that you have very little to brag about, and even less finesse when it comes to using it."

His face reddened as he drew back and raised his hand. She steeled herself for the blow, when she heard her name being called.

"Caradoc," she gasped, relief coursing through her.

Iain let go of her, stepped backward and yanked his sword from its scabbard. Before she could move, he put the tip of the blade at her throat. "Make a sound—*one sound*—I'll slit your throat."

Nervous now and tense, he glanced again toward the sound of pounding hoof beats, and she saw her chance. She dodged away and around the horse's rump. At the same time, Caradoc galloped into the clearing and pulled his horse to a halt. As she stumbled toward him, he swung down and unsheathed his sword as he ran to meet her.

When she reached him, he shoved her behind him, out of harm's way.

"Hold, or I'll kill you!" he ordered Iain, his face red with rage.

Holding his sword loosely in his hand, Iain strolled closer, not a whit upset as the horses shifted, more nervous than Iain, it seemed. "Well, well, well, Fiona, so this is the man you married. I was told he looked like a bear, and I see the description wasn't far off the mark."

Caradoc glanced at her, puzzlement in his eyes, his guard lowered.

"Be careful, Caradoc," she cried out, pointing. "He killed Ganore."

Caradoc followed her gesture and stiffened when he saw the body.

"He's stolen and slaughtered your sheep, too!"

Ominously enraged, Caradoc's brows lowered. "My men are on the way," he growled to Iain. "You had best give yourself up."

"To be hung? I think not," Iain scoffed, a mocking smile on his face. "Do you think I have come here alone? Fiona should remember that I have plenty of friends."

From the wood, a gang of men stepped out, their weapons drawn and like Iain clad in *feileadh mor* and *cuarans*. "You remember Fergus and the others, Fiona."

"You know these men?" Caradoc demanded. He pointed at Iain with his blade. "You know this one?"

Before she could answer, their hunting party appeared at the edge of the clearing. The outnumbered Scots began to move back as Lord Rhys, Jon-Bron and the rest reined in their mounts and regarded the scene before them with surprise and suspicion.

"Hold and stay where you are!" Iain shouted at his men. "Are you cowards, or Scots?"

The Scotsmen exchanged wary glances, but they halted nonetheless.

"Caradoc, what is happening here?" Lord Rhys demanded, walking his horse closer to him. "Who is this Scot and these men?"

"They have done murder and slaughtered my sheep," Caradoc declared, by the tone of his voice barely containing his rage.

Then, with dismay, Fiona spotted Cordelia in the middle of the group of men, Jon-Bron close beside her, for protection, no doubt. It would not be long before Cordelia saw Ganore's body, and Fiona's own heartache increased. Whatever she had felt for Ganore, Cordelia would be grief-stricken.

Iain sauntered toward Lord Rhys, apparently quite calm, but Fiona saw that his grip on the hilt of his sword was so tight, his knuckles were white. "Who the devil are you?"

The mounted nobleman regarded Iain scornfully. "I am Lord Rhys of Wales, Scotsman, and you had best watch your tongue, whoever you are."

"*I* am Iain MacLachlann, lately betrothed to Fiona MacDougal. I have come to demand recompense for her broken promise."

Oh, heaven help her, to see such a look on her husband's face—shock and dismay, and something worse besides in the depths of his brilliant blue eyes.

"Is that true, Fiona?" he asked, his deep voice deathly calm.

She was tempted to lie and deny what Iain had said.

To deceive him again.

He did not deserve to be lied to. He never had, and if Iain had been evil to mislead her, so she had been not to tell Caradoc the whole truth about why she had sought him out.

Iain was right. She had behaved no better than he. She, who had come here silently denouncing Iain, had acted no better, and the realization utterly humbled her.

But she would be honest with her husband now, come what may. He deserved no less. "Yes, I was betrothed."

"I knew it!" Cordelia cried out from the midst of their soldiers. "And Ganore knew it, too! I told you not to trust her, Caradoc. She's a lying *slut!*"

Caradoc didn't so much as glance at his sister and the others. Fiona likewise ignored them as she faced her husband. She stood before him, guilty, full of remorse, and as she looked at him, the light in his eyes seemed to change to something brilliantly bitter, like ice glittering on a freezing yet sunny day, or the way a loyal man regards a traitor.

Oh, God, what had she done? Whatever shame and distress she had felt the morning Iain left her, it returned a thousand fold, and more. She had lost nothing when she left Iain. She would lose all if she lost Caradoc.

"Yes, I agreed to marry him, until I learned he wanted my money, and not me," she desperately explained to her stoic husband, his lack of response terrifying her more than being on the runaway horse. "When I did, I left Dunburn and came here."

"Of course I wanted you, or there would be no money," Iain jeered. "Wasn't that why this man wed you, Fiona? For money?"

"I *offered* it to him. He did not think to take it from me—and he never claimed to love me, as you did."

Not until after. Not until last night.

"How can you say that, Fiona?" Iain demanded, his voice mocking. "You know I *loved* you."

She saw the triumphant gleam in his eye. Felt him as good as raise his sword to strike her dead. He was going to tell Caradoc everything.

As she should have done.

As she must do now, regardless of who would

hear. "Caradoc, we made love, this blackguard and I, to my eternal shame. He wanted to be sure of me and my money. Afterward I realized that I had been a fool."

"Whore!" Cordelia screamed. "Harlot! Deceiving him with the blood on the sheets!"

So, Ganore had looked and talked of it, too, Fiona thought, too numb to be more upset. She had expected it, and it had come to pass.

Cordelia's outburst appeared to have no effect on Caradoc. He might have been carved from stone, so still did he stand. Even his eyes—he looked at her like she was a stranger to him.

Then he moved at last, shifting his weight as if life were returning to his limbs before he pivoted to glare at Iain. "I am going to kill you, MacLachlann, as I will be well within my rights to do, for you have murdered my servant and killed my sheep, too."

It was then Cordelia saw Ganore. A great wail burst from her throat, and she dismounted despite Jon-Bron's attempts to make her stay with him and the soldiers.

Fiona watched with dismay as Cordelia ran to the chestnut tree and threw herself on her knees beneath Ganore's body. Sobbing, she begged someone to cut her down. None of the men moved, for their attention was fully on the two men in the center of the clearing, and their hands were all on the hilts of their swords.

"I did not kill that woman or his sheep," Iain retorted, not a whit disturbed by Cordelia's grief. "I found her hanging here the same as you. And a kinsman of King William of Scotland would never have to stoop to stealing sheep."

She had known he was a clever actor, but this was brazen beyond anything she had ever seen or thought to.

"He's upset because he's just found out his wife was supposed to marry me," Iain went on over Cordelia's keening wails, "so he's made these foolish accusations. Why on earth would I murder an old woman? What would I want his sheep for?"

"My lord, he himself told me he killed Ganore," Fiona declared. "And the sheep. He wanted me to pay for his silence about my broken betrothal and to prove how serious he was, he killed Ganore. As for why he killed the sheep, I expect he and his men ate them, for Iain MacLachlann has barely two coppers to his name."

"She lies, my lord," Iain said—but his knuckles were whiter yet.

"So it is the word of Lady Fiona against yours, MacLachlann," Lord Rhys declared.

"The word of a merchant's daughter against the word of a kinsman of King William?"

That was why he was so bold. He thought that even if Lord Rhys believed him guilty, he would not want to risk offending William.

Oh, God, she fervently prayed, *do not let that be so. And please, please, oh, God, let Caradoc see that I am sorry for what I have done and forgive me.*

"I believe my wife, my lord," Caradoc said, coming to stand beside her—but not close enough to touch. "I accuse this man of killing my maidservant and slaughtering my sheep. He has also insulted my wife. I will settle these matters here and now. By combat."

"Don't be a fool, Caradoc!" Jon-Bron cried, hurrying to him. "You can't fight a man like that. He's probably been fighting every day of his life, one way or another, brute that he is. You've got no chance."

Caradoc turned to his friend with a determined, cold-eyed stare. "I said I will settle this matter by combat. As I am overlord to you, you have no right to challenge my decision."

Thus rebuked, Jon-Bron flushed and went back to rejoin men, and terror for Caradoc destroyed the first hope that his declaration about believing her had created. Jon-Bron was right—Iain was a well trained, ruthless fighter. She had never even seen Caradoc draw a sword.

But if he would not listen to Jon-Bron, what could she say to stop him? He was filled with savage, grim determination. He didn't even really look like her loving husband at all.

In desperation, she turned to Iain, prepared to offer him the money he wanted, no matter what Caradoc said. Anything, rather than have Caradoc risk his life.

Iain was afraid. True fear was in his usually confident eyes, and he nervously licked his lips.

He should see the wisdom of leaving, for Caradoc looked enraged enough to kill without compunction, especially a man he believed had done murder. "Iain—"

Caradoc grabbed her arm. "Do not speak to that

man. Not now and not ever again. This is between the two of us now, not you."

A wail built in her throat at his cold, heartless words. *What had she done?*

"I will be delighted to fight you," Iain announced with the merest hint of a quaver in his voice, "if Lord Rhys approves—"

"He does not have to approve. I am lord here, by order of the king of England. I issue the challenge and you will agree, or you will put your tail between your legs and run back to Scotland, never to set foot on my land or in Wales again."

"Don't fight him, Caradoc!" Cordelia cried out as she struggled to her feet. "He'll kill you."

Her brother silenced her with one stern look.

"Very well, Caradoc, if this is what you want," Rhys said with obvious reluctance.

Rhys surveyed the other men, both Scots and Welsh. "You hear how thin is, then? One man against the other, and thus the matter will be determined. Is it agreed?"

The Scots nodded. The men of the hunting party looked far less convinced, but they did not protest. How could they, when Caradoc stood so firm of purpose, his very visage daring anyone to try to deny him this fight?

Rhys backed his horse away, until he was closer to his men, leaving the center of the clearing to Caradoc and his opponent.

"My lady, come stand by me," Rhys ordered, as imperious as Caradoc.

Despite the nobleman's command, she hesitated,

trying to think of some way to stop this fight before Caradoc was hurt or even killed.

"Fiona, go to Lord Rhys," Caradoc said, his expression stern and unyielding, his voice as firm as the ground beneath her feet, his whole body ready to fight.

He would brook no dissent, and thus she had no choice but to watch and wait, and pray that God would grant Caradoc the victory.

Cordelia sank weeping to the ground once more and Fiona wanted to join in her lamentations.

But she could not. Not yet. Now she needed her strength to look and see the final outcome of her deception, to live with the anguish of knowing that she was responsible for Iain's presence here.

When she reached Lord Rhys, he called out, "Let it begin!"

Caradoc crouched, while Iain, smiling with what was more like a grimace, began to circle him.

"Not a swordsman, are you, Taffy?" he jeered, using the common slang for a Welshman that set the Welshmen muttering. "You're holding your weapon like an ax, not a sword. Too bad Fiona's going to be widowed. She'll look like a fright in black."

Caradoc slowly, silently pivoted, following his adversary with his eyes.

Please, God, give him the victory.

"Did she moan for you, too, Taffy, when you took her, as she did for me? And make those little whimpers in the back of her throat?"

Humiliation swept through her. More punishment, as she felt the stares and looks of the gathered men. But she would gladly have endured a thousand times worse if it could have prevented this confrontation.

Iain suddenly stopped circling and his sword lashed out like a snake, slicing through the sleeve of Caradoc's tunic. A damp red patch appeared and expanded around the torn fabric.

Fiona fell to her knees, unable to breathe, while Cordelia's scream pierced the air as Iain's knife had pierced the cloth.

Oh, God, oh, God, she inwardly keened, her hands clasped as she rocked, but her eyes wide open as if closing them would kill him. *Save him. Help him. This is not his fault. It is mine, all mine. Do not make him pay for my folly and my pride with his life.*

"Is she worth it, Taffy?" Iain mocked, the sight of the blood making him bolder as he danced around Caradoc. "No beauty, Fiona, to die for. As for that old woman, I did you both a favor there. The tongue on her!"

Caradoc's grim expression didn't alter as he regarded his enemy. Still he pivoted slowly as Iain danced, as if he was uncertain what to do.

"Patience, man, patience!" Jon-Bron called out. "Wait for an opening."

Did Caradoc hear his friend? She could not tell. Around her, the noise increased—Cordelia's panicked cries, the men muttering, her own heart pounding as if it wanted to flee her body or kill her trying.

"You should have stayed in Dunburn, Fiona," Iain sneered as his sword lashed out again, making Caradoc jump back. "Married the better man. Look at him—useless with a sword. Probably useless in every—"

Suddenly Caradoc swung his sword not at Iain's chest, which was protected by the way he held his sword upright, or his arms, but at the calf of his leg.

A cry went up from the watching Welshmen as the blow connected with a sickening sound. Then, with a shriek of pain and dismay, Iain crumpled and fell, his sword dropping beside him. Fiona held her breath as Iain clutched his wounded limb, the blood pouring out from between his fingers while he groaned in writhing agony.

"Still think I'm useless?" Caradoc growled as he raised his sword to strike.

Chapter 15

"He just stood there looking at the man's body for a while," Jon-Bron said later in Bronwyn's tavern, his mood as grim as a lost cause. The ale in his mug, and that of Dafydd and his brothers, warmed as it sat untouched on the table. "Not a word, not a sound. And then he walked over to Ganore. Cradled her like a child as he cut her down."

Every man listening looked grave, and the place had been crowded with curious and concerned villagers as the tale of that day's event spread like rushing wind down the valley.

"He said nothing to Fiona?" Bran-Bron asked softly.

"Nothing, and her kneeling there as white as a pillar of salt. He talked to Cordelia as he helped her to her horse and led her home, but he just left Fiona."

Eifion wet his lips anxiously. "Didn't *she* say anything? Or cry?"

"No. She went to her horse and followed them. I sent two of the men with her. I couldn't leave myself, because we had the rest of the Scots to deal with. The leader of them that was left was quick enough to say the dead fellow was their clansman, so they had been duty-bound to come with him, but they had no quarrel with Lord Rhys or Caradoc, so they would go back to Scotland and call the matter settled."

"Cowards," Emlyn-Bron muttered under his breath.

"What, would you have had a battle?" Jon-Bron demanded, cuffing his younger brother on the back of the head. "A war between Welsh and Scot started here at Llanstephan?"

"Jon's right," Dafydd said. "Bad that would have been, to have something like that laid on our doorstep." He returned his attention to the garrison commander. "Where is he now?"

"You know how he is," Jon-Bron replied. "Goes to ground like a wounded bear. He's in his solar, and who knows when he'll come out?"

Dafydd sighed. "I'm that glad I wasn't there to watch. I would have been beside myself, expecting him to be cut down like Goliath."

"He's improved, but by God, I never thought Caradoc would ever be able to beat anybody in a fight," Jon-Bron agreed, "let alone kill a man. Not got it in him, I thought. I tried to talk him out of it, but the eyes of him! He would have attacked me if I had touched him, I think. A warrior after all, our

Caradoc, for that Iain was as good as any I've seen. Fast, like a fox."

"Caradoc got him in the leg first, eh?" Emlyn-Bron asked as he wiped up a bit of spilled ale with his finger. "Not the usual thing to do."

"Aye, but it worked. Then brought down his sword like a headsman's ax," Jon-Bron said.

"I wish I'd seen that," Bran-Bron remarked. "Must have been some blow."

The others gave him a disgusted look.

"Well, I do," he mumbled, finally lifting his ale either because he was truly thirsty or to hide his embarrassment. "He's strong, is Caradoc."

The others grudgingly conceded his point.

"What about our lady?" Bronwyn demanded as she set down new mugs of ale. "How is she?"

They started, not having seen Bronwyn approach in the dimness.

"I don't know," Jon-Bron replied, taken aback by both her appearance and her question. "I didn't go into the hall. Too much weeping and wailing for me over Ganore. Cordelia crying a storm, and the other women sobbing." His expression hardened. "Besides, it's all Fiona's fault with her secret lover—"

Bronwyn rapped him on the head so hard and so sharply with her knuckle, the brawny soldier cried out in pain.

"All her fault!" she chided, her hands on her hips and her eyes fairly glowing with disgust. "She made a mistake. She had a lover who tricked her so she left him and found a man who deserved her. It's as obvious as that nose of yours, Dafydd, that the man was a lout. What other kind of man would come all the way here after her and demand to be compensated because she jilted him? He should have been too ashamed of himself."

"You seem to know a great deal about what happened," Dafydd muttered into his mug.

Bronwyn tossed her raven tresses. "One of Lord Rhys's men stopped by here and told me about it. And I've met a few smooth, handsome men like that Scot. Fairly live to trick honest women, they do, and it's a mercy to my sex that Caradoc has rid the world of one of them. Aye, and not just women, I don't doubt. A dishonorable blackguard like that cheats everybody." She waved her hand at them. "Now drink up and be gone. I'm that put out with the lot of you!"

She turned on her heel and marched off toward the kitchen.

"Well, she's certainly on Fiona's side," Jon-Bron unnecessarily noted after a moment's silence.

Dafydd cleared his throat. "So am I. She loves Caradoc dear, and I think we should give her another chance. I hope he will, and if he asks my advice, that is what it will be."

"I doubt Cordelia will agree," Eifion observed. "I'm foreseeing a leaving, and I don't think it's going to be his sister."

Dafydd sighed wearily. "I hope that proves as true as the rest of your predictions."

"Dafydd?" a woman's voice whispered in the still of the night.

Sleepless, he swiftly sat up and peered into the

darkness surrounding him. "Who is it? What do you want?"

"It's me, Rhonwen."

"Rhonwen? What is it? What more has happened?"

She reached out and patted him comfortingly on the arm. "Nothing more," she assured him. "But I must speak to you nevertheless."

Dafydd quickly got out of bed. He struck flint and steel to make a light. The rush flared up before settling back into a steady flame, revealing Rhonwen's face still red and puffy from crying.

Her gaze flicked down his naked body. Surprisingly embarrassed by her swift inspection, although plenty of women had seen him naked before, he pulled on his breeches and tunic.

"Now then," he said, sitting back on his bed. "Why have you come to me in the dead of night, Rhonwen? I hardly think you intend to seduce me."

"How can you say such a thing at a time like this?" she demanded as her eyes filled with more tears. One slipped and caught on her lash, trembling for a moment before it fell upon her cheek.

"I'm sorry. Habit, that is, and wrong of me now." He took hold of her slender hands in his and rubbed them to warm them. Very small and very frail they felt, despite the calluses of hard work.

"What brings you here?" he asked with gentle sincerity.

"Lord Caradoc has gone into the solar and he hasn't come out. You know it might be days before he does."

"Aye. He's acted this way before. He'll come out eventually."

Rhonwen's expression turned fierce. "But in the meantime my sweet and gentle lady is sitting outside the solar waiting for him. She's been there since she returned, and she refuses to leave that drafty tower. She says she's going to stay there until he'll talk to her."

"By the saints," Dafydd murmured, running his hand over his forehead. "Do you think she means it?"

Rhonwen grimly nodded. "Aye, she does, and she looks that resolved, I think she will, no matter how cold or stiff she gets."

"He'll come out when he's hungry," Dafydd offered, trying to be hopeful.

"That doesn't mean he'll talk to her. You know how he can be, like after his parents died." She clasped her hands and regarded Dafydd anxiously. "He'll listen to you, though. You can make him come out."

Dafydd shook his head, a mournful expression on his face. "No, I can't. I've tried before when his parents died and it was no use." He eyed Rhonwen speculatively. "What about Lady Fiona? Can't you try again to get her to go? She likes you, and justly so."

A look passed over Rhonwen's face, as if his words had been a compliment she hadn't expected.

The look disappeared as quickly as it came.

"I've tried," she said despondently. "I've been trying all night, but she just says she has to talk to her husband and she'll wait there until she can. I took her a stool and a blanket, but she's going to get sick if she sits in that tower too long. If he won't come out and she won't leave, what are we to do?"

He sighed and once more warmed her cold hands in his. "I don't know if there is anything we *can* do. I think they're both that stubborn."

"But won't you *try*?" Rhonwen pleaded, her soft brown eyes begging him in a way that went straight to the hidden, serious center of his heart. "They love each other and it's breaking my heart. I heard all about it in the kitchen. I don't say my lady was right not to tell him everything, but I can understand why she didn't. He should, too. His pride is hurt, but that's no reason—"

She burst into tears and covered her face with her slender hands.

Dafydd pulled her into his arms and gently embraced her. "It just so happens I agree with you, and so do other people."

After a moment, he sat back and wiped her tears from her cheek with his thumb. "I'll see what I can do."

Sniffling, she smiled, her lips quivering. She reached out for the rushlight as he drew on his boots.

As she led the way to the door, the glow illuminated her face, and it occurred to Dafydd that it would be a wonderful thing to wake in the night with that pretty, loyal woman lying softly beside him.

Her forehead resting upon her knees, her back against the unyielding stones of the wall, Fiona waited as she had waited for hours before this. Inside the solar, Caradoc made no sound. He had made no sound since she had arrived. She had knocked and pleaded and knocked again, all to no avail.

She could imagine the thoughts running through his head, and she did not fault Caradoc for them. She had drunk from the same cup of bitterness. She, too, had been deceived, as Caradoc had been deceived by her.

For whatever reason, she had tricked him with that blood. She had been wrong not to tell him about Iain, and foolish to believe that she could put her past completely and secretly behind her. She should have realized that Iain would not countenance anything like a rejection, for unlike Caradoc, he was a vain and selfish man.

But now, after hours had passed, she could not accept Caradoc's continuing solitude, or that their situations were exactly the same. She had offered Caradoc only her dowry and her body, but she had given him her heart. She felt *more* for Caradoc than she had promised, not less. Surely he could see that. Surely he would realize that she was not like Iain. Yes, she had been wrong to deceive him on their wedding night, but at the time, she thought she had no choice. She had not known Caradoc well then, and feared that he would demand an explanation that her pride made her loath to give.

He had said the Welsh didn't put as much stock in virginity as others. Had that been a lie? Or had the Norman part of him proven stronger than the Welsh when it came to that? Was his pride so sorely wounded, their relationship was destroyed?

She had to find out, and she would stay here until she could.

Weary from her long vigil, she closed her eyes, hearing again Cordelia's wrenching sobs that had not abated by the time she had returned to the hall. Indeed, coupled with the crying of the other women, it seemed worse.

And then had come Cordelia's fierce accusations. "She would still be here if not for you! She would still be *alive*!"

It was the truth. Remorse for this, too, filled her, even as she tried to convince herself that the woman's death was not her fault. Iain had done the deed. His hand had struck the fatal blow.

Yet it was she who had brought Iain here, however unknowingly. It was because of Ganore's connection to her that she was dead.

Sighing and clutching the blanket Rhonwen had brought her, Fiona got stiffly to her feet and, putting her hands on the curve of her back, arched to relieve the ache.

A man's voice broke the silence. "My lady?"

She started and peered at the stairs. Dafydd stepped out into the shaft of dawn's first light coming in through a loophole.

"Rhonwen is right to want you gone from this drafty place lest you take sick," he said with soft-spoken sympathy that both surprised and relieved her.

She had not only been thinking of Caradoc as she sat here in the dark. A part of her had been worrying about the opinion of everyone else in Llanstephan.

"She is preparing the brazier in your chamber

against the damp and chill," he continued. "Will you not retire? I will take up your vigil while you rest, and I promise to fetch you if he comes out."

She shook her head. "If he comes out, I intend to be here." She lifted her arms, making the blanket flare out like a sail. "I have this, so I am warm enough, and Rhonwen also brought me a stool to sit upon."

"Do you want to get sick, then, to punish him for staying in his solar? Is that it?"

"No!" she retorted, his charge offending her. "It is not for that I wait. I will not go from here until I speak with him." Her gaze faltered, for she had not realized how much she valued Dafydd's merry friendship until she feared it was destroyed, too. "Do you think ill of me, Dafydd?"

He gave her a small smile and shook his head. "No, I don't. You should have been honest with him, of course, but I do not think he is right to behave this way. Caradoc, of all men, should understand wounded pride. That is what keeps him in that solar, for one thing. But regardless of where the hurt comes from, when he's upset, he goes to ground, like a wounded animal, and if he didn't care so much for you, it would have hurt him less."

She nodded. "I have wounded him very deeply."

"You're not the first."

She sat on the stool again. "It does not comfort me to think that I am like everyone else who has hurt him," she said quietly, regret for her subterfuge eating at her once more.

"Look you, my lady, give it time," Dafydd pleaded. "Give *him* time. He'll come out eventually."

"To act as if he has not been wounded, I don't doubt. His misery will be buried, but still there, festering, sickening what was once good between us." She shook her head. "No, Dafydd. I made a terrible mistake, and I admit it. I will not leave here until I can apologize and try to make him understand."

Dafydd frowned. Then he mused a moment before briskly stepping up to the door and knocking loudly. The sound reverberated through the stairwell as Fiona anxiously got to her feet. Maybe Dafydd would succeed where she had failed.

"Caradoc!" he called out. "It's Dafydd."

She held her breath.

Caradoc made no response.

"It is dawn and your wife has been sitting out here all night getting chilled through her bones waiting to talk to you," Dafydd continued. "Will you not speak with her?"

Still silence.

Dafydd held out his hands in surrender as he turned back to her. He gazed at her face a moment, then tried again. "Lord Rhys will be leaving. Will you come out to say your farewells?"

Only more silence rewarded his question.

"The wool merchants will be here soon, too, Caradoc. You will want to deal with them, won't you? Or should we leave that to your wife?"

The door abruptly opened. Caradoc stood there, pale, majestic, his face stubbled, dried blood caked on the torn right sleeve of his tunic, and his eyes gleamed. Hard and cold as ice on the river in the dead of winter they looked as he glared at them.

Hell was not eternal flame and fire. Hell was freezing cold, hardening hearts and making what had been warm and alive as frigid as a corpse in the snow.

"I am still the lord of Llanstephan Fawr, and I will do my duty," Caradoc rumbled, his words hoarse and stern. "I will bid Lord Rhys farewell in due course. I will conduct my business with the wool merchants when it is necessary." He ran his hostile gaze over Fiona. "As for my wife, I will deal with her in my own way."

He went to close the door.

She rushed forward and blocked the opening with her body. She would not let him shut her out again. "I have things to say to you!"

He regarded her disdainfully, as scornful as ever Ganore had been. "I am done with talking."

"You may be, but I am not. Not until I tell you everything and explain. I understand how you feel—"

"You know *nothing* of how I feel!"

"I do! Why do you think I ran away from Iain? I—"

Caradoc grabbed her arm and pulled her into the solar, slamming the door in Dafydd's startled face.

"Will you have this out in front of an audience, too?" he demanded. "By the saints, woman, didn't you reveal your sin in front of enough men yesterday?"

She straightened her shoulders. She was finally alone with him, and he was finally talking. If she had to bear a few insults, that was a price she was willing to pay. "If you had let me in sooner, he wouldn't have been there."

He planted his feet and crossed his arms, regarding her with that same scorn. "What excuse will you offer for what you have done?"

"I'm sorry I didn't tell you about Iain, but I was ashamed of how I let myself be duped by his false vows of love. I didn't want anybody to know about that, especially you. Nor did I expect Iain to follow me here."

The depths of his eyes flickered, but his visage did not alter. "Go away and leave me alone, Fiona. Tell Dafydd to go, too."

Not yet. She would not leave yet. "Caradoc, you must listen—"

"Are you *deaf*?" he roared, his face reddening and his hands balling into fists. "I am tired of talk! I am sick unto death of lies and truths revealed that are better buried! Get out and leave me *alone*!"

The easiest thing to do would be to do as he commanded. To give up trying to make him understand, and go away. But that would mean the end of all the wonderful intimacy and affection that had been between them, and she was sure the breech would be irreparable.

She was not willing to have her folly ruin their chance for happiness together, at least not until she had tried her best. "No, I will not go away. Not until you have listened to what I have to say."

He continued to glower, but he did not order her to leave, so she said. "When I left Dunburn I did not wish to tell anyone about Iain. I thought he would give me up and leave me alone, but even I underestimated his greed and his vanity that could not bear to lose anything, not even a woman he did not love."

"So you came here to escape your greedy lover and get a title, too."

Still cold, still like a rock in winter.

"Escape I craved, because I was ashamed. And I thought a title would be a reason you would accept without question. Not only did I want to forget Iain, I didn't want to admit that I had thought about you for years, and dreamed of you, and hoped to marry you. I spoke only of practicalities and not of my heart, for it was raw and wounded then. I was glad—aye, and relieved, I will confess—when you agreed to marry me. Yet you were always more than a means to escape or get a title to me. You are, and always have been, ten times the better man."

"A bargain, then, I was," he replied, his voice calm, as the very sick are calm, too ill to react more strongly. "A good thing Connor was not here, or not so much of a bargain would you have had."

He sat in his chair like a judge behind his table, while Fiona stood anxiously before him. "I didn't want Connor. I wanted *you*."

How much Caradoc wanted to believe her! To still be under the pleasant delusion that he was her first choice, not one made out of desperation and despair.

That she had come here because she thought him worthy, not because she sought refuge and escape, and he was the first man who came to mind who could offer both.

He yearned to believe that she was honest and plainspoken, and that he could trust her. That she had not purposefully misled him until now he did not know what was truth and what a lie anymore. "If it was as you say, why not tell this Iain how you felt to his face? You had no qualms about criticizing my temper when Sir Ralph came here."

"Because I didn't care enough about him to explain, and he didn't care about me."

He must pay no heed to the anguish in her eyes or the remorse in her voice. She was so obviously capable of duping him, he could not take anything about her at face value anymore. "Was he your only lover?"

Why not ask? He was too benumbed to feel any more pain.

She grabbed his arms and looked at him with fervent, pleading eyes. "Yes! That is the truth. You must believe me."

He could feel his frozen heart beginning to melt with the heat of her impassioned words. But the cold bitterness of his pain was still too new, too unbearable, for the warmth to best it. "I would have believed you had you told me this of your own volition when you first arrived. The loss of your virginity I could have overlooked, as long as you did not bear another man's child. It is the deliberate deception I cannot countenance, Fiona. I remember the blood upon the sheets. Ganore said it was a whore's trick, and now I find that she was right."

"But Caradoc—"

"It is the *deception*, Fiona!" he shouted, rising to his feet as his temper surged into life out of the ruins of his feelings. "How can I ever trust you? What else might I discover about my wife? I told you what Ganore said to me about my mother. I trusted you with that." His temper died as the thing he feared most found a quieter voice. "Is the love you said you felt for me a lie, too?"

Her anxious gaze searched his face. "How can you say that after the nights we have shared?"

"Because you have not been honest with me," he retorted as he strode toward the window, then turned back to face her, glad of the distance he had put between them. "Because I should have guessed that Caradoc of Llanstephan was nobody's first choice. Because I should have understood that you are as mercenary as this man you claim to hate."

"Mercenary?" she gasped, her palms folded flat against her chest as if to shield it from a blow.

"What else would you call it? What else am I to believe? You came to me to hide, not to love. You gave me your money in exchange for my title, my protection and sharing my bed at night. A bargain we struck, and I was a fool to think it was more."

"No, from the first it was more than that for me!" she cried, splaying her hands on the table between them. "I do love you, Caradoc. You must believe me! I never loved him, not as I love you."

"So you say now that the truth is out."

He turned away, unable to look at her, ashamed of what he had felt and how he had been fooled.

Ashamed of what he still felt, despite everything. What he feared he would always feel, because he cared for her so much. If he loved her less, the truth would not—*could* not—hurt like this. This pain, though . . . Could the torment of eternal damnation be worse?

She hurried to him and grasped his upper arms, making him face her. "I never *loved* Iain! He made me feel pretty and desired and I was lonely, so I let him seduce me. But I had already chosen you, long before I ever met Iain MacLachlann. Then I lost my way. When I realized what he was, I found it again and came here, to where my heart had always been. You must believe me, Caradoc."

Oh, God, he wanted to! He wanted to think that it was as she said—that she had wanted him and only fallen victim to a clever seducer who preyed upon her weakness.

But she was no feeble female. He had seen her strength. God help him, he had admired her for it. "How *can* I believe you, Fiona? You robbed me of that choice when you spread the blood in our bed."

The vital sparkle in her eyes dimmed, and she stepped back, away from him.

"Caradoc, I should have told you all," she began, her voice steady but flat, as if all her feelings had departed from her. "I didn't because I was *afraid*. Afraid you wouldn't want me, despite the dowry. Afraid you wouldn't respect me—as you do not now. Have you never been afraid, Caradoc? Have you never feared that your past was going to utterly ruin your present, and your future?"

"Of course I have, Fiona," he grimly replied. "I knew that fear when Ganore told me Edgar of Llanstephan was not my natural father."

"Think then how you would feel if someone came to tell you that her words were indeed a lie. The relief, the happiness, the hope—those are what I felt when you agreed to marry me and we first made love. I had real hope then that I could put the past behind me, and keep it there. But I could not. Yet I swear to you that you now know all there is to know, and I do love you."

Her chin came up, and the life returned to her glimmering green eyes. "But apparently my secret has destroyed whatever love you felt for me. If I do not have your love, if you think you can never trust me again, if you cannot understand or forgive, I will go from here."

She meant it. He saw that in her eyes, her face, the very stance of her body as she spoke. She would leave Llanstephan if he told her to.

Despite everything, he loved her. He would always love her.

But trust her? Could he ever have absolute faith in her again?

To trust Fiona or let her go was the ultimate ultimatum. His whole future, his happiness, his fate, rode upon it.

Trust her, or let her go, never to see her again, to be with her again, to hear her voice or feel her body beside his in the still, small hours of the night.

Suddenly, the answer was as simple as taking one breath after another.

No one could ever take her place in his heart, for it was a place she had created. She had made the opening and broken through the walls. She had filled his heart and his life with joy and happiness. He loved her, he needed her, and as she stood before him, still proud despite everything, he believed all that she had said.

As he loved her, he would trust her.

He took her hands in his and spoke haltingly, trying to find the words he needed. "I do know what it is to be afraid, Fiona. I have been afraid every day of my life. Afraid I was not good enough. Afraid no one could ever love me, not even my parents. Afraid I was going to lose my home.

"And then you came, and for the first time, the fear lifted. More than that, I was truly proud of myself, not for my rank or my family, but for *me*."

Her soft eyes filled with sympathy, and hope. "I . . ."

He put his finger gently to her lips. "Let me finish, Fiona, or I may never be able to bring myself to say this again."

She nodded, then moved her mouth a little, giving his fingertip a kiss.

He took hold of her hands again, determined to say what was in his heart as best he could. "To think that I was wrong about you, that you had lied to me and I had been a fool not to see it . . . that was the worst pain of all. Or so I thought, until you told me you would leave me. *That* would be the worst, Fiona. Please, do not go. Do not leave me alone."

She took his face gently between her palms and kissed him. Tenderly. Lovingly. "I will stay, but only if you can truly trust me."

"I can."

Then he gathered her into his arms and sealed his vow with a kiss. She was Fiona the Fair, the princess of his heart who had rescued him from his prison of isolation and despair, and he would never let her go.

He had come so close to losing her! He had nearly pushed away the one person who had ever made him feel that he was enough, just as he was. The thought made him weak.

He shivered as she ran her fingers through his curls to pull him even closer. His heartbeat thundered like galloping steeds as their kiss deepened, and her tongue sinuously entered his mouth.

She drew back and regarded him with a mixture of concern and dread as she put her hand to his forehead. "You're so warm. And you're sweating."

What was wrong with that, he vaguely wondered. "It's warm in here."

"And you're so pale."

She shoved up the torn sleeve on his wounded arm, to reveal the filthy, ink-covered rag he had wrapped around it when he first came into the solar. Dried blood was caked upon it.

She untied the rough bandage and then recoiled, for the wound was a horror of blood and bruise.

And infection.

She stared at the wound, aghast, then pulled him to a chair. "Sit down."

He thankfully obeyed, for he felt weak and sick. "It's just the sight of it," he mumbled more to himself than to her as an explanation for the nausea that was fast overtaking him.

"I must fetch a physician, or an apothecary," Fiona said as she ran to the door.

"Fiona!" he uselessly called after her, for she was already gone.

He wanted to tell her that there was no such person in Llanstephan.

Chapter 16

"**W**hat do you mean, there is no physician?" Fiona demanded incredulously, staring at Jon-Bron and his brothers as they stood before her in the barracks.

Necessity had driven any fears about what these men must think of her out of mind. All that mattered was Caradoc. His condition was serious, and time was of the essence. So was the proper care, and she did not know enough about healing to give it.

The men, far from looking at her with anger or hostility, looked as upset as she.

"Llanstephan is too small a place," Emlyn-Bron explained, buckling his belt around his leather tunic.

"Where is the nearest one?" she desperately demanded of Jon-Bron. "We must send someone to fetch him at once."

327

"Shrewsbury," he answered, his eyes burning with dread. "That's a good ways—"

"I don't care if it's the end of the earth," she cried. "Send your best rider on the fastest mount to Shrewsbury at once. Tell him that he is to bring a physician, or if he cannot find one, an apothecary, but a physician would be best."

"He may not—"

"Tell him!" she commanded as sternly and imperiously as Caradoc. Then her gaze faltered, and her voice trembled as her fear returned. "Otherwise, Caradoc may . . ."

She could not bring herself to say more.

Jon-Bron nodded, turned and nearly collided with Cordelia, who marched up to the grim group, her red-rimmed eyes blazing and her chin lifted. As Caradoc had seemed an Olympian god that first day, she looked like a Valkyrie.

"Is it true?" she demanded. "Is Caradoc sick from the wound he got yesterday fighting your lover?"

Fiona clenched her jaw at the word she used to describe Iain, then annoyance slipped from her mind. "Yes. The wound is infected."

"Fetch Bronwyn," Cordelia ordered Emlyn-Bron.

"Bronwyn?" Fiona questioned.

"She knows much of medicine." Cordelia's lips turned up in a condescending smile. "She is not only famous for her skills in bed."

Fiona didn't care what the woman did or where, so long as she helped Caradoc. "I am sending Jon-Bron for a physician, too. I have seen infected wounds before, and this one is very serious. No matter how skilled Bronwyn may be in anything—"

"It will be a waste of the money Caradoc sold himself for to bring a physician here. Bronwyn will—"

"No," Fiona said, shaking her head and firmly resolved. "I will have the best for Caradoc, and spend whatever it takes of the money I gave him. I will not have him die for want of coin."

Cordelia's pale face blanched. "Die?" she mouthed.

"I hope not, but I will not risk it. Go now, Jon-Bron, as fast—"

"*I* am the best rider in Llanstephan with the fastest horse," Cordelia interrupted, her eyes bright with sudden determination as the color returned to her cheeks. "I will fetch the physician."

Fiona suddenly realized she was staring at a mirror image. Not of looks, for Cordelia was by far the more beautiful, but in spirit. And pride. And stubbornness. The same in strength, unwilling to yield.

The very qualities that had enabled her to leave Iain and come here were those Cordelia had marshaled against her all along.

These were the qualities that would bring a physician to her beloved as fast as humanly possible.

Yet even with the image of Caradoc pale to the lips in her frantic mind, she could not put them both at risk. It was dangerous for a woman to travel alone, and if something were to happen before Cordelia reached Shrewsbury . . . "You cannot. It is too risky for—"

"I'll go with her," Jon-Bron offered. "I'm not so good a rider and my horse is not so fast, but I can keep up if she stays on the road."

"I'll stay on the road," Cordelia vowed.

Fiona looked from one to the other, and made her decision. "Go, then."

As Cordelia turned on her heel, Fiona put out her hand to hold her back a moment. "Tell the physician that I will pay whatever he asks if he comes immediately."

"I will," Cordelia answered. "I will bring him back if I have to threaten him with death."

"And he'll believe you, too."

At Fiona's vote of confidence, Cordelia made a little smile that was so like Caradoc's, a sob caught in Fiona's throat. "He's strong, that brother of mine, like a rock that nothing can break, and heaven knows, I've tried."

Fiona embraced her swiftly, then stepped back. "I hope you're right. Now go with God, and hurry."

A short time later, Fiona nervously watched Bronwyn examine Caradoc's wound. Then the dark-haired, full figured beauty straightened and fixed her eye on the lord of Llanstephan.

"You didn't even wash it, did you?" she charged.

Caradoc shook his head. Lying there so pale, sweating and weak, he seemed to put the lie to what Cordelia had said about his strength. "I had other things on my mind."

Bronwyn gave him a sour frown. "Men," she said with disgust. "Lackwits, the lot of you, when it comes to such things. Well, you'll remember next time, after you have to drink the potion of chickweed I shall make you. Aye, and you'll have a poultice of it, too, and it will stink."

She turned to Fiona. "I'll make up the potion and poultice directly."

"Thank you."

"And you sleep, nit," she ordered her overlord, who did look like a sick little boy propped up in their bed, chastened and remorseful. "I'm going to have a little word with your good lady."

She took Fiona by the arm and steered her outside into the hall.

"It's not good, this," she said, and the relief Fiona had felt disintegrated. "It could get beyond my skill."

Weak with fear and fatigue, Fiona leaned against the wall. This was all her fault and if Caradoc did not recover . . . if he died . . .

"I've seen worse, though. The potion may work, and Emlyn tells me you sent to Shrewsbury for a physician?"

"Yes," she whispered.

"Good, is that," Bronwyn said with a brisk nod of her head that made Fiona feel a little better. "He's strong, is our Caradoc."

"That's what Cordelia said, too."

"Well, there then!" Bronwyn cried, as if that confirmed it and thus Caradoc must recover.

A knowing, friendly smile grew on her face. "But I am thinking that you, of all women, should know how strong he is."

Fiona did know, and she began to feel a little better still. Not only did talk of his strength help; so did the woman's bantering manner. If she could joke, Caradoc could not be so very ill.

Footsteps sounded on the steps, and in the next moment, Lord Rhys appeared. He halted and ran a favorably appraising gaze over Bronwyn, who didn't seem at all bothered by it.

But then, Fiona supposed, she was probably used to it.

"My lord, this is Bronwyn," she said by way of introduction. "She has come to tend to the wound in Caradoc's arm, which I fear has become infected."

"So I heard," he replied, his attention still on Bronwyn more than her.

"Well, then, I'll leave you to see to your husband, my lady," Bronwyn said, flicking a lock of her thick dark hair over her shoulder as she passed Lord Rhys.

"My lord, if you don't mind," Fiona said, "I think my husband should rest."

Rhys stopped watching Bronwyn as she disappeared down the steps and turned his wayward attention to her. "I did not think it was very serious."

"It may be. I have sent for a physician."

"Good. I would take it very amiss indeed if he died."

He spoke as if he thought she wished that.

She clenched her jaw and struggled not to betray her annoyance. "As would I."

"I set a great deal of store in Caradoc. He is everything a lord seeks in the people with whom he is allied."

Anger rose within her. To think Rhys believed she, of all people, did not appreciate Caradoc's merits! "I know that, and that is why I sought him out, despite what you heard yesterday. That is why I offered him my money, to save his home and him from disgrace. A pity it is, my lord, that you should value him so much, yet you could not bring yourself to come to his aid."

Rhys colored, and his brows lowered as if he wasn't used to being criticized. She didn't care if he was or not, after what he had said to her and the way he had treated her husband.

"Do you think he would have taken money from me to pay his taxes if I had offered? You should know him better than that by now."

"If he was desperate enough to marry a Scottish merchant's daughter he barely knew to keep his home, don't you think he might have? But of course, thinking him too proud saved you the trouble, and the coin."

"Of course I value him. Why do you think I cared so much who he married?" Rhys demanded, crossing his arms. "Why else did I take the trouble to come and see you for myself? Because he, the best of men, is worthy of the best of women."

His eyes narrowed and she steeled herself for the onslaught, which was not long in coming. "So let me ask you, my lady, was it true, what you said about that villainous Scot? He seduced you and you left him to come to Caradoc?"

She faced him squarely. The truth was out, and Caradoc had forgiven her. Therefore, she didn't care very much at all what this man thought. "Yes, my lord."

"And Caradoc did not know?"

"No. I didn't want him to know I had been a fool."

"Yet you admit that you were wrong to deceive him?"

"Yes, my lord, and he has forgiven me the deception."

Rhys did not mask his surprise.

"It is the truth, my lord, and when he is better, he can tell you for himself."

"Perhaps I should ask him now."

Her feet planted, her hands balled into fists at her sides, Fiona faced the most powerful man in Wales with a fierce righteousness that would have given anyone pause. "I think not. He needs to rest and I will not allow you to interrogate him on a matter that we have settled."

Rhys blinked and looked at her for a long moment, as if expecting her to change her mind.

When she did not, he yielded. "Very well, my lady, I shall not intrude either into your husband's bedchamber or upon your hospitality. I take my leave of you. Tell Caradoc I hope he recovers quickly."

"I shall, my lord. Farewell."

He turned to go, then glanced back to survey her head to toe one more time. "So this is the kind of women Scotland breeds. I think I shall have to be careful of your sons."

Fiona wiped Caradoc's feverish brow and changed the sweat-soaked linen as she waited anxiously for Cordelia and Jon-Bron to return with a

physician. She had been waiting for three long, ago-
nizing days, during which she never left the bedchamber. Rhonwen, as steady and competent a
helper as she could ever want, had run herself
nearly to exhaustion fetching cold water, hot water,
broth, bread—anything Fiona requested.

While Caradoc grew worse. How much longer
could he endure with this fever raging through him?

He started to mutter again through dry, cracked
lips. He tossed his head upon the damp pillow, un-
consciously revealing his innermost thoughts and
feelings. He murmured of the deep vulnerability
felt by a boy trying so hard to please and being rejected. He talked of his envy for a cherished, popular brother, and his own disgust that he should feel
that way. He whispered of his anguish over
Cordelia's scornful treatment and Ganore's tale of
his true father.

And listening, she grew to love him even more.

She also sent fervent prayers to heaven that he be
allowed to live. He was too young to die. They had
not had enough time. It was not just. It was not fair.

Especially when she was beginning to believe
that she carried his child.

Where was Cordelia and Jon-Bron? Why had they
not come back? What if they were too late?

Then she heard a sound that brought her leaping
to her feet and rushing to the door: the booted foot-
falls of someone taking the steps two at a time. Before she reached it, the door banged open and
Cordelia ran into the room. Her hair was a tousled,
wild mess, her clothes mud-stained and sweaty, her

boots filthy—but her triumphant smile made everything else unimportant.

"We've brought Arundel of Shrewsbury, the best physician outside of London," she declared, coming to a panting halt and smiling at Fiona. "He's coming up the steps behind me."

Then she stared at her stricken brother. "Tell me we're not too late."

Fiona went to her sister-in-law and embraced her, full of gratitude for what she had done. "He lives, and while he lives, I hope."

A middle-aged man, his dark hair flecked with gray, and wearing a long black tunic, swept into the room. He ignored them and went directly to the bed, where he set a wooden box with a leather handle beside Caradoc.

"I told him what happened," Cordelia explained, clutching Fiona's hand as they watched Arundel examine Caradoc's face, his eyes, and the strength of his pulse.

Arundel lifted the poultice and sniffed. He likewise sniffed the wound before he sat back. He was so grave and silent, all the joy that Fiona felt began to seep away.

She glanced at Cordelia and saw that she looked just as frightened.

"How serious is it?" she asked, too tense to do more than whisper.

"Leave such concerns to the physician, my lady," Arundel replied with a patronizing smile. "Your husband is in good hands now. Lady Cordelia, please ask the cook to prepare a nice beef stew and some clear chicken broth."

"I'm not sure Caradoc will be able to eat stew," Fiona said warily and with a horrible doubt about the man's abilities if he thought Caradoc was in any state to eat.

"The stock is for Lord Caradoc, and the stew will be for me," the physician replied. "It has been a hard day's ride."

"I'll go at once," Cordelia said, and after giving Caradoc a final, worried glance, she hurried from the room.

Arundel rose and began to roll up the sleeves of his tunic, and the white linen shirt exposed beneath.

"Now it would be best if we could keep the visitors to this chamber to a minimum, my lady," he announced. "Too many people makes for agitation, and the balance of your husband's humors has already been disturbed enough. That includes you, my lady. I'm sure there is another chamber you may use while I tend to your husband."

She had no intention of leaving Caradoc for any length of time while he was so sick. "This is my chamber, too. I shall do whatever you ask of me, but I must be allowed to help tend to my husband."

Arundel did not look happy, but he must have understood that she was not asking his permission. She was telling him how it would be. "Very well, my lady. If you can be quiet."

She fought the urge to frown or otherwise betray any animosity to this man who was, after all, also a guest in their household. "Yes, I can be quiet. Now, how serious is his condition?"

He gave her another condescending smile. "You must not worry, my lady, for a *physician* is here."

He spoke to her as if she were a child he was patting on the head. She wouldn't have been surprised if he had added, "Run along."

She was not a child, and she would not be condescended to, especially now. "I asked you a question, Arundel. How serious is my husband's illness?"

Arundel's eyes flared with indignation, as if she presumed far too much by asking that. "Since you insist upon knowing, his blood is poisoned, and although the chickweed was a good course of action, it may have been too little, too late. I fear he is going to die, and soon."

She felt for a chair and sat heavily. She had thought the rational part of her mind had realized this, but *no* part of her was prepared to accept that Caradoc's wound was mortal.

Arundel seemed mollified by her dismay, for suddenly his indignation disappeared, and a compassionate look appeared upon his face. "Fortunately, it appears your husband is a strong man, and healthy before this, and there are still other remedies to try."

He smiled when he finished, as if he had just pronounced Caradoc cured.

She would abase herself at his feet if he made Caradoc better. She would keep silent and defer to him, and she would forgive this arrogant, pompous fellow anything so long as he cured Caradoc.

His fingers on Caradoc's pulse, Arundel frowned. Caradoc was still insensible with fever, although Arundel had been there for two days and tended to him with everything in his power. Like Fiona, he had rested little and eaten sparingly as they changed poultices and made medicines and bled him. He had been as dedicated to his patient as she could have hoped, in spite of his arrogant manner, yet nothing seemed to work.

Outside, the rain fell, the gray skies so dark, she had lit candles to help Arundel see.

She looked at the physician expectantly as he slowly lowered Caradoc's hand, and the expression on his face made her stomach plummet. She began to tremble uncontrollably, her whole body quaking with a fear such as she had never known, not even when Iain had held his sword at her throat.

"If the fever does not break tonight," Arundel said slowly, "I fear we must expect the worst, my lady."

Staring down at her husband's pale, gaunt face, she refused to accept it. "There must be more we can do. Another potion... different herbs... There must be *something* ..."

With a face full of pity, and no vestige of the patronizing learned man confident in his abilities to hold back the Angel of Death, Arundel patted her on the arm. "There is nothing more to try. I have done all I can. The rest is up to God." He heaved himself to his feet. "Now I am going to sleep. Call me at once if there is any change."

He was abandoning them. Not even his pompous pride could compel him to remain.

It must be hopeless.

She knelt beside the bed and tried to accept the inevitable, as she had accepted so many other things in her life. Her mother's death so long ago. Her father's. The realization that Iain had never loved her.

The knowledge that she had grievously erred by not being honest with her husband.

She must accept this, too.

She pressed a kiss upon Caradoc's hot hand, thinking of the brief joy they had shared. *Too brief.*

She must be grateful for the time they had together. *Too brief.*

She wet Caradoc's lips with cool water from the ewer on the table beside the bed. She changed the poultice and forced more of the chickweed brew down his parched throat.

Then she knelt and began to pray.

For it was as Arundel had said, as it had always been.

Caradoc was in God's hands.

She was kneeling still when Arundel returned at dawn, her forehead on her husband's outstretched hand.

But when she raised her head to look at the physician, a glorious smile blossomed on her face and tears filled her eyes. For a long moment, she could not speak. Her heart was too full of relief and gratitude, as her prayers had been since the first rays of the morning sun had streaked the sky.

For after the long and desperate days of nursing, the countless urgent prayers and her final, fervent vigil, she had touched her husband's limp hand.

And discovered that the fever had broken.

Dafydd bit his lip as he walked toward Cordelia. She sat in the kitchen, her shoulders slumped and dark circles under her eyes. None of the inhabitants of Llanstephan, castle or village, had slept easily lately. Only now, as Caradoc lay near death, did the realization that he might someday be gone and another overlord come to take his place seem to occur to them.

Difficult it was to imagine the castle without him in it, more difficult yet to imagine another lord in his place, even Connor the merry, the laughing, the tempestuous. Connor was a charming fellow, they all agreed, but what kind of master would he be? A pleasure for feast times and festivals, but what about the rest of the time? Responsible and dutiful? Not likely.

Eifion had finally angered Bronwyn so much with his gloomy predictions of the future that she had banned him from the tavern.

Gwillym, the maidservants, the spit boy, and the scullery maids warily watched as Dafydd sat on the bench beside the weeping Cordelia.

"No change?" he asked softly.

She shook her head.

"Rhonwen's taken up some soup," Gwillym offered quietly, lifting the ladle from the broth he had been stirring in a big iron pot on the massive hearth.

"And something for the physician and my lady," Lowri added, sniffing and wiping her eyes with the edge of her sleeve. "Worn to nothing, she is."

"Aye," Una said, setting out some bread before Dafydd and laying a knife nearby. "She's going to kill herself taking care of him."

Dafydd sighed and nodded his agreement. "Many a Welsh noblewoman would leave the nursing to the servants. I think our Caradoc chose well for himself."

"Yes, he did," Cordelia declared, raising her tearstained face, her gray eyes blazing. "And I'll hit anyone who says otherwise!"

Dafydd stroked her arm, as if she were a dog who suddenly snapped. "Aye, but I don't think there will be anyone saying anything against her now. And thank God for you, too, Cordelia, for fetching the physician. Ah, Rhonwen!"

He jumped to his feet as the young woman appeared at the entrance to the kitchen, a tray covered with a linen napkin in her hands. The activity in the kitchen came to a halt and all eyes turned to Rhonwen as she set the tray down.

"How is he this morning?" Dafydd asked, his whole body tense with anxiety.

A smile bloomed upon her face, as welcome and unexpected as a flower after months of drought. "The fever broke last night. Arundel says he's going to get better."

"God be praised!" Dafydd cried.

Then he grabbed her hands, tugged her to him and kissed her full on the lips. And a long kiss it was, too, for it seemed Rhonwen was in no hurry to end it.

Cordelia rose unsteadily, her expression hopeful, yet still wary. "You're sure?" she asked when they finally parted.

Rhonwen dragged her gaze away from Dafydd's equally flushed face. "Aye, that's what he said," she confirmed. "And look."

She pulled the covering off the tray she had carried and triumphantly pointed to an empty bowl. "He ate all that soup this morning."

"Thank God I made his favorite!" Gwillym cried, clasping his hands and raising his eyes to heaven as if his soup was the cure.

Rhonwen addressed Cordelia, sympathy joining with the joy in her expression. "Lady Fiona says you are to come right away to see him."

Cordelia didn't hesitate. She ran out the door at once.

Smiling, Rhonwen spoke to Gwillym. "She also says there must be a feast tonight, even if my lord cannot come down for it, or she, neither, for she still won't leave him, but it's joyful she is, and the eyes of her when she looks at him—!"

She seemed to realize that she had been rattling on without interruption or censure.

Dafydd sat on the bench and gestured to a spot beside him. "Come sit by me a moment, Rhonwen-the-steadfast-and-fair, and tell us what else the physician said."

With a shy smile that made her even more beautiful in Dafydd's eyes, she did.

Fiona reached out to caress Caradoc's stubbled cheek. "How do you feel?"

"Like I've been dead awhile," he whispered hoarsely, and meaning it.

He had no idea how long he had been abed because of his wound, but judging by the weariness in Fiona's face, it must have been a long time.

She quickly filled a goblet with water. Sitting sideways on the bed she lifted his head and helped him to drink. That took more effort than he expected, and he fell back, astonishingly weary. "How long have I been sick?"

"Too long. Five days, in fact. You frightened me, Caradoc," she gently chastised him, happy and tearful at the same time as she again caressed his cheek, his five-day growth of beard rough against her palm.

She assumed what struck him as a distinctly maternal pose. "I *never* want you to do anything like this again," she said. "First you draw your sword like some sort of tournament champion and nearly get yourself killed, then you hide yourself away like a hermit while your blood gets poisoned."

His blood had been *poisoned*? God save him, no wonder he had been so sick.

"You must promise me that you'll never be so foolish and stubborn again."

"I shall do my best not to be." He mustered a smile. "But I confess I could grow to like the tending."

"I shall soon be too busy," she said pertly.

"I really must stop trying to make jokes," he muttered. "They never work."

She smiled, and beautiful happiness sparkled in her green eyes. "I shall be too busy, because I shall have a truly helpless babe to tend. *Our* helpless babe."

"Fiona!"

Surprise and delight tumbled through him. He grabbed her hand with all the strength he possessed and struggled to sit up. "Stop!" she commanded, gently pushing him back down. "You are to rest. The physician says so."

He obeyed, but he pulled her down beside him and kissed her deeply, ardently, joyfully. Wonderfully.

To think she was with child—their child!

A new happiness beyond anything he had ever known, even Fiona's love, filled him. A new life. A new beginning—for both of them, too.

Panting, she broke the kiss and sat back, out of reach. "You're supposed to rest. The physician says you are not to exert yourself, in *any* way." She tilted her head to regard him critically but with love shining from her eyes. "Shall I have Jon-Bron detail a guard to make sure you obey your physician's orders?"

Caradoc scowled, half serious in his annoyance. He wanted to kiss her more than he wanted to sleep.

But she needed to sleep, too. He could see how tired she was, and if she was with child . . .

Then he got an idea. "Lie here beside me and rest with me."

Her lips turned up in a wonderfully wicked smile of approval. "Rest, you say?"

"Caradoc!"

Cordelia rushed into the chamber and, unaware of how she had startled and interrupted them, skittered to a halt beside the bed as Fiona rose. She clasped her hands together as if she might fly out the window if she did not contain her excitement.

"I've been so afraid you were going to die, Caradoc," she said fervently. "If you had, I would never have forgiven myself for quarreling with you all the time. I'm sorry for that, and for everything else I've done to upset you. And I'm glad you married Fiona. She saved your life, Arundel says, and I believe him. I'm sorry I was cruel to her, too."

Then she threw herself on his chest and started to sob.

Her tearful confession was nearly as surprising as Fiona's revelation. Not quite, but almost—and as welcome, too.

"It's all right, Cordelia," he said softly, stroking her back and smiling at Fiona over her shoulder.

"It was Cordelia who went for the physician, Caradoc," his lovely Fiona told him. "With Jon-Bron as escort."

"So you see, all that riding had some use after all," Cordelia declared as she straightened, her apparent defiance reduced by her sniffling and her tremulous smile.

"I'm glad I let you, then," he replied with mock gravity.

"You *let* me? I didn't think you even knew what I was doing."

"Of course I knew. I knew every time you gave your guards the slip. I was just too wary of your temper to try to stop you."

"Wary? Of my temper?" she demanded incredulously. "You never seemed to care how angry I was."

"Well, I did."

"Cordelia," Fiona interjected gently, "he really should rest now. There will be plenty of time for talk later."

Cordelia nodded and obeyed without protest,

and he was most impressed. It seemed his illness was having one benefit, at least.

"Until later, Caradoc," his sister said in farewell. "And do as Fiona says."

"Always has to have the last word," Caradoc noted to his wife as he patted the bed beside him. "Come here, Fiona," he crooned.

"You really should rest, my love."

"Then sing me a lullaby in your beautiful voice," he wheedled, truly hoping for a song, but more for her to sit beside him.

Before she could, Dafydd careered into the room. "Saints be praised, there he is, awake at last."

"Are you drunk?" Caradoc inquired, his momentary frustration at this new interruption giving way in the face of his friend's obvious delight.

"Only with joy, my friend, only with joy," Dafydd retorted as he bounced toward the bed. He airily kissed his hand to Fiona. "A wonderful day, my lady, is it not?"

"I know you're glad to see him, but he's supposed to rest," Fiona said, by her tone a little peeved and frustrated herself.

Regardless of her admonition, Dafydd plunked himself on the bed. "Oh, I have permission from Arundel. In the kitchen he is now, bragging how he saved your life, Caradoc. Me, I think it was Fiona. And sweet little Rhonwen, too. Either way, estate business I have, you see. I promise not to take long."

"Very well," Fiona conceded. She sat on the stool beside her dressing table and, with her elbow resting on it, leaned her head on her hand.

In the next moment, she was asleep.

She must be exhausted, and while he appreciated her nursing and her concern, he worried she had done too much.

Dafydd playfully punched his leg, drawing Caradoc's attention from his worried contemplation of his wife.

"What the devil were you about, man?" he demanded. "Thought to be the center of things, did you? You picked a poor way to do it, if you ask me. Half the women been in tears and the other at prayer. A man could hardly get a bite to eat or so much as a word from one of them."

Caradoc gave him a skeptical look. "What about *sweet little Rhonwen*?"

"I tell you, it's ashamed of myself I am, to think all this time she was right there under my nose." He grinned, as irrepressible and merry as always. "Maybe that was the problem, eh? I couldn't see her in the shade of it."

"What is this business you mentioned?"

"The wool merchants have come to buy the fleece. They've been hanging about waiting, because nobody dared to deal for you. That Heribert is driving Bronwyn mad with his gossip, and the rest of them have drunk nearly all the ale in her tavern. It's getting to be a serious state, Caradoc, so somebody had better deal with them. Who shall it be if you can't get out of bed? Me?"

Caradoc shook his head. "Fiona."

"You want your wife to sell the fleece?"

Caradoc nodded, absolutely certain that this was

the perfect thing to do. "She's a wool merchant's daughter, after all."

"Ah, you're right. She ought to know something of the trade."

"And she drives quite a bargain."

Dafydd chuckled. "Back to your old self in no time, you'll be. Eifion's been predicting your death these past five days. I'll be glad to be able to tell him he's wrong again."

"Not so glad as I am. Is Lord Rhys still here?"

"No."

Caradoc sighed and closed his eyes, relieved. "Thank God."

"Aye, he's a trouble. I think he'll be back sooner rather than later next time, though. He kept talking about Fiona's voice. Mind, he seems wary of her, too, for all that, and last I heard, he was muttering something about your sons." Dafydd fixed him with a sharp and shrewd look. "So, are you keeping more secrets from me, Caradoc, or what?

Caradoc thought it was too early to tell the world Fiona's joyous news, but he couldn't help giving a hint, so he winked.

Dafydd's eyes lit up like a bonfire on a winter's night.

"Keep it a secret, Dafydd, though," Caradoc urged, suddenly regretting he had revealed that news. "It's early days yet."

Dafydd put his hand to his heart as if mortally offended. "I can keep a secret. Why, did I announce to all and sundry that you were passionately in love with your wife?"

"I never told you I was."

"Eyes in my head I have, and I've known you all your life. Indeed, I think I knew it before you did."

"It might have made things easier if you'd told *me* what I was feeling," Caradoc growled.

Dafydd chortled. "Ah, you're on the mend, all right." He sobered when Caradoc yawned, for he was still weak and weary despite his joy. "About the sheep those louts stole . . . I am thinking we could ask for compensation from King William since that bastard you killed was so proud of his connection to the king."

Caradoc wanted nothing more to do with King William or any man from Scotland. "Leave it."

Fiona's head jerked up. "I must have nodded off," she said, stifling a yawn. Her beautiful eyes narrowed. "How long have you been here? He's supposed—"

"To rest. I know," Dafydd finished as he got to his feet. "We're done with business." He grinned. "Caradoc here says you're to deal with the wool merchants."

Obviously taken aback, she limply pointed to her chest. "Me?"

"Yes, you," Caradoc answered, giving her a loving smile that could not convey all the love he had for her in his heart, but was better than words. Yet he would tell her some things, too. "I trust you absolutely."

Her loving smile blossomed.

Blushing as if he had interrupted them making love, Dafydd backed toward the door. "I think it's time I left and let you rest like you're supposed to. And your lady, too, I should think."

"We shall rest," Caradoc promised.

"You had better, you bloody great git."

"Blackguard."

At the threshold of the chamber, Dafydd's homely face shone with a beaming smile of warmth and relief. "I'm glad you're not dead, you nit."

"So am I," Caradoc murmured as he reached for Fiona and pulled her down beside him, to nestle against him at last. "So am I."

Chapter 17

Four weeks later, on a warm and mellow August evening, Caradoc was finally well enough to come down to eat in the hall. Everyone was there for the occasion, except Arundel, who had gone back to Shrewsbury, fully intending, Fiona was sure, to brag of how he had cured Caradoc of Llanstephan with his incredible skill.

Dafydd sat close beside Rhonwen. In fact, he was so close to her, Fiona wasn't sure how Rhonwen was going to move her right arm to eat. But she looked so happy, and he looked so totally besotted, she was sure food was not uppermost on either of their minds.

Father Rhodri, who had been offering thanksgiving masses for days, rose to say grace.

"Oh, God and St. David, patron saint of Wales," he began humbly, in a normal voice, although loud and resonant enough to reach the back of the hall, "thank You for shining Your countenance upon us, especially those who have been ill. We also give thanks for those who live Your love in the care they give to others.

"Oh God, I would also ask Your forgiveness for those who have not acted with Christian goodness, mercy or charity, but who have seen the error of their ways and seek to reform.

"And finally, Heavenly Father, we thank You for this bounty before us. Amen."

As the priest sat down in the silence that followed, Caradoc held up his hand to command the attention of everyone there.

"I want to thank you all for your good wishes," he said, his voice not as strong as it had been, but firm and steady. "And I have some joyful news I would share with you now." He looked at Fiona with love blatant in his blue eyes. "My wonderful wife is with child."

The hall erupted into spontaneous cheers and claps and stamping feet, and in the next moment, Fiona was being nearly strangled by an over-enthusiastic Cordelia.

"Oh, I am so happy," her sister-in-law sobbed as she hung about her neck. "So happy! I shall be the *best* aunt!"

Whatever else she said was muffled as she wept into Fiona's hair.

Caradoc disengaged her. "Sit down, Cordelia and dry your eyes. This is a time for celebration, not tears. And let's eat. I'm sure Gwillym has outdone himself. Look you—isn't that fish?" He winked at Fiona. "I do enjoy a nice bit of fish."

Never had Fiona enjoyed a meal more. It was like Christmas and Easter and every other holiday rolled up in one marvelous celebration of thanksgiving. The food was superb, Gwillym having exerted himself once more. The stock of ale had been replenished and flowed freely, and it seemed Caradoc and Dafydd were determined to outdo one another regaling her with tales of their youth.

"So there he was, his head in a bucket," Dafydd concluded at the end of one such recitation. "Just sitting and not saying a word, like he was in holy contemplation, while I had to fetch the shears."

"I was too angry to speak, you nit," Caradoc growled with a bogus scowl. "You're lucky I couldn't see or I would have knocked you down. Haven't been able to stand the smell of honey since, or *braggot*, either, although not such a loss there, I grant you."

"But I was dying a thousand deaths fearing what our fathers were going to do when you came back with your hair looking like some beast had torn out pieces. I thought they might think I'd decided to practice the shearing on you. And hell to pay there was, too. Why, I couldn't sit for a week."

"I looked like I had the mange for more than that," Caradoc countered.

"Why don't you two stop quarreling about past times better forgotten and let Fiona sing?" Cordelia demanded, having heard this story—and the mutual accusations—about a hundred times before.

"Next thing we know, we'll be hearing again about the Bull and Crown."

"What happened at the Bull and Crown?" Fiona asked innocently, although she had her suspicions about what sort of thing had happened when Caradoc glanced sheepishly at Dafydd and blushed.

"Nothing," her husband said.

"Farther afield, is it?" she inquired.

Caradoc looked as if he had swallowed a bug.

"No, no, not far at all," Dafydd swiftly lied, but he was not fooling her for instant. "Close by, really. About five miles over the hills to the south."

Fiona leaned close to her blushing husband. "Whatever happened at the Bull and Crown, not a shame, is it, for the Welsh?" she teased, putting her hand on his thigh and quite shameless fondling his leg.

She was also thinking of what might happen later. When they would be alone.

"Cordelia's right," Caradoc announced, his voice slightly strained. "A song, my lady, if you please. Otherwise, I'm going to embarrass myself, you temptress," he finished in a mockingly chastising whisper.

"For you, my lord, my love, anything," she replied, giving him a seductive smile.

"Been hanging about too much with Dafydd, you," her husband chided, his tone grave but his eyes dancing with merriment. "No way for a lady to speak, that."

"I was not born a lady," she pertly reminded him as she rose. "I am a merchant's daughter, remember?"

"Aye, I remember a lot of things, especially when we were in the solar."

She warmed beneath his steady, passionate gaze as she cleared her throat. Then she began to sing.

She delighted the gathering with a rollicking Welsh ballad Cordelia had taught her. When she got to the chorus, she gestured for Cordelia to stand up and join her, and the two women's voices joined and blended and filled the hall with joyful music.

Bang!

The door to the hall burst open and hit the wall. A man stood on the threshold, limned in the afternoon sunlight.

"A celebration for the return of the prodigal son, is it?" he asked, his deep voice very like Caradoc's, and his hair just as savagely long. "Have you killed the fatted calf, too?"

"Connor!" Cordelia screeched as she rushed from the dais and threw herself into the arms of the stranger, who was really no stranger at all.

Connor of Llanstephan was a rather unforgettable personage—not nearly so impressive as Caradoc, of course, Fiona thought, but he did have a fairly commanding presence, too. Tall, dark-haired, so handsome it could make a woman gasp, he had the build of a warrior, and the confidence of a champion of tournaments, which he was.

The soldiers and servants, the brothers of Bronwyn, Bronwyn herself, Father Rhodri—as excited as a boy—and Dafydd hurried to cluster around Connor. They all talked at once, asking questions and trying to tell him about Ganore, Caradoc's injury, his subsequent illness, and the visit of Lord Rhys.

Caradoc slowly got to his feet and she wondered what he was thinking, for here was Connor, the favorite in the flesh.

"Give me your hand, Fiona," he said quietly.

As they approached Connor, Fiona noticed that Rhonwen hung back, and she knew exactly how she felt. For days now she had been living with a happy confidence and security such as she had never known but now, suddenly, she was once more Freckled Fiona, sure she was lacking and trying not to show it.

"Watch the shoulder, rabbit, watch the shoulder," Connor genially warned as he embraced Cordelia with his right arm, his left held against his chest. "Out of joint twice it's been, and if I hurt it again, my wife will be having my head on a plate. And one at a time, the lot of you. I cannot make out half of what you're saying."

Tall enough to look over the women and several of the men, Connor saw them draw near, a curious smile on his face as the crowd parted to let Caradoc and Fiona through. Tension began to replace the merriment, and she realized everybody was watching them very keenly. No doubt there would be tales about this reunion, too, in time to come.

"Greetings, brother," Caradoc said, his tone considerably cooler than anyone else's had been.

Fiona glanced at him uncertainly, then back to Connor.

"Greetings, Caradoc." Connor smiled, as charming as always, his features lighting with it. "This must be the bride of Llanstephan."

Fiona tried to look pleased to see him.

Sudden recognition dawned on Connor's face. "Why, it's little Fiona MacDougal all grown up, isn't it?"

"I am," she answered, stunned. She had no idea he had even known she existed.

She slid another glance at Caradoc, who looked as dumbfounded as she.

"How could I forget the only girl who never paid a jot of attention to me before I went on Crusade?" Connor amicably demanded. "Hurt my feelings and my pride, you did, Fiona MacDougal, but I forgive you. You must be quite a woman to win my brother's hand in marriage."

He gave Caradoc a condemning look. "You might have let a brother know you married."

Caradoc stiffened. "So might you—and by a swifter method than Sir Ralph de Valmonte."

Instead of taking umbrage at his brother's tone, as she had expected, Connor chuckled. Perhaps he had learned to curb his temper, as impossible as that seemed. "Ah, the good Sir Ralph de Valmonte."

"Good?" Caradoc rumbled as his grip on her tightened with agitation. "The man took six weeks to get here."

"I meant that in a general way," Connor explained. "The man's as big a dolt as they come, but he has his uses."

"Why do we not all sit down?" Fiona suggested, hoping to prevent another quarrel, especially so soon after Connor's arrival. "I'm sure you must be weary after your journey, Sir Connor."

"As a matter of fact, I am. And since we are related, do not call me by my title." His expression brightened as he looked at the food on the tables. "Is that fish? How the devil did you get Gwillym to cook fish when it's not Friday?"

"As you said, my wife is a very special woman," Caradoc growled as he turned and led the way to the dais, holding Fiona's hand as if he feared she might take it into her head to bolt.

Father Rhodri quickly made way for Connor to sit at the high table. He went to join Jon-Bron and his brothers and his sister below the dais.

"Why the hell did Richard trust Sir Ralph with such a message?" Caradoc demanded before Connor was even fully in his chair.

"Is that what he told you, that Richard sent him?" Connor threw back his head and laughed. "Richard went back to Europe weeks ago, right after I was married. *I* sent Sir Ralph with the message because I could not come myself. The physician wouldn't allow me to ride, and my wife wouldn't, either."

Caradoc was obviously not mollified. "Pretty poor choice of messenger, brother."

Connor flushed and seemed most fascinated with the fish, for he kept his gaze on the dish before him as he answered. "I wasn't sure how you would take the news, so I thought a little delay might not be amiss."

Caradoc brought his fist down on the table so hard, the goblets rattled. "*Amiss?* It was very *amiss* of you to keep me worrying when all had been made well. It would have been a relief to me to know about the taxes, at the very least. How else did you think I would take the news?"

Worried where this would lead, Fiona gave

Cordelia a pleading look, silently urging her to intervene, but Cordelia simply shrugged her shoulders.

"I thought you might not take kindly to my help," Connor said.

"It was you caused the problem in the first place, with your temper," Caradoc declared, leaning forward on his elbow to glare at his brother.

Connor raised his head to fasten a steadfast gaze on his brother. "I know that. But you are as proud and stubborn as Cordelia and I. I was afraid you would take it as an insult to your ability to run Llanstephan, or think it charity."

Just like Lord Rhys, and Fiona was no more impressed that Connor used the same reason. To be sure, her husband was an expert at hiding his feelings and behaving as if he wanted no assistance, but surely they should have offered.

"Do you honestly believe I would put my pride before keeping our home? Or that it would not wound my pride worse to lose it?"

Connor shrugged his broad shoulders and looked apologetic. "I could never figure out *what* you were thinking, or feeling, from the time we were children."

Caradoc brought his fist down on the table again. "Just because I don't go flying into a temper the way you do—"

"The way you are now," Fiona observed, afraid this would herald another argument on a day she wanted everything to be pleasant, in spite of Connor's unforeseen advent. "Caradoc, Lord Rhys used the same excuse when I asked him why he did not offer to help."

"You asked that of Lord Rhys?" Caradoc demanded incredulously. "When?"

She swallowed hard. Every person in the hall seemed to be watching her with rapt attention, especially Connor and Cordelia. She wished she had spoken of this to Caradoc alone, but the fleece was off the sheep now. "Before he left."

Caradoc's brows lowered, and more than ever she wished she had not broached this subject. "I don't imagine he took kindly to your criticism," he said.

"No, he did not."

His lips curved up in a smile. "Good."

Her jaw dropped at his pleased response.

"You are not the only one who thought the offer should have been made, but I liked your offer of marriage better." He studied her face and his smile was warm, and gentle. "Don't worry about Rhys. I've been dealing with the man for years and he makes a fearsome noise, but he's not a fool. He would think twice before he would move against the lord of Llanstephan Fawr."

Relief coursed through her and she let out her breath.

"Especially one whose brother is close enough to the king of England that he could call on him for help," Connor added. "And you see, Caradoc? *Everybody* thinks you are too proud to accept money."

"Which doesn't mean I wouldn't have if I stood to lose Llanstephan," Caradoc retorted. "Nor does that absolve you from sending that fat dolt with such important news."

"That *fat dolt* is what brought me here," Connor replied, folding his arms over his chest. "He sent a very odd message to me telling me I had best go home for a visit. He seems to be under the impression that you are on the verge of madness."

"Madness?" Fiona gasped.

"He thought he should let me know before the king found out."

Caradoc scowled. "I am no more mad than he is."

"So I see, but what exactly did you do when you read my message?" Connor asked, raising a quizzical brow. "He implied you were likely to go on a murderous rampage, at the very least, and suggested I should get here as quick as I could. I thought I had better come see what had happened and why my brother, the most steady and stable of men, had given him the impression that he was about to go off like Attila the Hun."

"He lost his temper," Cordelia said.

Caradoc glared at her as if he was about to go on a murderous rampage.

"Well, it's true. Isn't it, Fiona?" she protested, appealing to her sister-in-law.

Fiona wasn't quite sure how to respond. Caradoc had most certainly flown into a temper, as she very well remembered, but she didn't want to be in the middle of an argument.

Before she could answer, Connor smiled with sly satisfaction, which was not, Fiona thought, the way to mollify her husband. "So now you know how I felt the day I berated Richard and started all our troubles."

Caradoc blinked. Then he lowered his brows.

"Our troubles started when you insisted upon going on Crusade."

Connor met his glare with the beginning of a glower. "It was my Christian duty to free the Holy Land. I won't apologize for wanting to do my duty, disastrous though it was in the end."

This was going to lead to disaster here, and she wouldn't have it—not now and not ever.

"A fine way this is to treat your brother when he's just arrived, Caradoc," she said, putting her hand on his arm. "Let the past be in the past. It doesn't matter anyway. You are not in debt, you both have fine estates. Stop quarreling like bickering children and behave like civilized knights of the realm."

"Fiona," Caradoc warned.

"Or, if you cannot do that, perhaps it is time you finally fought it out. What say you, Cordelia? Shall we let them brawl like boys until all is settled between them?"

Her rebuking gaze going from one brother to the other, Cordelia said, "What a wonderful suggestion. That may be best. They are like two boys with one bow between them. Shall we ask Jon-Bron to oversee the fight?"

"No, he'll favor Caradoc," Fiona replied, taking great satisfaction talking over their heads as if they weren't there. "I think Eifion."

Cordelia rubbed her chin, as Caradoc did when he was thinking. "He'll whine about the time it will take."

Caradoc and Connor exchanged the baffled looks of men caught with their breeches about their ankles.

"Emlyn-Bron, then?" Fiona suggested, still ignoring them.

"What about Bronwyn?"

"Maybe we don't need anyone to oversee it. They're both wounded, so I think it will be generally fair."

"Wounded?" Connor demanded, looking at his brother in amazement. "How in the name of the saints did you get wounded? You've never fought a battle in your life."

"He most certainly has," Cordelia retorted, finally paying attention to him. "That's what Jon-Bron was trying to tell you."

"Aye!" Jon-Bron shouted, reminding them that they had an audience. It also sounded as if he and his companions had been sampling the *braggot* again.

"The wound nearly killed him," Cordelia continued. "It would have, except for Fiona's nursing."

Connor sat perfectly still for a moment, regarding his brother. The mood in the hall shifted, to one grave and serious. "You nearly died?"

Caradoc nodded.

Connor slumped back, staring at him with shocked disbelief.

Then Caradoc gave him a sardonically proud smile. "I am finally going to have a scar better than any *you've* got."

Connor straightened and the spark of brotherly competition lessened the grim mood. "I doubt it."

Caradoc shoved up the sleeve of the shirt beneath his tunic, exposing the bandage on his healing wound. "We'll compare, shall we?"

"Caradoc, you keep that wrapped," Fiona cried, afraid that he was going to tear off the bandage then and there.

"All right," he agreed. He got to his feet. "Come, Connor, let's go to the solar where men may talk in peace."

He gave his wife and sister a wry look. "I promise I will do my best to keep my temper, but if you hear the furnishings being tossed about, you may interrupt."

"And we will," Fiona vowed.

A long while later, Caradoc sighed and leaned back in his chair. He sat behind his table, and Connor in front, so they looked like two generals conferring about strategy. The warm glow of the beeswax candles in the stand encircled them and added to the congenial atmosphere that Caradoc was determined to keep, now that he was over the first shock and irascibility his brother's unheralded arrival had occasioned. "So now you know all that has happened while you've been gone."

Connor shook his head. "You married, a babe on the way, Ganore dead, and Dafydd and little Rhonwen to wed. It is a lot to take in all at once."

"So was the news of your wedding and how it came about," Caradoc replied. He took a deep, strengthening breath, determined and sure of what he was about to say next. "There is one thing more. The day I sent her away, Ganore told me something, Connor, and now I must tell it to you."

Grimly resolute, Caradoc related the gist of Ganore's sordid story.

When he was finished, Connor studied him as if trying to see the truth of it in his face. "What did she say the man's name was?"

"DeFrouchette. Do you know it?"

Connor nodded slowly, his eyes as grave as Caradoc had ever seen them, or more. "I know it very well. I knew the man himself. Him it was tried to kill the king. Him it was *I* killed preventing it."

Shocked, Caradoc struggled to come to grips with what Connor was saying. If DeFrouchette was his natural father, and the same man Connor had killed, his real father was not just a rapist and a villain, but a traitor.

A wild, desperate hope flashed through him. "Even if Ganore's story is true, maybe it wasn't him, but a relative—a cousin, or brother."

"I have to tell you, Caradoc, the age would be right, and he had blue eyes. He was tall, like you."

"And you."

"Aye, and I have been searching your face for any other likeness." Connor smiled with compassion. "I do not see any."

Caradoc heard his words and saw his smile, but it was to the depths of his brother's eyes that he looked for the truth.

He saw it, and it was different from his words. "Don't lie to me, Connor. If there is a resemblance, say so."

Connor frowned with frustration as he got to his feet and started pacing. He threw his hands in the air. "Who can say? There may be, but he was older and thinner, not so dark as you."

He halted and faced his brother. "I absolutely refuse to believe this story, and I don't think you should, either."

"It would explain some things," Caradoc answered quietly, nevertheless grateful that his brother wanted to deny it.

Connor returned to his chair and sat heavily. "Aye, it would," he admitted. "Things I've wondered about, too. And tried not to remember."

Again Caradoc took a deep, strengthening breath, for he had come to the most important thing, beyond his personal pain. "If I am a bastard, Llanstephan may not be mine by law."

The familiar, fierce expression of temper appeared on Connor's face. "What, you think it should be *mine*?"

Slapping his hands on the arms of his chair, Connor rose abruptly once more. This time he did not pace, but glared at his brother, hands on hips, as righteously indignant as Caradoc had ever seen him. "You are still our mother's son, and Llanstephan comes from her line, not our father's. Besides, nobody deserves to rule here so much as you—and nobody will be able to do it so well, or be as welcome. I know that as much as anybody and I'm insulted—*insulted!*—that you would even *imagine*—"

Caradoc held up a placating hand. "All right," he said, secretly pleased—and relieved—by Connor's declaration. "Stop before you start frothing at the mouth. Very well, I shall keep Llanstephan."

"*Good!*"

"Sit down, brother."

Connor threw himself into a chair, and scowled. "Insulted, that's what I am," he muttered.

"Whether it's true or not, I think we should tell Cordelia."

That calmed Connor down. "Why?" he demanded. "It will only hurt her, and there is no proof. It could just be Ganore's spiteful lie."

To keep this secret from Cordelia had been his first reaction, too, but having thought long and hard upon it as he had recovered, Caradoc had decided otherwise. "I have seen what secrets and deception can do. Ganore may not be the only one who knew, other than those directly involved. Cordelia may come to hear rumors or stories. I would have her prepared."

Connor did not look quite convinced, but he shrugged his shoulders nonetheless. "You are the elder brother, Caradoc. Whatever you decide, that is what will be done."

"Oh, so in this you will listen to me?" Caradoc chided, only half joking. "Now you will give me respect?"

Connor regarded him steadily, and sincerely. "I've always respected you."

This, too, was difficult to believe, given the teasing he had endured from this supposedly respectful sibling. "You have an odd way of showing brotherly respect," he observed with a hint of his past displeasure.

"Well, I did, in my own way," Connor protested. "And envied you, too."

"*You* envied *me*?" That was *impossible* to believe.

Connor raked back his long dark hair with his slender yet powerful fingers. "I've envied you all my life, Caradoc. That's why I teased you the way I did."

Caradoc continued to stare at him with skeptical disbelief.

"I envied the way you stayed so calm and in control all the time." He spread his hands. "Look you all the times Cordelia and I tried to get a rise out of you—and nothing. I could never understand how you managed it, because try as I might, I could never rein in my temper. And there were times, brother, I dearly wished I had.

"The envy it was made me goad you, you see, and comfort myself with thoughts that you were jealous of me for my skill at arms and," he flushed a bit, "other things. I'm sorry."

Caradoc didn't know what to say. Once again, his heart was too full of feeling to find expression in words.

"And you are to have a child—another thing to envy you for, Caradoc."

As Caradoc looked at his brother, the last of his bitterness and jealousy ebbed away, never to return.

"You have not yet been married long enough to fret about that," he replied, wanting to offer some comfort.

Not that it seemed Connor needed any comforting, for a broad grin came to his face. "No, and I'm doing my best to remedy that lack."

Which reminded Caradoc that Fiona was surely awaiting him in their bed.

"If you'll excuse me, Connor, I'm tired," he said, pushing back his chair and coming around the table.

"You must be, too. Why don't we retire for tonight? I trust you'll be staying awhile."

Connor grinned his devilish grin as he rose. "A few days, but no more. My wife will be missing me too much, and I her—and I do not mean only for genial, marital conversation."

Connor had never jested this way with him before, the way he did with Dafydd and the other men, and Caradoc suddenly had the pleasant sensation that he had been admitted into some kind of secret fraternity.

Then his brother clapped his hand on his shoulder, and despite the merriment that had been in his eyes moments ago, Caradoc saw brotherly love there, too. "I'm glad you didn't get killed, Troll."

For the first time in his life, Caradoc didn't bristle when he heard that name. "I'm glad you didn't, either, brother."

Fiona sighed and nestled against her husband, secure against his shoulder. Her fingers traced the edge of the bandage on his arm.

"And you truly didn't quarrel?" she asked tentatively, not wanting to imply that he had been less than truthful, but he had been somber since he had joined her in their bedchamber.

For a moment, she feared he wasn't going to answer, that he would shut her out as effectively as if he was in the solar with the oaken door between them.

"We didn't quarrel again," he replied softly. "I told him what Ganore said before she left."

So that explained his state. "What did he say to that?" she asked, knowing how it must hurt him to speak of this.

"He refuses to believe it and denies any claim to Llanstephan."

Relieved, she breathed again. "Is that not an end to it, then, if he does not wish to question it?"

"Until I tell Cordelia, as I think I must. She must be prepared, in case there are rumors."

She would not disagree with his urge for honesty. Lies and deception had cost her too dear to protest.

"And there is more," he said, his voice soft in the darkness.

He raised himself on his elbow to regard her. "The man Connor killed when he saved the king's life—he may have been the man who raped my mother."

She sucked in her breath, her eyes wide with the shock. "Then he would be—"

"My natural father, and a traitor as well as a villainous rogue."

Hearing his anguish, knowing his inner pain, she caressed his rough cheek. "You cannot help what he was, if indeed Ganore spoke the truth, and I, for one, am not willing to accept her words at face value." Nevertheless, she had to ask the question uppermost in her mind. "Did Connor see any resemblance between you?"

Caradoc lay back down and held her close again, closing his eyes as if he was too ashamed to look at her. "I think so, but he would not say it."

"I don't care if the meanest, most despicable lout in England was supposedly your father," she declared. "You are the best, most wonderful, generous, kindhearted . . ."

He took her by the shoulders and pulled her to him for a passionate kiss. She rolled so that her breasts crushed against his chest as his mouth claimed hers.

"Cease your compliments," he ordered when they broke the kiss, "or I will be getting conceited. I am not used to such fulsome praise."

She shifted back, the sensation of his aroused body beneath hers wonderfully provoking. "Well, you will have to get used to it, my love," she murmured, her voice a low, seductive purr, "because I'm going to compliment you every chance I get."

She kissed his chest. "You are owed much there, and I intend to make up for the lack." She raised her head and gazed up into his handsome, rugged face. "I mean what I say, Caradoc. It doesn't matter who your father was—not to me, not to anyone who knows you. Llanstephan is yours and should be. You have worried and worked for it all your life, and nobody deserves to rule it as much as you do."

He nodded and toyed with a strand of her hair, yet she could see that he was still distressed. "That is what Connor said, too," he murmured.

"Then let us leave the matter to rest, Caradoc. De-Frouchette is dead, and so are your parents. Connor does not dispute your right to rule Llanstephan, so nobody else will." She sighed. "I suppose we should be glad Ganore could keep a secret as well as she did. Maybe that's why her mouth was so tight all the time."

Caradoc's chest quaked with the low rumble of his chuckle. "I cannot thank God enough for you, Fiona," he said when he stopped laughing.

His voice lowered to that deep, seductive growl she found so alluring as he trailed a finger down her arm, sending delicious shivers outward along her body. "I do not have to tell Cordelia right now."

"No, I think it can wait," she agreed with a tremulous sigh.

His hand began to slide along the curve of her hip. "I seem to recall a certain day in the solar when I sat upon the chair . . ."

"A chair?" she whispered as the heat of desire stirred within her.

He stroked her breast, his long, strong fingers moving with deliberate, delicious enticement. "Is your memory failing, my love?"

She lifted his hand and, gazing steadily at his desire-darkened eyes, brushed it across her lips. The pulse in his neck started to throb. "At least your brother recognized me without being told who I was."

"I remembered who you were," he retorted, shifting closer so that she could feel more of his flesh against hers.

She slid her fingertips across his nipple, then playfully tweaked it. "Only after I told you my name."

She thought she had been playful, but the low moan he made suggested to her that it had felt somewhat more than playful.

"I had a lot on my mind in those days," he muttered as he pressed his warm, soft lips to her shoulder. The excitement flashed from there to the rest of her.

He regarded her with mock sternness. "Since when have you and Cordelia become thick as thieves?"

Was this sudden shift in mood designed to tease her, and increase her already surging ardor? "Since you two proved grown men can still act like boys."

He frowned.

Well, he had asked, and if he didn't like her answer . . . "This is hardly a time for questions, my lord," she noted, letting her hair sweep over his chest.

His frown disappeared, and in an instant, desire shone in his brilliant blue eyes.

"It's a pity Connor didn't bring his wife, though. I would like to meet her," she remarked.

It seemed he regretted starting a conversation, for he grabbed her shoulders and pulled her forward, bringing his mouth to hers for a passionate kiss.

She arched back and his lips trailed across her chin and down the slender column of her throat. "We could go to your brother's estate," she offered breathlessly as she tried not to give in just yet to the passion throbbing through her. "Wouldn't that be nice, to travel?"

"I would rather stay right here with you. Right *here*," he repeated. "In this bed."

As he took her mouth again, she willingly and joyfully gave herself up to the hunger coursing through her.

Mindful of that day in the solar, and excited by the memory, she maneuvered herself to sit on his hips, then put her hands beside his head and leaned closer, inviting him to pleasure her breasts.

With delicious, deliberate slowness he did. He swirled his tongue around the hardened peak of her nipples, making her pant and sigh.

Stroking and caressing, kissing and touching, she explored his body as he did hers, until the excitement seemed too much.

Yet not enough.

She raised herself and guided him into her, then slowly, slowly, lowered herself until he filled her. Thus joined, she tried to move with equal leisure, to take the time to enjoy every element of their passion.

But she could not. For years upon years she had dreamed of being loved by her Dark Prince, and more. To be cherished. To be safe and secure. Appreciated. Wanted. Needed.

Thus it was at last. All the past known, no more secrets between them, she was loved and cherished, safe and secure.

That wonderful realization drove her on, and spurred her to bring him to the zenith, to share her passion and her joy, until at last she cried out in completion, and he with her.

Their breathing slowed as they rested, then she moved away to lie beside him in his tender embrace. "I love you, Caradoc," she whispered.

Caradoc sighed as joy washed over him and through him, and made him feel truly whole for the first time in his life. He was at peace at last, blissfully content, and finally free. "And I love you, Fiona the Fair."

*The weather is getting warmer, and things
at Avon romance are getting hotter!
Next month, don't miss these
spectacularly sizzling stories . . .*

MARRY ME by Susan Kay Law
An Avon Romantic Treasure

Emily Bright has found a place to call her home, but imagine
her shock when she is awakened in the middle of the night to
discover a tall stranger who claims she is sleeping in *his* bed!
Should she marry Jake Sullivan and make this claim come true?

MY ONE AND ONLY by MacKenzie Taylor
An Avon Contemporary Romance

When Abby Lee strides into the office of Ethan Maddux and
begs for his help, he barely agrees to give her ten minutes out of
his busy day. So how *dare* he ask her to spend time with him at
night? Abby knows that when business and pleasure mix—look
out!

A NECESSARY HUSBAND by Debra Mullins
An Avon Romance

He's the long-lost heir of the Duke of Raynewood . . . she's a
delectable society lady who learns it's her role to turn him into
a proper Englishman. Of course, there are rules about these
things . . . but sometimes the rules of society are meant to be
broken.

HIS SCANDAL by Gayle Callen
An Avon Romance

Sir Alexander Thornton has a reputation as the most dashing—
and incorrigible—man in England. He wagers he can win a kiss
from any lady in the land . . . but that's before he meets proper
Lady Emmeline Prescott.

REL 0402

Avon Romantic Treasures

Unforgettable, enthralling love stories,
sparkling with passion and adventure
from Romance's bestselling authors

Have you ever dreamed of writing a romance?

*And have you ever wanted
to get a romance published?*

Perhaps you have always wondered how to
become an Avon romance writer?
We are now seeking the best and brightest undiscovered
voices. We invite you to send us your query letter to
avonromance@harpercollins.com

What do you need to do?

Please send no more than two pages telling us
about your book. We'd like to know its setting—is it
contemporary or historical—and a bit about the hero,
heroine, and what happens to them.

Then, if it is right for Avon we'll ask to see part of the
manuscript. Remember, it's important that you have
material to send, in case we want to see your story quickly.

Of course, there are no guarantees of publication,
but you never know unless you try!

*We know there is new talent just waiting
to be found! Don't hesitate . . . send us
your query letter today.*

**The Editors
Avon Romance**

MSR 0302